PAINTING OVER CRACKS

a novel

LEE BUKOWSKI

Painting Over Cracks
Red Adept Publishing, LLC
104 Bugenfield Court
Garner, NC 27529
https://RedAdeptPublishing.com/
Copyright © 2026 by Lee Bukowski. All rights reserved.

Cover Art by Streetlight Graphics[1]

---

1. http://StreetlightGraphics.com

For my beloved father, Sam, whose years were long but not long enough.

And our precious Audrey, who filled our hearts sooner than expected.

One heart departed, another just begun—both forever a part of me.

Chapter One

"*H*e *doesn't look great.*" *Why does everyone keep saying that? He looks dead.* Beth put on a stoic face—as stoic as possible, considering she stood next to her husband, laid out in a casket in his best suit.

"They really did a nice job with the makeup, didn't they?" one mourner remarked.

"Mmm," Beth managed through the numbness permeating her.

Another mourner opined, "It's amazing what they can do. You can't even tell he was in an—"

"Yes, well, thank you very much for coming. I know my sister appreciates it. Don't you, Beth?" A frustrated puff of air escaped Hannah's lips.

"Mmm. Mm-hmm." Beth stood rooted to one spot like an ancient tree.

Hannah led her away from the receiving line and lowered her onto a velvet sofa then plopped down next to her, careful not to bump Beth's casted left arm.

"Jesus, these people are idiots. You okay?"

Beth sighed and adjusted her sling. Her head throbbed. Her body ached as if she had the flu.

"Who even are some of these people?" Hannah scanned the room. "Like that group sitting in the back with their heads together. Do you know them?"

Beth shook her head. She looked around and realized she didn't know many of the people attending the service. "Maybe Danny's business associates? They introduced themselves, but I wasn't really listening. I think one of them said he just saw Danny last week in New York. He did some contract work there for his friend's firm."

The line to view Danny's body stretched out of the room and down a corridor. Beth mindlessly accepted condolences, nodding dutifully as mourners extolled her husband's virtues.

Her thoughts drifted to eight years ago. Beth and Danny had met at a fundraiser for some politician or another. Though he'd been a solo law practitioner for the last five years, when they'd met, he'd been working for a law firm that was supporting the candidate, and Beth's boss at the mortgage company had sent her to make pleasantries and deliver a check. She'd noticed Danny first, the way his dark hair flopped over his right eye when he laughed, giving him a hint of youthful charm beneath his designer suit. At some point during the evening, they'd wound up in the same circle of idle chitchat, and the attraction had been mutual. They'd started dating the following week.

That seemed like yesterday.

Laura, Beth's mother, approached and took her arm. "Honey, the funeral director just told me the pastor is ready to begin Daniel's service. He wants everyone to take a seat."

"I'm starving," Nicole, Beth's youngest sister, complained.

Hannah glared at her. "Shut up," she hissed. "For Christ's sake, Nic, really? Even today?"

"What? I'm just saying..."

"I know what you're saying. I also know what you're thinking about—the same thing you always are—yourself. Should we ask Beth to have the pastor rush through her husband's funeral service so you can have a sandwich?" Hannah practically spat the words.

"Sorry. Sue me for being hungry." Nicole looked around for her mother and located both her parents sitting in the front row of mourners.

Beth was not quite two years older than thirty-year-old Hannah, but people mistook the sisters for twins because of their dark-blue eyes, auburn hair, and nearly identical small noses and angled cheekbones. Though Hannah was younger, she had a domineering temperament that Beth had called bossiness when they were children but appreciated now that they were adults. When something needed to be done, Hannah stepped up.

In the conventional sense, Nicole, the youngest at twenty-six, was the most striking, with her honey-gold hair and chiseled features. But she was often so unkempt that people had to piece her together in steps to appreciate her whole look. She wore her hair long and parted in the middle, creating the illusion of curtains shading her view of the real world. She dressed as though it were an afterthought, forgetting an earring or throwing on a tattered skirt purchased at a flea market for dinner in a posh restaurant with her parents. Richard said Nicole had his own mother's carefree and oblivious personality.

Beth turned in her seat, scanning the crowd for Molly, her best friend, and spotted her a few rows back. Molly's expression was pained, but her look said, "I've got you." Beth had to look away in order not to burst into tears.

"On behalf of Daniel's family, Beth, and her family, I'd like to extend warm thanks to all of you for attending this service to honor the life of Daniel Collins..."

Beth struggled to pay attention to the pastor. Her mind floated for the hundredth time to the night of the accident. She closed her eyes as if to block the memory.

"...particularly difficult when such a young man is taken so suddenly..."

As she remembered that early December night, Beth's body tensed, and she absentmindedly placed her hand on her abdomen. She saw the flash of bright light and heard the deafening crush of metal and glass. Then the part she struggled to remember but couldn't—

"Daniel's brother, Joshua, would like to say a few words about his brother. Josh, please come up to the podium."

Josh paused and touched Beth's shoulder, momentarily bringing her back from her reverie. She managed a grateful half smile at Josh, two years younger than Danny but with the same dark, wavy hair, clear blue eyes, and determined jawbone. On Beth and Danny's honeymoon, she had remarked that Danny's eyes were the exact color of the Aruba sky.

"Danny was not only a model son and husband. He was a talented lawyer, a loyal friend, and the best brother anyone could hope for..."

Beth only half listened to Josh talk about her husband. It still hadn't sunk in. Danny had only been thirty-six years old. People didn't die when they were thirty-six. People died when they were eighty-six or ninety-six. She stared at the fingers sticking out of her arm cast, the fingers that had instinctively flown to her face when a speeding car had torn into theirs and ripped her life to shreds.

Is this what I deserve? Is this my punishment? Tears balanced on her dark lashes, threatening to spill.

Josh finished speaking and gave Beth a pained look as he returned to his seat. The pastor concluded the brief service, and the mourners poured out of the funeral home into the bright December day that belied the grim occasion.

Molly walked out with Beth and pulled her sunglasses down from her head, releasing her nearly black mane of curls and shading her chocolate-brown eyes. "I'll see you at your parents'. I don't know what to do or say. Just, you know, whatever you need, I'm here. I can't make this better with flowers or a casserole. If you need to talk, drink wine, punch someone, or scream at them, I'm here."

Beth hugged her, thankful to have a friend she didn't have to pretend with. Molly would be there for her no matter how erratic Beth's moods got through this horror show.

As they hugged, Molly whispered, "And by the way, who invited the hooker?" She gestured to a young woman wearing a very short, skintight dress and strappy four-inch heels. "With those tiny boobs, I bet she charges a flat rate."

Beth dropped her head onto Molly's shoulder and smiled. She could always count on Molly.

Since Danny's parents lived out of town and his mother's health was poor, Richard and Laura hosted the postservice luncheon at their modest home in a suburb west of Philadelphia. Mourners filed in, again offered condolences, and headed for the buffet the caterers had set up in the dining room.

Beth hated this part of funerals most of all. To her, the gathering after the service too closely resembled a party. It seemed as though no one even spoke about Danny. A group of guys whose ties had long been loosened and sport coats tossed aside sat on the enclosed back deck, drinking beer, scrolling through their cell phones, and laughing at shared stories. In the living room, women sipped wine and picked at crackers and dip as though they were attending a book club instead of a funeral luncheon. Their cheery talk about upcoming Christmas plans was more than Beth could bear. Children running around and playing games completed a picture that was too festive for her.

She'd made small talk on autopilot for as long as she could stand it. Her parents' holiday decorations added to the incongruence of the sorrowful occasion, and gradually, she drifted away to be alone. Now, she stood at her parents' kitchen island, holding an untouched plate of food someone had handed her an hour ago.

"Who gave you this sandwich? Obviously, someone who doesn't know you can't eat gluten." Hannah took the plate from her sister's hand and sighed. "How are you doing? Oh, great, I've joined the ranks of well-meaning people asking you stupid questions."

Beth pinched the bridge of her nose. She'd gathered her long hair into a low ponytail. She hadn't bothered with makeup this morning other than foundation and lip gloss. The foundation did nothing to hide the dark circles under her eyes. Her natural resting expression was one of seriousness, and now that look carried the additional weight of loss. "I just want everyone to leave. I'm exhausted."

"I figured as much and put a bug in Mom's ear. 'No-filter' Laura can clear a room like no one else. They're starting to head for the exit. Dad's too nice. He'd start out thanking them for coming and end up refilling their wineglasses." Hannah looked around. "Nic will head out as soon as there's any talk of cleaning up. And probably leave her kids with Mom."

Beth's thoughts returned to the hospital after the accident. *I'm so sorry, Beth. We did everything we could...* "Yeah, our little sister is definitely detached from reality. Sometimes, I wish I were more like her. Not a care in the world."

"Oh, please. She's an adult and needs to start acting like one. I mean, I love her, but I can only handle one of her." Hannah led Beth out to a chair on the now-empty deck and put a glass of cabernet in her sister's hand. "Sit. Relax. Drink." She lowered her voice. "Hey, did you see the police officer at the funeral home? The one who was first at the scene of the accident? I saw him talking to Danny's parents, but then I think he left without going through the receiving line. Did he say anything to you?"

"Yes, Officer Kingston. He didn't talk to me at the funeral, but I have a voicemail from him. He wants to talk to me about our wallets and phones being stolen from the... car wreck. Maybe he has an update. I don't know." Her voice trailed off, and she sipped her wine, gazing at the trees gently swaying in the breeze. "Hannah, I want to tell you something." She closed her eyes and was silent for a few moments. "At the time of the accident, I... I was..."

"Finally, everyone is gone!" Laura walked through the open French doors with Richard trailing behind. Shaking her head, she tucked a strand of her chin-length bob behind her ear. She gathered her chenille shawl in front of her to ward off a chill despite the unseasonably warm December-evening air.

"The last group was slow to read the cues until your mother handed them their jackets." Richard winked at Beth.

"Well, for goodness' sake, people can't take a hint. It was a luncheon to thank the mourners, not a class reunion. It's almost five o'clock." Laura turned to Beth. "Hon, Danny's parents and brother are leaving. His poor mother isn't doing very well between Danny's death and her health issues. Maybe you want to say goodbye to them?"

"Oh, yes, sure, be right back." Beth dragged herself to her feet and went inside, but before she was out of earshot, she caught their hushed words.

"How is she holding up?" Richard asked Hannah.

"I don't know. She's calm, but that worries me. I think I'd feel better if she were crying and screaming. It's like she's numb."

"Give her time. She's still processing. It's a terrible shock." Richard lowered his head. "We're all devastated by Danny's death."

"Hey, Mom, I'm taking off!" Nicole's voice rang out from the kitchen. "Okay if Zoe and Ethan spend the night here? Some of my friends are going out in Manayunk."

Laura sighed.

Hannah raised her eyebrows. "Not everyone is devastated. Some of us have no clue what it means to care about anyone but themselves."

"Oh well," Laura offered. "It's not like Nicole staying here will bring Daniel back."

No, it won't, Beth thought. *It won't bring any of them back.*

Chapter Two

Beth lay on her side of the bed and reached out to touch the empty space left by Danny. Despite her mood, the late-January sky outside her window was an optimistic blue, unmarred by clouds. The sound of air brakes on a garbage truck slowing in front of the house reminded her she'd forgotten to take out the trash—again. Danny had always taken care of that. One more thing she would have to get in the habit of remembering.

Beth's parents and Hannah had all invited her to stay with them as long as she wanted, but what she wanted was to be in the house she'd shared with Danny until his death.

Her mind wandered back to their first date. Danny had asked her out to dinner but hadn't specified a place. When Beth answered the door in jeans and a sweater, she and Danny both took in his sports coat and pleated slacks and laughed.

"Well," she joked. "I'd say we need to work on our communication skills, but since we've only known each other for twenty minutes, I think there's hope."

"I should have been more specific. I want to take you somewhere nice."

"So, you think my clothes aren't good enough?" Beth had raised her eyebrows playfully.

"No, no, that's not what I meant." Red blotches worked their way up Danny's cheeks. "I mean, I was trying to impress you."

"Try a different way. Fancy restaurants won't do it."

"Fair enough. Where do you want to go?"

Beth grabbed her jacket. "I know just the place."

They ended up at a taco joint across town whose decor consisted of neon sombrero wall hangings and rope lights. Beth ordered for both of them—spicy margaritas and a variety of tacos served in red plastic basket boats lined with checkered paper.

"Oh my God," Danny exclaimed, wiping salsa from his chin. "This food is fabulous!"

"Impressed, Counselor?"

"Very," he'd said.

A buzzing noise interrupted her thoughts and brought her back to the present. It took a few seconds to realize it was her cell phone on the nightstand. She figured it was her boss calling to ask how she was doing but really wanting to know when she would come back to work. Turning to grab the phone, Beth winced at the pain from her bruises. She was only mildly surprised to see that it was almost nine a.m. She'd been sleeping later than usual. She didn't see much point in getting up.

Beth recognized the number on the screen. "Hello, Officer Kingston."

"Hi, Beth. And please, call me Adam. Do you have a minute?"

I have nothing but time. "Sure, Offic—Adam."

"First, how are you? I mean..."

Beth let him off the hook. "I'm okay, I mean, physically, I guess. Emotionally, well, you know." She heard the dullness in her voice. "It's just..."

"Don't feel you have to explain. Take one day at a time. I can't imagine." Adam cleared his throat. "Listen, I hate like hell to bother you, but when I stopped at the hospital to talk to you, you weren't in any shape to answer questions about your phones and wallets. May I stop by today for a chat?"

Beth closed her eyes and drew in a breath. "Sure," she answered, releasing the breath. "I'll be here all day."

"Okay, great. I'll be there around noon. Bye, now."

Beth gingerly got out of bed, made her way to the bathroom, and ran a hot bubble bath. As the tub filled, her mind drifted again to that night. It had been raining hard, most likely a contributor to the crash. She carefully pulled on a plastic cast cover, lowered herself into the tub, her left arm hanging over the side, and sank up to her neck beneath the foamy bubbles.

The car had come out of nowhere. She and Danny were dissecting the party they had just come from.

"Margot was hammered! She seemed annoyed at Joel spending so much time talking to you... What were you guys talking about? It looked serious."

Danny brushed it off, his arm casually draped over Beth's seat. "He was asking me if I want a case that the firm just gave him. A personal injury thing. I'm not sure it's right for me."

They moved on to the delicious appetizers and made a mental note to get the caterer's name when—Beth's world changed forever.

The car hit the front of theirs on Danny's side and threw him from the vehicle, even though he'd been wearing a seat belt. All Beth could remember was the thunderous sound of crushing metal and bright flashes of light.

When she regained consciousness, she was in the back of an ambulance. A female EMT worked swiftly, hooking up monitors and starting an IV. Beth murmured to her so softly that the EMT removed the stethoscope from her ears and leaned down to listen closer. She'd nodded to Beth sympathetically and made a note on the file she'd started. Danny had been placed in an ambulance behind her, and that was the last time she saw him alive.

At the hospital, it was chaos. Amid the acrid smell of alcohol, antiseptic, and sickness, doctors and nurses rushed around evaluating injuries and ordering tests. Beth had suffered bruises on her face and ribs, but her most serious injury, bone fragments breaking through the skin on her arm, took priority. An X-ray revealed a complex fracture in her left elbow, and she was informed she would have surgery early the next morning.

No, she thought. *I can't have surgery.* She'd lain awake all night, time passing not in minutes or hours but in waves of hope and fear. Praying, reasoning, bargaining—anything to keep hope alive.

The following morning, in the sterile operating room, Beth blinked against the bright lights above her head as the staff bustled around her, attaching tubes, administering IV drugs, and tapping at keys on monitors. She heard the doctor's voice from earlier that morning, compassionate but definitive... "So sorry for your loss... the impact was too great... You are the lone survivor of the crash..."

An anesthesiologist arrived, and the voices around her became thicker, as if spoken underwater. She was soon transported to a blissful sleep. The doctor repaired the break, using metal rods to set the bone in place while it healed. When Beth awoke in recovery, a masked surgeon informed her that the surgery had been successful and her injuries would heal.

He hadn't said anything about the injuries he couldn't see—the ones she deserved.

Beth shivered in the bathwater, now cooled. Rising, she dried off and dressed in jeans and a long-sleeved T-shirt. Her jeans sagged against her flat abdomen, and she tried to remember when she'd last eaten. Proper nutrition no longer seemed like a priority. Dragging a comb through her tangled hair, she peered at her reflection in the mirror. Her facial bruises continued their colorful healing trek from dark purple to sickening greenish and finally pale yellow. She didn't bother with foundation but applied a thin layer of gloss to her dry, cracked lips. After fastening her arm sling, she padded downstairs in her bare feet.

A pile of unopened mail lay on a table in the foyer. A few pieces had slid onto the floor, and Beth picked them up and threw them onto the heap. She contemplated opening some of the envelopes but didn't think she could bear more sympathy cards before a cup of coffee. In the kitchen was more evidence of the last few weeks' crushing reality—unwashed dishes in the sink; sour smells emanating from the fridge's days-old covered dishes baked by neighbors; wilting, thirsty plants lining the windowsill.

As Beth brewed coffee, her thoughts turned to her upcoming conversation with Officer Kingston. It was hard to believe people could be so horrid, but someone had apparently approached the accident scene on foot and taken both Danny's and Beth's wallets and phones. Beth had been so distraught, she hadn't realized it until she was released from the hospital. The police had given Laura Beth's personal items from the car, but her wallet and phone were missing. Danny's parents had reported the same thing about his, but they were too devastated to care.

She pulled coffee creamer from the fridge, and a photo on the door caught her eye. It had been taken in Hawaii. Their tanned faces glowed against the sunset behind them. She missed everything about him—the musky scent of his cologne, the way his smile started at the corners of his eyes and bled into the whole of his face, the tip of his tongue poking out of the corner of his mouth when he concentrated intently on writing a legal brief.

When their relationship had begun to get serious, Danny had shared with Beth that he worried about getting married. He suspected his parents—like many people married several decades—were just going through the motions. They had a comfortable marriage that he described as "fine." He confided that he found it bizarre that people in their twenties or even thirties vowed to love one person for the rest of their lives. He wondered how anyone could make such a promise, believe that they would grow and change in exactly the same ways, and stay madly in love forever. Danny said he didn't want "fine." If he were to marry, he wanted her to be "the one." When he later proposed, he tearfully professed to Beth that she was his "one." His favorite person. He felt strongly that their relationship was based on one crucial point: They were friends before they became a couple. They *liked* each other. Beth felt the same way about Danny. They were meant to be.

The doorbell jostled Beth back to reality, almost causing her to spill her coffee. She carried her mug with her and pulled open the door. The officer was dressed in jeans and a light- blue striped button-down shirt. He wore his light-brown hair short, which accentuated hazel eyes that had seen their fair share of sadness and loss. Stomping crusted snow from his shoes, he released his breath in clouds as he greeted Beth.

Beth squinted against bare branches glittering with ice. "Come in, Adam. It's freezing out there. Would you like some coffee?"

"Sure, that would be great."

He followed her to the kitchen, and Beth noticed him taking in the surroundings.

"Yeah, excuse the mess. Haven't been in a cleaning mood." Beth inspected a ceramic mug. "Don't worry, though, this mug looks pretty clean. Cream and sugar?"

The officer accepted the steaming coffee and sat at the table. "No, black is good. And I've seen worse messes. For the record, if you ever find yourself at our precinct, don't drink coffee unless it's in a Styrofoam cup. Just sayin'."

"Noted. Let's go into the family room. I think something may be living in the fridge, and the smell is starting to get to me." Beth led the way and sat on the overstuffed cream-colored sofa Danny had picked out. Beth had complained that she sank so far into it, she felt like she was tumbling down a well every time she sat.

"Don't worry, babe, I'll pull you out," he'd told her.

Who will pull me out now?

Adam sat in an upholstered chair opposite the sofa and pulled out a pad and pen.

Beth managed a smile. "Old-school. I like it."

"Oh, this. Yeah, I hate using technology when I talk to people. Just seems so impersonal." He flipped past a few pages and frowned, his brow creasing. "So, here's what we have so far. As you know, the driver of the car that hit you was alone. He was pronounced dead at the scene. We'll get back to him." His expression softened. "Danny was thrown from the vehicle. We've searched the surrounding area several times and found no sign of his wallet or phone. At first, we thought we just hadn't found them yet, but we found your purse, and your wallet and phone were also missing. Remember, it was pouring that night. Your car was forced off the road by the impact. Thanks to the rain and mud, there were several sets of footprints around the scene. We've identified most of them as belonging to the EMTs who arrived on the scene." He paused and consulted his notebook. "But we haven't been able to identify one set of footprints. We know they belong to a male because of the size and shape of the shoe. Our initial thought was the person who called in the accident, but that call came from a couple who drove by and saw your car." He glanced at his notes again. "They pulled over, got out of their car, and were at the scene when the ambulances arrived. We've confirmed the mystery set of footprints doesn't belong to them."

Beth rubbed her forehead. "So, your theory is that someone saw the accident from the road, approached the scene on foot, and robbed us. Nice guy."

"Yes." Adam shook his head in disgust. "Hard to imagine someone could be that cold, but you'd be surprised at the shitty—'scuse my French—things people do." He closed his notebook. "Beth, I hate to make you think back to that night, but you're the only eye-witness. I know you lost consciousness, but before that, do you remember seeing anyone approach the scene? Did you hear anyone speak? Any detail, no matter how small, could help us."

Beth gripped her coffee mug and stared out the window. She searched her memory for anything that might lead the police to the thief but came up empty. She couldn't remember anything between the impact and waking up in the ambulance with the EMT.

"Please... my husband... I have to tell him... He doesn't know..."

A lone tear escaped her left eye, and her voice was raspy when she spoke. "I'm sorry, Adam. I just don't remember seeing anyone. I don't remember much of anything at all."

"It's okay," he said softly. He flipped through a few more pages. "It's weird. The driver of the car that hit you? We found no wallet or identification on him. No phone either. The car was a rental from an agency in New York that didn't mind dealing in cash. The name on the paperwork is William Schotz, but no such person exists, and the manager admitted to us that his New Jersey license looked fake. He paid cash and waived the insurance, so it's a long shot to ID him. We can't notify any next of kin about his death until we know who he is. His prints aren't in any database, so he doesn't have a record. But it gets even weirder. No footprints lead to his car, so we believe that means no one robbed him."

"I'm not following."

"It's just strange that a guy has absolutely no identifying information in his possession. It's like he's a ghost."

Beth considered this and shuddered. "So, what are you saying? Do you think we were targeted? That the driver meant to hit *us*?" She sat up straighter.

"Hard to say. It's possible, but that doesn't make sense. Why would someone target you and Danny? I think it's more likely the driver was fleeing a different scene, and unfortunately, you two ended up in the way. It's an unimaginable tragedy—such a young life taken so needlessly. These are the ones that keep me up at night." Adam closed his notebook and rubbed his hands up and down his thighs. "I've kept you long enough. I'm sure you have things to do. Thanks for talking to me. And if you do think of anything—no matter how insignificant it might seem—give me a call."

"I will." Beth showed the officer out, closed the door, and leaned against it. Hugging herself tightly and sliding down to the floor, she wondered for the thousandth time if she'd gotten exactly what she had coming to her.

Adam's words reverberated in her head. "An unimaginable tragedy."

You have no idea.

Chapter Three

Two Months Later

Sunlight spilled generously across the front lawn, warming areas of grass that had only recently shed patches of snow. Birds returned to the trees with their unique songs, and the breeze, though still brisk, held the promise of spring.

Beth heard her parents' car doors slam and checked her appearance in the foyer mirror. She did what she could to smooth her hair with her hands and made sure no mascara was smeared under her eyes. Before she even opened the front door, she swore she could hear her mother's fretful footsteps approaching. Beth appreciated her mother's concern, but it stressed her out. She wished she'd asked Hannah to pick her up instead of agreeing to drive to lunch with Laura and Richard. But then she would have had to endure Hannah's stories of the happy chaos at her house with her husband, Eric, and their two kids, six-year-old Sydney and four-year-old Henry. She wasn't sure she was up for that.

"Hi, Mom. Hi, Dad."

"Hi, honey." Richard pulled her into an embrace. He was beginning to gray at the temples, but his face still retained the handsome ruggedness of a man ten years younger. Recent hours of yard work gave his skin a golden-tan hue.

"Now that spring is coming, we'll have to get some flowers for your planters," Laura remarked, pulling at the tangle of dead vines trailing from the terra-cotta pots on Beth's front porch. "Something low-maintenance, like begonias or zinnia."

"Find something no-maintenance, and you're on," Beth answered while Richard smiled, gently shaking his head.

"Here, Richard, throw these away." Laura handed the debris to her husband and turned to Beth. "Oh, Beth, how are you? You've hardly returned my calls."

Richard dutifully headed toward the kitchen despite Beth's comical *don't-leave-me* look.

"Mom, really, I don't know how I'm doing. I guess I'm doing my best. I don't return your calls because I don't have anything new to talk about."

Beth noted that, as usual, Laura was put together. It seemed effortless, as though her outfits arrived at her door exquisitely fitted and complete with shoes and accessories. Today, she wore slim, cropped tan pants and a crisp white blouse. Around her neck hung a dainty gold chain with a capital L dangling from it, and modest diamond studs sparkled on her earlobes. Her black flats—the season's newest style—matched her croc-patterned shoulder bag, which she threw on the bench in Beth's foyer before hugging her daughter. Beth frowned at her own wrinkled drawstring pants and T-shirt, feeling disheveled by comparison.

Laura studied Beth's face. "I'm just worried about you." Laura wore little makeup: lightly shadowed eyes, a soft bronze dusting on her cheeks, neutral gloss on her lips. Her bob was stylish but not severe, more "game-night fun" than "ladies-who-lunch stuffy." At fifty-three, she was often mistaken for an older sister rather than the girls' mother.

"I know, and I appreciate it. I'm so lucky to have all of you, but I feel like I need to work through this myself."

Laura could be a bit much at times, but the girls loved her quirks and mannerisms. Laura didn't mind them teasing her about them, and Richard always served as a buffer when his wife strayed out of her lane. Her "Laura-isms" were part of her appeal. Laura and Richard had loved Danny, too, and Beth tried to remind herself that his death was devastating to them, but she couldn't be their support system. *Danny's death.* The words sat on her heart like a fifty-pound weight, pressing on her chest and making the smallest tasks required to get through each day overwhelming.

"We should go. Hannah will be waiting." Richard returned from the kitchen and handed Laura her purse.

"Okay. Beth, do you want a barrette to tie back your hair? I think I have one in my—"

"Mom," Beth said at the same time Richard said, "Laura."

City Tavern was a popular lunch spot in town. Located in a quaint area that boasted shopping, dining, and walking areas, it drew both locals and visitors. Beth and her family loved living in Stradmore, a suburb of Philadelphia, because it offered the perfect combination of city-like bustle and small-town charm. Hannah and her kids were already seated when Beth and her parents arrived.

"Aunt Bethie! Look at my nails!" Sydney shrieked, waving her manicure wildly at Beth. "Mommy and me got mandiques! The color is called Cotton Candy Pink!"

"Wow, beautiful!" Beth made a fuss over her niece's nails while cringing at her own, bitten down to the skin. Another thing she'd let go.

Henry had three crayons in his fist and was furiously drawing on construction paper. When Hannah went out with the kids, she packed her bag as if going on a month-long cross-country road trip.

"What are you drawing?" Beth asked.

"A dinosaur. A bwontosawus!"

Sydney wrinkled her nose. "It doesn't look like a brontosaurus. You're just scribbling."

"It is!" Henry cried. "See his long neck?" He furrowed his brow, his clear blue eyes shooting daggers at his sister.

Hannah gave her daughter a stern look. "Syd, leave your brother alone."

"I see it!" Richard said as he and Laura took their seats between their grandchildren. "Nice work, Henry!"

Henry smiled proudly and went back to his masterpiece.

"Sydney, your nails look lovely! You're becoming quite the young lady," Laura remarked.

Sydney beamed and shook her wavy light-brown mane. "Mommy said if I don't pick at it, next time, I can get a petticue. That's when you get polish on your toes." Pleased with herself, she flashed a big smile that showed her dimples—and the gap where one of her front teeth used to be.

"How are you going to do that?" Laura asked. "Your feet are ticklish!"

"LaLa." Sydney's expression grew serious. "They're going to tickle my feet?"

Laura assured Sydney that the nail tech would be careful.

Before any of the grandchildren were born, the girls had playfully tormented Laura about what they would call her. She'd constantly remarked that she was far too "young and cool" to be called Grandma. "'Grandma' is for old grandmothers. I refuse to answer to that."

Zoe, the first grandchild, had settled it. When she'd started talking, she'd dubbed her LaLa, her version of her grandmother's first name. Laura loved it, and it stuck.

"Where are Nicole and the kids?" Beth asked.

Hannah snorted. "Are you kidding? Like she could get herself *and* the kids out the door without Mom there to tie their shoes. And I'm not just talking about Zoe's and Ethan's."

Beth smiled at the image. Where Hannah made working and raising a family look easy, Nicole lacked her instincts and organizational skills. Of course, it helped that Hannah's husband, Eric, was an attentive, hands-on dad. Nicole, a single parent, struggled to keep it all together. Zoe and Ethan were the product of a high school relationship turned brief, tumultuous marriage. Though Hannah was never short on jibes and Beth agreed with her, she usually held her tongue about their younger sister.

"Hannah, really," Laura chided. "Stop exaggerating. Nic manages fine without my help."

"Is that so? Like the time she called Dad to come over because Ethan messed up the buttons on the remote and she couldn't get *Bubble Guppies* on TV to occupy the kids while she cleaned up the kitchen from breakfast—which was probably two cereal bowls and two spoons? Or the time she forgot she signed up to bring cupcakes to Zoe's kindergarten class, so you canceled your book club to bake them and personally deliver them to the school?"

"I remember that," Beth said. "That was the Halloween party. Mom, didn't you pipe little icing ghosts on each one, complete with M&M eyes?"

"I wonder if they have their chicken salad today. I love how they put grapes and walnuts in it." Laura studied the menu, pretending not to hear her daughters, while a small smile spread across Richard's face.

Hannah wasn't finished. "Or my personal favorite..." She looked like a stand-up comedian ready to deliver the punch line. "The time she totaled her car, so you gave her *your* brand-new car."

Laura huffed. "Nic needed a car to get to work."

"And yet she was fired from that job for taking too many days off." By then, Hannah's eyes watered from laughing. She sank back in her chair and covered her face with her menu.

"Mommy." Sydney frowned. "We're not supposed to act so silly at the table."

"That's right, Syd," Laura agreed. "Maybe your mommy needs a time-out."

Beth gazed at Sydney and Henry, her eyes misting over. She loved her nieces and nephews with all her heart, but they had become a stark reminder of what was missing from her life. She'd always imagined a gaggle of kids—hers and her sisters'—running around the backyard, having sleepovers, building sandcastles...

"Beth, honey, the server is telling us the specials. I asked him for a gluten-free menu for you." Laura's voice brought Beth back to the present.

They ordered lunch, and the conversation turned to more neutral topics—the unseasonably cool weather, summer-camp offerings for Hannah's and Nicole's kids, their annual July family trip to Avalon, New Jersey.

But no matter the subject, no matter how carefully selected by her family, all Beth felt was loss and pain. She wondered how much one person could cry. *Is the reservoir of tears endless, or does the supply eventually run out? How long does a young widow grieve?* It had only been two months since the accident, but Beth felt as though she had also perished that night. The credits had rolled at the end of Beth and Danny's movie. The final words of their story were written. The end. Done.

She hated the pitying looks on people's faces when they saw her. They approached awkwardly, as if she were made of glass and might shatter. Many of them stopped calling or dropping by. Maybe they worried that death and bad luck were contagious. *Hang around Beth Collins, and it might get you too.* Beth understood. The messages she appreciated most were ones expressing that someone was thinking about her without expecting a response. She much preferred *Thinking of you* to *How are you doing?* Only her family and Molly had continued regular visits and invitations.

After lunch, Hannah asked Beth if she wanted to walk around town with the kids and her. Beth agreed, and they said goodbye to Richard and Laura, Beth promising to return her mother's calls. Hannah pushed Henry in a stroller, and Beth held Sydney's hand as they walked. Beth's left arm itched inside her cast. She looked forward to having it removed the following week.

Sydney filled Beth in on the palace intrigue of her first-grade class. "And Sara likes Ben, but he runs away from her at recess to play kickball with the boys. I don't know why she even likes him. He wipes his nose on his sleeve. It's sooooooo gross!" Sydney made a gagging noise.

"Tell Sara not to give up hope. I'm sure, even at the ripe old age of six, she'll find a boy out there for her," Beth assured her niece.

"Are boys different when they're older, Aunt Bethie?"

"Yeah," Hannah chimed in. "They're taller."

They walked along a brick path lined with flowers and came to a park with playground equipment. "Go ahead and play, but stay on this side where we can see you," Hannah instructed.

The sisters found a bench in the shade. They sat in silence for a few minutes, watching the kids, Hannah occasionally calling out warnings and instructions to Sydney and Henry. Sydney was on the slide with a few other kids who looked about her age, while Henry crawled through a tunnel shaped like a giant caterpillar.

"So," Hannah began, not looking at Beth. "When were you going to tell me?"

"Tell you what?" Beth stared straight ahead, but relief crossed her face as she realized Hannah had figured out her tragic secret.

Hannah turned to her sister. "Oh, Beth, I should have known. I can see it all over your face. It hit me at the restaurant when you were watching Syd and Henry."

Beth faced Hannah but said nothing.

"How far along were you?" Hannah took Beth's hand.

For a moment, neither of them spoke.

"Eight weeks at the time of the accident. I hadn't even told Danny yet." A light breeze blew a strand of hair across Beth's face. She didn't bother to move it. "I intended to tell him that night. But he'd been so distracted and working crazy hours. We were running late for the party, so I decided I'd tell him afterward. I knew he would be suspicious if I didn't drink at the party. I just kind of held the same glass of wine in my hand all night so he didn't suspect anything." She absentmindedly placed her hand on her belly. "When I came to in the ambulance, I told the EMT so she wouldn't give me any meds that would be dangerous for the baby. I hadn't even seen an obstetrician yet. My first appointment was scheduled for two days after the accident."

"Jesus."

"Then, in the hospital, they told me Danny had died. I asked them about the baby, but I already knew. I could just tell." Tears streamed freely down Beth's face. "The doctor gave me medication to induce labor." Her breath caught, and she choked back a sob. "They did the procedure the next morning."

Now Hannah was crying too. "My God, Beth. Did you...? Did they let you hold...?" She covered her face with her hands.

"Yes."

Neither woman spoke for a few minutes. Hannah still clutched Beth's hand in hers.

"Mommy! Henry's eating dirt!" Sydney's voice rang out from the playground.

"Am not!" Henry protested. "You're a tattletale!"

Hannah wiped her face with her sleeve. "I guess that's my cue. Be right back."

While her sister investigated the dirt-eating situation, Beth attempted to compose herself. She had seen the tiny fetus, no bigger than a kidney bean. Though the doctor hadn't said—she wasn't even sure they could tell—Beth knew in her heart that the baby had been a girl. She felt bonded to her in a way she knew could never be severed. Though she'd never had the chance to hold her in her arms, Beth hoped her baby had felt the connection too.

The feeling she couldn't shake, no matter how hard she tried, no matter how tightly she squeezed her eyes shut against the vision, was that she had gotten exactly what she deserved when that car slammed into them.

Hannah returned and sat so close to Beth, their arms and legs touched. "It's overwhelming. What you've lost. I can't wrap my head around it."

Beth released a breath she didn't know she'd been holding. "So, now I have to figure out how to build a future for myself. I had a husband and a baby on the way, and now I'm alone."

"You're not al—" Hannah started to object but stopped mid-sentence, as though she knew what her sister meant.

"I know Mom means well. She casually mentions things like 'I saw Grace from your office at Stop & Shop. She asked about you,' when what she really wants to say is 'Are you ever going back to work, or are you giving up on everything?'"

"Yeah, she's about as subtle as a freight train. But you're right, she means well. They're both worried about you. We all are." Hannah paused. "Will you tell them about the pregnancy?"

"I don't know. I guess. Why not give them one more thing to fret about, right? I'm a ray of sunshine, aren't I? No matter how shitty your life is at the moment, my life can top it." Beth studied her hands, her oval diamond sparkling on her left ring finger. *Should I still wear this? I'm not married anymore. I'm not anything anymore.*

"Stop it. It's not your fault. And anyway, it's about time the drama came from somewhere other than Nic, right?"

Beth managed a sad smile. "Has Mom told you she thinks I need to 'talk to someone'?"

Hannah didn't answer and instead busied herself with shoving the kids' jackets in her bag.

"Oh my God, you think I should too. You all think I'm going crazy!"

"Not crazy, but come on, Beth. You've suffered a terrible blow. Losing Danny is bad enough. But the baby. Anyone would have trouble coping." Hannah looked so sad that Beth felt sorry for her. "If not a therapist, maybe a support group? You know, with people who've gone through the same thing. Maybe you'd feel better talking to them. Let's face it, as much as we love you, we can't know what you're feeling."

Beth considered this. Maybe Hannah was right. But she felt so numb with loss, she wasn't sure she could open up to strangers, even if they'd had similar experiences.

"Promise me you'll at least think about it."

Beth nodded, and Hannah called out to Sydney and Henry that it was time to leave. They walked back to the parking lot near the restaurant and loaded the kids and the stroller into Hannah's SUV.

"So, what *about* your job? Have you decided when you might go back?"

Beth sighed. "I don't know. I'm thinking I might not."

Hannah's eyes opened wide in surprise. "Really? Why?"

Beth got into the passenger seat and fastened her seat belt. "I keep imagining the pitying looks, the kid-glove treatment I'll likely get. I don't know if I'm up for it. I've been thinking about changing careers—trying something completely different."

As they drove away, Beth spotted a storefront across the square with a For Lease sign in the window. Sunlight shone on the large bay windows, showing dirt and streaks of neglect. "Hey, wasn't that the bakery with the bagels you all said were so delicious? What's it called? Something catchy, I think."

"What? Oh, yeah. Cake My Day. I'm so bummed they closed. The owners retired to Florida. All their stuff was delicious. I mean, I know you can't eat most of what they made because it was loaded with gluten. I've been going to the one on Seventh Avenue, but it's not as good."

"Huh."

Hannah steered the car out of the shopping district. Beth turned back to the vacant storefront and fixed her gaze on it until it disappeared from view.

Chapter Four

Three Weeks Later

Beth stood at the entrance to her kitchen with her hands on her hips. She shook her head at the mess. *What am I doing? Becoming a hoarder won't bring them back. It will just make me a depressed person with junk piled up around me.* It was a slippery slope. One day, there were a few dirty dishes in the sink, and the next, she wouldn't be able to get to the shower with all the used toys and rusted tools blocking it.

She had to accept that it was her life now. No Danny. No baby. She'd been marinating in her sadness, letting it drench her, pull her under. No more plucking T-shirts from his dresser drawer, desperate to inhale her husband's scent, his essence. It wasn't there, anyway. Only the fragrance of laundry detergent lingered.

She needed to find a new normal.

Leaning against the doorframe, Beth closed her eyes. *I miss you so much, Danny. I miss our inside jokes and our silly nicknames for each other and reading to you with your head in my lap. I miss the unspoken way I knew when you needed time to yourself and you knew when I needed time with Molly. Mostly, I miss how we couldn't wait to get back to each other after those times apart. But this is where I am now. You're gone, but I'm still here. I'm incomplete, like a book without pages, a ballad without words. I have to find my way. I'm fraying, and I need to find a way to patch myself back together.*

Strengthened by her internal pep talk, she rolled up her sleeves and got to work loading the dishwasher, wiping down the counters and tables, and mopping the floor. She raised the window shade above the sink and let the morning sun's rays stream into the now-sparkling kitchen. Then she moved to the foyer, stooping to retrieve unopened mail from the floor. She separated it into neat piles of bills and sympathy cards and tossed the junk mail into a trash bag. Tackling the family room next, she gathered mugs and wineglasses from the coffee table and took them to the kitchen. After loading the mugs into the dishwasher and hand-washing the glasses, she returned to the family room to dust the coffee table and straighten the sofa cushions.

Grasping the unopened bills and cards, she drew back the curtains and sat cross-legged on the sofa. Energized by her organized surroundings, she began opening cards. Most were from friends and business associates of both hers and Danny's, bearing the usual sentiments: *Sorry for your loss, Our thoughts are with you,* and *If you need anything...*

One envelope with no return address caught her attention. On the front of the card was a familiar sympathy card scene—the sun peeking through trees after a rainstorm, the quintessential representation of hope after darkness. She opened the card and furrowed her brow in puzzlement. There was no writing inside, no compassionate message, and most baffling, no signature. Nothing. She flipped over the envelope and looked at her name and address to see if she recognized the handwriting, but she didn't.

Hmmm. Weird. It was postmarked in New York, so Beth figured it was from one of Danny's associates or clients. Danny traveled to New York periodically to do contract work—specifically estate cases—for a small Manhattan firm run by one of his law school classmates, but Beth didn't know anyone's name in that office.

She was still pondering this when another envelope caught her eye. She recognized the penmanship on it as her boss's. Sheila had been more than supportive these last few months, giving Beth time to grieve and heal with an indefinite leave of absence. Beth had to admit that, as careers went, hers as a mortgage broker was, well, fine. She was good at it. She enjoyed negotiating with lenders to help her clients secure their dream of owning a home. Few things pleased her more than brokering the perfect deal for hopeful homeowners. She often developed friendships with couples and families she worked closely with as she assessed their needs and fought to find the right lending option for them. Happy clients invited her over when they moved into their new homes and sent her thoughtful cards and gifts to thank her for her tireless efforts.

Still, is "fine" what I need after losing both Danny and my pregnancy? Since the accident, she'd gone from finding fulfillment in her job to viewing it as monotonous and pedestrian. The aspects of it that she'd thought she enjoyed—regular hours, steady income—now struck her as rote and unsatisfying. She'd taken a leave of absence after the accident, and while her boss was gracious and understanding, Beth knew she had to make up her mind soon. She couldn't expect the mortgage company to hold her job forever.

She didn't know why, but the vacant bakery shop in town had monopolized her thoughts ever since she and Hannah had driven past it. It was as if it were calling to her, crooking its finger, beckoning her to bring it back to life. *But in what way? What do I know about running a small business?* Yet something told her if she wanted to move past her life with Danny and their hopes for a family and a future together, Beth would have to completely reinvent herself. Beth the mortgage broker tragically lost her husband and unborn baby, but Beth the—*what? Shop owner? Bakery owner? Café owner?*—had never existed, so neither did her tragic past. For so long, Beth had been convinced that a husband and children were the only things that could fill the void and make her complete. *But were they?*

The thought tugged at her. A fresh start, a way to put the past behind her. *What a crazy idea,* she thought, even as she grabbed her purse and keys and hurried out the front door.

Midday traffic was light, and Beth made it downtown in fifteen minutes. She pulled into the square, where the vacant shop sat nestled between a boutique and a gift shop. Cutting the engine, she sat behind the wheel for several moments, staring at the storefront. Finally, she got out of her car and walked across the square to an indie bookstore called Can't Put It Down. She ordered a latte from the coffee bar in the store's front and took a seat facing the square.

As she gazed at the dirt-splattered windows of the vacant shop, a vision began to take shape. Instead of counters covered in musty drop cloths, Beth saw sparkling glass cases displaying house-made artisan sandwiches, salads, and desserts. She envisioned a large kitchen open on one end to the customers, a cheery staff bustling around, good-naturedly ribbing each other as they worked. Just inside the bay windows, Beth could see round tables surrounded by chairs with curlicue wrought iron legs where people gathered to start their days or meet for lunch.

Beth had an unhealthy relationship with food, but this venture could change that. She suffered from celiac disease, an autoimmune disease for which there was no cure. The only way to manage it was to adhere to a strict gluten-free diet. Everywhere Beth went, celiac disease followed her like an unwelcome companion, ruining visits with friends, parties, outings at restaurants. Even worse was the way many people made fun of or disparaged people who ate gluten free. Some viewed it as a fad and others as a way to get attention. For Beth, eating gluten free was far from a fad. She'd been sick for years and had consulted countless doctors before they'd finally figured out what was causing her debilitating abdominal pain.

She sipped her latte and wondered if opening a café with numerous gluten-free options could have the dual effect of helping her move past her loss and helping her create delicious homemade foods that everyone could enjoy—whether they suffered from celiac disease or not. One of the things that infuriated Beth was when people—even though they meant well—said things like "This tastes so good, you'd never know it was gluten free!" as though anything that lacked gluten also lacked taste. Ever since she'd been diagnosed, she constantly experimented with substitutions in recipes to make them gluten free. It wasn't difficult once she knew what she was doing, and contrary to what the jokesters thought, food was every bit as good when made with gluten-free flours, breadcrumbs, and other substitutions.

Beth felt a rush of something she hadn't felt in the months since the accident: hope. Her heart beat rapidly, and a reel of her future café played in her head.

She didn't realize she was smiling until a woman took the seat next to her and remarked, "Maybe I should have ordered what you're drinking."

Grabbing her purse as she stood, Beth answered, "It's a beautiful afternoon, isn't it? Have a nice day!"

She practically skipped across the square and cupped her hands against the grimy glass storefront window. The seed was planted, and she saw it growing, flourishing. She dug her phone from her purse and punched in the realtor's number.

Chapter Five

"Oh, Beth, I'm so glad you're feeling better and moving on, but really? Quitting your job? Opening a café?" Laura carried a salad to the table, and her eyes pleaded with Richard for help.

He placed his hand on top of his wife's. The family was gathered for Sunday dinner at Beth's parents' house, and she felt she had enough details about her plan to share with her family.

"Laura, let's hear her out before going off the deep end." Richard scooped up a portion of chicken parm and passed the casserole dish to Hannah.

Hannah filled the kids' plates and began cutting the gooey creation into bites.

"Here's a thought, Mom. How about not going off the deep end at all? She's opening a small business, not building a campfire in Death Valley." Hannah patted her mother's shoulder.

Nicole added, "Yeah, Mom, I think it's cool. Let her talk. Life is shor—"

Hannah's eyes widened, and she loudly cleared her throat.

"I mean, go ahead, Beth. You were saying you're thinking about offering mostly gluten-free options?"

Beth smiled. "Yes, and by the way, you don't need to tiptoe around me so much. You're right. Life *is* short. Danny's was too short. My baby never even got a chance to live." Everyone's expression sobered at the mention of Beth's miscarriage. "But I'm here, and they're not. I have to carry on." She turned to her parents. "Mom, you suggested I join a support group, and I did, and it's helping. I even spoke at the last meeting. I told the group about feeling that I need an entirely fresh start, and they were so supportive. They understood the need to do something completely different from my life with Danny."

"So, you're doing this to forget Danny?" Laura rubbed her temples. "I'm a bit confused."

"No, of course not, Mom. I'll never forget Danny. Or the baby. Nor do I want to. But losing them has made me entirely rethink things. I don't know... I just feel like I *need* to do this. I can't explain why the empty store spoke to me, but it did."

"Beth, your eyes light up when you talk about the café. It's so great to see you looking forward to something—something you can pour some positive energy into." Richard smiled. "And I happen to have some free time on my hands. I'd be happy to help. My woodworking skills are rusty, but I'd love to take them out for a spin."

Laura wasn't convinced. "But, honey, just abruptly quitting your job? The renovations will be costly. Will you be able to manage until your café is up and running? And even then, it will take some time before you make a profit."

"Oh, for God's sake. Other than that, Mrs. Lincoln, how did you enjoy the play?" Hannah scolded her mother, and Nicole laughed so hard she snorted.

"Yeah, Mom, do you need a paper bag to breathe into?"

"The girls are right, Laura," Richard said softly. "You're only concentrating on the cons. Try to look at the pros."

Beth frowned. "Money isn't an issue. It's not the way anyone wants to come into it, but when I probated the will, it was clear Danny had his affairs in order. Between his life insurance, his 401(k), and his investments, I'm financially well-off." A prolonged pause followed Beth's declaration.

Nicole broke the silence. "Well, I think it's great, Beth."

"Me too," Hannah added. "Nic, maybe you could even work there. You might even last longer than six months."

Nicole rolled her eyes.

Richard laughed. "Beth, so tell us a little more about what you're thinking in terms of food. You mentioned offering lots of gluten-free options. You're certainly an expert in that field."

"Yes, that's right. You know what a pain it is for me to go out to eat. Always scanning menus, trying to figure out what I can eat and what I can't. One of the things that aggravates me the most is choosing something then being told by the server that it has gluten. When I go to my second choice, the same thing happens. By the time I find something safe, it's not even something I want to eat. Not just that, but I get embarrassed and anxious watching everyone at the table either pity me or get frustrated because I'm holding up the ordering process."

Laura nodded. "Well, that's certainly true. It's not easy."

Beth leaned forward, her folded arms on the table. "One thing I really feel strongly about—maybe more than anything else—is dispelling the incorrect notion that gluten-free foods cannot taste as good as foods with gluten. Society has put that idea into people's heads, and it drives me crazy. I've been cooking gluten free since I was diagnosed with celiac. You guys eat at my house, and I don't see any of you spitting your food into your napkins. Sure, it took some research and finagling, but most recipes can be made gluten free with very simple substitutions. And okay, I've had some epic fails, but that happens even when cooking with regular flour, breadcrumbs, and sauces. I also have another idea."

Ethan, Nicole's four-year-old, played with his pasta, attempting to twirl it around his fork.

Beth pulled him onto her lap. "Ethan, remember the cookies we made when you and Zoe slept over last time?"

Ethan's face lit up. "Oooh, yeah, they were sooo good! And you let me put sprinkles on top!"

Beth squeezed her nephew and rested her head on top of his. "Right! So I was also thinking I'd offer gluten-free cooking and baking classes for adults and kids. I want people to see how easy it is to do and, most of all, that gluten free does not mean taste free. Listen, I really need you guys to get on board with this. I know it won't be easy, but for the first time in a long time, I feel hopeful about the future. Excited, even. I can't go back to my old job. I just can't. I need a fresh start to move on."

Sydney had been listening intently. "Aunt Bethie, you're going to be a boss lady!"

The next week, Beth's cheeks flushed with excitement as she showed her family around the former bakery.

"Okay, yes, I can picture it." Richard nodded and stroked his chin as he, Laura, and Hannah followed Beth around the empty shop.

Maria, the real estate agent, stood off to the side, giving Beth space but remaining on hand to answer any questions.

"Right?" Beth stood next to the chest-high glass cases and spread her arms. "These display cases were here when the shop was a bakery, and they're fine. But I'd like to add a counter that extends on one end of them. At that end will be room for takeout orders." She motioned to an area about ten feet from the display cases, where she could already see perfectly arranged sandwiches, salads, and pastries. She could offer samples and daily specials. Her food items would appeal to all the senses. She remembered hearing somewhere that people experienced food through smell before any other sense. "The kitchen would be behind this space but open to the dining area. Dad, I'm hoping you'll work your magic and build me a sturdy butcher-block workspace back there."

"You may need one or two people just handling takeout. This square is crazy at lunchtime because of all the businesses in the area," Hannah offered.

The space was about twelve hundred square feet, with clean grayish-brown laminate flooring. The walls were painted a soft gray that shone in the afternoon sunlight streaming through the large windows. Overhead lights with bamboo shades cast a soft glow, and Beth could picture customers reading or chatting at tables beneath them.

"I love the floors," Laura remarked to Maria.

"Aren't they great? And practically new. They look exactly like hardwood but are much easier to clean and maintain."

Beth gazed out the windows at the side area. She envisioned a paved courtyard surrounded by a gate. Socket-style lights strung overhead through a pergola and greenery would allow people to enjoy the café outdoors. Maybe even a firepit. She could hear Danny's voice in her head saying, *No, you don't want a firepit. It would be a liability nightmare.* It struck her that the thought of Danny's voice made her smile instead of filling her with instant sadness.

Richard asked, "The space is available immediately?"

Maria looked at the papers in her hand. "Yes. I mean, we'll need to work out the terms of the lease and the financing. The sellers want to lease the first year, but you'll have an option to buy after that period expires."

Beth rubbed her hands together. "Lucky for me, I come from that world and speak the language. Do you have a copy of the lease with you, Maria?"

"Yes, you can take a look at this copy, but I'll also email you one so you can take your time going over it before making a final decision."

Beth flipped through the pages. "It looks pretty straightforward, but I definitely want to look at it more closely at home. Let's see... the rent does not include operating expenses like utilities, maintenance, property taxes, insurance, and property management."

"You have to pay property taxes even though you'll be renting for the first year?" Laura asked.

"Yes, that's fairly common in Pennsylvania. The renter pays in one form or another. The Lord giveth, and the government taketh away." Beth chuckled. "However, I know from experience that everything is negotiable."

"Can I get an amen?" Maria pecked at her phone. "There. I sent you the lease electronically. Go over it and get back to me. I should tell you, I have other people looking at the space. They don't seem as motivated as you, but I want you to know there is interest. It's a great location."

"It is," Beth agreed. In her head, the shop was already hers.

Chapter Six

One Month Later

By late May, the southeastern Pennsylvania suburbs had burst into green. Trees towered, full and leafy, casting spotted shadows on the sidewalks. The scent of lilac and freshly mowed grass permeated the air. After the gloom of winter—particularly the last one—Beth found comfort in cool mornings, bearable heat, and the occasional sudden shower that left everything glowing.

She marveled—not for the first time—at how bizarre it was that life went on despite her own imploding a few months ago. Spring was ready to hand the baton to summer. The sun rose every morning and set every evening. People got out of bed and went to work or school. They loved and fought and worked and dreamed as though nothing had changed, as though a freak car accident hadn't taken the lives of Danny and their unborn baby. Even the flowers seemed indifferent, as if the earth had decided that beauty must persist, no matter who was missing. And yet, as hard as it was to grasp, life somehow simultaneously seemed to go on exactly as it should.

Beth drew in a deep breath as she stepped into the dimly lit store. As of that morning, it was hers—now all she had to do was clean and renovate it, find employees and vendors, and create recipes for foods that would entice customers. She flipped on the overhead lights, a stark contrast to the dull light struggling to penetrate the filthy bay windows. Wandering around the space, she tried to grasp the reality that she was a small business owner.

Things had happened quickly after she'd made the final decision. After combing through the lease, Beth had Maria draw up the paperwork before she could change her mind. She and Maria had a virtual meeting with the previous owners, who were gracious and happy for Beth. They loved that someone with such passion would be taking over the space that had meant so much to them for so many years. Following a flurry of tears and congratulations, they imparted vital information such as how to install netting to keep birds from building nests in the light fixture over the front steps and how to "unstick" the back screen door when the humidity caused it to swell in its frame. They had wished Beth the best and promised to stop in when they visited family in the area.

Beth was anxious to start the renovations. She had three contractors scheduled in the next few days to give her quotes. Two had come out to their house when she and Danny had decided they wanted to add a sunroom off their kitchen. They'd never gone through with it, though. At the last minute, Danny had become concerned with the cost of the project, even though he'd initially been gung ho about it. He was often that way—one day buying a brand-new car and the next canceling a weekend getaway, claiming it was too expensive. Though Beth had always had everything she'd wanted or needed, Danny's vacillating attitude about money had often confounded her. When she'd tried to talk to him about his change of heart, he had snapped at her. Aware he was dealing with stress at work, she'd backed off and never mentioned her desire for the renovation again.

Before she met with contractors, she would begin cleaning. Returning to her car to retrieve buckets, brooms, mops, and other supplies, she encountered a woman power walking around the square.

The woman waved and shouted, "Hello there! Are you the new owner?"

Beth smiled at her frankness. *Jeez, get right to the point, why don't you?*

She approached, and Beth stuck out her hand.

"Yes, hi. Beth Collins. I'm opening a café."

"Lucy Herrera. Pleased to meet you." The woman tucked a wayward strand of hair under her visor and wiped her sweaty hands on the front of her walking shorts before shaking Beth's hand. "That's awesome! Such a shame to have a great space sitting empty. I used to work for Tom and Sylvie at the bakery. Nice people. Hated to see them go."

Beth estimated Lucy to be in her late forties. Her shoulder-length dark-brown hair was pulled back in a ponytail, and Beth spotted a few errant grays threatening to escape. Her striking amber eyes lit up when she spoke about working at the bakery, as though the experience had left her with fond memories and a plethora of stories.

A few brooms and mops slid from Beth's grasp.

Lucy grabbed them as they fell. "Here, let me give you a hand with those."

Beth started to protest, but Lucy headed toward the door before she could form a sentence.

Lucy's eyes widened as she stepped inside, and she let out a low whistle. "Holy dirt and grime!"

"Yeah, I have my work cut out for me, huh?"

"You can say that again." Lucy dragged her finger over the filthy windowsill and kicked a dust bunny on the floor. "You planning to tackle this all by your lonesome?"

"No, not entirely. My parents and sisters will help. My best friend too. It takes a village, right?" Beth looked around and wondered for the thousandth time if she had bitten off more than she could chew. She willed Danny to whisper in her ear, encourage her to push forward.

Lucy seemed to sense Beth's doubt because she hurriedly added, "You know what? I have some time on my hands. I wouldn't mind helping. I haven't found another job since Tom and Sylvie left, and I love a good project."

"Oh, I couldn't ask—"

"Honey, you didn't ask, I offered." Lucy gestured toward the parking lot, where Beth's car doors stood open. "Go get the rest of the supplies. I'll open the blinds so we can see exactly what we're dealing with. Then you can tell me what you have in mind for this place."

Beth did as she was told, chuckling and shaking her head the whole way. She had the feeling Lucy wasn't someone people argued with.

Retrieving the last of the items from her car and dumping them inside the door, she waved her arm in front of her as if presenting a prize on a game show. "Well, you know the layout, but I'm going to make some changes." She explained to Lucy her battle with celiac disease and her vision of a café that offered fresh, mostly gluten-free dishes.

Lucy followed her around the space and nodded as Beth relayed her ideas. The more Beth spoke, the more real it became to her. As she articulated her vision to Lucy and imagined what it would look like, a warm flourish of anticipation filled her insides. Shiny floors, pleasing wall colors, soft lighting, and comfortable seating for both dining and conversation. Add to that an original menu that appealed to people of all ages. She didn't realize she was smiling until she saw Lucy's face.

"What?" Beth stopped to catch her breath.

"If that light in your eyes is any indication, you'll do just fine here. You know, if you don't mind my saying so, I thought I detected apprehension on your face when I first ran into you outside. Maybe I did, maybe I didn't. But when you talk about your café, there's nothing but sheer joy on that pretty face of yours."

Beth thought about Danny, and a calm permeated her belly. His voice was in her head now, urging her to do this, telling her he believed in her.

Lucy grabbed a bucket and a bottle of Mr. Clean and headed for the sink. "So, we better get started. This place won't clean itself."

The two women talked easily as they worked. Beth told Lucy that her father dabbled in woodworking and was going to build a butcher-block island in the kitchen and fix up things like the walls and trim, which had seen better days. Lucy admitted that Tom and Sylvie knew the bakery was falling into disrepair but had constantly put off making improvements. They'd installed the new flooring recently, and the stress of that project—backorders, wrong materials, installers showing up late—had led them to conclude they wanted to retire.

"So, this family of yours, are they going to work in the café when it opens?" Lucy asked as she finished wiping the glass on the front of the display cases.

"Oh, no. I mean, I think they'll help out if I'm in a jam, but they all have their own lives. My parents are retired, so they'll pinch-hit if necessary. My sister Hannah has a full-time job and two little kids. In fact, she was a regular at the bakery, so you may even recognize her. My younger sister, Nicole, also has two little ones and is usually 'between jobs,' so I might be able to corral her help once in a while." Beth smiled at the thought of Nic getting up in time for the breakfast shift.

"So, how did you discover you have celiac disease?"

"Ugh. It was rough. I was sick for years. Every time I ate, I had mad stomach pain and, well, digestive issues, if you know what I mean." A pink hue spread across Beth's cheeks. "I went to doctors for years, but no one could figure out what was wrong. It was crazy.

When you have debilitating abdominal pain and digestive issues, what do you typically do?"

Lucy thought about it for a second. "Eat a bland diet?"

"Bingo! Crackers, pretzels, dry toast. Things like that. I stopped eating butter, cream cheese, sauces... all the things you would assume aggravate an angry belly. Turns out, it wasn't the butter or cream cheese. It was the bread and crackers and all the other bland foods I was eating, which are loaded with gluten!"

"Ain't that something! You gave up the usual belly crampers and opted for the foods that were *actually* making you sick."

"Yes, crazy, right? So, anyway, I went to an array of doctors, none of whom could figure out what was wrong with me. One even told me no one gets that sick from eating plain crackers and suggested I see a psychiatrist." Beth rolled her eyes.

"He may have been onto something. You probably felt like you were losing your mind from all those incompetent doctors." Lucy peeled off her rubber gloves and blew a strand of hair out of her face.

"It was stressful because I kept getting sicker. In their defense, though, this was years ago, when celiac disease was not as prevalent. And it's often misdiagnosed because of the number of different symptoms."

"Well," Lucy said. "You'll make a lot of people very happy. Celiac is so common now, people will love having a place in the area where they can safely eat delicious food."

"That's the thing." Beth sighed. "Dining at restaurants is so stressful for me. I want people with or without celiac disease to come here to eat without even *thinking* about whether their order is gluten free. Always *thinking* about what I can and can't eat is what drives me most crazy. Does that make sense, or do I sound loony?"

"Makes perfect sense to me. Maybe you even have a tagline in there somewhere. You know, 'All the taste, none of the stress' or something like that."

Beth laughed. "Or 'Gluten is for gluttons!' or 'Life is sweet without wheat!'"

Lucy applauded. "You are obviously much better at this than I am."

"Well, unfortunately, due to necessity, I'm constantly thinking about it."

"Here," Lucy directed as she tossed a garbage bag to Beth. "Start gathering paper towels and other trash and stuff it in this bag."

Beth couldn't help but smile. *Yes, ma'am,* she thought, but she enjoyed Lucy's take-charge attitude. A thought formed in her mind. "Lucy, earlier, you said you haven't found another job. Would you consider working for me, here, at—whatever I'm going to call this place?" She waved her arm at the empty but now clean space and looked hopefully at the woman she'd met only a few hours earlier.

Lucy leaned on the long handle of a push broom and chuckled. "Don't you want references or something? What if I'm a serial killer? Or worse—an Aquarius?"

"Ha! See? You're perfect! You'd keep me in line and teach me a thing or two. Plus you have just the personality customers would love. And you know the business... I mean, I know a café is a little different from a bakery, but still. And—"

"Whoa, easy there. You're gonna get dizzy and fall over!" Lucy shook her head and laughed. Her iWatch dinged, and she glanced at it.

Beth's hand flew to her mouth. "Oh my God! Here I am going on and on about myself and my life, and I didn't ask you anything about yours. I've kept you too long!"

Lucy shook her head. "Gurrrrl, we need more than a few hours if we're going to talk about my life. That's a conversation best had over a martini. Or two. Or three." Her infectious smile was genuine.

"Listen, I didn't mean to put you on the spot. Think about my offer, and we'll talk more later. And thank you so much for all your help today. At the very least, even if you don't take the job, let me treat you to lunch when I open."

"You're on." Lucy pushed open the door and turned around. "How do you like that? I go out for a walk and come back with a job offer."

Beth gave a little wave. "And hopefully what you consider a new friend."

"Definitely a new friend. I'll be in touch!"

Lucy crossed the square in the direction of her house. If she noticed the man staring at the storefront from his parked car, she didn't let on.

Chapter Seven

Four Weeks Later

"Dad, you're the best!" Beth hugged Richard, who beamed with satisfaction. "It's exactly what I envisioned. Lucy and Frank will love preparing meals on this beauty!"

The entire kitchen had gotten a facelift. Beth ran her hand over the smooth finish of the butcher-block island Richard had installed in the middle of the square space. On the wall to the left of it were rows of cabinets he had hung the day before. A new counter with spacious drawers separated the low and high cabinets. Additional counter space took up the right side. Above the counters were hooks for utensils of all sizes. An eight-burner cooktop, wall ovens, three large sinks, and a dishwasher occupied the far wall. Off to the side, a small room that had once been a walk-in closet now served as a butler's pantry with its own shelves, cabinets, drawers, a sink, a range, and a small refrigerator. Any food containing gluten would be prepared in this space, so Beth's main kitchen could be rightfully declared a dedicated gluten-free food preparation space.

The square buzzed with late-summer shoppers and diners. Many had stopped in during the renovations to inquire about what sort of new business they could look forward to. They didn't hold back their enthusiasm about Beth's plan.

The café was scheduled to open in a few weeks, and Beth labored over what to name it. Every name she came up with felt wrong, like it would alienate some sect of the community. If she emphasized healthy food, she worried people might think she served only salads and smoothies. If the name was overly general, she was concerned people would view it as just another breakfast and lunch spot with nothing new to offer. And her worst fear of all—if the title mentioned gluten-free items, people would wrongly assume her dishes tasted like cardboard.

Beth had lain awake night after night, trying to come up with a memorable and original name. She was hopeful the café would be what she needed to truly move on after the accident. Danny's death and her miscarriage had carved a hole in her that she was desperate to fill. In the end, that loss guided her to her business name. After much fist clenching and teeth gnashing, Beth settled on Fresh Start. She loved a good pun, and this one described both the food she served and her lot in life. The agony of losing Danny and their baby was part of her story, a part that had left a permanent scar inside but that she camouflaged on the outside. She wished for the café name to be both an invitation and a mystery that would attract all manner of customers in all life situations—agony and ecstasy and everything in between. People could come here during happy times or when they needed a friendly conversation and something delicious to eat. She wanted it to be a place they could find comfort in one form or another. Happy with the name, Beth contracted an artist to design both indoor and outdoor signs. She couldn't wait to replace the Coming Soon sign that currently occupied the front window.

To Beth's delight, Lucy accepted her job offer. Since she had experience in the food industry, Lucy would run the kitchen. Ads in the local newspaper and on social media resulted in Beth finding Frank, a cook who had recently relocated to the area and had experience working in various diners and cafés. Lucy immediately deemed him "second in command," a title to which Frank happily agreed. He had no interest in upstaging Lucy—not that it seemed possible. Not surprisingly, Lucy and Molly hit it off instantly. Beth had no doubt her longtime best friend and her new chief employee would add a never-a-dull-moment element to the venture. They good-naturedly poked fun at Beth's suggestion that having fresh fruit on the menu every day would be a cheery item to draw people in.

"Gurrrl," Lucy chided. "I've had more bad days than I can count, and never once when I was at a low point did I say to myself, 'You know what would really rev my engine? Some fresh fruit!'"

Molly was quick to pile on. "She's right, Beth. You know what never disappoints? A chocolate muffin with chocolate chips on top."

The ads also produced a server named Gemma, a twentysomething grad student with a pleasant disposition and strong work ethic, a rare combination. She also dabbled in art and had some creative ideas for decor and social media.

"What time do you expect your next interviewee?" Richard emerged from the kitchen, covered in paint splatters and wiping his hands on a cloth. "I'll be finished with the touch-ups within the hour."

Beth looked at her iWatch. "Any minute now. This girl sounds promising as a server. She has experience and has lived in the area for years, so she knows a lot of local people."

The door opened, and Beth and Richard turned, expecting to see Allie Davidson, age thirty-two, with eight years' experience in the food industry. Instead, a tall man with an angular jaw and deep-set brown eyes stepped inside. His face broke into a tentative smile as his chocolatey eyes took in Beth and the café.

"Can I help you with something?" Beth asked. "We don't open for a few more weeks."

"Oh, I wasn't sure. I've seen a lot of activity here over the last few months." He looked around. "Are you the new owner?"

"Yes."

"Are you opening another bakery?"

"No, it's going to be a café serving breakfast and lunch." She approached the man and stuck out her hand. "I'm Beth. This is

Richard, my father." Beth studied the black polo shirt and slim jeans that covered his lean frame and tilted her head. "Are you looking for a job?"

The man's hand flew to his chest. "Me? Oh, no. I have a job."

Beth and Richard exchanged puzzled looks.

Richard made an attempt next. "Good to meet you, er..."

"Oh, where are my manners? Andre." He shook Richard's hand and cleared his throat. "I live not too far from here, and I hang out in this square for meals and coffee. Some cool bars too. All your recent activity piqued my interest." He wore his sandy hair longish on top and shorter on the sides and back. Raking his hand through it, he looked around at the renovation.

Beth broke the awkward silence. "Um, would you like a quick tour? I've got someone coming in for an interview in a few minutes, but I could show you around."

"Oh, I don't want to—I mean, sure, that would be great."

"Go ahead, I'll watch out for Allie," Richard offered. "I need a break anyway. My boss is demanding!" He winked at Beth and pulled out one of the new chairs.

Beth led Andre around and gave him the *Reader's Digest* version of her vision for Fresh Start. She couldn't help noticing how intently he listened then asked thoughtful questions.

"You've really done a remarkable job here, Beth. Has it always been a dream of yours to own a café?"

Beth lowered her eyes and hesitated before answering. "Actually, no. I never even thought about it until a few months ago. I've had a... well, a rough year... and I'm trying to move on by doing something completely different." A pink hue spread across her cheeks. "Maybe I'll regret it, but I hope not."

"Ah, hence the café's name." Andre nodded as though the magnitude of the name registered in his head. "I think you'll do great. Your enthusiasm alone has to translate to success."

Beth surveyed Andre from head to toe. His dark clothes made him seem taller somehow. He was handsome in a boyish, unassuming way, and Beth found herself thinking of the first time she saw Danny. The thought made her feel slightly dizzy, and she shook her head to dispel the memory.

Andre continued, his face softening. "I'm sorry you've had a rough time lately. But you seem to be channeling your energy in a positive way. That's no small thing."

Embarrassed that a stranger would offer such a compliment, Beth stammered, "Well, I mean, thank you, I—"

Richard's voice interrupted the moment. "Beth, Allie is here."

Andre cleared his throat. "I'll leave you to it. It was great to meet you, Beth. Thanks so much for the tour. I really admire what you're doing here. I look forward to seeing you again when the café opens." He nodded at Richard and walked out the door.

Beth watched him make his way across the square. He didn't get into a car. Instead, he kept walking until he was out of sight.

Chapter Eight

Tomorrow was the soft opening of Fresh Start, but though it was autumn, it felt like opening day of baseball season. No errors yet made, no strikeouts, everyone in first place. Not that Beth didn't have her doubts—she'd had plenty of them over the past few weeks.

Laura meant well, but she couldn't help herself. "Are you nervous, Beth? Running a café is not easy."

Beth groaned, but Lucy always came to the rescue. "That's why she has me, Laura." She nodded toward several small vases filled with chrysanthemums and baby's breath. "Now, how about you make yourself useful and put a vase in the middle of each table. The larger one goes on the counter."

Beth's eyes sent a silent *thank you* to Lucy. Laura's words needled Beth more than she wanted to admit. *What if she's right? What if I'm diving off a cliff with no life raft below?* When her doubts got the better of her, when she was ready to scrap the whole idea, she heard Danny's voice propelling her forward. *You can do this, babe. You can do anything you set your mind to.*

Danny never let anything rattle him. Sure, sometimes he'd been moody and sullen after a bad day, but he'd had a high-pressure job. Beth knew he'd tried to shield her from the unpleasant aspects of his work, often going outside to take a call when his expression at the incoming number promised a hostile exchange. Early on, she'd asked him about the tense calls, but his curt responses had quieted her, and in time, she'd learned it was best to leave Danny alone when he was in the middle of sticky situations. Though Danny's sharp words had sometimes hurt her feelings, she'd told herself that legal issues were messy and lawyers had the unbearable job of making their clients see what was in their best interests, even if they disagreed.

She summoned her burgeoning *I-can-handle-anything* attitude today so she could concentrate on Fresh Start's soft opening.

"You're right, of course," Laura said as she carried out her task. "I believe in you. I really do. I just worry—"

"Nope, nope, none of that, my love. Not today. Tomorrow is day one of the rest of Beth's life." Richard charged through the door, holding a large cardboard box. "We're so proud of you! Right, Laura?" He walked through to the kitchen, calling over his shoulder, "This was on the front step. Should I open it?"

"Oh, yes!" Beth's expression brightened. "I bet it's the coffee mugs I ordered with our logo! I was so worried they wouldn't get here before we opened."

Richard tore off the top of the box and peered inside. "Yep, you're exactly right, hon."

Laura put her hand on her daughter's shoulder and beamed. "I really do believe in you. My daughter—the business owner!" She headed for the kitchen. "The timely arrival of those mugs is a sign. I'll wash them by hand so they're ready to go when the first guest arrives."

"Thanks, Mom. For the record, I love that you worry about me. But I really want this. It's the first thing I've felt excited about in a long time. I need your support."

"You have it. You're so brave to do this. I have every faith in you. Now, let me get to those mugs."

Beth had also hired Norma, a fiftysomething woman who had decades of experience baking breads and pastries. Because Norma hated her name and her long hair was a beautiful flaming crimson, she preferred to be called Red. She claimed people had called her Red for so long, she sometimes forgot her given name. Tall and extraordinarily thin, she appeared as though she'd never tasted a single carb she'd baked, and she'd laughed off the notion when Beth had joked about it. "You'll see, honey. When you're around something day and night, it loses its appeal. Come to think of it," she said with a wink, "that's what happened with my husband."

Lucy and Frank had worked tirelessly on the menu to offer a variety but not an overwhelming number of breakfast and lunch options. Because Beth felt so strongly about dispelling the incorrect notion that gluten free equaled taste free, they expertly crafted naturally gluten-free dishes without changing or substituting a single ingredient. The pair coordinated with Red and created a combination of sandwiches, muffins, pastries, fruit, and egg dishes for breakfast. For lunch, they went with soups, sandwiches, wraps, grain bowls, and salads. Each had ideas for specials and novelty items but agreed it was best to get off the ground before venturing too high above the clouds. Beth's panicked expression when they excitedly talked about specials such as falafel, empanadas, crepes, and poke—"Raw fish? Where will we get raw fish?"—told them they needed to tread lightly and not scare their new boss as she ventured into the food business. Beth hoped to eventually contribute to the café's cooking and baking, so she was overjoyed with the staff she'd found.

Beth went over the details for the following day for the hundredth time. She'd done extensive research into how to have a successful café soft opening. She'd invited her staff's friends and family, a few area food critics Gemma had found on social media, and other local business owners. Allie knew a food blogger and had extended an invitation to her. In order to introduce customers to the various menu options, Beth had elected to have a one-day soft opening and serve both breakfast and lunch, as opposed to breakfast one day and lunch the next. She hoped this would give customers an idea of the various items available and allow Beth and her staff to focus on perfecting each dish. She anticipated her guests drumming up interest by telling their friends and social media followers about their experience before Fresh Start officially opened. Beth vowed to use their feedback on everything from the food to the service to the atmosphere and decor. Gemma, a social media whiz, touted Fresh Start's impending opening on Facebook, Instagram, and X.

The front door swung open, and a sweaty delivery guy entered, wiping his brow with a bandana and looking at a clipboard. "Um, Beth Collins?"

"That's me."

"How you doin'? Sign here, please." The man handed Beth a pen and tapped the bottom of the paper. "Looks like you're getting two high chairs and three booster seats." He looked around. "Guess you're running a kid-friendly place here."

Beth watched the man wheel in two large boxes on a dolly. He then trotted back to the truck and returned with three smaller ones. Her mind flashed to the baby she'd lost. Before the accident, when no one knew she was pregnant but her, she'd spent hours on her laptop, searching cribs, high chairs, car seats, and changing tables. Too excited to stop, she'd inevitably found herself on sites advertising tiny onesies, bibs, and booties. Now, a familiar sadness crept into her heart, reminding her she wouldn't need any of those things—reminding her of what she had done...

"Um, ma'am?" The delivery guy cleared his throat, eyeing the clipboard she still held.

Beth stared at him, unable to move.

Hannah came in right behind him and gently took Beth's arm. "Beth, sign right here."

Beth tried to steady her shaking hand and do as her sister instructed. Hannah took the clipboard from her and gave it back to the driver.

"Thanks. Have a good day." She turned back to Beth. "You okay?"

Lucy had witnessed the incident and brought Beth a glass of water. She opened her mouth to ask a question, but she and Hannah exchanged a look that made her close it without speaking.

Hannah guided Beth to a chair. "Sit for a few minutes. You've been working nonstop to get this place open. You need a break." She offered Lucy a small smile. "She's okay. Just overworked."

Lucy retreated to the kitchen, and Hannah turned back to Beth. By this time, Richard and Laura had joined them, Laura rubbing her daughter's back. They spoke in hushed tones as the staff went about their tasks.

"What was that all about?" Red asked Lucy.

Lucy continued chopping broccoli and cauliflower. "I have no idea. How does a woman who seems ready to take on the world get spooked by some high chairs?"

Aside from a few unexpected last-minute glitches that needed handling—a refrigerator that kept blowing a fuse and a mix-up with the bank handling their credit card transactions—Beth was pleased with the state of things for the soft opening. The contractors had done a great job and even finished ahead of schedule. The color scheme she chose, soft grays and browns, worked well with the natural morning sunlight, and the overhead light fixtures cast a welcoming glow when the afternoon rays moved behind the building. Rows of pastries, muffins, and cookies were arranged like little soldiers in the display case, and salads and side dishes lined the refrigerated case beside it. The new tables and chairs gleamed as if they couldn't wait to be used.

In the kitchen, Lucy spoke to her crew, beaming in their starched white pants and aprons. "Okay, guys, it's go time. We've got this. Remember, whatever happens, we smile and keep going. We handle any problems—not that I'm anticipating any—quietly and calmly. No angst in front of the guests. Any kvetching can be saved for later, after the doors are closed. Any last-minute questions or concerns?"

As Lucy reviewed instructions about keeping the main kitchen a dedicated gluten-free space, Beth stood at the counter, grateful for some time alone. The last weeks had been a haze of manic activity and preparation, leaving precious little time for reflection or relaxation, let alone sleep. Now it was time to turn the sign on the door from Closed to Open, and she needed a chance to savor the moment and think about how far she'd come since the accident.

She felt Danny's comforting presence, and oddly, it seemed to her as if *she* had risen from the dead. She'd been so lost, gutted, and aimless, and here she was about to open the doors to her very own café. Staring at the freshly painted and newly hung sign next to the front door, Beth blinked back tears and whispered softly, "I did it, Danny. I really did it. I'll never stop loving or missing you, but I think I'm going to be okay."

Chapter Nine

All in all, Beth and the staff felt Fresh Start's soft opening was a huge success.

When the last guest departed, Frank sank into a chair. "Nice work, gang! Nailed it!"

"You mean besides that damn credit card machine that the bank promised was fixed! Beth, thank God your mom is a math whiz and could quickly calculate the tabs when the machine acted up!" Gemma shook her head.

Beth hugged each employee, happy tears shining in her eyes. "You guys are the best. You took a chance on a rookie and really stepped up, every one of you. I'll never forget it. And I'll contact the bank—again—and get the issue straightened out."

"Yes, boss, we're the bomb, aren't we? Now enough of that huggy-kissy mushy stuff. We have work to do." Lucy took a pen from behind her ear and scribbled notes on a clipboard. "Red, let's work on the pumpkin muffin recipe. They look a little too crumbly. And the sweet potato chili is really good, but I want to kick it up a notch. I'm thinking a little cayenne pepper."

"Aye, aye, Captain." Red gave Lucy a mock salute and followed her into the kitchen.

Beth chuckled and called after them. "Don't work them to death, Lucy. This was a great dry run. Sure, we have some small kinks to work out, but I feel much better about the official opening next week."

After hugs and thanks, Beth insisted her parents and sister go home and get some rest. They'd been a big help, allowing Beth to circulate among the guests as the café had filled up. Hannah had explained in great detail all the fresh ingredients in the menu items, and Richard had helped deliver orders to tables. And Beth had to admit that Laura had been amazing in action, keeping her eyes on everything, warmly welcoming people, and silently troubleshooting with a nod or glance to the staff when a guest had a question or needed special attention. She had even been as cool as could be when the credit card machine failed.

Laura opened the door to a draft of crisp autumn air.

As Richard ushered his wife and daughter out, he paused and turned back to Beth. "Hey, hon, isn't that the guy who stopped in a few weeks ago? What was his name?"

Beth stopped busing tables and followed her father's gaze to a familiar figure sipping coffee on a bench in the square. "Oh, Andre. Yes, that's him."

Andre, who was reading a newspaper, smiled and waved as the trio exited the building. He strolled over, and Beth could tell her parents were gushing about the soft opening. They got into their car, and Andre walked toward Fresh Start. Beth subconsciously smoothed her hair and did a quick swipe under her eyes for any makeup smudges.

"Hey there, it sounds like everything went well today. That's great!" Andre folded the newspaper under his arm and gave Beth a thumbs-up.

"Yes, it really did, all things considered. I have some kinks to work out, but the staff did a fabulous job, and my family was clutch. People really seemed to enjoy the food and the atmosphere."

"You missed giving credit to one person. You've been working so hard. Looks like it paid off."

Beth blushed. "Thanks, I have been giving this place my all. My feet are killing me. I can't wait to crawl into bed tonight."

"Oh, okay, I was going to ask you... But I'm sure you're beat."

"You were going to ask me what?"

Andre's dark eyes took in Beth from head to toe. "If you would have a drink with me."

Beth froze, unable to answer for a moment. She finally managed, "I, um... I... I don't do that."

"You don't do what? Drink? No problem. We could grab a coffee or—"

She cut him off with a wave of her hand. "No, I mean, I don't... I don't date." She groaned, embarrassed at her assumption. "I mean, I'm not suggesting you're asking me out. It's just... It's just..."

"I'm sorry," Andre said softly. "I didn't mean to put you on the spot. You seem like a nice person. I just thought maybe you'd like a break from everything for a bit." He shrugged and flashed a smile that revealed white teeth, one eyetooth slightly crooked, which gave him a rakish look. With his hands out in front of him, palms up, he added, "Can't blame a guy for trying."

Beth smiled. "No, that's true."

"Hey, congrats again on the successful event. Get some rest. From the sound of things, you'll be busy when you officially open." He turned toward the door.

"Come back when we do!" Beth called after him, but he was already gone.

Lucy emerged from the kitchen with two cherry turnovers on a plate. She sat and pushed out a chair for Beth with her foot. Watching Andre retreat to the square, Lucy commented, "He looks yummy. Maybe we should put him on the menu. Friend of yours?"

Beth's cheeks burned as she took a bite of the pastry. "Andre? No, I barely know him. I mean, I don't know him at all."

"Mm-hmm. Okay. If you say so."

"What? What do you mean?"

Lucy tilted her head, one brow raised. "So you don't know him, huh? But talking to him for a hot second made your cheeks as red as the cherries you just bit into. And I'm not one to eavesdrop, but did I hear him invite you out for a drink?"

Beth licked a crumb off her thumb. "No big deal."

"And my hearing must be failing me because I swear I heard you turn him down."

Beth pushed away her plate. "It's complicated."

Lucy's expression softened. "Listen, I don't mean to pry. I've spent a lot of time around you these last several weeks. I see the look in your eyes. It says that the world has taken something from you, something important. It's there, just under the surface of your enthusiasm for this place." She fiddled with her napkin. "Okay, full disclosure. I googled you. I read about the accident and your husband's death. I can't believe I didn't know about it before, but I pretty much keep to myself. I don't get a newspaper or go on social media. God, Beth, I'm so sorry."

Beth exhaled. "Thank you. I wasn't sure if you knew or not. Do the others know?"

"Beats me. I doubt it, though. Frank and Red are new to the area. Allie and Gemma are young, and I mean no disrespect, but young people's worlds tend to revolve around themselves."

"I was going to tell you. I just wanted to throw myself into this place. You know, put all my energy into something positive. I didn't want to look like a damsel in distress who needed rescuing."

"I totally get it. You want to move on. You wanted—Oh!" She hit her forehead with the heel of her hand. "A Fresh Start!"

"Yes."

"Listen, even knowing the truth, I don't see a damsel in distress. I see a person who, like everyone, is a collection of all her experiences—good, bad, happy, sad. I think it's great that you wanted to

open a café where people can gather and have fresh food and pleasant conversation no matter what's going on in their lives. We're going
to give them that."

"Thanks, Lucy."

Lucy stood to clear their plates. "Can I give you one bit of advice?"

Beth grinned. "Can I stop you?"

"Good point. But seriously, I love that you're channeling your
loss in a positive way with this place." Lucy looked Beth square in the
eyes. "Just save a bit of that energy for your personal life too. Who
was it who said something about the cracks letting in the light?"

"Leonard Cohen, in his song 'Anthem,' I believe."

"That's right." Lucy touched her shoulder. "All I'm saying is,
don't be afraid to let in some of that light."

Chapter Ten

With autumn drawing to a close, the crisp, sharp air felt to Beth like a collective exhale before the first breath of winter. As fall faded like a photograph left too long in the sun, she was certain that opening Fresh Start instead of returning to her job at the mortgage company had been the right decision. Last year at this time, Danny had been alive, laughing over breakfast, running late, picking up takeout.

As the season slipped toward winter, Beth realized that changing careers lessened the pain from the memory of that night almost a year ago. It was always there, but starting completely over had given her a brand-new place to exist. Slowly, the unfamiliar environment became a kind of shelter. The air as winter approached again didn't choke her with loss the way it had before. In the moments when the past reached for her, she had something to reach back with—a purpose, a life that hadn't existed when Danny was alive.

The lunch rush over, she sat at a table, checking and double-checking her list. Her first baking class was coming up, and she wanted to make sure all her *i*'s were dotted and *t*'s crossed. She chewed on the end of her pen as she went over the ingredients for the holiday cookies she planned to feature in the class.

"Good job, Santa, making a list and checking it twice," Lucy joked. "You and Red will kill it. Great idea, making it a parent–child event."

"Thanks, Lucy. I think it will go well. I actually got the idea from baking with my nieces and nephews last year. Sydney will be my cohost for the class. She can't wait! Hannah and Nic will bring the other kids too. I just hope more people sign up. I'm trying to figure out the cutoff number."

"You'll fill this place. We've been getting busier every week. And Allie and Gemma have been talking it up on social media."

"I hope you're right."

"I am. You'll see. Then I think you should host a follow-up class that teaches kids how to clean up a kitchen covered in flour and sugar. Now *that* would be a sure hit!"

Beth laughed. "Oh, I know. After cookie day at my house last year, I was cleaning up flour remnants all winter. It looked like we shot flour out of a cannon."

The door chimed, and Beth froze when Officer Kingston entered the café.

"Hey, Beth. How are you?" He looked around and smiled. "The place looks great. I'm really happy for you."

"Hi, Adam. Thanks." Her mouth suddenly felt dry. "What brings you...? I mean, do you have any new information about...?"

"Oh, no, sorry, I just stopped in to say hello. I meant to come by sooner."

Beth exhaled. "Oh, okay. Can I get you a coffee? Black, right?"

Lucy interjected, "You sit, boss. I got it."

Adam sat across from Beth. "I wish I had something to report. But don't worry. Just when we think the trail has gone dry, something turns up. That's always the way. You never know what seemingly insignificant detail will break open a case."

They chatted for a few minutes, Beth filling in Adam about the café and Adam listening so intently that they didn't hear the chime or see the door swing open.

Andre, clad in slim black pants, a tan sweater, and a fitted quilt jacket, breezed in the door. He raked his fingers through his wind-blown hair and sat at a nearby table. "Hi, Beth. Good to see you. You're not closed for the day, are you?"

Lucy approached him. "No, the rush is over, but we're open for another hour. What can I get you?"

Andre scanned the menu. "Hmm. Everything looks good. How about the pesto chicken and roasted red pepper wrap? And unsweetened iced tea."

"You got it. I'll put a rush on it. Wouldn't want you to be late for your *GQ* shoot." Lucy hummed as she retreated to the kitchen.

Beth shot her a look that said, *You're incorrigible.*

Andre laughed and shook his head. "So, how are you, Beth?" He regarded Adam and added, "Oh, sorry, didn't mean to interrupt."

"It's fine, you're not interrupting. Adam, this is Andre. Andre, Officer Adam Kingston."

Andre rose to shake Adam's hand, and they exchanged pleasantries.

"Officer? Beth, are you in some kind of trouble? Your food is so good, it's a crime?"

He winked at Beth, who laughed nervously.

"No, nothing like that. Adam and I have gotten to know each other over... well, over the last several months. He's helping with... um—"

"Here we go. One chicken pesto and roasted red pepper wrap. And iced tea." Lucy set down the plate and broke up the awkward moment. "Enjoy!"

"I should get going." Adam stood and addressed Beth. "Congrats again on the café. I'll be in touch with any developments." On his way out, he added, "Nice to meet you, Andre."

While Andre ate, Beth joined Lucy and the staff in the kitchen. "Lucy, could you be any more obvious?"

Lucy raised her hands, palms out. "Hey, I'm just enjoying the scenery. I'd make a move myself if I were fifteen years younger. Seriously, though. You think he keeps stopping in here for the chicken? Now, get out there and make nicey-nice before he hightails it out of here in those delicious Italian leather loafers." She made a shooing motion with her hands.

"He is awfully easy on the eyes, boss." Gemma peered around the corner.

"Oh, jeez, you too?" Beth shot her staff a warning glance as she backed out of the kitchen. "Okay, okay, I'm going."

Andre had just finished lunch and was dabbing his mouth with a napkin. "That was really good. My compliments to the chef." He nodded toward the kitchen, a mischievous smile playing on his lips. "I'm guessing she's one of the crew spying to see if you came out here to talk to me." He waved playfully toward the kitchen.

"Don't mind her. She fancies herself a matchmaker."

"Hmm. Well, I'd hate to disappoint her. Call me a glutton for punishment, but are you free tomorrow night? How about that drink?"

From the kitchen, Lucy loudly cleared her throat as the others looked on.

Beth groaned. "Wait here while I go back there and fire them all."

Andre laughed. "I think they mean well. So, what do you say?"

"Sure. A drink sounds great."

Someone dropped a lid in the kitchen. Beth could only hope it drowned out the light clapping.

"**I** think I should cancel."

"What? Are you nuts?"

Beth switched the phone to her other ear and chuckled as she listened to Molly apologizing to the checkout clerk at Stop & Shop.

"Sorry, not you. You're doing a great job and are clearly not nuts. I'm talking to my friend who *is*, in fact, nuts."

Beth could hear the shuffling of bags and the screech of Molly's shopping cart wheels then the sound of her car starting.

"Give me a sec to switch to Bluetooth... Okay, now, what is this nonsense about you canceling?"

"I don't know. Maybe it's not a good idea."

"I'll tell you what's not a good idea. Singing 'Total Eclipse of the Heart' at karaoke night after three dirty martinis."

"You didn't."

"Oh, but I did. I'm praying I don't become a YouTube sensation." Molly regaled Beth with the hilariously cringeworthy night, and Beth laughed until she cried. "Now, back to your situation. How is a drink with Andre not a good idea? From what you've told me, he's a good-looking guy who's an above-average conversationalist, and he may or may not have his shoes imported from Europe. What's the problem?"

"I mean, I don't know. I guess I feel a little guilty."

"There it is. I knew that's what you were thinking. Hang on, I'm home and getting out of the car. Switching you over to speaker."

Beth heard more muffled shuffling as Molly made her way into her house.

When she spoke again, her voice was soft and sympathetic. "Okay. Beth, I worry about you thinking you don't deserve happiness. You do."

Beth spoke so softly, it was a wonder Molly could hear her. "Mol, you know what I've done. Maybe my sentence is to be alone forever."

"You can't possibly believe that."

"I don't know. I've made some mistakes. Some big ones. One really big one."

"Stop that. Who hasn't? Listen to me. The past is the past. Danny is gone. You miscarried. It sucks. But that's the reality. You've been dealt a truly shitty hand. You, my friend, are still very much alive. And look how far you've come these last several months. You got out of the mortgage company crypt and opened your own café. You're a business owner!"

"Yes, but—"

"I'm not done. You've put yourself out there professionally, and that's great. Now, don't you think it's time you did the same thing in your personal life?"

"I don't know. It's scary."

Molly sighed. "Of course it's scary. Anything new is scary. But I'll tell you what. I'm looking around the empty house I just came home to. If a hot, nice guy asked me out for a drink, I'd say yes so fast, your head would spin."

"Maybe you're right. It's a drink. What's the harm?"

"That's my girl. I expect full details."

Beth laughed. "Should I record our conversation?"

"I'd say yes, but I don't think that's legal. And, Beth, one more thing. If you go to a place where there's karaoke..."

"I know, I know. I won't even think about it."

Chapter Eleven

Two Brothers Brewing Company was crowded for a Wednesday night. Beth had suggested meeting Andre there. She honestly wanted to curl up with her comforter and hide just like she'd been doing for nearly a year. But after the cajoling from her staff, she had to admit her life wasn't just the café, no matter how much she tried to convince herself it was enough. So she ignored the sweaty palms and gazillion misgivings and relented. When she arrived, Andre was already there, waiting in the vestibule. He flashed his smile and touched her arm. Beth self-consciously watched him take in her skinny jeans, fuchsia liquid leather jacket, and black fabric boots.

"Hi. You look great!"

Beth stifled a chuckle. While FaceTiming Molly, choosing an outfit for tonight had been nothing short of a runway fashion show. She pictured the ten or so items that hadn't made the cut strewn across her bed. Playing it cool, she answered casually. "Thanks. So do you."

"Should we sit at the bar, or do you prefer a table?"

"Either is fine." She peered inside. "It looks like a few high-tops are available in the bar area. Why don't we take one of them?"

"Perfect." Andre spoke to the hostess, who led them to their seats.

Two Brothers was outside of town in a nearby suburb of Philadelphia. A large farm had once occupied forty acres of space where the restaurant was located, and the owners had retained much of the rustic charm of the original buildings. Heavy wooden beams lined the arched ceilings, and many of the original windows and walls, though restored, remained. Beth loved living near but not in Philly. She went there periodically, but she wasn't a city girl. She preferred the many unique, picturesque towns with bars, restaurants, and attractions away from the hustle and bustle—and traffic.

"Have you been here before?" Andre asked as he pulled out Beth's chair.

"A few times. You?"

"Yes, they have an amazing selection of craft beers. Are you a beer drinker?"

"No, I don't—actually *can't*—drink beer."

Andre looked mortified. "Oh, I'm such an idiot! I should have asked. We can go somewhere else." He looked around for their server.

"No, no, it's fine. I have celiac disease, so I can't drink beer. But as luck would have it, wine and liquor are fine."

Beth smiled, and Andre appeared to relax. He opened his mouth to ask a question, but an approaching server halted him.

"Hi, you two. I'm Kate, and I'll be taking care of you. Have you decided on drinks?"

Andre gestured to Beth, who said, "I'll have an extra dirty martini. Blue-cheese-stuffed olives."

"Vodka preference?"

"Grey Goose."

"Perfect." Kate nodded at Andre. "And for you?"

"I'll try the Atomic Pumpkin Ale. And may we see an appetizer menu?"

"Sure thing." Kate returned momentarily with two menus.

"So, celiac," Andre started. "What is that, besides something that allows you to drink vodka and not beer?"

"Ugh. It's a pain. It's an autoimmune disease with no cure. The only treatment is adhering to a strict gluten-free diet."

"Oh, gluten free! I'm familiar with that. But I've never heard of celiac disease. I thought people eat gluten free to be healthy. Or cool." Andre smiled sheepishly. "And you're very cool."

"Well, thanks." Beth rubbed her sweaty palms on her jeans while she returned Andre's grin. "A lot of people think it's a fad. It's one of my missions at Fresh Start—to dispel preconceived notions about gluten-free food."

Andre rubbed his hands together as he looked at the menu. "Consider me a willing student. What looks good?"

Beth went over the menu with Andre and explained the options. They chose a flatbread on a cauliflower crust. The drinks arrived, and they talked easily while they waited for their food. The atmosphere was warm and inviting with its long mahogany bar, uplit with bronze sconces. Beyond the bar, a solo musician set up his amp and microphone. He took out his guitar and began warming up. Kate brought the flatbread as the musician began his first song, "Settle Me Down" by Josh Abbott Band.

"He's really good," Beth commented between bites.

"He is, and I'm not going to lie—so is this flatbread. I never in a million years would have ordered butternut squash, shaved brussels sprouts, and ricotta cheese on a flatbread, but this is freakin' delicious!" He reached for another slice.

"It really is. I'd like to start serving flatbreads at the—"

A chair screeching on the floorboards at the bar interrupted Beth as a burly, red-faced man stood abruptly. "I'm so sick of your shit!" he yelled at the woman next to him, towering over her like a sequoia.

The embarrassed woman's eyes darted around wildly. She spoke to him in hushed tones, but he wasn't having it.

"Don't shush me! All you do is nag, nag, nag, and now you want me to shut up?"

The couple had everyone's attention in the bar area. Before Beth knew what was happening, Andre was at the belligerent behemoth's side.

"Hey, dude, take it easy." Andre spoke in a measured voice, but Beth noticed him clenching and unclenching his fists.

"Sorry, was I talking to you? Maybe you should mind your own effing business, *dude*." Spittle flew from the man's snarling mouth.

Andre took a step toward him, fists poised. The woman jumped up so quickly, her barstool toppled to the floor.

"Okay, that's enough." The bar manager appeared and wedged himself between the two men. "You—out! We called you an Uber." He pointed at the angry man then turned to the woman. "Are you going to be okay?"

"Yes," she answered, her hands shaking like tree leaves in a breeze. "He gets like this sometimes. He'll sleep it off."

"Okay. Just be careful." The manager regarded Andre as the woman made a quick exit. "Thanks for stepping in, but it's risky mixing it up with big guys who have a snootful. Can't exactly reason with them."

Andre glared out the window at the drunk getting in his Uber. "Tomorrow, she'll act like it never happened, and the cycle will continue. A-holes like that need to be put in their place."

"Not our problem, buddy. Everyone has free will. We can stop serving him, but what she's willing to put up with is her business." The manager nodded toward Beth, who watched the scene with interest. "Listen, why don't you and your friend have a drink on the house? Sorry for the disturbance." He gestured for Kate to bring them another round.

Andre returned to their high top and slid onto his seat. Beth studied him. His cheeks slightly flushed from the incident, he was even more handsome, dangerously so in a way that flustered her.

She spoke first. "So... that was... something." She leaned in on her elbows, closer to him. "Weren't you worried that idiot would take a swing at you?"

"Listen, I don't go looking for trouble." He leaned back and exhaled loudly. "I just hate guys like that. Thinking they're so tough because they can intimidate a woman half their size." His sculpted features were more pronounced by his set jaw. The muted light from the sconces played on the sheen of his dusky eyes, enhancing his dangerous guise.

Beth shook her head. *No, no, no. I'm not ready for heart palpitations and butterflies in the pit of my stomach.* "Well, I won't argue with that. He was definitely a jerk. I hope, if that's a regular occurrence, she comes to her senses and kicks him to the curb."

"I hope so, too, but it's not always that easy." Andre fixated on his beer, the froth slowly shrinking with every burst bubble.

Since he appeared lost in thought, Beth gave him a moment. She listened to the music until Kate approached with the free round of drinks. Andre took a deep breath, and they chatted amiably again.

Finishing her second martini, Beth called it a night, citing her early opening time at Fresh Start.

Andre walked her to her car and leaned against a lamppost. "Despite the drama, I had a really nice time tonight, Beth. I'd love to see you again."

"I did too. I'd like that." She playfully punched his arm. "Next time, I'll bring my referee whistle and yellow flags."

Andre laughed. "Good idea. You never know when drunk-guy drama will break out."

As Beth drove away, she thought about Danny. *I'm moving on, but I'll never forget you.* She wished she could talk to him. She wondered what Danny would have thought about her asking Andre if he was worried the drunk would take a swing at him. She couldn't shake the feeling that Danny would have told her it seemed Andre was more worried he wouldn't.

Chapter Twelve

"Okay, every detail. Don't leave anything out." Molly's chin rested on her hands, her elbows on the table. Only the district attorney was better prepared than Molly with questions.

Hannah, Nicole, and Lucy joined the interrogation.

"Let her catch her breath," Hannah said.

Lucy dramatically folded her hands over her chest. "She wants to tell us. She's *dying* to tell us!"

Beth chuckled. "It's really amusing how you talk about me as if I'm not even here. Your lives must be dreadfully boring if my Wednesday-night date is big news." She turned to Lucy and Nicole with feigned annoyance. "You two are supposed to be working on the details for the baking class. You know it's only a few days away, right?"

"We're on our union-mandated break," Lucy quipped.

"Mm-hmm. Only we don't have a union."

"Well, I know the boss, and she doesn't want her staff to be overworked," Nicole added, winking at Lucy. "Besides, the lunch rush is over. C'mon, Beth! Don't keep us in suspense!"

"Good Lord, you guys are pathetic. Okay, okay, I'll tell you all about my Wednesday evening out with my tall, dark, handsome guy."

Beth started with her quest for the right outfit.

"You should have seen her," Molly teased. "Emptied out her closet before finally deciding. I bet he complimented you, and you gave him the 'This old thing?' line."

Beth cringed. "Something like that."

She entertained the girls with the details of the evening, giving special weight to the incident with the drunk guy at the bar.

"Wow!" Hannah shook her head. "That's quite a bit of excitement for a Wednesday night. God, my life *is* boring! I spent the evening folding laundry and helping Henry write his name."

Beth bit her bottom lip, her heart twisting. *I'd love to spend an evening like that.*

Molly chimed in. "Yeah, meanwhile, I spend hours trolling dating sites, and you have a tall, dark stranger fall at your feet."

"Having any luck with those sites?" Lucy asked Molly. "Aren't there some bizarre ones? Like guys with weird fetishes?"

"I stay off of those. Besides, been there, done that. My ex had a really weird fetish. He used to dress up in his own clothes and act like a gigantic asshole."

Amid the girls' howling, Beth stared at the ceiling, lost in thought.

"What?" Nicole asked.

"I don't know. It's just..." She squinted, recalling the scene at the bar. "It was strange. When that idiot was being aggressive and loud... it was like Andre took it personally or something. The way he jumped right in."

"Well, maybe he has a low tolerance for jerks," Hannah said.

"Maybe." Beth shrugged. "You're probably right. I'm overthinking it."

"Yeah, I think it's cool, you know, in a chivalry's-not-dead way," Nicole added.

"Right?" Molly quipped. "After most of my dates, I have the sinking feeling that while chivalry might not be dead, it's unconscious and throwing up blood."

A male voice interrupted the revelry.

"Is this a party?" Andre approached the group. "I don't want to crash."

Beth's hand flew to her chest, her eyes the size of saucers. "Andre! No, um, I mean, no, it's not a party," she stammered. She took in Andre's black turtleneck, light-gray wool pants, and the black leather jacket flung over his shoulder, then his shoes. *Does he own any pairs that aren't designer?*

Coming to her rescue, Molly stuck out her hand. "Nice to meet you, Andre. I'm Molly, Beth's friend. She was just telling us about your evening. Beats the pants off our dull Wednesday nights. Sounds like you're a good man to have around in sticky situations."

"Oh, I don't know about that. Right place, right time, you know?" He rocked on his heels. "I just hate seeing a drunk with beer muscles bullying a woman."

"Well," Hannah added, "I think it's admirable. I wish more guys stepped up like that."

The girls murmured their agreement and scattered, giving Beth and Andre some space.

He took a seat next to her. "So, interesting evening, huh? Go out for a bite and a cocktail and almost get into a brawl. How about another chance? I was thinking maybe we could go somewhere a fight isn't likely to break out—like a hockey game."

"Ha! My dad has a joke about that. 'I went to a fight last night, and a hockey game broke out!'"

"Good one!" Andre laughed. "So, I know an excellent Italian place in the city. The only fighting I've ever seen there is the owner cursing loudly in Italian if the vodka sauce isn't perfect. What do you say? Saturday night?"

Beth smiled and shrugged. "Sure. What do we have to lose? Except maybe a few teeth."

He chuckled at her attempt at humor. "Let's hope it's a calmer evening. Okay if I pick you up this time?"

Beth hesitated but agreed. She gave Andre her address and phone number, from which he created a new contact in his phone.

"I'll pick you up at seven on Saturday. Looking forward to it."

Chapter Thirteen

Salvatore on Pine was a quaint BYOB in a converted row house off Broad Street in Philadelphia. If not for the twinkling white lights outlining the large front window and the sign hanging from a wrought iron bracket, it would be impossible to tell the building from the other row homes lining the street. Andre led Beth up the steps and into the tiny foyer, where they were greeted by the owner, a wiry sixtyish man with tufts of wispy white hair on the sides of his otherwise bald head.

"*Benvenuto!* You have a reservation, yes?"

Andre gave his name to the hostess and asked for a table near the window.

After they were seated, Beth looked around and nodded her approval. "This is nice. Good choice."

A server approached the table with wineglasses and a corkscrew and introduced herself as Sophia. Andre handed over the bottle of cabernet he'd brought.

Beth smiled. "It was nice of you to text and ask me about my wine preference."

"My pleasure. No one wants to pair a great meal with a wine they don't like."

Sophia promised to return in a minute with menus and bread.

"Oh, no bread for us," Andre commented. "And we'd like gluten-free menus."

Sophia smiled broadly. "Oh, we have excellent gluten-free bread. I'll be right back."

Beth and Andre clinked glasses.

"To a drama-free evening." Andre winked.

"I'll drink to that."

Sophia returned in a minute with a basket of warm bread. "Here we go. Gluten free." She handed them menus. "Most of our entrées and all of our pizzas can be prepared gluten free." She went over the specials and left to give them a few minutes to decide.

"Should we start with sautéed calamari?" Andre asked while perusing the appetizers.

"Yes, sounds good," Beth agreed as Sophia approached once more. After they ordered, pasta a la vodka for her and veal with prosciutto for him, Beth looked intently at Andre. "So, tell me a bit about yourself. You're kind of a mystery man."

Andre pointed all ten fingers at his chest. "Who, me? Nah. I'm not that interesting." He looked at Beth's raised eyebrows and leaned back in his chair. "Okay, let's see. I grew up in Philadelphia. My mom still lives here. I have two sisters, both of whom are college graduates and productive members of society. I tried the college route, but it wasn't for me. I lasted about two and a half years."

"Wasn't for you? What do you mean? Not that college is for everyone or even necessary in a lot of cases." She sipped her wine, watching his reaction through the fan of her eyelashes. To temper her inquisition and sound less harsh, she said, "Just curious."

Andre looked out the window, and the twinkling lights reflected the chocolatey hue in his eyes. "I got tired of taking classes I felt were useless. I was a business major, but you know how higher education works. You have to take a bunch of gen eds before you really get into your major. They made me lose my focus, and I guess I got restless. I wanted to get out and find a good job."

Sophia arrived, placed a platter of calamari in the center of the table, then poured more wine.

"So, you quit?"

"Yes. Well, I had been thinking about it. My mom really wanted me to finish college, but as I said, I got antsy."

"What about your dad?"

Andre dropped his eyes then stared out the window again.

Beth, worried that she'd made him uncomfortable, quickly added, "Sorry. I'm asking too many personal questions."

"No, it's okay." He folded his arms across his chest. "I didn't have a very good relationship with my dad. Let's just say he wasn't a stand-up guy. My mom finally left him some years ago. I haven't seen him since."

"I'm sorry. That can't have been easy." She changed the subject. "So, you were talking about leaving college."

"Yes, so I met a guy at college—Chaz—whose family ran their own business. They were looking for summer help. I worked for them between my sophomore and junior years. We spent a lot of time together and really hit it off. I fit in well, and they were happy with my work." Andre shook his head as if remembering his early days working for his friend's family. "In those days, I was so happy to be making money, I took whatever work they offered me. Sometimes, it felt like I was doing more personal favors for the boss instead of actually working for the company. When those 'opportunities' come up now, I steer clear of them."

Beth looked at him quizzically, and Andre rushed on, seeming to want to change the subject. "Anyway, at some point during my junior year, they offered me full-time employment, and I accepted. I left school and went to work for them."

The delicious aroma of their food wafted through the air before Sophia made it to the table. She set two steaming plates in front of them. "Enjoy! I'll be back to check on you."

"Mm, this looks fabulous! I really like this place. It's a casual atmosphere, but it feels like fine dining." Beth beamed at Andre. They ate in silence for a few minutes, then she asked, "What kind of business did you say it was?"

Andre dabbed at his mouth. "I didn't, but it's a consulting business. They deal with a lot of compliance issues. Between what I learned in school and what Chaz's dad taught me, I was a quick study and moved up in the ranks. I've been working for them ever since." He refilled their wineglasses. "How about you? What's your story? How did you end up opening a café?"

Beth took a moment to gather her thoughts. "Well, a café wasn't part of my plan. Just last year, I was happily married and working as a mortgage broker. And then..." She hesitated.

Andre set down his fork and leaned in. "Go on. I mean, if you want to."

"Yes, I think I want to talk about it." Beth cleared her throat. "I was married to the love of my life. His name was Daniel, Danny to me. He was an attorney."

"Was?"

"Yes. We were very happy. All we wanted was a family, to raise our children and grow old together. Boring, right?" She gazed out the window. Now it was her turn to be mesmerized by the twinkling lights. "I used to look around our house and picture it with a few kids. The thought of the noise, the mess, the chaos... it gave me a feeling of peace. I'm jealous of my sisters. I can't help it. I want what my sisters have. I almost had it. Then, last winter, we were driving home from a holiday party. We were chatting just like any other night. Chatting like two people who don't know the world is about to change forever. It was pouring outside, one of those rainstorms where it comes down in buckets and you can't see a foot in front of the car and the wipers are useless against the deluge hitting the windshield."

Sophia approached. Andre gently but wordlessly let her know they needed a minute.

"The other car came out of nowhere." Beth squeezed her eyes shut against the memory. "It slammed into Danny's side of the car. He died almost instantly. The driver of the other car was also killed. I was the only survivor."

Outside, on the street, a couple meandered by. The woman pushed a stroller, while the man fussed about the baby, making sure a blanket was tucked securely around it.

"I was eight weeks pregnant at the time," Beth said dully.

Andre gasped. "Oh, Beth."

She huffed out a long breath. "Danny didn't know I was pregnant. I planned to tell him that night. Instead, the big news that night came from the attending doctor in the ER. After they assessed my injuries, he told me Danny had died and I had miscarried."

The color drained from Andre's face. "Jesus. Beth, I don't know what to say." He put his hand over hers on the table.

She didn't hear him, not really. She just stared as if he weren't there. The words opened up a hollow cavern in her heart she'd thought she had closed. "Just like that, everything that mattered to me. Gone."

Andre spoke softly. "So, Fresh Start. It was a way for you to completely start over."

"Yes." Beth breathed in deeply and managed a shaky smile. "I just felt like I had to leave behind my old life and its ghosts if I stood a chance of moving on."

"And has it been one? A fresh start?"

"Absolutely. It's a lot of hard work, but I enjoy it. And it has helped me heal. I mean, I'll never be completely over losing Danny and my baby, but I'm moving in the right direction."

"What about the driver of the other car? Was he drunk? Speeding?"

Beth sighed. "That's a whole other strange story. He had no ID, no wallet, no phone on him. The car was a rental, paid for in cash.

The police still don't know who he was. They have no way of notifying a next of kin. They have a few theories, but it's all speculation."

Andre let out a low whistle. "You're right. That's very strange."

"Thank you for listening. It felt good to talk about it." Beth sat up straight and shook her head as if to clear it. "Sure, I have scars, but I'm trying to think of them as a positive thing. They mean I survived."

"Don't thank me. I like you, Beth. I want to get to know you better. Knowing your story is part of that. I appreciate you sharing it with me."

Sophia collected their dinner plates and handed them dessert menus. "The flourless chocolate tart is to *die* for."

Beth and Andre tried unsuccessfully not to burst out laughing at Sophia's unfortunate choice of words.

"Well," Beth said. "In that case, we'll try it!"

Chapter Fourteen

Early December settled over Fresh Start like a sigh. There was a certain stillness to everything, as if the earth itself were holding its breath. It felt to Beth as though the world teetered between quiet tranquility and festive anticipation.

Fifteen people signed up for the parent–child gluten-free baking class at Fresh Start. Hannah, Nicole, and Laura draped garlands across the display cases. They wound tiny white lights through it and tied in holiday cookie cutters with red and green ribbon. Beth had arranged the tables in an L formation so everyone in the class could see and hear her as she instructed them in the fine art of gluten-free cookie baking. Six baking stations were set up at various points around the table. Participants had been asked to bring their own cookie sheets, scoops, and tins, but Fresh Start would supply all the cookie ingredients. Beth and Red assembled bowls, cookie sheets, and utensils, checking and rechecking that they hadn't missed anything. Sydney and Zoe would assist Red and Beth, while Henry and Ethan would participate in the class with their mothers. Richard and Laura were on troubleshooting and cleanup detail.

"A bunch of kids let loose with flour, sugar, and sprinkles... How much of a mess can it be?" he quipped, scooping up Ethan and throwing him over his shoulder.

"Yes, I may have made a mistake wearing this black sweater," Laura joked.

"Hey, Beth," Hannah called over her shoulder as she stood back and admired the garland. "You said Andre is coming tonight, right?"

"Yes, that's what he said at dinner on Saturday, though I haven't heard from him at all today." Beth placed a large poinsettia on either side of the café's entrance. "Also, great job, guys. It looks like a holiday postcard in here!"

Hannah smiled slyly. "He'll be here. He's smitten."

"We'll see."

The first group of bakers arrived, and Beth turned her attention to them.

"Welcome! So glad you're joining us!"

Laura and Richard took their coats, hats, and gloves, and Beth led them to one of the stations. The group consisted of a mom and her two children, and they unpacked their supplies as more people filed in.

When everyone was in place and ready, Beth and Red began the class. Red distributed ingredients, while Beth explained to the parents the differences in gluten-free baking.

"It's very much the same as baking like people are used to. Usually, the only difference is the type of flour used. Typical baking requires wheat flour, which causes cookies and cakes to trap the air released by leavening agents. This is the main reason these baked goods rise easily and are light and airy. We'll be using gluten-free flour, which can cause cakes and cookies to be dense and crumbly. But wait until you see my work-arounds. Absolute magic!" The kids began squirming, so Beth switched gears. "Okay, who's ready to bake?"

Amid cheers from the young participants, Red handed out the first recipe. Beth couldn't help scanning the parking lot in the square for a sign of Andre, but he was nowhere to be found.

Beth caught herself frowning and turned back to her students with a smile. "Let's start with a fan favorite—chocolate chip cookies! Now, moms and dads, if you've ever made gluten-free chocolate chip cookies, did you find anything frustrating about the experience?"

A tall, thin woman called out, "They came out flat. I like my cookies puffy!"

"Exactly," Beth answered. "With a few minor adjustments, we can fix that. First, go ahead and cream the sugar and butter. When you get to the step where you mix the dry ingredients, be sure to sift the flour. This will eliminate clumping. Another easy trick is to use baking powder in place of baking soda, since baking powder is a leavening agent. The general rule of thumb is two teaspoons of baking powder per cup of flour. I put that in the recipe I gave you. Now, if you happen to like a flatter, crispier cookie, you can skip these tips. It's pretty simple—baking soda causes spreading, and baking powder causes puffiness."

Red supervised Zoe and Sydney mixing up their dough while Beth walked around, assisting and answering questions.

"Another trick is to chill the cookie dough before baking if you want puffier cookies."

A dad in black horn-rimmed glasses asked, "I always thought it was a pain to make gluten-free flour. Don't you have to mix a bunch of ingredients to make a flour that is the same as an all-purpose flour?"

"Great question. That used to be the case, but now, there are several one-to-one all-purpose gluten-free baking flours. A real game changer!" Beth replied.

"Henry, stop eating chocolate chips. We won't have any left for the cookies!" Hannah grabbed the bag from him.

"I'm not eating them!" Henry complained, but the dark circle around his mouth gave him away.

She handed him a measuring cup. "Here, you and Ethan measure out two cups of chocolate chips." When Beth walked by, Hannah whispered, "Where is he? Do you have any texts or missed calls from him?"

"I haven't checked. I have no idea where he is." Beth shrugged and returned to the front of the room. "Is anyone ready to put your cookies in the oven? Every station has a Sharpie. Write your initials on the bottom of your cookie sheet so there's no confusion."

"We've got plenty of confusion over here," Richard said jovially, using his hand to brush flour out of Henry's and Ethan's hair. "Beth, I think we have two future chefs you may want to hire!"

One by one, the groups baked and carefully scraped their cookies onto cooling racks. As the cookies cooled, the adults cleaned up while Laura led the kids in singing holiday songs. The groups chatted easily as they packed their cookies into tins to take home.

"This was great," one mom remarked to Beth. "My daughter doesn't have celiac disease, but she is gluten intolerant. It's good to know how easy it is to bake gluten free."

"I'm glad you found the class useful. I started with a simple cookie so I could point out some of the nuances of gluten-free baking. I'll do another one next week where we make cutouts. They're a bit more labor-intensive, but I think it will be fun. You can sign up online, just like you did for this one. I hope you'll come back." She smiled warmly and said goodbye to the mom and the other participants.

When the last group left, she turned to her crew, a satisfied look on her face.

Before she could say anything, Red jammed her fists into her hips. "Well, where is he? I hope he has a good excuse!"

Hannah burst out laughing, and Nicole cringed.

Beth's shoulders almost touched her ears as she shrugged, palms out, face up. "No clue."

"Sorry." Red shook her head. "Everyone knows redheads have impulse-control issues."

Beth retreated to the restroom. Leaning against the locked door, she pulled her phone from her pocket. No texts or missed calls.

Chapter Fifteen

"Beth, I'm so sorry! As soon as I get this mess under control, I'll be on my way." Frank sounded frazzled over the phone.

"Oh my gosh, don't worry about the café. Ugh. Five inches of water in your basement, what a nightmare!" She shrugged into her coat and grabbed her bag and keys. "I'm headed there now. I have to do payroll and inventory today. Then I'll help out in the kitchen. Or I'll see if Nicole is available." Beth had been impressed by how her sister had stepped up and become more responsible and less self-centered since the opening of Fresh Start. The café had proven good for them all. "I'll figure something out."

"Thanks, Beth. Listen, one more thing. Being new to the area, I don't know of any water restoration companies. Do you know anyone? The drywall and trim are damaged in the finished part of the basement."

As Beth placed her phone in her car's holder, a text notification from Andre lit up the screen.

"Actually, I do. Danny and I had water damage a few years ago." She pressed her fist to her forehead, eyes squeezed shut. "Oh, I'm drawing a blank. But I'll look through my bank statements online when I get to Fresh Start and text you the name. They were great to work with."

Her phone lit up again. Another text from Andre, which Beth ignored.

Driving to Fresh Start, she racked her brain for the company name, momentarily putting Andre and his texts out of her mind. She arrived at the café to a bustle of activity. Frank had called with the news of the water disaster, so the staff was up to speed. They assured Beth everything was under control.

"I'll be in the office," Beth said, pouring a mug of coffee on her way. "I need to look up something for Frank, then I'll start payroll. Let me know if you need anything."

Grabbing her phone from her bag, she opened Andre's messages.

Andre: *Hey there, so sorry I missed your event. Can we talk?*

She chewed her thumb cuticle and tossed aside her phone, eager to turn her attention elsewhere. *It's no big deal. We just met.* At her desk, she logged on to her bank and found the account she and Danny had used to pay bills.

Brow creased, Beth sat back in her chair and folded her arms. "Weird. Why can't I find it?"

"Find what?" Lucy appeared in the doorway with inventory sheets.

Beth looked up. "Oh. It's just an invoice payment to a water restoration company we used a few years ago. I want to give the name to Frank."

"Maybe you're looking at the wrong month," Lucy suggested.

"No, that's the thing. I remember exactly when the burst-pipe catastrophe happened because it was an inopportune time—not that there's ever a good time for your basement to flood." She continued clicking and moving the cursor. "I remember it vividly because it was the week of our anniversary. We had plans to go out to dinner, but Danny's mom was admitted to the hospital. She has a musculoskeletal condition and often suffers from complications. Anyway, I know that's when our basement flooded because we had just canceled our reservation and were headed upstate to see her."

"Jeez, a literal when-it-rains-it-pours situation."

"Yeah. It was a stressful week all around. Danny had been in a mood, and I'd been tiptoeing around him for days. Then the pipe burst, so we didn't leave to see his mom until the next day." Beth tapped her fingers on the keyboard, trying to ignore the uneasy feeling creeping into her belly. "This makes no sense. We have a few accounts, but we always used this one to pay bills, repairs, home improvement projects, that sort of thing."

"Maybe Danny used a different account for some reason?" Lucy placed the sheets on Beth's desk. "I'll leave you to it and get back to work. The Tuscan soup won't cook itself!"

Beth hardly heard Lucy. "Huh? Yeah, sure." She began searching for a payment for their kitchen renovation. As she scrolled through checks and credit card payments, the uneasiness increased with each missing record.

Trying not to overreact, she logged into their two other bank accounts and resumed the search, though to her knowledge, she and Danny had never used those accounts for things like repairs and house projects. Maybe he had used funds from one of them without mentioning it to her. She scrolled through statement after statement. Nothing.

Hurrying past the kitchen, she shrugged back into her coat and called out, "You guys good? I need to run a quick errand."

Red wiped her hands on her flour-covered apron, eyebrows raised. "Uh, sure, boss. We'll be fine."

Lucy tasted her broth. Without looking at Red, she said, "That girl's on a mission."

"No, I don't have an appointment," Beth answered impatiently. "But I need to talk to an associate about my accounts." She spoke to a representative at the Bank of Philadelphia branch that looked exactly like every other bank she'd ever seen. Velvet ropes attached to brass stands formed lines in which customers waited their turn for the next available teller. High ceilings outlined with ornate crown molding created a cavernous feel as associates and managers, their names and titles engraved in cursive on nameplates, spoke in hushed tones to customers seated across their desks.

"Come this way, ma'am." The woman led Beth to a man behind a cherry desk next to a large artificial floor plant.

"Hello, I'm Ted Haines, one of the assistant managers here. Please, have a seat."

He held out his hand, which Beth shook before sitting down. Ted Haines wore large plastic-framed glasses that accentuated his receding hairline. He steepled his fingers on his meticulous desk, and Beth wondered idly if the neatness signified he had no work to do.

Only when she folded her hands in her lap did she realize they were shaking. "I'm Elizabeth Collins. I have some questions about my bank accounts."

Ted Haines began typing Beth's name into his computer.

"My husband... er, late husband, Daniel Collins, died last year."

"I'm so sorry, Elizabeth."

"Beth. Thank you. Anyway, I'm the executrix of his estate and sole beneficiary. We have no children."

Ted nodded but said nothing.

Beth licked her lips and continued. "The thing is, I was looking through our accounts. We always used one for bills, repairs, those kinds of things. I have our account numbers here." She handed him a slip of paper with three lengthy numbers written on it. "The top one is the account I'm referring to. Today, I was looking for specific transactions—withdrawals from this account that I know occurred. But I couldn't find them. Then I checked the other accounts. The payments weren't taken from them either."

"You say your husband's name was Daniel? Daniel Collins?"

Beth nodded and tried to relax.

Ted looked at the paper and resumed typing. "Hm," he mumbled, frowning.

Beth scooted to the edge of her seat. "What?" She could see his puzzled expression reflected in the desktop screen.

Ted scrolled and clicked a bit more then sat back and looked up. "Do you have proof of your executrix status and a death certificate?"

"Proof of—yes, but not with me. Why?"

"Any executor or administrator needs to produce a copy of the death certificate, proof of administrator status, and a valid ID to withdraw funds. I assure you, it's standard practice."

"But I don't want to withdraw money. I just want to find the record of the transactions I'm looking for." She shook her head. "Also, I'm confused. My name is on the accounts, so why do I need any documentation?"

Ted's pursed lips indicated he was not sure how much further to take the conversation. Appearing to measure his next words, he handed the paper back to Beth. "Yes, that's true. Your name is on *these* accounts."

Beth huffed impatiently. "Right, so why do I need...?"

Ted pushed up his large glasses frames, never taking his eyes off her.

"Oh." A tidal wave of realization washed over Beth. "You mean there are other accounts? Ones in Danny's name but not mine?"

Ted stood and offered his hand again. "Come back with those documents, Mrs. Collins."

Chapter Sixteen

Beth's head pounded. On the face of it, the fact that Danny had opened additional bank accounts without her knowledge wasn't cause for hysteria. There must be a million explanations. But she couldn't seem to come up with a single one.

Danny, what were you doing? Why the secrecy?

The truck horn's loud honk made Beth jump. She waved off the obscene gesture from the driver behind her and stepped on the gas. "Jeez! Sorry!" She automatically steered toward Fresh Start but abruptly changed her mind. Knowing she would accomplish nothing until the mystery was sorted out, she made a U-turn and headed home.

At a red light, she noticed a truck with a familiar logo. She studied it and read the ad: *Eastern Pennsylvania Fire & Water: Serving Your Restoration and Reconstruction Needs.*

"That's the company!" Before the light turned green, Beth texted the name to Frank. "At least I can solve one problem today."

As the text flew through cyberspace, she noticed Andre's messages and remembered she hadn't responded. She would deal with him later.

At home, she called the café to make sure they were functioning without Frank or her.

Lucy said Nicole had come in to help and assured Beth everything was fine. "How about you?" she asked. "You ran out of here like you had a plane to catch. Everything all right, boss?"

"Yes... I mean, I think so. I just have something I need to deal with. I'll see you a little later."

Riffling through the filing cabinet in her home office, she found the folder she was looking for. She thumbed through the documents before tossing the whole thing into her bag and heading back to the bank and Mr. Large Glasses.

Dinging from her phone momentarily broke her concentration. More texts from Andre.

Andre: *I hope you're not too mad at me... Can we talk?*

She sighed. "Oh, what the hell. This day is already a shit show. Let's hear what the guy has to say for himself." Beth hit the phone button on her console and called Andre as she backed out of her driveway.

He answered on the first ring. "Hey! I'm glad you called. How are you?" Andre sounded groggy, like she'd woken him up.

"I'm okay. How are you?"

"I've been better. I'm a little under the weather." He cleared his throat. "Listen, I'm so sorry I missed your baking class last night. I was really looking forward to it. Then, after work, I started feeling awful."

"Awful how?"

"Kind of like a truck hit me. My whole body ached, and I could hardly move. I came home to change, fell into bed, and passed out for the rest of the night. I'm really sorry."

Andre sounded sincere, and Beth said sympathetically, "Sounds like the flu. There's a bunch of stuff going around."

"Yeah, I guess."

"It's no big deal. There will be other classes if you're really interested in gluten-free cooking and baking."

"Well, I'm interested in a girl who's into gluten-free cooking and baking, so..."

Beth couldn't help smiling at Andre's charm. "Is that right? Well, I bet, if you played your cards right, she'd bring you a fresh-baked loaf of banana nut bread and a piping hot cup of tea—"

"No!" Andre said a bit too abruptly.

"I'm... I'm sorry. That was presumptuous of me." Beth was glad Andre couldn't see the rosy hue spreading across her cheeks.

"No, sorry. I just mean I wouldn't want you to catch whatever bug I have. I think I'm better off lying low for a few days."

"Sure, yeah, good idea." She steered into the bank's parking lot and assumed a more businesslike tone. "Listen, I'm kind of in the middle of something. I'll talk to you later. I hope you feel better."

"Thanks, Beth, talk soon."

Beth ended the call and walked through the same doors she had that morning. Ted Haines was with another customer, and Beth chose to wait until he was available. She had no desire to go through the whole story from the beginning with someone different.

Her mind drifted as she sat in the lobby. Andre definitely hadn't sounded well, so she had no reason to doubt his explanation. It also made sense that he wouldn't want her dropping by if he had a contagious virus. Regardless, she was uneasy.

But she had a more pressing issue at the moment, namely, why Danny had bank accounts in only his name, which Beth had known nothing about. They'd always discussed financial matters and made decisions together. She tried to remember back to when the pipe had burst in their basement. *Had Danny mentioned anything about payment for the repairs using a different account? Or the kitchen renovation?* She couldn't recall any such discussion, but she had to admit that while she and Danny had talked about repairs and projects, when it came time to pay the bills, Danny had taken care of it.

"Mrs. Collins, nice to see you again. Come on over and have a seat." Ted Haines guided Beth toward the same chair she'd occupied earlier. "I take it you have the necessary documents."

"Yes." Beth handed him the folder containing Danny's death certificate and a document naming her both the executrix and sole beneficiary of his estate.

Ted briefly glanced at the paperwork and nodded. "And you have a valid ID?"

"Yes, I have my driver's license."

Ted gathered the materials. "I'll be right back."

As Beth waited, she tried not to let her imagination run away with her. After the accident, she tended to think the worst, see doom around every corner. She'd temporarily lost hope. But since she'd opened Fresh Start, she had worked hard to think more positively. There had to be an explanation for the mix-up with their accounts.

One thing was certain. Though he'd liked being a lawyer, Danny's work had caused him a lot of stress. He'd left a corporate firm to open a practice on his own, but it had done little to allay the pressure. In fact, without partners or associates, it seemed the workload only increased. Beth winced at the recollection of phone calls that soured his mood for hours or even days. Countless phone calls he took in his home office, behind closed doors, trying to keep his voice even. Beth couldn't make out the words, but she could tell by the tone that the calls were contentious. When she asked, he said opposing counsel was being unreasonable or his clients weren't listening to his advice.

Then there was the traveling. Several clients from the firm stayed with Danny when he went out on his own. Plus he sometimes did estate work for a law school buddy's small New York firm, and the headache of traveling to meet with those clients took a toll on him, especially, it seemed, during the last year of his life. He often came home sullen and quiet for a period of time until his cheery, playful mood returned. Beth didn't push him to talk when he was like that. She let him come around on his own.

The fact that he earned a nice income took away some of that tension and allowed the couple to enjoy the spoils. They'd always had enough money to live comfortably and do things they'd enjoyed, like taking vacations and fixing up their house.

Maybe Danny opened an additional account to save money for special-occasion trips to surprise me with? Maybe he was putting away money in case I decided not to work outside the home when we started a family? Maybe—

Ted returned and handed back the folder. "Well, everything is in order. Thank you for keeping such organized records. Now then, let's take a look at what we have here." Ted typed, scrolled, and made that annoying repetitive clicking noise with his tongue that people made when they searched for something. His printer spit out a few pages, which Ted grabbed and separated into two neat piles on his desk. "Okay. Besides the three accounts bearing both your and Daniel's names, three additional accounts are in his name."

He handed one of the stacks to Beth, who hung on his every word.

"These pages show transactions for each account dating back a few years, except for this one." Ted stabbed his finger at one of the pages. "This account was only opened fifteen months ago, which looks like—" More annoying tongue clicking. "Only three months prior to your husband's passing. That one, as you'll see, has some deposits but no withdrawals."

Beth blinked hard several times and stared at Ted Haines. Thoughts too unorganized to form actual questions swirled around her head. She looked at the sheets in her hand, but the numbers were a blur. "I... I don't understand. What was Danny...?" Her voice trailed off.

"Mrs. Collins, if I may?"

Beth nodded, so Ted continued.

"Go home. Look through the account activity. I'm sure you'll find the answers you're looking for. You know, I hope I'm not being too forward, but I've sat across from many people in your situation whom I've had to tell that there are little or no funds available to them. You've just learned you have more money than you thought. It could be worse."

Beth thanked him and shoved the papers into her bag. She sat in her car for several minutes without starting it. She'd come in for answers and left with more questions.

Chapter Seventeen

Beth arrived at Fresh Start to find every table occupied and several people picking up takeout orders. After her harrowing morning at the bank, she welcomed the bustle of the café. Instead of immediately holing herself up in her office, she stopped by several tables to chat with customers. The short, pleasant diversion did wonders for her state of mind.

Lucy stepped out from the kitchen, carrying something Beth imagined heaven might smell like. "How about something to eat, boss? You look like you could use a bowl of my Tuscan soup right about now."

"You know what? That sounds perfect. Thanks, Luce."

Beth accepted the steaming bowl and carried it to her office. She threw her bag on a chair, the paperwork from the bank peeking out of the top as if beckoning to her. As she savored the soup, she decided to put aside the bank account mystery for a while and instead tackle some of her café work. Moving her mouse to wake up her computer, she opened the payroll program and set about entering the appropriate information.

An hour later, feeling better at having completed the task, she leaned back in her office chair and stretched. Her thoughts returned to Danny and the mysterious banking saga, but she forced them away. Needing to get up and move around, she turned her attention to inventory. She entered the kitchen, where activity was winding down. The café was closed, and one by one, she bid the staff goodbye.

Red and Lucy were the last to remain. "You want help with inventory, Beth?" they asked.

"No, you guys get going. Thanks so much for running the show today. Frank will be back tomorrow." She shook her head, her shoulders slumping. "And I'm sorry I bailed on you this morning."

"Aw, no sweat, boss. It's not like you do that much anyway," Lucy joked, playfully punching Beth's arm.

Red's shocked look made Beth chortle. "It's okay, Red. She's right! That's the brilliance of my leadership style. Hire great people, then leave them in charge while I run around town on a wild goose chase."

"Seriously, Beth." Lucy headed for the door. "You looked like you saw a ghost."

"I wish I had." Beth locked the door behind the two women. "I have a lot of questions for him."

At home in her sweats, curled up on the sofa with a glass of wine, the bag containing the bank documents at her feet, Beth thought about her life with Danny. The stress of his career aside, their personal life had been wonderful. Their love had felt so easy and natural, like the first kiss of sunlight on a summer morning. She'd felt lighter, freer with Danny. She'd had a few serious relationships before him, but it wasn't until she met Danny that Beth had felt she could truly be herself. They'd talked about anything and everything, and she'd never had that with anyone before. It hadn't mattered if they were cleaning out the garage or attending a formal dinner event, they'd had fun because they were together. So deep was their connection, they would catch each other's eye across a room and wordlessly communicate their thoughts.

So, why, Danny? Why the secrets? Why didn't you trust me?

Sighing, Beth sipped her wine and opened her bag. She started with the activity in the accounts with both their names. At first glance, nothing jumped out at her. There were regular recurring deposits of both their paychecks, along with larger quarterly deposits reflecting Danny's bonus distributions from his firm. The bonus amounts varied, but nothing suspicious stood out. The printouts also indicated funds withdrawn for purchases and bills. Again, nothing seemed out of order. She refilled her wineglass and turned to the accounts in Danny's name, reaching for them slowly, as though they might burn her fingers.

The activity on these sheets was foreign to Beth. There were more deposits than withdrawals or payments, but the deposits followed no pattern. Not only did the amounts vary, but the intervals between deposits were random. Beth chewed her bottom lip as she studied the statements, trying unsuccessfully to make heads or tails of what she was looking at. Rows and rows of numbers and dates made her head spin, blurred her vision. She could find no consistent patterns that might lead her to answers. Finally, her head pounding, she gave up for the night.

Alone in her bed, Beth couldn't quiet her mind. Besides the obvious question of why Danny had secret accounts, something else about the bank statements nagged her. She tossed and turned, unable to put her finger on the source of her angst. Flopping onto her back, she stared at the strip of moonlight visible through her window shade.

She had just started to doze off when a jarring thought made her sit straight up. Throwing back the blankets, she shot out of bed as if fired from a cannon. Taking the steps two at a time, she ran downstairs to the sofa, where the bank papers still lay. On her knees, she arranged the documents into neat piles according to their account numbers. She found the three accounts bearing only Danny's name and traced her finger up and down the columns of each statement.

Stunned, she sat back on her heels. "It has to be here." Again, she went through each document, line by line, only to arrive at the same result. Just like on the statements in both their names, she could find no record of the payment she was looking for—a payment to Eastern Pennsylvania Fire & Water.

"What the...? How did Danny pay them?" Then other questions took shape, ones that made the hair on her neck stand up. *Are there more accounts? But why didn't Ted Haines know about them? Does Danny have accounts at other banks?*

Beth stared out the window, unable to posit answers to any of her questions. She sat that way for a long time, wondering if, for the past year, she'd missed a man who had never existed.

Chapter Eighteen

After a fitful night's sleep, Beth crawled out of bed. She hoped a hot shower would wake her enough to clear her jumbled thoughts.

The truth she hated to admit was that she was mad at Danny. She'd spent the last year mourning the everyday loss of him, their lazy Saturday mornings in front of the fire, drinking coffee, the meals they'd cooked together and eaten in front of the TV, meeting after work to decompress at the local dive bar. It was hard to separate her feelings for that man from the anger she felt toward the one with a treasure trove of secrets.

She saw him in every corner of the house they'd shared, in the chipped granite where he'd dropped a full coffee mug, the weathered recliner he'd refused to get rid of when they'd redecorated, the cluttered shelves in his home office that she couldn't bring herself to clear out.

His office. Of course! Maybe something on those shelves or in his desk drawers will provide some answers.

Stepping out of the shower, Beth vowed to search Danny's office from top to bottom. Tomorrow was Monday, the only day of the week Fresh Start was closed. She would ask Molly to help. If Danny had left clues there, they would find them.

Beth walked from her car across the square and relished the comforting calm she felt at Fresh Start. The café had come to feel like home, her staff more like family than employees, and her regular customers more like familiar friends. After the accident, Fresh Start had become her sanctuary, a place not haunted with memories of her life with Danny—a life suddenly clouded with so many questions, like a miniseries revealing new twists with each episode.

As she entered through the kitchen, she mused at how daunted she had been at first about owning a business. Now, it was the place she felt safest. It was rewarding to have created a space for people to gather. Many of the "regs"—as Lucy called them—had already formed friendships, and Beth loved seeing them greet each other warmly and exchange pleasant conversation.

The kitchen was in full swing, and enticing aromas enveloped her like a favorite blanket. Lucy and Frank often involved her in the cooking, making her more like a part of the team, not a disengaged owner. They'd started her with mainstream recipes then moved on to more inventive ones. Beth had always loved to cook, but her chefs had shown her how rewarding it was to take simple ingredients and create masterpieces for their valued guests. Red had done the same with pastries and other baked goods, teaching Beth the nuances that transformed baking from a skill to an art form. And her entire staff had embraced her goal of incorporating gluten-free ingredients into their recipes as a simple way of preparing delicious food rather than a fad that suggested bland or complicated dishes.

She frowned, thinking that the most complicated part of her life was no longer navigating a gluten-free diet but unraveling Danny's secrets. The thought was still with her as the crew apprised her of the day's specials. She was glad for the distraction.

"And let's eighty-six the strawberry cheesecake bars. Strawberries are terrible this time of year." Red updated the whiteboard on the wall. "I came up with a new cinnamon roll recipe. Something that'll stick to the ribs in this cold weather."

"Sounds great." Beth studied the board. "I'm glad we're keeping the cornflake-crusted chicken with cheesy mashed potatoes for a few more days. Frank, nice work finding gluten-free cornflakes. People love that dish. Real comfort food."

"Yes, minus all the grease. But, shh, let that be our secret." Frank moved his index finger to his lips. "I mean, how can breaded chicken taste good without the grease, right?"

"In fact"—Beth's face lit up—"after the holiday baking classes, let's do one where the adults make the chicken and the kids make the dipping sauces. They can do... hmm, how about a honey mustard, a dill, and a barbecue sauce. That would be fun."

"Boom! And we'll call the class 'Something to Crow About,'" Lucy added.

Allie arrived for her shift and poked her head into the kitchen. "Do chickens crow? I think roosters crow."

"Roosters are male chickens, and they all crow. Female chickens cluck. I think," Frank yelled from inside the walk-in fridge.

"Then we'll call the class 'A Cluckin' Good Time'!" Lucy doubled over laughing. "That'll surely make parents wanna bring their kids."

"Well, it would get their attention." Beth's eyes watered from laughing, showing her appreciation for the sense of family she and her staff had developed. "I love you guys. Seriously, you're the best."

"Everyone's getting in on the action." Red smiled. "Beth, Nicole has been helping out with the new baked goods and pastries. I daresay she's turning into a grown-up right before our eyes."

"I know. She's been great. Even Hannah has noticed, though it kills her to admit it. Will wonders never cease?"

As the staff continued to go over the upcoming week's menus, Beth felt her phone buzz with an incoming text. Thinking it might be Andre, she pulled it from her pocket. Instead of his name, Molly's lit up the screen.

Molly: *Happy Sunday! You okay? Texted a few times yesterday, but you didn't respond.*

Beth scrolled up and saw the unanswered messages.

Beth: *Yeah, sorry. Crazy story for you. Feel like helping me with some sleuthing?*

Three dancing dots told Beth she had piqued Molly's interest.

Molly: *Tell me where and when.*

Beth: *My house, later. FS closed tomorrow, so it could be a late night.*

Molly: *I'll be over right after work. I'll bring wine.*

Beth gave Molly a thumbs-up and dropped her phone back into her pocket. "Hey, Frank, did you call the water restoration company I told you about?"

Frank wiped his hands on his apron. "Yes, they're coming out to the house tomorrow. Thanks for the tip." He shook his head, a low whistle escaping his lips. "What a mess. We cleaned up as well as we could, but we definitely need pros for the wall and trim damage. I just hope they're not too expensive."

I wish I knew, Beth thought as she headed for the coffee pot.

The rest of the day felt like it dragged on forever. Beth couldn't wait to get home to start digging through Danny's office. Trying to keep busy, she tossed around notions that might explain the additional bank accounts. She was busing a table when the door swung open, bringing with it Andre and an icy blast.

Andre shuddered as he removed his scarf and gloves. "Brrrrrr. It's freezing out there!"

Beth studied his chiseled features. His cheeks glowed from the cold, and his windswept hair somehow looked better disheveled.

"Well, looks like you've rejoined the land of the living." Head tilted, Beth crossed her arms.

"Yes, I have. Whatever bug I had has thankfully gone to bother someone else. It knocked me off my feet for a few days, though."

Beth narrowed her eyes and nodded toward Andre's mouth. "Is your lip swollen? And it looks a little discolored."

He touched his lip, and redness colored his face. "Oh, yeah, this. It's stupid, really. When my fever was at its worst, I dragged myself out of bed and stumbled to the bathroom for some water. I was so disoriented that I walked into the doorframe. I had no idea the flu could turn me into such a klutz."

Beth furrowed her brow, processing.

Andre took a seat and unbuttoned his navy-blue wool coat. "Anyway, I'd love something hot to drink."

"What's your pleasure? Coffee, tea, hot chocolate?"

"Hot chocolate sounds amazing. Thanks." Through narrowed eyes, Andre watched Beth make his drink. When she set it in front of him, he asked, "So, how are you? You don't seem like yourself."

Beth shook her head. "No, I'm fine. Just ready for this day to be over." She wasn't going to share with Andre what she'd learned in the last two days. She liked him, was even attracted to him, but it was too personal to share with him until she had more answers.

Andre blew on the hot chocolate, causing ripples on the surface. "I can understand that. I bet when you get home, you'll put up your feet, pour a glass of wine, and gaze at the lights on your Christmas tree. A totally peaceful evening." He leaned back and folded his hands over his chest.

Beth didn't answer. She longingly stared at Andre's hot chocolate. *Christmas. The second one since Danny died.* She and Danny had kept a tradition of going to a local Christmas tree farm and chopping down a tree while sipping hot chocolate from thermoses. The accident had taken place only a few weeks before last Christmas. When she'd been released from the hospital, she couldn't bear to look at the tree. She'd asked Hannah's husband to take it down and get rid of it. This year, she couldn't bring herself to put up a tree or decorations at the house. They would be too painful a reminder.

But now she wasn't sure what was real and what wasn't. *Had our life been like a snow globe, perfect and peaceful at rest but swallowed by a blizzard of snow when shaken?*

"Beth?"

"Um, well, the thing is, I didn't put up a tree or any decorations at my house." She shifted nervously from one foot to the other.

"Come here, sit down." Andre stood and pulled out the chair next to him.

Beth sat and folded her hands in her lap. Not raising her head, she said quietly, "The accident, when my husband died, it was a few weeks before Christmas. Remember I told you we were driving home from a holiday party when it happened?"

"Oh, yes, I'm sorry. I hadn't put that together." He gently lifted her chin. "Is that what has you off kilter today?"

His fingers were warm on her skin. "No, well, maybe a little. I just have a lot on my mind."

Andre took both Beth's hands in his. "I'm here if you want to talk."

Beth stood, his touch sending a pleasant tingle through her. "Don't mind me. I'm not usually such a downer. It's been a crazy few days, and I'm just kind of distracted."

"Anything I can help with?"

Only if you know why my husband was keeping secrets about our finances. Not trusting herself to avoid flinging herself back into the chair and spilling the whole sordid mess, she turned away. "No. But thanks. I'll be fine."

Chapter Nineteen

Dusk arrived, and the forecast called for a light snowfall. Beth had just changed into loungewear and heavy wool socks when the doorbell rang.

"I brought red and white. I figured, why choose?" Molly stuck the bottle of white in the fridge and took two wineglasses from Beth's cabinet. "Where's your wine opener? And are you going to tell me what this is about? The suspense is killing me!"

Twenty minutes later, sitting at the kitchen island, Beth came up for air while a stunned Molly refilled their glasses. Beth had the stacks of bank records laid out in front of them.

"Holy hell." Molly held her head in her hands, elbows on the island. "Okay. Let's not get crazy. So Danny had some bank accounts he didn't tell you about. The question is obviously 'Why?'" She drummed her fingers on the island. "Did he ever mention being worried about money? Were things at the firm not going well?"

Beth shook her head. "No, never. I mean, sometimes he was busier than other times, but that's true in any business. He never seemed concerned. He never said we had to control our spending or modify anything about our lifestyle. I mean, he could be erratic, change his mind about things suddenly, then change it back. Remember the kitchen renovation? After months of planning, looking at cabinets, tile, granite, paint colors... one morning, out of the blue, he said he thought we should scrap the whole project, then a few days later, he was full steam ahead again. I didn't want to agitate him, so I didn't push him for an explanation. It's just how he was." She gazed at the ceiling as a thought occurred to her. "Hey, now that I think of it, I don't remember seeing all the payments to the contractors for the kitchen reno on the bank statements. I was so focused on the water restoration company, I didn't look for that."

The girls spent several minutes combing through the statements, highlighting withdrawals and payments for the kitchen project. When they finished, Beth sat back, confusion knotting her brow.

"Weird. So, some of the payments are accounted for. Let's see..." She clenched the highlighter between her teeth and ran her index finger up and down the pages. The highlighter bounced onto the island as she expelled an exasperated breath. "The cabinetry and painting payments are here, but not the granite or tile. How on earth did Danny pay those bills?"

Molly topped off their wine. "You thinking what I'm thinking?"

"There has to be more money somewhere. Other accounts."

Molly slid off her stool. "Well, then, let's get sleuthing." They headed for Danny's office.

Beth swore she still felt traces of Danny. The sandalwood scent of his cologne, his eucalyptus shampoo, the bourbon he sipped while reading all lingered on the edges of Beth's memory, now weighty and unsettling given his clandestine activities.

The girls worked methodically, Molly taking the built-in shelves while Beth searched the desk drawers. "Maybe you should ask Danny's parents or Josh if they have any idea what was going on."

Beth flipped through papers in the top drawer. "I thought about that. But Danny's mom is so sickly, I don't want to give them another thing to worry about. And Josh, I don't know, I just get the feeling he doesn't know anything. I feel like I would have picked up on something when he was with us. I won't rule it out, but for now, I don't want to involve him. At least until I know more."

An hour later, Molly had gone through half the shelves, and Beth was combing through the last desk drawer. So far, they'd found nothing of note. The shelves primarily held books, legal journals, case law, and articles. The few files she uncovered were mostly Danny's notes from phone calls and meetings. The center drawer held what most did—paper and binder clips, Post-it notes, a few random keys, and some coins. Other than files containing copies of briefs and decisions from judges, his other desk drawers revealed little more than notes scribbled on legal pads.

"I've been thinking." Beth closed a folder. "I'm going to contact the water restoration company directly and ask them how the bill was paid. If it was paid with funds from a different bank, I can contact that bank to get access to any accounts they have in Danny's name. I'll do the same with the cabinetry and painting invoices. Something, somewhere has to lead me to answers."

"Good idea. We're not finding anything here. Whatever Danny was up to, he didn't leave a paper trail in his home office."

"He does have a laptop here. I haven't opened it since he died. No reason to until now. I don't even know his passwords. And of course, the firm took over his files on his work computer. I'm sure they've all been redistributed or closed by now."

Beth had just shut the last drawer when the doorbell rang, startling both women.

Molly raised her perfectly shaped brows. "You expecting anyone?"

Beth sat back on her heels. "Nope."

Molly followed her out to the foyer. Through the beveled-glass panes next to the door, they could barely make out a man wearing a Santa hat, his arms wrapped around something about a foot shorter than him. Beth smiled and pulled open the door.

"Ho ho ho?" Andre asked sheepishly. He nodded toward the tree in his grasp, wound tightly with plastic netting. At his feet, strands of lights spilled out of a large shopping bag. "Don't be mad. I'll take it away if you want. I just thought maybe a small tree might bring you some holiday cheer."

Molly took in the comical scene. "You gonna let poor Santa stand out there in the cold all night?"

"No, that would put me on the naughty list, wouldn't it?" Beth's grin spread. She opened the door wider and swung out her arm, palm up, like a game show host. "Come on in, Santa."

Andre leaned the tree against the doorframe. "I have a stand and some lights too." He handed Molly the bag. "I didn't want this to be any work for you, Beth."

"Very considerate. Why don't you show Andre where you'd like the tree? I'll grab the white wine. It should be chilled by now." Molly dropped the bag in the family room and headed to the kitchen, leaving Beth and Andre alone in the foyer.

Beth's expression swelled with heartfelt gratitude for Andre's gesture. "This is really nice of you. I guess I could use a little holiday cheer."

Andre exhaled, never taking his eyes off her. "Whew. I was afraid I was overstepping. But when the idea came to me after talking with you today at the café, I literally ran with it."

"Here, let me have your coat and scarf."

"Thanks. I think I should take off my shoes too. As is the case with most of my brilliant ideas, this one was sudden, so I didn't have time to go home and change into boots before traipsing around the tree farm. Also, it's starting to snow." Andre grabbed the tree and followed Beth into the family room.

"How about over there, in the corner by the window?"

Beth removed the stand from the bag and placed it on the floor so Andre could wiggle the tree into it. They tightened the screws into the trunk, and Beth retreated to Danny's office for scissors to cut off the netting.

"I'm sorry if I interrupted a girls' night." Andre fluffed out the tree's branches, standing back and examining his work. "Does that look straight?"

Beth nodded.

"Well, it wasn't exactly a movie night or anything like that." Molly returned with the wine and clean glasses. "We were on a mission."

Beth shot her a stern look and changed the subject. She hoped he would be so intent on the tree that he wouldn't ask what the girls were doing before he arrived. "No, you're not interrupting. Here, let me help you with the lights."

"Uh-uh," Andre said. "You sit and relax. I'll do the lights. As I said, this is my brainchild. I didn't want my kooky idea to create any work for you."

Molly raised her eyebrows and nodded approvingly at Beth, who ignored her. "So, you look like you're feeling better."

Andre, who'd been unraveling lights from a plastic case, froze. "What?"

"Beth said you had some kind of nasty bug. You look like you're on the mend."

"Oh, that." He resumed draping lights on the tree's branches. "Yes, the flu. It knocked me for a loop."

Andre squinted, and his tongue poked out the side of his mouth as he worked, a sight so reminiscent of Danny that it stole Beth's breath. She shook her head and sipped her wine.

"Yes, and he missed the cookie class. I'm only a tiny bit suspicious he faked his illness so he wouldn't have to help clean up the mess," she teased.

"No chance. I was looking forward to it. Sign me up for the next one!"

"I don't know," Molly joked, pointing at Andre's brush-burned knuckles. "Baking can be dangerous. It looks like you have a few wounds there. Did you get those wrestling with this tree?"

Andre shoved his hands in his pockets, away from Molly's probing gaze. "Yeah, I guess I should have worn gloves."

Molly yawned and stretched her arms over her head. "I'm about to turn into a pumpkin. You two can take it from here." She gathered her coat and purse. Hugging Beth, she whispered, "He's a keeper."

Beth rolled her eyes and playfully pushed Molly toward the door. "Say good night, Molly."

"Good night, Molly!" Molly laughed at her own silliness and waved at Andre. "Bye, Santa!"

After Beth returned, Andre said, "She seems like a good friend. And a lot of fun."

"Molly's the best. I don't know what I'd do without her."

Andre finished the tree and stuffed the empty light boxes back in the shopping bag. Beth sank onto the sofa as he plugged in the lights. The tiny white bulbs bathed the room in a soft glow, making it instantly feel five degrees warmer. When he moved next to her, Beth couldn't be sure if the heat was due to the twinkling lights, the wine, or her proximity to Andre.

They drank without talking for a bit. Then, slowly, he put his arm around her shoulders. She stiffened, but only for a moment before leaning against him. They sat that way for a minute until Andre turned to Beth and searched her face. Beth thought he was silently seeking permission, and she granted it by moving closer to him. His lips softly closed over hers. It struck her like a lightning bolt that she'd wanted Andre to kiss her since their first encounter at the café. She just hadn't been able to admit it to herself out of loyalty to Danny. The tumble was risky, but she knew, in that moment, it was a risk she was ready to take.

When Andre pulled away, he rested his forehead against hers and sighed. "I've wanted to do that for quite some time."

They kissed again, slowly, deliberately, then Beth rested her head on his shoulder, and they held hands, contentedly gazing at the tree.

Eventually, Andre broke the spell that had encircled them. "I should go. Roads might be getting slick, and you've had a long day." He kissed the top of her head and pulled her to her feet. Throwing his scarf around his neck, Andre shrugged into his coat and shoes. He tilted Beth's chin up and kissed her tenderly one more time before leaving.

Beth watched him walk carefully to his car. She waved as he drove slowly away until nothing remained of him but the sweet reminiscence of his kiss and his perfect footprints in the snow.

Chapter Twenty

About four inches of snow fell during the night, and Beth was surprised to find the walk outside the café already shoveled. She went in the kitchen entrance and kicked the stoop to loosen the snow stuck to her boots. "Hey, Frank," she called. "Thanks for shoveling!"

"Wish I could take credit, boss, but it wasn't me. It was done before I got here." He resumed chopping vegetables for the stir-fry he was making for one of the day's specials. "I think you have an admirer. Or a guardian angel."

"Definitely an admirer. One in designer shoes. Guardian angels don't shovel snow. They miraculously make people miss planes that crash." Lucy hummed as she stirred pots of soup.

"Really? You think—"

The staff collectively raised their eyebrows.

"We don't think, we know. Seems like you're the only one who doesn't see Mr. GQ has it bad for you," Red agreed. "And if I'm not mistaken, the feeling is mutual."

Beth felt heat rise from her neck to her cheeks. "I mean... I do like him, sure, but do you really think he came out early this morning to shovel?"

As they nodded in unison, Beth pulled out her phone to text Andre and saw a text had already come in from him.

Andre: *Good morning! Just happened to drive by with a snow shovel in my trunk ;) Have a great day!*

A smile plastered to her face, Beth typed.

Beth: *First the tree, now this? How can I thank you?*
Andre: *How about by letting me take you to dinner?*
Beth: *Sounds good. Talk later!*

Beth beamed and started toward her office. With a hair tie she'd had on her wrist, she gathered her unruly mane into a knot on top of her head and woke up her computer.

She sighed. *Now back to my husband's mysterious past.*

A quick Google search revealed that Eastern Pennsylvania Fire & Water had three locations in the greater Philadelphia area. Sipping coffee, Beth called the first number, and a pleasant woman named Anne informed her that no work for a Mr. and Mrs. Daniel Collins had been performed through her office.

"Thank you, anyway," Beth told her. "I'll try the other two."

"What is it you're looking for?" Anne asked.

Beth hesitated before beginning her practiced speech. "Well, it's a little embarrassing. You see, your company did some work for us a few years ago. My husband has since passed away, and—"

"I'm so sorry!"

"Thanks." Beth cleared her throat and tried to sound casual. "The thing is, he passed away, and I'm trying to reconcile our finances. I can't seem to find a record of any payments to your company. But as I said, I'll try one of your other locations."

Beth could hear the tap of computer keys and the click of a mouse. "Hang on. If all you want is a record of payment, I can find it in our system, even if the work was performed by one of our other offices."

"Really? That would be very helpful."

"Yes." More clicking. "You said your husband's name is—sorry, was—Daniel Collins?"

"Correct."

"C-o-l-l-i-n-s?"

"Right."

"Mrs. Collins, may I put you on a brief hold?"

"What? Um, sure."

Instrumental music from a Broadway show whose name Beth couldn't remember—the one with all the female murderers—filled the space Anne left. Chicago, *that's it*. Beth listened to the music of "Funny Honey" for what felt like hours before Anne returned to the line.

"Mrs. Collins?"

"Yes, I'm here." Beth sensed Anne's pleasant tone had changed to one of unease.

"Can you confirm your home address?"

After Beth recited it, Anne continued. "So, first of all, your service was performed by our Jenkintown office."

"Okay." Beth scribbled the name on her notes. "But you said you could tell me how the bill was paid even if your location wasn't the one that did the work."

"Yes, I did say that. However, this appears to be a bit more... complicated than I anticipated."

A dull ache started in Beth's head. "Complicated how?"

"Well, um, the invoice for the work at your residence was paid for by an LLC."

Beth was momentarily speechless. *What?* She rallied and asked, "An LLC? Are you sure?" An icy tingle wove its way up her spine. She pinched the bridge of her nose. *Come on, Beth. You have banking experience. Think.*

"Yes, I'm quite sure." Anne sounded sympathetic, as though she sensed Beth's ignorance of the situation.

"What is the name of the bank affiliated with this LLC?"

"I'm sorry, but I can't provide you with any additional details without proof of identification, but if you contact the Jenkintown office and supply them with that, they will give you all the information they have."

Beth stared at the phone. "Yes. Okay. I'll do that. Thank you for your help."

"Have a nice day, Mrs. Collins."

Beth left her office and wandered out to the front of the café. It hummed with activity, the morning crowd packing every table. She mingled among them, chatting with regulars and introducing herself to newcomers. Craving mindless tasks to distract her from the news of the LLC, she took a tray of pastries from Red and arranged them in the almost-empty case.

Her thoughts turned to Andre and the previous night. For the first time since Danny died, she felt open to the idea of getting involved with a man.

Those kisses. Those. Kisses. She'd thought of little else since last night. The way his tongue gently touched her parted lips. The way her body overflowed with sensation. She'd had no hesitation. With Andre, she didn't feel weighed down by the past or worried about the future. She just felt... present. Her past, her mistakes, the one she couldn't forgive herself for, felt lesser somehow, like a long-ago broken bone that occasionally ached dully instead of a constant hurt.

"You gonna just stand there holding that empty tray, boss?" Red leaned on the counter and observed Beth through narrowed eyes. "You look like you have more than chocolate croissants on your mind." She took the tray from Beth. "And I daresay your giddiness from this morning seems to have vanished. What's up?"

Beth leaned on the pastry case and held her head in her hands. "You ever wish you could talk to the dead?"

"What do you mean?"

"You know, like literally summon someone who has passed away and ask them some questions."

"Like a séance."

"Yeah," Beth agreed.

"Be careful talking like that. Next thing you know, two guys with nets will come throw you in the back of a van."

"I'm being serious."

"Nah, I have all I can handle dealing with the living. I prefer to let sleeping ghosts lie." Red studied Beth while she wiped down the glass case. "I hope I'm not being too forward, but is this about feeling guilty getting involved with Andre? You know, feeling like your husband wouldn't approve?"

"No, nothing like that." Beth shook her head vigorously. "I mean, the questions I have are for Danny, but they're not about Andre."

Red looked skeptical. "Well, a word of advice, if you don't mind. Letting ghosts get inside your head is dangerous, especially the ghost of past loves. Best to let them stay where they are."

Beth drummed her palms on the counter. "So, I guess that means I have to find the answers myself."

She pulled herself up to her full height and smoothed her sweater as Red turned back toward the kitchen.

"Hey, Red," she called over her shoulder. "Do you think you'll come back as a ghost one day?"

"Honey, I hope so. I want to haunt my ex by screaming every time he sticks his fork into a slice of cake!" Red's laughter filled the air and buoyed Beth's spirits as she went back to her office.

Okay, you've put this off long enough. Get to it. She moved her mouse, and the screen popped up with the addresses and phone numbers of the other two water restoration company offices. "Okay, let's do this." She dialed the number of the Jenkintown location.

After several rings, a man with a deep voice asked how he could direct her call.

"Um, billing, please."

"Okay, I'll connect you." More elevator music then finally a human came on the line.

"Billing, this is Carrie. How may I help you?"

Beth took a deep breath. "Hi, Carrie. My name is Beth Collins. Your company did some work for my husband and me a few years ago." She paused to find the details in her notes.

"Can you give me those dates? We guarantee our work for one year—"

"Oh, I'm not calling to dispute the bill or complain about the work. What I'm trying to do is figure out how our bill was paid."

"How the bill was paid?" Carrie sounded confused.

Beth could hear the all-too-familiar typing and clicking.

"Yes. You see, my husband passed away last year, and I'm going through our bank records, trying to reconcile some financial issues. The person I spoke to at the other location told me our bill was paid by an LLC but couldn't give me additional information about it."

"I'm sorry for your loss," Carrie said sympathetically.

"Thanks. What I'd really like to know is the name of the LLC, what bank it's affiliated with, and anything else you can tell me about it."

"Okay. Let's take a look. What was your husband's first name?"

"Daniel."

"Can you spell your last name for me?"

Beth felt like a broken record. "C-o-l-l-i-n-s."

"Hm. May I put you on hold for a minute, Mrs. Collins?"

"Sure." *If she comes back and says I need to show up there with proper identification, I'm going to reach through the phone and—*

"Sorry to keep you waiting. Mrs. Collins, I'm afraid we'll need to verify your identification before we can give you the information you're looking for."

Beth almost burst out laughing. Not a wow-this-is-funny kind of laugh. More like an I-think-I'm-losing-my-mind kind of laugh. "For the love of God, can't I somehow verify who I am over the phone? I'm just looking for some answers!"

"I understand your frustration," Carrie said in a calm tone that suggested she had no comprehension of Beth's frustration. It was very unlikely that Carrie also had a dead husband who had taken a boatload of secrets to his grave.

"Why, exactly, do I need to provide identification? Isn't my name on the work order and invoice?" Beth struggled to remain calm. *It's not Carrie's fault.*

"No, only your husband's name is on any of our records. Unfortunately, to give you access, we'll need you to bring—"

"Let me guess," Beth snapped. "The death certificate and proof that I'm executrix of his estate."

"Yes." Carrie's tone softened. "I'm very sorry. I can hear how upset you are. It's just, well, we'd rather not get involved in our customers' personal business. I hope you can understand."

Beth spoke quietly. "I can. I'm sorry I snapped at you, Carrie. None of this is your fault."

"No apology necessary. Come in with your ID and the other documents, and we'll hand over everything we have."

Chapter Twenty-One

"An LLC? What the fuck?" Based on the horns blaring through the phone, it sounded like Molly had almost driven off the road. "When I saw you calling, I was sure you were going to tell me you'd gotten some answers from the water restoration company. I did *not* expect this! What the hell was Danny up to?"

On Lucy's assurance that they were fine at the café without her, Beth had left right after her call with the water restoration company. The stumbling blocks she'd encountered might slow her down, but she was determined not to let them stop her.

"Right? I mean, every time I think I'm getting somewhere, I end up with another layer to the onion. And this onion is really starting to stink!"

"All onions stink, honey, but I'm trackin.'"

Beth laughed, grateful for Molly's sense of humor. "Seriously, though, Mol, this is messed up. I feel like I didn't know Danny at all. I thought we were so close." She breathed out a melancholy sigh.

"I know it's overwhelming. But, Beth, both things can be true."

"What do you mean?"

"I mean that even though Danny had some secrets, it doesn't mean he didn't love you. God, everyone could see it. He adored you. You two were a great couple."

"I thought so too. But he obviously didn't trust me enough to share what was going on. Just think of everything I've uncovered in the last few days. It's making me question our entire relationship." A tear threatened the corner of her eye.

"Try not to do that, Beth. No one knew Danny better than you. True, he had some secrets. Maybe he got himself into something and he had it all under control, but his sudden death prevented him from finishing whatever it was. I don't know, I'm spitballing, but we'll figure this out. We'll keep pushing and searching, and we won't stop until we find answers."

Beth was warmed by Molly's use of the word "we." Knowing that she wasn't alone was a huge weight off her shoulders. "Thanks, Mol. Listen, I'm pulling into the parking lot of Eastern PA Fire & Water armed with paperwork that proves I am Beth Collins—widow of a man of mystery and sole heiress to the mess he left behind. Wish me luck!"

"Go get 'em, girl."

Beth entered the lobby and approached the counter.

A thirtyish woman with short, spiky hair looked up and smiled. "Hi. Can I help you?"

Beth laid her folder on the counter. "Yes, I'm Beth Collins. I called this morning about an invoice and was told I needed to provide proof of identification for the information I'm requesting."

"Oh, yes. Just a moment. I'll let Brent know you're here."

Beth nodded. *Please let Brent—whoever he is—lead me to some answers.*

"Mrs. Collins, I'm Brent Yerger, manager of the Jenkintown office. Come right this way." Brent was tall and lanky with dark, wavy hair and deep-set eyes. He extended his hand to Beth before leading her down a short hallway to an office. He took a seat behind his desk and indicated the chair across from him then eyed her folder and cleared his throat before continuing. "I'm sorry for what must seem like a very inconvenient formality. It's just—"

"No, it's okay. I understand." Beth flipped open the folder and handed Brent documents one by one. "Here is my ID. This document is Danny's death certificate, and this one names me as executrix of his estate." She sat back heavily and watched Brent examine the documents.

"Yes, well, thank you for these." He opened a file folder in front of him and began removing papers. "So, let's get right to it. Your husband paid for the work we did at your residence from an LLC." He watched Beth closely as if to gauge her reaction, but she stared at him without blinking. "The name of the LLC is—let's see—RCF Services. Are you familiar with it?"

Beth's brow knit, and her foot tapped rapidly. "RCF. No, that means nothing to me. Is that a business name?"

"I wouldn't have any way of knowing. My only concern when collecting payment is that the source has sufficient funds. The payment went through without incident."

"Forgive me, but this is outside my wheelhouse. How does one go about starting an LLC?"

"It's not really my area of expertise either. I do know there are many reasons people start LLCs, though. I think the bank could better answer your questions."

"And what is the bank affiliated with this LLC? I know it's not the Bank of Philadelphia."

"No, it's—" Brent thumbed through the paperwork. "Here it is. Bank of Greater Pennsylvania."

"Bank of Greater Pennsylvania," Beth repeated, mostly to herself. "We've never banked there. I don't even recall seeing branches in this area." She rotated her stiff neck and grabbed her folder. "May I have the record of payment for your services?"

Brent handed over the papers. "I'm sorry I can't be more helpful, Mrs. Collins. You need to contact someone at the bank. And make sure you provide—"

Beth didn't hear his last words. She was already on her way out the door.

She knew her next move had to be speaking with someone at the Bank of Greater Pennsylvania. Needing some time and distance from Danny's money mysteries, she decided to go back to Fresh Start. She arrived just in time to help clean up for the day.

"Good lunch rush today, boss," Frank told her. "The paninis sold like hotcakes!"

"Excellent. I'm really happy with the bread from that vendor. Next time he comes in, I want to talk to him about other products." Beth cleared a two-top and was on her way to the kitchen when she spotted Andre approaching the front door. The smile spreading across her face was a dead giveaway if she even thought of hiding her pleasure at seeing him. "Late lunch today?"

The tension in Beth's shoulders and neck eased when Andre hugged her.

He loosened his scarf and pulled off his gloves. "Nope. I've come to collect on my bill."

"Your bill?"

"Yes. I brought you a tree—all the while looking ridiculous in a Santa hat, I might add—and shoveled your walk. Now I've come to collect. Remember, you agreed to let me take you to dinner. How about tonight?" He grinned, looking proud of himself.

"Oh, yes, that! You're right. I do owe you the privilege of taking me out to dinner. And I always pay my debts," she teased. *And I even know where the money comes from.* Not wanting to ruin the moment, she shook the troubling thoughts from her head.

"Have you heard about the new Asian fusion place in Wynnemede? It's only been open a few weeks."

"Yes, I think it's called Jade Garden. Hannah and Eric had dinner there with friends and raved about it. Gemma follows them on social media and says the food looks amazing. I've been wanting to try it."

"Perfect. I need to get back to work, but I'll make a reservation and text you the time I'll pick you up." Andre kissed her on the cheek before tossing one end of his plaid scarf over his shoulder.

Beth waved as Lucy strode out of the kitchen and watched Andre cross the parking lot. "What kind of work does Andre do?"

"I'm not totally sure." Beth resumed cleaning tables. "Something to do with compliance."

"I'd comply with whatever that man wanted," Lucy mumbled with a smile.

Later, at home, before getting ready for her date with Andre, Beth looked up nearby Bank of Greater Pennsylvania branches. She entered the addresses one by one into the navigation app on her phone. Looking at the directions for each one, she frowned at what she'd learned. The closest branch was two towns away, more than thirty miles from her house.

She sat with the knowledge, staring out the window at bare tree branches, wondering what it might mean. The most obvious conclusion was that, given the distance, Danny chose it because he wouldn't see anyone he knew there. But that didn't make sense. *Why would he need to go there in person?* They'd both had direct deposit for their paychecks, and they'd paid all their bills online. They'd made the occasional cash withdrawal, but they'd done that at ATMs where they had bank accounts. *What were you mixed up in, Danny? Gambling? But then why the LLC?*

A *ding* from her phone interrupted her reverie.

Andre: *I'll pick you up at 6:30. Can't wait to see you!*

Beth responded with a thumbs-up.

Beth: *Me either!*

She headed upstairs to take a shower, Danny and his secrets remanded to the back burner until tomorrow.

Chapter Twenty-Two

Jade Garden was housed in a bustling downtown area rife with trendy shops and restaurants. Its decor was an eclectic mix of retro and contemporary with herringbone wood flooring, high-backed upholstered booths, and teahouse pendant lights.

"I don't know what to look at first," Beth told Andre as they took their seats. "I would never think to put some of these styles together, but it all works really well."

"I agree. Look behind the bar. The wall is wood but in a wavy pattern. The lighting is really cool too."

A cheery server dropped menus on the table. "Hi, I'm Sara. I'll be taking care of you tonight. Would you like to start with drinks?"

After ordering cocktails, they perused the dinner menu.

"So, you're the food expert. What exactly is Asian fusion food?" Andre's eyes widened. "The menu is huge."

Beth laughed. "I'd hardly call myself an expert. Remember, I kind of fell into the café life unexpectedly. In my previous life, I'd have helped the owner get the mortgage for this place. But thanks to my staff, I have learned a lot since opening Fresh Start. My understanding of Asian fusion is that it combines multiple cooking traditions and cultures. It's a great way for chefs with different backgrounds to come together and create unique dishes."

"So, do all the dishes have Asian influence?"

"More or less. I think most of the recipes start with traditional Asian-style ingredients and cooking methods, but they are combined with other ethnic recipes."

"Ah, hence the 'fusion.'"

"Yes, and the mashups make it a very popular concept. Frank always talks about it. He says chefs love the idea because they can create signature dishes that set their restaurants apart from others."

Sara arrived with their cocktails and asked if they had any questions about the menu.

"Do you have a separate gluten-free menu?" Beth asked.

"No, but many of our dishes are gluten free or can be prepared gluten free. If you tell me what you're considering, I'd be happy to help you. Off the top of my head, I know most of the sushi can be prepared gluten free if you get it with grilled protein instead of tempura."

"So, you have gluten-free soy sauce?"

"Yes. Take a look at some of the other dishes, and let me know what you're thinking. If I'm not sure about an item, I'll check with the chefs. They use rice noodles in all the noodle dishes, so those should be fine unless there's a thickener in the sauce. I will tell you, the dan dan noodles are my favorite. The honey garlic spareribs are a close second." Sara laughed and held her stomach. "I'm slowly working my way through the entire menu. I'll need bigger pants soon!"

"Too funny! Maybe give us just a few more minutes? You're right. Everything looks good."

"Of course. Take your time. I'll be back." Sara hurried off to another table.

Andre rubbernecked to check out a tray of food another server carried to a party near them. "I don't know what that chicken dish is, but it looks delicious. And are those crab legs?"

The server heard him and chimed in, pointing to the food Andre mentioned. "This one is black pepper chicken, and that one is Singaporean crab legs. Both great choices."

"They smell as good as they look," Beth said. "I wonder what the spices are on the crab legs."

Sara returned in time to hear Beth's question. "It's a mixture of garlic, turmeric, and ginger. Awesome, right?"

Narrowing down their choices, they finally decided on a sushi roll and dan dan noodles to share.

When Sara left, Beth placed her hand on top of Andre's. "I'm really glad you came over last night. Thanks again for the tree... and for shoveling the walk at Fresh Start... and..."

"You don't have to thank me. I'm trying to go slow, to give you space if you're not ready, but I just really like you. I hope you feel the same way, but I don't want to push you." He moved closer to her. "Then, when we kissed, well, it felt so natural, so comfortable. I'd really like to keep seeing you."

Beth smiled. "I'd like that too."

"Honestly, yesterday you seemed so out of sorts when I stopped in the café, I almost didn't do the Santa thing. I wasn't sure you'd be happy about it."

"Oh, I guess I was a little off, but it isn't just holiday blues." She sighed, not sure how much she felt like talking about her recent revelations. "It's just that I've been trying to settle some financial issues involving Danny, and I'm running into a brick wall at every turn."

Sara returned with their sushi. The restaurant had filled up, and she looked frazzled. Wisps of hair escaped her ponytail and stuck to her damp forehead. As she turned to leave, Andre ordered another round of drinks, and Beth asked if the dipping sauces on the table were gluten free.

"Oh, right." Sara motioned to a server rushing by. "Hey, can you snag that bottle of soy sauce from the table over there, where those people just left?" She turned back to Beth and Andre. "She'll grab that for you, then you're good to go."

The other server, equally overwhelmed, sped to a nearby empty table and picked up a bottle.

She placed it in front of Beth. "Here you go. Enjoy."

Beth, remembering when she first opened Fresh Start, empathized with the harried servers. "Thanks so much. It looks like the word is out. It's packed in here."

The server smiled gratefully and trotted off to wait on a newly seated party of six.

Andre picked up his chopsticks. "You were saying something about financial issues. I don't mean to pry, but shouldn't all that be settled by now?"

Beth nodded and filled a small dish with soy sauce. "Yes, it's nothing to do with probating the will or anything like that. That all went smoothly." She plucked a piece of sushi from the plate with her chopsticks and dipped it in the sauce.

"I'm sorry, it's none of my business. Forget I asked."

"No, it's okay. It's just, well, obviously, Danny's death was unexpected, to say the least. And I'm discovering some... discrepancies with our bank accounts." She smiled sadly. "And the person with the answers isn't here to ask."

"That sounds frustrating. No wonder you seemed miles away yesterday."

"It is, for sure. But on a brighter note, this sushi is delicious." Beth helped herself to another piece as Sara approached with their drinks.

"It really is. I have to tell you, Beth, you're helping me expand my palate. Besides how much I enjoy your company, you've gotten me away from my steady diet of pizza in front of the TV."

"Nothing wrong with that—once in a while," she teased. "I like hanging out with you too. And it's good to get away from spending every minute that I'm not at the café trying to reconcile our banking. It's easy to get bogged down by it."

Sara arrived and placed a steaming platter and two plates on the table. "Enjoy!"

It was Andre's turn to tease. "Well, I'm happy to serve as a distraction from your headaches," he joked as he spooned food onto each of their plates.

"That's not what I meant!"

Andre played it up with a sly smile. "Who knows, maybe your roof will start leaking and you'll go out with me again to take your mind off that?"

"Oh my gosh!" Beth couldn't stop laughing as she sprinkled soy sauce on her noodles. "I really have a way with words, don't I? I should write greeting cards!"

When the food was gone, Andre leaned back in his chair and threw his napkin onto the table. "I'm stuffed, but that was so good."

Approaching, Sara smiled and cleared the plates. "So, I guess that means you don't want to take a peek at a dessert menu."

Beth groaned. "I may have to loosen my belt a notch or two. I wish I had room for dessert, but even the thought of it makes my stomach feel like bursting."

"Coffee? Cappuccino?"

Beth shook her head, and Andre said, "Just the check. Thanks."

A few shops in the area were still open, so despite the cold, the couple decided to attempt to walk off dinner. Hand in hand, they strolled, chatting and window-shopping, occasionally ducking into a store to escape the chilly night air.

Beth stopped in front of a shop that sold trendy kitchen items. She indicated an eclectic display and chuckled. "I don't even know what some of these things are. I need Frank and Lucy's expertise."

Andre nodded and pointed to a funky-looking gadget. "That one looks like a fancy label maker."

"It does, but I think it's a sushi roller machine."

Andre's brow knit in puzzlement as he indicated another item. "Why is a kitchen shop selling hair straighteners?"

Beth laughed. "It's actually a bag sealer. I guess it works somewhat the same as a hair straightener."

"All I know is I burned my hand on my sisters' straightener more times than I can count. When we shared a bathroom, they had a habit of leaving it out on the counter and forgetting to unplug it." He squinted and shook his finger at the window. "And the dastardly contraption looked a lot like that."

"Well, keep your hands off if you see one of those in their kitchen. Safety hazards galore." They merged into the crowd of last-minute shoppers. "How long have you lived in this area?"

"I bought my house a few years ago. I rented in Jersey for a while because Chaz's family had me covering territory from Pennsylvania to New York, but I got tired of throwing money away on rent. I like this area, and it's easy for me to get to Jersey or New York if they need me. Lately, they've been giving me more accounts in Pennsylvania, which is good."

Beth listened but vigorously rubbed her arms.

Andre pulled her close. "Are you cold? We can start walking back to the car."

"No, it's not that. My arms are really itchy. I've never worn this sweater before, and I guess I thought it would be more comfortable."

"Well, the color looks great on you. Come to think of it, I can't imagine a color that wouldn't. Let's make our way back. In a minute." He tilted Beth's face up to his and kissed her tenderly.

Beth sighed, and they stood without moving for a moment, foreheads touching. Finally, they pulled apart and turned back toward the restaurant parking lot.

Beth lay in bed that night thinking about her capacity to love again. She wasn't sure what she felt for Andre was love, but it was the promising start of it, falling slowly, the way one might drift off to sleep. She closed her eyes, basking in the exciting newness of their relationship and where it might take them.

In the middle of the night, Beth woke up to a different feeling—an itching, burning sensation on both her arms. She pulled up her sleeves, rubbed her left arm, and felt raised bumps. Dragging herself to a standing position, she ran her hand up and down her right arm and felt the same roughness. Beth flicked on the bathroom light and stared at her arms in shock. Angry red bumps covered her forearms, and the mirror revealed that the worst of it was on her elbows.

"Jesus, what the hell?" The rash itched like poison ivy. She wanted desperately to scratch it, but she knew that would only make it more inflamed. Yanking open the medicine cabinet, she rummaged through bottles and tubes until she found a cream that touted a calming effect on rashes and burns. Gingerly, she applied the ointment to her skin and pulled her sleeves down to cover the redness. She lay back down and tried to fall asleep.

Daylight shone through Beth's bedroom blinds, but what roused her was the burning sensation of the rash. Grunting, she grabbed her phone and searched for the number to her doctor's office. After getting an appointment, she called Lucy.

"Hey, boss."

"Hi, Lucy. Listen, I won't be in today."

"You know, I'm starting to think you have another job," Lucy joked.

Beth groaned. "Very funny. No, my arms started itching before I went to bed, and it got worse during the night. I have some kind of angry-looking red rash. I don't know what it is or if it's contagious. I'm going to the doctor to get it checked out."

"Ugh. Yes, you and your rash should stay far away from our kitchen and my boilermaker chili. We're good to go here."

Beth could hear the behind-the-scenes sounds of the café coming to life.

"My arms feel like they're simmering in a pot of your chili." She pulled on jeans and a sweater as she talked. "My appointment is in forty minutes, so I have to hustle. I'll keep you posted."

As Beth buckled her seat belt, she was dismayed to see the rash had worsened. It looked blistered in places, and the itching drove her crazy.

In the waiting room, a text came through from Andre.

Andre: *Good morning, beautiful.*

Beth smiled despite the fire under her sleeves.

Beth: *Morning, yes—good, not so sure. At doc office with mysterious rash on arms.*

Andre abandoned texting and called her. "Hey, what's going on? I remember you saying last night that your arms itched. Was it the sweater?"

"I don't know. All I know is I look like I wrestled with a poison ivy plant and lost. And the itching is enough to drive me out of my mind."

"Beth?" A girl with a clipboard stood at the doorway that led to the exam rooms.

Beth stood. "Gotta go. I'll call you later."

She followed the girl to a room at the end of the hall.

"Go ahead and have a seat. I'm Amelia. I'll take your vitals and go over your history before Dr. Roth comes in." Amelia was professional but pleasant.

Though Beth hadn't been to the office in quite some time, she remembered her from previous visits. Beth sat on the paper-covered exam table and rubbed her arms.

After reviewing her chart and medications, Amelia took Beth's blood pressure and pulse. "So, what brings you in today?"

"My arms began itching last night. I was wearing a new sweater and thought maybe the fabric had caused it. But after I took the sweater off, it continued to get worse." She pushed up her sleeves.

"And now it looks angrier than ever. I think it might even be blistering on my elbows."

Amelia looked at Beth's arms. "Ooh, that looks sore." She typed a few notes on Beth's chart. "Have you changed soaps or laundry detergents recently?"

Beth shook her head. "Nope."

Amelia pecked out a few more sentences. "Okay, Dr. Roth will be in shortly." Before she left the room, she turned back to Beth. "I was really sad to hear about your husband. I'm sorry for your loss." Amelia smiled sadly. "I don't know if you know this, but my parents hired him to handle my grandfather's estate when he passed."

"No, I wasn't aware of that. Danny was private about his clients' cases."

"Of course. That makes sense. Anyway, my parents really liked him. They said he was very thorough and nice to work with, even though..." Amelia's cheeks reddened, and she shuffled her feet uncomfortably.

Beth waited silently, not wanting to pry or embarrass the girl.

"Even though it didn't work out exactly as my parents thought. Um, my parents thought my grandfather—he was my mom's dad—had quite a bit more money than he apparently did. He'd had a lucrative career with a great retirement plan, and he'd invested well—or so they'd thought. They figured my grandmother could afford to live out her days comfortably with no money worries, but..." Amelia cleared her throat. "Anyway, it didn't work out that way. I guess Granddad didn't invest as wisely as they'd believed. My grandmother lives with my parents now. It all seems to be going okay. But I wanted you to know they thought the world of your husband. He helped them through a rough time."

Beth took in Amelia's story, easily visualizing Danny in that role—the professional but compassionate lawyer sorting out the family's financial difficulties. A thought tugged at the corner of her brain, trying to take shape.

Dr. Roth breezed into the room, breaking Beth's concentration.

Amelia left with a small wave, and Beth's thoughts returned to her itchy, inflamed arms.

"So, let's see what we have here." Dr. Roth was in her forties, with curly blond hair that she wore in a braid. She perused Beth's chart and Amelia's notes. "Hmm. A rash on your arms. May I have a look?"

Beth rotated her arms from side to side and bent them so the doctor could see her elbows. "It was so strange. I was out to dinner—that new Asian fusion place in Wynnemede—and my arms were fine. It was only later that the itch started, then in the middle of the night, the rash came on with a vengeance. I was wearing a new sweater, and I thought that might have caused it, but now I'm not so sure."

Dr. Roth examined the rash with gloved hands. "I don't think sweater material, no matter how itchy, could cause a rash to this extent, especially after taking it off." She leaned against the counter and folded her arms. "What did you have for dinner?"

"Oh, the food was fabulous. We started with cocktails and a sushi roll, then we shared one of their signature entrees, a noodle dish with chicken. It was to die for! The place was mobbed. Have you been?"

"No, but I've been meaning to get there. I'm sure the food was great, but I'm asking for another reason. Hang on a sec." She minimized Beth's chart on her computer and tapped the keys. A minute later, several images appeared on the screen. The doctor scrolled through them and stopped on a page filled with photos of angry blistering rashes that looked just like Beth's. "Take a look at this."

Beth wrinkled her nose as she studied the photos. "Ew. Yuck. Looks just like mine. What is it?"

"Well, you have celiac disease."

"Yes, but I'm not following you. My stomach is a little unsettled, but I don't have digestive symptoms. I have a rash."

Dr. Roth pointed at the caption under one of the photos.

Beth read aloud, "Dermatitis herpetiformis. Uh, what's that?"

"It's the skin manifestation of celiac disease. It's much less common than digestive symptoms. Only approximately ten percent of celiac patients experience it." She looked at Beth's confused face and continued. "Dermatitis herpetiformis—or DH—is an external manifestation of an abnormal response to gluten. Typically, if I didn't know the patient had celiac disease and presented with such a rash, I'd want a biopsy to properly diagnose it. But we already know you have celiac."

"I don't understand. I didn't eat gluten last night. I made sure to ask about every dish and sauce before I ordered."

"I'm sure you did." Dr. Roth closed the tab. "But restaurants make mistakes. You said yourself it was mobbed."

Beth remembered the frazzled servers and nodded. "But why did I get this derma—DH—instead of my usual gastrointestinal problems?"

The doctor shrugged. "Hard to say. It could be a fluke. But it happens."

"So, can you give me something for it? It really itches. Not to mention, it looks gross."

Dr. Roth lowered herself onto her black swivel stool and typed a script into her computer. "I'm going to prescribe dapsone. It's an antibacterial drug. There's a topical cream, but the oral medication will work faster. Do you still use the same pharmacy?"

"Yes. Thanks, Doctor."

Beth started toward the door, but the doctor's soft, sympathetic voice stopped her.

"Beth, I haven't seen you since the accident. You've been through such trauma. I'm really sorry for your loss. I hope you're healing not just physically but emotionally. Let me know if you need anything. Ever. Just call."

"Thanks. I'm doing better. One day at a time, right?"

Beth crossed the waiting room to the exit. Amelia, who was leading another patient to see the doctor, caught her eye and offered a sad smile.

Chapter Twenty-Three

"Derma—what?" Andre sounded confused.

"Dermatitis herpetiformis, or DH as it's commonly called in the live-gluten-free-or-die world I inhabit. Apparently, there's a skin form of celiac disease to add to the fun. I've never experienced it before. When I mistakenly eat gluten—and I rarely do—my symptoms are more of the angry-alien-in-my-gut-trying-to-bust-out variety." Beth curled her legs under her on the sofa and spread a blanket over her lower body. She'd taken one of the pills Dr. Roth had prescribed and planned to catch an afternoon nap, both to escape the itch and because she'd slept poorly the night before.

"But, how? We checked everything we ordered. Oh, wait—remember when you asked Sara about the soy sauce? She commandeered another server to grab a bottle off another table. Is it possible she grabbed the wrong one? The place was a zoo at that point."

"Huh. You may be right. And I doused my food with that sauce like my plane was going down." Beth stretched and yawned. "Sorry, I didn't sleep very well last night since my arms were on fire. I'm going to catch a few z's now, but do you think I should let the restaurant know what happened? I don't want to get anyone in trouble, but they need to know how important it is to be careful if they're offering gluten-free options."

"I agree. I have an idea. We'll go back soon for dinner and let them know what happened. Your people skills are great. You'll gently but clearly make them understand the seriousness of people with celiac disease ingesting gluten. But the fact that we're back to eat will be a kind of olive branch. You know, 'No hard feelings, but get your act together.' How does that sound?"

"Perfect. I like it." Beth slid farther under the blanket and murmured, "Now, if you'll excuse me..."

"Pleasant dreams, Beth."

She awoke a few hours later to the winter sun dipping behind the mountains in the distance. Dusk gradually invited darkness outside her window, and Beth pulled the blanket up under her chin. Her arms still itched, but the medicine quelled the burning a bit. She reached for her phone. Almost five o'clock. Sitting up, she remembered everything she had to do. She needed to get to a branch of the bank affiliated with Danny's mysterious LLC. Not to mention, with Christmas less than a week away, she needed to finish her shopping. Laura called daily to ask her if she wanted to hit the stores in the evening after Fresh Start closed—and to ask repeatedly if Beth would be bringing Andre to Christmas dinner. The rash had thrown a monkey wrench into her day in more ways than one.

Rotating her neck to loosen the stiffness, she examined her arms. Still red, but definitely less blistered and angry looking. She stumbled up the stairs and changed into jeans and a soft cotton top. After brushing her teeth and hair and splashing water on her face, she took another pill and assessed her options. It was too late to deal with the LLC issue today, so she decided to head out to the local shops alone instead of meeting up with her mother. She had gifts for her nieces and nephews, sisters, and parents but still needed presents for her staff. And Andre.

What to get Andre? Their relationship was still new. She didn't know the comfortable, familiar gift ideas exchanged by couples who'd been together for years. She hadn't even been to his house yet, so she didn't know his taste in decor. Something told her he was not an upside-down-wooden-crate-footstool-that-doubled-as-a-kitchen-table kind of guy, but he had mentioned pizza nights in front of the

TV. One thing she knew: Andre was, without a doubt, one of the best-dressed men she'd ever known. Armed with that fact, she headed to a men's shop near her café.

Upon entering the store, Beth was quickly approached by a salesperson who directed her to displays of the "latest trends" in men's fashion.

"These faux fur coats are all the rage this season. They dominated the runway in the fall show in Milan."

Beth stifled a giggle at the image of Andre trussed up in a long faux fur while sipping a latte at Fresh Start. "I'm sure they did. I'm looking for something a little less... um..."

"A little less what, ma'am?" The salesperson sniffed lightly, as though an unpleasant odor had suddenly filled her upturned nostrils.

Ma'am? Is she kidding? "A little less furry, I guess. I think I'll browse, if you don't mind." Beth thanked her and scurried off to a display of scarves and hats as the woman set her sights on a presumptive mother and daughter. Next, she perused the shop's shoe selection and found several pairs she could picture Andre wearing.

She moved to a table bearing Italian leather wallets when the two women casually strolled over.

The younger of the two picked up a slim bifold design in dark leather. "Mom, how about something like this for Dad? That tattered old fabric thing he uses is embarrassing!"

The older woman chuckled. "But this wallet doesn't have a Velcro closure. You know how Dad loves seeing us cringe when he tears that thing open!"

Her daughter laughed.

The saleswoman was back. She sensed a fish on the hook. "You have excellent taste, miss."

Oh, she's a miss, and I'm a ma'am. I see how it is. Beth stood back and observed the reel in.

"The leather these wallets are made from is sourced from premium, handpicked tanneries in Western Europe, most predominantly from Tuscany, Italy—the epicenter of the leather industry." She made that sniffing noise again in Beth's general direction.

Beth rolled her eyes.

"Honestly, hon." The mother examined the wallet. "I could see your grandfather using this before Dad. Somehow, he's more fashion-forward than his son. Go figure!"

"Why not get them both one? We have complimentary gift wrap."

Oh, you're good. Beth refrained from chiming in that if they purchased two wallets at that price, they wouldn't have any money *left* for gift wrap. She could just hear Richard if she presented him with a wallet sourced from a Tuscan tannery. He would smile and comment on how beautiful it was, then insist she return it because it was too expensive—without ever knowing the cost.

She offhandedly realized that she couldn't wait to tell Andre about the experience. That happened more and more lately—she looked forward to sharing even seemingly innocuous daily events with him.

Beth held up a jacket and mused at how Andre's clothes fit him like a superhero, as though everything were expertly handsewn onto his body. She finally decided on a quarter-zip sweater in heather gray. She also found a pair of casual shoes she liked for him, but she would have to do some detective work to learn his size. As she paid for the sweater and waited for it to be wrapped, she made a mental note to check his size the next time he came over and kicked off his shoes to curl up on the sofa and watch a movie.

Back out in the chilly December air, Beth's thoughts returned to the mother and daughter at the men's shop. The mention of the girl's grandfather brought to mind the story Amelia had told her earlier that day at the doctor's office. Beth could easily picture Danny helping Amelia's parents and grandmother navigate such a sensitive sit-uation. Despite the clandestine activity Beth was uncovering, when it came to his clients, Danny had maintained a stellar reputation for rigorous and fair representation. He knew just what to say—and more importantly, just how to say it—when analysis and evaluation of the decedent's estate revealed considerably fewer assets than believed by the family. Her feelings about Danny had become complicated by recent revelations, but she was heartened to hear that Amelia's family had had a positive experience with him as their attorney. That was the Danny she knew.

Beth passed a shop that made customized holiday ornaments and stopped in to see if there was still time to fill orders before Christmas. Told by the store owner that it wouldn't be a problem, she selected various ornaments for her staff, deciding she would give each employee an ornament and a cash bonus, something personal and heartfelt accompanied by something everyone needed at that time of year.

Though her arms felt better, the rash still itched, and she was anxious to get home and out of her heavy coat. As she turned back toward the lot where she'd parked, several blocks away, she felt her phone buzz in her purse. She retrieved it, and the screen lit up with a text from Andre.

Andre: *How's the arm fire? Feeling any better?*

Beth paused her brisk steps to respond.

Beth: *Better. I'm out finishing some shopping but heading home soon.*

Andre: *Wanna come over and watch a movie? I have hot chocolate and popcorn :)*

Beth: *Sounds perfect.*

Then she realized she didn't know where Andre lived.

Beth: *Text me the address.*

Her stomach growled, reminding her she hadn't eaten dinner. She ducked into a small store boasting artisanal cheeses and bought two varieties, some rice crackers, and a cranberry walnut spread. Andre was always bringing her thoughtful gifts, so she was happy not to show up empty-handed.

In fifteen minutes, she was heading to Andre's, which her GPS told her would take twelve minutes. She drove onto his street, found his address, and pulled up to the curb. The modest brick two-story house looked decades old but meticulously maintained. As she made her way up the walk, Andre appeared in the doorway, wearing jeans, a red sweater, and no shoes. He rocked back and forth on his heels, hands shoved deep in his pockets against the cold. When Beth reached the door, they embraced, and Andre led her inside. He took her coat and hung it on a wall-mounted wooden rack in the entryway.

Underneath it, several pairs of Andre's shoes were lined up like kindergarteners ready for recess. A sly smile crossed Beth's lips. She feigned stumbling over a shoe, a leather slip-on in a rich butterscotch color. It flipped over, and she bent to put it back in line with the others.

"Don't worry about that." Andre took her hand and led her into a cozy living room with a fireplace, but not before she managed to catch a glimpse inside the shoe.

Size eleven.

Chapter Twenty-Four

The next day, Fresh Start hummed with its usual early-morning activity. In the kitchen, Frank and Lucy simultaneously went over the specials and discussed holiday plans. Pots and pans clanged, and comforting aromas wafted to the dining room, making Beth's mouth water. It distracted her from the task waiting for her that afternoon—visiting a branch of the bank linked to Danny's LLC. As she filled condiment containers, she pushed up her sleeves and was relieved to see that Dr. Roth's medication was doing the trick. Some redness remained, but the rash was much less severe.

After the lunch rush, she grabbed her coat and purse and said goodbye to the staff. The trek to the Berwyn branch of the Bank of Greater Pennsylvania seemed endless, but it could have been due to Beth's anxiety over the LLC she was going to inquire about. Following her GPS along scenic streets adorned with colonial and Tudor-style homes, she tapped her fingers nervously on the steering wheel and wondered how many times Danny had navigated those roads without her knowledge. She passed a commuter rail station and entered a section of businesses, scanning company signs for the bank.

Finding the building and pulling into a parking space, Beth drew in a deep breath and held it. *You can do this. Whatever it is, you can handle it.* She exhaled and swung open the car door.

Once inside, Beth approached a teller and said she needed to speak to a representative who could answer questions about an LLC affiliated with the bank. The teller spoke quietly into her headset then directed Beth to a waiting area. Clutching the folder with the documents she was sure she would need to obtain any information, she perched on the edge of one of the matching upholstered chairs to wait.

Jangling her nerves even more was the fact that she knew so little about LLCs. She wasn't even sure where to start her questions. Thanks to the soy sauce–induced rash outbreak, she'd had scant time to do research since learning that Danny had an LLC. The little digging she'd done had revealed that in Pennsylvania, a person had to register with the Department of State, most likely apply for a separate taxpayer ID, and determine how many registered agents the LLC would have. None of that came remotely close to giving Beth any insight as to why Danny had formed one. And the name—RCF Services. *What on earth does that mean?* By the time a woman with a bad dye job approached her and extended her hand, Beth's head had already begun to pound.

"Hello, I'm Penny Hartline, one of the branch managers here."

"Hi, I'm Beth Collins."

"Follow me. My office is just down this hall." Penny wore an olive-green jacket and skirt, and her nylon stockings made a shushing sound when she walked. She held the door open for Beth and indicated a chair across from a large cherry desk. The sun streaming in the window behind Penny accentuated the brassy tone of her hair.

"So, you're here to discuss an LLC? Are you interested in forming one?" Penny folded her hands on her desk.

"Oh, no, nothing like that." Beth exhaled audibly. "My husband died suddenly about a year ago."

"I'm so sorry, Mrs. Collins."

"Beth. Thank you. Well, the thing is, I've been going through our finances, and I learned that my husband formed an LLC and that the funds go through your bank. This is strange for many reasons, the two most obvious ones being: one, we don't bank here, and two, I have no idea why he would form an LLC or what he would have used it for." Beth's cheeks reddened, knowing how it must sound.

Penny's brow knit. "Okay. What was your husband's name?"

"Daniel Collins." Penny woke up her computer and began typing. Before she could ask, Beth laid the folder on the desk. "I brought his death certificate as well as a document naming me as executrix of his estate."

Penny smiled sympathetically. "Thank you. That will make things much easier." She licked her index finger—a habit that had always irritated Beth—and leafed through the papers Beth had produced. Seemingly satisfied with the authenticity of the paperwork, Penny resumed typing and scrolling.

Though not two minutes passed, it felt like an eternity to Beth as this person she'd never met combed through her personal affairs. Penny stopped periodically, cocking her head and resting her chin on her hand as she read. It was all Beth could do not to blurt, "Penny for your thoughts!"

Finally, Penny leaned back in her leather chair. "You're correct. Your late husband formed an LLC two years ago. He is the only registered agent, so he owns one hundred percent of the membership interest. Of course, now that he is deceased, that interest will be passed on to his estate—that would be you."

Two years ago. About a year before the accident. Beth filed away the detail for later. "And my understanding is that the name of the LLC is RCF Services."

"Yes. Do you have any idea what the initials stand for? Is it an acronym?"

"Those letters mean nothing to me. I can't think of anything with those initials." Beth paused, thinking about what to do. "I'd like everything you have—statements, history, activity, a copy of the operating agreement—all documents related to the LLC."

She waited while Penny scrolled, typed, and printed out a stack of papers. Penny sat quietly while Beth perused the documents.

Beth looked puzzled as she held up one of the sheets. "What are these large monthly transfers? It looks like they're wire transfers."

Penny studied the paper. "Yes."

Beth combed the sheets again. "And the transfers are to a trust account?"

"That's correct."

The information hit Beth like a gut punch. "Wire transfers? To a trust? For whom?" Beth grasped the chair's arms to steady herself.

"We don't have that information. The trust account is not set up here. It's at a different banking institution." Penny grabbed a sheet of paper and wrote down what she was looking at on her computer screen.

She handed the paper to Beth, who studied it as her head spun.

"Northeast Trust. That's the bank?"

"Yes." Penny nodded. "It's a boutique investment bank. They deal primarily with estate planning."

Beth's head spun as she digested the bizarre information. Just then, a sixtyish man with a combover and a stomach that strained his shirt fibers stuck his head into Penny's office.

"Sorry to interrupt. Penny, when you finish here, can I steal you for a few minutes?"

"Sure. Hey, Phil. You handle a lot of business accounts and have more experience with LLCs than I do. Can I pick your brain for a minute?"

He leaned against the doorframe. "Of course. Shoot."

"In your experience, how do people go about naming LLCs?"

Phil stroked his chin. "Well, that depends on a few factors, but most often, the name reflects the nature of the business."

Beth spoke up. "But this one wasn't set up for a business. In fact, I have no idea what it was set up for."

Penny filled in the blanks. "This is Beth. Her husband formed an LLC through our bank a few years ago without her knowledge. He passed away suddenly last year, and Beth is trying to ascertain why he formed the company."

"What is the name of the LLC?"

"It's three initials." Penny glanced at Beth, and Beth nodded her approval for Penny to continue. "RCF Services. Beth doesn't know what the letters might stand for."

"Or," Beth added sheepishly, "what 'services' the 'company' offers."

Beth looked at Phil hopefully, and he returned her gaze with compassion. "Well, I can see from where you sit how the name might seem cryptic. But it could be innocent. Sometimes, names or words are long, so people use initials or acronyms. Sometimes another LLC already has the name they want, so they shorten it to just letters. Could be any number of explanations."

"Thanks, Phil," Penny said.

Phil gave a mock salute. "Good luck, Mrs. Collins."

Beth's thoughts returned to the water restoration company. Instead of using one of their bank accounts, Danny had paid them with funds from RCF Services. *And why was he wiring money to a trust account?* None of it made sense.

Penny interrupted Beth's reverie. "I'm sorry we couldn't give you better answers. But as I said, Daniel owned one hundred percent of the interest, and you are the beneficiary of your husband's estate, so all the funds are yours. I'll print out the documents for you." She pecked at the keyboard for a few moments, then the printer hummed again before it spit out another document. Penny handed all the papers to Beth, who barely held back a gasp.

The LLC had almost three hundred thousand dollars in it.

Chapter Twenty-Five

On Christmas Day, snow fell lightly, like powdered sugar from a sifter, outside the two-story windows in the Petersons' family room. At her parents' insistence, Beth had finally invited Andre to Christmas dinner, unsure if he would accept. He'd told Beth he understood if she would rather he not attend, but she'd assured him with a tender hug that she wanted him there. Her family had all met Andre at the café. It was time to let them get to know him better.

Flames danced in the fireplace as everyone engaged in awkward conversation, avoiding the elephant in the room. There was enough tension leading up to dinner to bounce a coin off, but it was Andre—seated at Laura's table in the chair that, until last Christmas, Danny had occupied for eight years—who put everyone at ease.

"Mr. and Mrs. Peterson, I want to thank you for including me in your holiday celebration. I also want to say I'm so sorry for your loss. Beth has told me how much all of you cared about Danny, and the last thing I would ever try to do is take his place." He paused to make eye contact with everyone at the table. "I get the sense you are purposely not talking about him, and if that's your way of coping or if that's what makes you comfortable, I understand. But please don't avoid talking about Danny on my account. Beth and I talk about him all the time. He was her husband and a very important part of her life. Our relationship is new. I don't know where it will lead—but I hope to be around for a long time." He placed his hand over Beth's and smiled shyly. "Anyway, thanks again for including me. I'm really happy to be here."

It was as if the heavy cloud over the room lifted and allowed sunlight to flood in. Hannah and Nicole audibly exhaled, and Laura tearily thanked Andre for his words. Richard raised his glass in Andre's direction. The kids—very hungry by that point—clamored for their favorites on the table, and the usual organized chaos ensued. Conversation flowed easily as the family enjoyed their traditional Christmas meal: honey-baked ham, pepper-crusted rib roast, sweet potato casserole, garlic mashed potatoes, and a variety of side dishes and salads. Andre playfully chided the kids, pretending to take Ethan's last bite of mashed potatoes and crowing over a broccoli dish Sydney refused to try.

Conversation revolved around the gifts they'd exchanged earlier, everyone's jobs, and how things were going at Fresh Start. Beth sincerely complimented Nicole on becoming a valuable part of the team. Hannah started to tease her youngest sister about finally buckling down and taking a job seriously but backed off when Laura loudly cleared her throat and glared at Hannah.

"It's okay, Mom. I've earned the jabs." Nicole rubbed Beth's arm. "Beth has been through so much. She could have easily shut down and thrown in the towel. But here she is, a proud new business owner. You made me take a look at myself and realize I needed to grow up. I'm happy to be part of the gang at the café. Red has even been teaching me some of her baking tricks. She gave me the recipe for the cake I brought today."

"Oh my God, Nic!" Hannah threw her hands in the air. "You're acting like a bona fide adult!"

Nicole stuck her tongue out at her sister.

"Okay, good, glad to know childish Nicole is still in there."

The sisters laughed as Richard and Laura observed, smiling at the girls' good-natured banter.

Talk eventually led to Andre's work.

"Beth tells me you do consulting? Or is it something to do with compliance?" Richard asked.

"Yes, sir, that's right. I do both. I work for a small company owned by a friend I met in college. Lately, I've been doing mostly consulting. We analyze businesses to determine where or if they're not reaching their goals or potential. Compliance is one area the company founder specializes in. We work with businesses who have any number of issues and develop a plan to get them back on track." Andre scooped up the last of his mashed potatoes. "This meal is delicious, Mrs. Peterson."

"Thanks, but it was a group effort. I'm lucky to have so many good cooks in the family."

Eric, Hannah's husband, chimed in while cutting ham on Sydney's plate. "I'm the dessert guy. I made an apple pie from scratch—gluten free, of course." He laughed and nodded at Beth. "But I have to admit, it's a little intimidating baking for the family now that we have an honest-to-goodness foodie in the house."

"Careful, hon. If it's too good, she may give you a job!" Hannah joked.

"My role is strictly taste-tester," Richard added. "Best job of all."

Laura shook her head vigorously as if a thought had occurred to her. "Oh, Beth, I almost forgot to tell you—I ran into Adam Kingston last week."

Hannah groaned. "Aaaaaaand, the Laura pin pops the joy balloon."

"What?" Laura waved off Hannah's comment.

Beth laughed. "It's okay. Go ahead, Mom. Did you talk to him?" She turned to Andre. "Adam was the police officer at the scene of the accident."

"Oh, right." Andre nodded. "I met him at the café once."

"Yes, I'd forgotten that." She turned back to her mother. "So, what did he have to say? He and his wife sent me a Christmas card."

"That was nice of them. He didn't really say much. We just made small talk. I did ask if they've made any progress on the investigation, but he said they haven't. I got the feeling they reached a dead end, though he didn't say that."

Richard spoke quietly. "It's hard to imagine they'll come up with anything substantive. It's been more than a year, and they haven't been able to ID the deceased driver of the other car."

Beth threw her napkin onto her plate. "I think he emailed me some photos from the scene a few months ago, when the investigation was in full swing. I imagine he was trying to jar my memory—you know, in case I recalled anything significant. I don't think I even looked at them. I didn't see the point after all this time."

Tired of sitting politely, the children squirmed in their chairs, complaining that they wanted to play with their new toys. Trying to avoid all-out bedlam, the adults cleared the table while Laura brewed coffee. They decided to take a break and digest before dessert. Andre fit right in, playing with the kids and talking easily with the rest of the family. Just after eight o'clock, Hannah, Eric, and Nicole escorted their exhausted children out the door, and Andre thanked the Petersons again for their hospitality.

Later, back at her house with Andre, Beth lit the tree and poured them each a glass of prosecco. The soft glow from the lights cast soothing warmth over the room.

"You survived Christmas at the Petersons," Beth joked, bending to retrieve her gifts for him from under the tree.

"Survived? Are you kidding? I had a great time. They're a lot of fun. It must be nice to have a big family." Andre retrieved a bag of packages from the foyer and sat next to Beth on the sofa.

"Most of the time, yes. I wouldn't trade them." She handed him his gifts and gave him a peck on the cheek. "Merry Christmas." Her heart beat faster, and for a moment, she second-guessed her gift choices for Andre. *Are they too much? Too little? Too personal?*

Not personal enough? She'd specifically planned the evening so they wouldn't exchange gifts in front of her family and Andre wouldn't feel like he was under a microscope.

Andre seemed to sense her sudden anxiety. He embraced her and placed a stack of presents next to her. "Don't worry. You're not the only one who's nervous. Merry Christmas to you too. You've made me appreciate, even look forward to, things like holidays, Beth. Thank you for letting me into your life."

Beth breathed a sigh of relief and opened her gifts first—a pair of gold hoop earrings, a cashmere scarf in soft blues and greens, and a combination calendar-appointment book with a soft leather cover displayed beautifully in a decorative box. Delighted, she threw her arms around his neck and thanked him profusely.

"I hope you like them. I confess, my sister helped me pick out the earrings and scarf. The appointment book idea came to me when I saw yours at the café. It's held together with paper clips and rubber bands, so I figured you heavily rely on it."

"I do, and this one looks much nicer than the one I have." She wrapped the scarf around her neck. "Okay, your turn."

Andre opened his sweater and shoes, and a look of genuine gratitude overtook his face. "I love them both. And you guessed right on the sizes." He held the sweater up in front of him. "Great color!"

"Well, I did guess on the sweater size, but I have to confess to a little snooping on the shoes."

"How did you do that?"

"Last week, when I was at your house, I only pretended to trip over the shoes in your entry so I could sneak a peek." Beth gave him a self-satisfied look.

He grasped her gently by the ends of her scarf and drew her in for a kiss. "Aren't you clever?"

"I want a better look at my new appointment book. I'll just grab scissors from the office desk. Why don't you refill our glasses?"

Appointment book in hand, she bounded into Danny's office and yanked open the top desk drawer. Careful not to nick the leather, Beth cut the plastic ties holding the book in place and removed it from the box to admire it.

As she threw the scissors back in the drawer, her eyes locked on the keys she'd seen when she and Molly had combed through the office weeks earlier. A few of them looked familiar, but one she didn't recognize jumped out at her because it had a series of numbers on the key bow. She hadn't noticed that before. On a whim, she plucked the key from the drawer and put it in her pocket.

Andre had refilled their glasses and was stretched out on the sofa, admiring his new shoes. "Seriously, Beth, I love these! You know I'm a shoe guy."

"I'm so glad." She settled beside him and held up the key. "Hey, check this out. Have you ever seen a key like this? Any idea what it might be?"

Andre examined it. "It looks like it might be a key to a safe-deposit box."

"What makes you think that?"

"See these numbers?" He pointed to them. "Some safe-deposit keys have the bank's routing number printed on the key bow so customers can identify and recognize the bank."

"You've seen one of these before?"

"Yes, I actually had one where I kept some of my mom's important documents and her few nice pieces of jewelry." Andre looked embarrassed. "Also, when I started making decent money, I tucked some away for her in there. I don't know why. I guess I thought it would be better to have some money hidden in case my dad came back, wanting to mooch off her. Anyway, the key had a routing number like that." He seemed to pick up on Beth's puzzlement. "The key isn't yours?"

"No, it was in Danny's desk drawer."

"Do you have a safe-deposit box?"

"No." She looked pointedly at Andre. "Not that I know of."

Thoughts of the last several weeks swirled around Beth's head. The mysterious accounts, the LLC, the wire transfers... now this. Another piece of the Danny puzzle. *But where does it fit in? If the key is to a safe-deposit box, where's the box?* Penny hadn't mentioned anything about it. *Could it be at the bank that manages the trust account? And what's in it? Possibly something that would explain what was going on with Danny?*

If the key was to a safe-deposit box, Beth finally felt like she had a lead to some answers. She just wasn't sure if that evoked excitement or dread.

Chapter Twenty-Six

RCF... RCF... For days, Beth had racked her brain for what the LLC initials might stand for. *RCF Services... What services? Danny's only service was lawyering.* Unable to come up with anything, she focused on her next move. If Beth was shell-shocked at the amount of money in Danny's LLC, it was nothing compared to her astonishment at learning he had been wiring money to a trust.

She'd tossed and turned in bed most of last night, plagued by the fact that she now had *two* mysteries to unravel—the LLC and the trust. She needed to figure out the connection. Adding to her puzzlement about why Danny had formed an LLC was how he'd gotten the money to feed into it. He was obviously paying some of their bills from this "company," but she had no clue where the money would have come from. *And the trust account? For whom did he set up a trust at an investment bank? For me?* The trust occupied her every thought and caused her to put aside combing through the LLC activity for the time being.

Christmas had come and gone. Early January in Pennsylvania was gray and heavy, holiday cheer replaced by the hum of routine, and Beth turned her attention back to Danny's mysterious finances. She'd casually mentioned to her family that Danny had opened a few bank accounts Beth hadn't known about, but she didn't elaborate so as not to worry them. It felt unfair to only give them part of the story with so many unanswered questions and loose ends, especially when she felt she was on the verge of finding answers. They had known a different Danny than the one shrouded in secrets.

Confiding in Andre—though she didn't tell him *everything*—assuaged her stress. Andre's levelheadedness had a calming effect. He advised her to follow the trail and get answers rather than fall down a rabbit hole by jumping to conclusions.

As soon as Fresh Start closed its doors that day, she would pay a visit to Northeast Trust.

She was chatting with a family of regular customers when the door opened and Officer Adam Kingston entered. He shivered as he removed his coat and took a seat.

Beth acknowledged him with a wave. "Hi, Adam."

"Hey, Beth." Adam perused the daily specials and gave Gemma his order. He was scrolling through his phone when Beth joined him at his table.

"Thank you for the Christmas card."

"Oh, you're welcome. It was nothing."

"No, I really appreciate it. I hope you and your wife enjoyed the holidays."

"Yes, we did. We don't have kids yet, but we have lots of nieces and nephews. Kids make the holidays more fun." He blushed and pressed his lips together, as though he wanted to take back his words. "I'm sorry. That sounded insensitive."

"No, it didn't. You're absolutely right. My sisters' kids make everything livelier." Beth hated everyone tiptoeing around the subject of kids with her. She wrestled with the subject ten times a day. Besides seeing Hannah and Nicole's kids often, many of Fresh Start's customers had babies and children. *Am I jealous of them?* Absolutely. But it wasn't a hateful jealousy. She loved her nieces and nephews and enjoyed the children who frequented the café. She didn't begrudge them their families. She just wanted one too.

They deserve their families.

Adam, who'd been studying the tabletop, cleared his throat. "Um, hey, did you get the photo of the footprints I emailed to you?"

"Yes."

"Beth, I'm so sorry that we haven't been able to identify the driver of the car that hit you. Obviously, he can't be punished since he died in the accident, but we were sure hoping to get you some answers. The driver is like a ghost. No ID, no phone, car rented under a phony name and paid for in cash. Dead end after dead end." He sighed loudly. "And those footprints. I'd feel so much better if we could at least nab the lowlife who robbed you and Danny at the scene." His cheeks puffed as he exhaled loudly.

"I know. I've often wondered how he sleeps at night."

Gemma approached with Adam's chicken salad wrap.

"I'll let you eat in peace." Beth started to walk away but paused and turned back around. "Adam, listen, don't beat yourself up. I know you've left no stone unturned trying to get to the bottom of what happened that night. Sometimes, it's best to put it behind you and move on. That's what I've tried to do. It was a freak accident. I've decided to put my energy into moving forward rather than digging into something that has no connection to Danny or me."

Adam gave Beth a look of appreciation, but she could see in his eyes that the unsolved case did not sit well with him. She supposed it was that way with all police officers when a trail ran cold. They wanted answers.

Driving to banking institutions is becoming a habit, Beth thought as she steered into the parking lot of Northeast Trust. She cut the ignition but didn't get out of the car.

In her pocket, she fingered the key she'd found in Danny's desk drawer. It wasn't lost on her that it could both figuratively and literally unlock Danny's clandestine activities. She felt an odd push and pull, one sensation pushing her toward whatever she was about to discover and another pulling her back, as if she wasn't sure she wanted to know—as if to preserve the last vestiges of blissful ignorance. Beth couldn't fight the feeling that everything she'd thought she knew about her husband was about to implode.

Only one way to find out.

She composed herself and gathered the all-too-familiar requisite paperwork. Inside the bank, it took a moment for her eyes to adjust from the bright sunlight outside to the dim glow of the bank's overhead lighting. Just inside the heavy doors, a framed poster-sized photo portrayed an older couple walking along the beach, hand in hand, with the words *Northeast Trust, Your Partner in Wealth Management* beneath them. Beth pushed her sunglasses to the top of her head and informed the first person she encountered that she needed to speak to someone who managed trust accounts. She provided Danny's name, and the associate retreated to find the appropriate manager.

A thin woman in a winter-white pant suit approached Beth and held out her hand. Beth guessed her to be in her late thirties. Her warm smile revealed a naturally attractive face that wore little makeup, just a bit of light blush and nude lip gloss. She wore her sleek blond hair in a low bun.

"I'm Toni Sandsdale. How can I help you?"

"Hi. I'm Elizabeth Collins. You can call me Beth. I'm looking for information about a trust account my husband set up at your bank."

Toni nodded, her expression stoic. "Why don't you follow me, and we'll talk in my office?"

She closed her office door and positioned herself behind her desk as Beth sat across from her.

"So, your husband has a trust account at our institution."

It sounded more like a statement than a question. "Yes, but I guess I should fill in some blanks. My husband, Daniel Collins, passed away suddenly a little over a year ago. I've had to sort through our finances, and it's come to my attention that, unbeknownst to me, he set up a trust account here. I didn't know anything about it. In fact, all I know now is that he regularly wired money from an LLC—that I also didn't know about—to this trust account. I want to see any and all documents and activity connected to it. I have all the paperwork naming me executrix of my late husband's estate." She pushed the dog-eared folder across the desk. "Oh, and I found a key in his home office that I believe may belong to a safe-deposit box. I'm hoping you can tell me if that's correct and if the box is at your bank." Beth was talking at warp speed and paused to breathe as she extracted the key from her pocket and placed it in front of Toni.

Unblinking, Toni looked at the key and back at Beth. She repeatedly smoothed the front of her suit jacket, and it struck Beth as a nervous gesture.

Beth leaned back and folded her arms over her chest. "Why do I get the sense that you're not surprised by any of this?"

Toni sighed. She gave Beth such a sympathetic look that Beth thought she might cry. After thumbing through the paperwork Beth had brought, Toni slid the folder back to her and picked up the key. She turned it over in her palm a few times before placing it back on the desk.

With her elbows on the desk in a tent formation, Toni laced her fingers together and rested her forehead on them for a moment before speaking. "No, I'm not surprised by anything you told me. I always knew this day would come. I've thought about it more times than I can count."

A chill snaked up Beth's spine. "Go on."

Toni looked Beth directly in the eye. "Your husband did set up a trust account and named me as a cotrustee. Sometimes, it's called a joint trustee. What that means is Daniel appointed me to share the responsibility of managing the trust's assets. A cotrustee can also temporarily fill in if the primary trustee is unavailable, such as during an illness or—"

"In the case of his death."

"Yes. Danny came to me because the situation was delicate and he felt he could trust me. You see, we go way back to our college days. I only recently learned of his death. In fact, I was alerted to it because the wire transfers ceased but the withdrawals continued. He rarely came here in person. All I did was approve money taken out of the trust, which in this case, happened regularly."

Beth felt time stand still as she prepared herself to ask the next question. Her voice sounded small. "Who is the trust set up for?"

Toni shifted uncomfortably in her chair. She turned to her computer and printed a few pages, which she held out to Beth. Beth gingerly took the papers from her, as though they might burn her fingers. She skipped over the usual legalese, her eyes coming to rest on the answer to her question. The trust Danny set up was "For the benefit of Reilly C. Fisher." *RCF.* Reading further, she saw that Antoinette—Toni—Sandsdale had been named a cotrustee, as was a person named Madison A. Fisher. The trust account was established as an investment account and had a checking account attached to it.

Beth blinked hard several times, and the color drained from her face. She was stuck in an awful place between wanting answers and dreading them because then she could never go back to not knowing. Finally, she managed, "Who is Reilly C. Fisher?"

The woman sighed, a sadness creating shadows on her attractive face.

"Please. Just tell me."

Toni took a moment before looking up from the floor. "Reilly is Danny's daughter."

Chapter Twenty-Seven

Someone handed her a bottle of water, but Beth couldn't say who. The pounding in her ears threatened to split open her aching head. She fought back nausea roiling in her stomach, and her breath came in anxious huffs. *Danny's daughter. Reilly is Danny's daughter.*

"Beth. Beth?" Toni's soft voice was barely audible. "Please drink some water. You've had quite a shock. Take your time, and when you're ready, I'll take you to the safe-deposit box."

Beth looked right through her. *This isn't happening. This can't be happening.* The bottle of water slipped from her trembling hands to the floor, creating a puddle at Beth's feet.

Toni quickly retrieved it and called out to someone nearby to fetch some paper towels. She squeezed Beth's shoulder gently and spoke quietly in her ear, but Beth couldn't make out the words.

After a few minutes, her breathing had just about returned to normal. Toni had handed her another water bottle, which she sipped slowly. She lifted her slumped shoulders and nodded at Toni.

"Come with me, Beth."

On shaky legs, Beth followed her to an elevator, and they rode down one floor. Toni started to make idle conversation but then seemed to sense Beth would prefer she didn't. The two women walked down a corridor to a large steel door.

"This is a very old institution. Though most banking is now done electronically, some banks—like this one—still have a physical vault for valuables and important documents."

Toni fumbled with a metal ring that held keys of varying shapes and sizes. She swung open the door and ushered Beth inside. Floor-to-ceiling rows of safe-deposit boxes comprised two walls, each box having two locks. Using her master key and the key Beth had brought with her, Toni opened one of the small doors and slid out a metal box that resembled a large shoebox. She then escorted Beth to a smaller room containing a wooden table and two chairs and placed the box on the table in front of Beth. Before leaving the room, she offered a sad but caring smile. "Take your time. I'll be right outside."

Beth shuddered despite the tepid humidity in the well-lit room. She sat unmoving, staring at the safe-deposit box as if it might suddenly grow fangs and bite her. A strange before-and-after sensation came over her—as though opening the box would plunge her from the Danny she'd known before to the Danny she'd had no idea existed, the one who'd secretly fathered a child. Her hands shook, and she had a difficult time swallowing as she lifted the lid.

Several envelopes lay inside the box. Beth tremulously opened the first one to find a document with paternity test results verifying Daniel Collins as the father of the female child Reilly Collins Fisher, born to Madison Fisher. She gulped and dropped the paper onto the table.

It was true. Danny had—has—a daughter. Before. After.

Though she felt weak enough to pass out, Beth took a swig of water and willed herself to examine the rest of the box's contents. The next paper was a copy of Reilly's birth certificate. It named Danny and this Madison person as her parents. Both parents' addresses were listed. Beth, of course, recognized Danny's. Madison Fisher had a New York address. Their occupations were listed, Danny's an attorney and Madison's a paralegal. With unsteady hands, Beth dropped the document onto the table.

Her head spinning, Beth moved on to the next envelope. From that one, she extracted a paper that she needed only to read a few lines of to realize that it was a trust document. It outlined a trust set up for "the health, maintenance, and care of the minor Reilly Collins Fisher." Several lines of banking legalese followed, and Beth struggled to concentrate and continue reading. The next section explained the terms and conditions of the trust to the beneficiary, Reilly Collins Fisher. That part struck Beth as meticulously worded. It gave Toni the authority to manage the trust and approve any funds drawn from it.

It went on to explain that Madison Fisher had the authority to withdraw funds but only with Toni's approval. The fact gave Beth pause. The child's mother could only withdraw funds with the approval of a cotrustee at the bank. She had no idea why Danny would set it up that way. Then again, she had no idea how any of this could be happening.

The next envelope contained copies of Danny's and Beth's wills. Having contributed to the creation of these, Beth skimmed their contents, anxious to return to the other paperwork.

She continued on autopilot to the last envelope in the box. This one was not an official-looking envelope. Rather, it was a standard white envelope anyone might use for daily mailing purposes. It was upside down, and when Beth flipped it over, she found her name handwritten in Danny's careful penmanship. The sight of it made her breath catch in her throat and tears sting her eyes. Picking it up cautiously, she held the envelope to her chest. She couldn't bear to open it—not yet.

Beth finally rose, ghostlike, from the chair. She felt as though she was swimming through murky water as she made her way to the door and pulled it open.

Toni, sitting on a bench outside, jumped up. "Beth. Are you okay? I mean, as okay as possible under the circumstances."

Beth didn't answer. As still as a stone, she clutched the envelope.

"Beth, can I call someone? Maybe to pick you up? I'm not sure you should drive." Toni's voice was strained, as though she desperately wanted to do something—anything—to make the situation bearable for the broken woman in front of her.

"I... I... Yes. I guess we could call my best friend. Molly." She pulled out her phone and made the call herself. In a barely audible voice, she asked Molly to pick her up at Northeast Trust. She would explain later but said she didn't think she could drive.

Of course, Molly responded that she would be there as soon as possible. After texting her the address, Beth scrolled until she came to her texts with Andre. She needed his strong shoulder, his clear head. Her trembling thumbs hovered over the keyboard for a few seconds before typing.

Beth: *Hey.*

Andre responded immediately.

Andre: *Hey, babe. What's up?*

Oh, not much, she thought, her inner voice dripping sarcasm. *I just found out my late husband has a daughter. Typical afternoon.*

Beth: *Too much to text. Can you meet Mol and me at my house in an hour?*

Andre: *I'll be there. You okay?*

Beth: *I'll explain when I see you.*

Beth sank onto a bench, and Toni joined her.

She studied Beth's face sympathetically. "I'm sure your head feels like it's ready to explode. Please, tell me what I can do. I may be able to answer some of your questions—at least the ones relating to the trust."

Beth felt small in the vast expanse of the situation. "I'm sure I'll have questions for you. It's just, well, right now, the enormity of it all... it's crushing me. I don't even know where to start. I think I need to take these documents home and go over them again to let everything sink in." She bashfully showed Toni the envelope with her name handwritten on the front. "Do you know what's in here?"

Toni placed her hand over Beth's. "No. I don't know what's in any of the envelopes. They're Danny's—and now your—personal property. I only know what Danny gave me authority to know as far as managing Reilly's trust."

Beth rested her head in her hands and stared at the envelope in her lap. She looked up at Toni with a quizzical expression. "Actually, I do have one question. This woman, the child's mother, why does she need your approval to withdraw funds if they're for Reilly?"

Toni folded her hands in front of her. She inhaled deeply and blew out a strong breath before answering. "Listen, Beth. My heart is breaking for you. Danny made me a cotrustee because, as I said, we go way back. He considered me a friend." Her eyes turned glassy, and she touched Beth's arm. "He's gone, and I'm going to talk to you not as a banker now but as your late husband's friend."

"I appreciate that."

"Danny wanted me to oversee the withdrawals because he learned that Maddie had gotten involved with some shady characters."

"Shady? Shady how?"

"I'm not exactly sure. That was the word Danny used. I think he believed Maddie may have been using drugs. When he established the account, he was adamant about making me a cotrustee to oversee the withdrawals. I think he was worried Maddie would take out money for her own, um, recreational activity. He was beside himself, Beth. He wanted Reilly to be well taken care of."

Beth's quivering lip forced a tear to fall from her lashes. "I just don't understand. Why wouldn't Danny come to me? As awful as this is, Reilly is a child! Did he think I'd be so cruel as to leave her in a dangerous situation?" She slumped back against the wall behind the bench.

"Beth, listen. Danny had only recently learned about Reilly. Maddie never even told him she was pregnant. Not to lessen the impact on you right now, but he was just as blindsided when she—"

"Wait." Beth shot upward and ran back into the room. She grabbed the envelope with the birth certificate and practically tore it open. Combing through the certificate, she gasped when her eyes rested on what she was looking for. She gripped the table's edge to steady herself. All at once, the world seemed out of focus. The words blurred on the paper.

Reilly's birthdate, though, was crystal clear. She was born eight years ago—just three months after Beth and Danny's wedding.

Chapter Twenty-Eight

"**B**reathe, Beth."

Molly was uncharacteristically at a loss for words. She hardly knew any of the story, but the little bits Beth had managed in the car on the way home had rendered her speechless. Now, she sat next to Beth on the sofa, rubbing her back. She threw a blanket over her friend's shaking shoulders.

Beth vacillated between bursts of disjointed information—"Danny's daughter...! Cotrustees...! Madison... drugs!"—and near catatonic silence.

The doorbell rang, and Molly led Andre to Beth. At the sight of him, Beth dissolved into sobs that racked her entire body. Andre held her and let her cry. He gave Molly a wide-eyed, imploring look, but Molly held up her palms in a give-her-time gesture.

Beth was numb. She was even more devastated by these revelations than she had been when Danny died. Dying was part of life—even dying young. As terrible as it was, every human being lived with the knowledge that *everyone* died at some point. No one got out alive.

But this?

Finding out her deceased husband had a secret life, including a child, was not part of life. That was the stuff of movies and Netflix series. And yet, there she was, starring in her own shocking drama.

Beth thought about how she'd finally moved on and begun to live again. Losing Danny had been unimaginable, but she'd somehow come to terms with it and started over. But now, she had to reconcile the husband she knew with a complete stranger. Danny's death felt like a punishment that was no one's fault. An accident. But this was worse—this was outright betrayal.

And now there was a child involved.

On the ride home from the bank, Beth had stared blankly out the window in silence as Molly drove. At a red light, she'd noticed a couple on the sidewalk, embracing. The man had leaned down to whisper something in the woman's ear. It must have been funny, because she threw back her head and laughed while he kissed her neck. *How dare they? Couldn't they turn their gleeful heads, look in the car window, and see how broken I am? What gave them the right to be so happy? And right in front of me?*

Beth pulled herself up and accepted the bourbon Molly handed her. Her eyes were red and swollen from crying, and her face had taken on a ghostly pallor. Little by little, detail by detail, she spilled the whole story to Molly and Andre. They sat immobile in stunned silence. From time to time, one of them would open their mouth as if to ask a question, only to close it again and continue listening. Beth told the tale in rote fashion, hardly altering her tone, so she might have been recounting an innocuous incident at the grocery store. By the time she finished, exhaustion overtook her, and she could barely keep her puffy eyes open. She closed them for a few minutes and let Molly and Andre absorb the drama.

"Jesus" was all Molly could manage.

Andre ran his hand through his hair and whistled. "My God. If I didn't know you, I'd say you have to be making this up."

"Danny has a daughter." Molly repeated the words as if only doing so made them real. "So, I guess the question is—now what? Where do you go from here?"

While they tossed around their reactions, Beth remembered what Danny had once told her about his younger years. She had complimented him on his work ethic after he'd spent months on a case and won it spectacularly. Danny had confided that he hadn't always been so focused or driven. He said his teenage years were wild ones, his parents fearful that underage drinking and partying with poorly chosen friends would keep him from pursuing an education and putting his natural intelligence to use. Despite having a perfectly "normal" upbringing—supportive, present parents who attended his games and school activities, nightly dinners around the table together, summer vacations at the Jersey shore—Danny was untethered and spiteful in his teenage escapades, a fact that baffled his parents. Many weekends, they sat up at night, either waiting for their son to come home or for a call from the police station—or worse.

But in his senior year, Danny shed that skin and got serious about his future, as though he woke up one morning and realized he needed to get out of his own way. He began working out, hitting the books, and visiting colleges with his parents. He became a better role model for Josh, urging his younger brother to stay on the straight and narrow and realize his potential. He severed his hoodlum ties and made new friends, who were as focused on their futures as he was. Danny was accepted into every college he applied to after high school and every law school he applied to after college. When he'd graduated from law school, he'd been courted by law firms up and down the East Coast before choosing one in Philadelphia.

Could it be that his reckless past self never really died? Could I have been totally wrong about him?

She was furious with a dead man, a man who wasn't who she'd thought he was at all.

Beth refocused on Andre and Molly's discussion. They batted questions and observations back and forth so rapidly, she felt as if she were on a tennis court.

"In the car, she mentioned contacting Danny's parents to find out if they knew. God, he has a daughter!"

"Yes, and she may want to go to New York to find Madison and meet Reilly, right?"

"Definitely." Molly, who'd begun jotting points on a notepad, rubbed her temples.

"Guys, you know I'm here, right?" Beth managed a tortured smile.

Andre put both hands on Beth's shoulders. "Sorry, baby. We're just trying to help you sort through this."

"I know, and I appreciate it. Believe me, that's why I called you two first. I need to be in a better headspace before I tell my parents and sisters. They're going to lose their minds. And I can't say I blame them."

Andre ran his hands through his hair and let out a low whistle. "It's unreal. I mean, I knew the guy had some secrets, but this—"

Molly's head jerked toward Andre. "What do you mean, you 'knew Danny had some secrets'?" She raised her eyebrows, waiting for his response.

"Noth—nothing. I mean... I just mean, I know about the financial mystery Beth has been uncovering recently. That's all I meant."

Molly sighed. "Of course. I'm sorry. We're all on edge."

Beth cleared her throat. She reached for the envelopes from the safe-deposit box, now strewn on her coffee table. "Let's talk about the elephant in the room."

Neither Andre nor Molly spoke.

"Reilly's birthdate," Beth practically whispered. "She was born three months after Danny and I got married. That means Danny cheated on me with her mother."

"Oh, honey, it makes me so mad I could spit. I wish Danny were alive right now so I could kill him!" Molly's face was bright red. "Of all the—"

Andre attempted to lower the temperature. "Listen, you're thoroughly exhausted, Beth. You need to process everything before you decide what to do next. Why don't you rest, and I'll fix us something light for dinner? If it's okay with you, I'll stay here with you tonight. I don't think you should be alone."

"Well, normally, that would be my role, but I think Andre's offer is more appealing," Molly agreed. "You know where to find me if you need me. The café is closed tomorrow, so you'll have the day to process and plan." She gathered her belongings, hugged Andre and Beth, and saw herself out.

Beth washed her face and padded out to the kitchen, where Andre had just finished making tomato-and-cheese omelets.

Beth pushed the food around on her plate until Andre joked, "I know I'm no Lucy or Frank, but is it that bad?"

"No, it's good. I just don't feel like eating."

"I'm not surprised. Go up and get ready for bed. I'll clean up and be right up."

Beth barely heard Andre enter the bedroom several minutes later. She let exhaustion claim her and slept in his arms until the winter sun peeked through the blinds the next morning.

Beth reveled in the drowsy state between asleep and awake, the first few seconds after opening her eyes, the blissful moments where sleep gave way to consciousness and previous events hadn't registered yet. Then the whole sordid story came back to her in frames, as though she were watching a film. Groaning, she covered her face with her pillow.

Andre appeared at the door with two steaming coffee mugs. "Good morning. I figured you could use this." He kissed her and set her coffee on the nightstand.

"You really are a savior, aren't you?" Beth excused herself to use the bathroom and brush her teeth before returning to bed. She sat cross-legged facing Andre and sipped her coffee.

"On a scale of one to I-just-had-a-bomb-dropped-on-me, how are you feeling?"

"I think a bomb would be less shocking. Definitely less painful." Beth stared into her mug. When she spoke again, her voice was soft and vulnerable. "Danny has a daughter. He's gone, but he has a child. That's the bottom line. The secret accounts, the LLC, the trust—all of that is connected to Danny's plot to keep his secret. At this point, I have more questions than answers, but looming large over all of it is that my late husband has a child. As angry as I am at him, I have to remember that."

"So, are you thinking of getting in touch with Madison? Do you want to meet Reilly?"

"Yes. But I think my first move has to be reaching out to Bruce and Louise to find out what, if anything, they know about this. Could they all have been keeping this secret? Reilly was born a few months after our wedding, but Toni said Danny had only recently found out. And then there's the issue of the LLC with several hundred thousand dollars in it. Where did that money come from? Oh God, and my family. I have to tell them." Beth's face twisted into a tortured grimace. "I have more of the pieces, but the puzzle is still unfinished."

Andre moved behind her and rubbed her shoulders. "It's overwhelming, for sure. Take your time figuring out how you want to proceed. And, Beth, I'm here for you—as much or as little as you want me to be. You're not alone."

Beth couldn't say why she decided at that moment to share her own painful secret with Andre. Maybe it was the compassion and strength in his eyes. Maybe it was the way they'd grown steadily closer by sharing parts of themselves and their pasts, both of which were far from fairy tales. Maybe she just felt so battle weary that her defenses were down. Whatever the reason, it was time to put all her cards on the table. Secrets weren't serving anyone well.

She inhaled deeply and turned to face him. "Andre, I'm going to share something with you. Something I did. It was years ago, but I've dragged it around with me like a bag of cement ever since." She fiddled with the bedsheet.

"What is it? You can tell me anything."

Beth paused, searching for the right words, pain creasing her face. "When I was in high school, I dated a guy for a few months. I liked him, but as I got closer to graduation, I knew the relationship wouldn't go the distance and it was just a matter of time until we broke up. Anyway, I slept with him a few times... and... a few months before graduation, I found out I was pregnant." Her face reddened, and she avoided eye contact with Andre. "I was devastated. I didn't know what to do. I didn't love the guy. I had already been accepted to the college I wanted to attend. I was in no position to have and raise a baby. For weeks, I agonized about what to do. I'm sure you've figured out by now what I did. I had an abortion." Tears filled Beth's eyes. She drew in a sharp breath. "At the time, I saw it as my only option."

"Did you tell the boy?"

"Yes. He was sympathetic but totally on board with terminating the pregnancy. He had a football scholarship and didn't want his life derailed. The only other person who knows is Molly. She took me for the... procedure. The boy and I broke up. I was depressed for weeks afterward. My family thought I was just stressed about the breakup or transitioning from high school to college. But they were wrong. It wasn't any of those things. I still think it was the right thing to do at the time, but I've never forgiven myself."

"Beth—"

"No, let me finish. I need to get this out." She sat up straighter. "Eventually, I pulled myself together. I graduated high school and started college. I got my degree and found a decent job. I really liked my job and the people I worked with. But I couldn't stop thinking about the abortion. The truth is, as the years went by, I realized that what I *really* wanted was a family of my own. A career is great, and I was glad I had one, but it didn't make me feel happy or complete. I don't know if it's because of what I did, but I believed only a spouse and children could fill the void inside me. I obsessed about it. It was all I thought about."

"Did you ever talk to anyone? A counselor?"

"Yes. I found a great counselor, and eventually, though I didn't fully forgive myself, I learned strategies to help me deal with the past, put it behind me, and move on."

"Then you met Danny."

"Yes. And I believed he was 'the one.' I thought our relationship was damn near perfect. We didn't just love each other, we *liked* each other too. Time went on. Everything was great. He proposed, and I started to believe I could feel whole again. I wanted so much to have a family and spend the rest of my life with Danny and our kids."

Andre looked as dismayed as Beth felt. He said quietly, "Then you found out you were pregnant, and before you even had a chance to tell Danny... dear God."

Beth buried her face in her hands. Her voice was strained when she spoke again. "I can't help feeling like I deserved to lose Danny and our baby, like I'm being punished—because of what I did. Like the universe said, 'Oh no, you had your chance and you threw it away.'"

Andre's face crumpled to the point that Beth thought he might cry.

"Beth. Jesus. That's not true. You're not being punished. You did the only thing you thought you could at the time." He embraced her, rocking her back and forth. "Oh my God. I feel so sad that you've carried this burden for so long."

"I thought I'd moved on to the point where, though I'd never forget about it, I could go on to live a full life. Then the accident. It hurled me right back to believing I'd gotten exactly what I deserved."

Andre took Beth's face in his hands. "Listen to me. I'm not trying to invalidate your feelings or minimize anything you've been through, but please promise me you will forgive yourself and stop thinking you deserve terrible things to happen to you. Everyone—*everyone*—has done things they regret or wish they could do over. If you had it to do over, you wouldn't have slept with that guy—or at least taken steps to prevent getting pregnant. The important thing is what we learn from those things and how we live our lives moving forward. I'd say, based on your relationships with your family, your friends, your staff, your customers, and thankfully, me, you've lived your life pretty damn well."

Beth sighed. "It's not even the fact that I had an abortion. Everyone has the right to choose what is best for them. I just can't stop thinking that it may have been my only chance to have a child, and I threw it away." She lay back on the pillows and swiped tears from her cheeks. "I feel better now that I told you. No one knows but Molly—and of course the boy."

"Hey." Andre kissed her forehead. "Thank you for sharing that. It means a lot to me." He stared past her, out the bedroom window, a faraway look on his face.

After a long period of silence, they went downstairs to the kitchen.

After refilling their coffee mugs, Andre led Beth to the table and asked her to sit. "Beth, you've shared something deeply personal with me, and there's something in my background I'd like to share with you too."

Beth searched his face. "Okay."

He cleared his throat. "On our first date... at the brewery... when I intervened in that couple's fight?"

Beth nodded. "I remember."

"When that brute was bullying his wife, it angered me so much because..." He exhaled loudly. "It made me see red because *my* dad was a mean drunk who abused my mom. It was brutal. She put up with it for far too long because she didn't think she had the resources to leave. The worst part was that, sometimes, he came after me, and my mom intervened so he would hit her instead."

Andre's face reddened as shock registered on Beth's face.

"I know... you can't even conceive of such behavior. Your dad is such a stand-up guy."

"My family is far from perfect, but you're right, he's never done anything like that."

"I hated my father. It got so that all I could concentrate on was getting my mom out of that house and away from him. That's why I dropped out of college after two years. Chaz's dad offered me a job where I'd make enough to help my mom, and I jumped at it. I took whatever work they had. Eventually, I helped her get her own place. It was only a modest house, but to my mom, it was better than a mansion. She finally had the freedom to live her life in peace, without fear."

"How did your dad react? Did he look for her? Wasn't he furious with you?"

"At first, he called a lot and left nasty messages, so I got us all new phones. He found her and showed up at her door a few times, but he soon realized he no longer had any power over her. He wouldn't assault her in public or at work. Like all abusers, he was too much of a coward. Mom having her own place disarmed him, and eventually, he went away. We haven't heard from him in years. Good riddance." He looked at Beth with tear-filled eyes.

"Wow. That's something. I'm sorry you and your family went through that, but I'm happy you're all safe now." She swiped a tear at the corner of his eye. "And it explains a lot. Thank you for telling me."

"There's something else." Andre's chin dropped to his chest.

"Okay."

"The night I missed your baking class at Fresh Start. Remember, I said I had the flu?"

Beth sat up straighter. "What do you mean, you *said* you had the flu? You weren't sick?"

"No. I mean, I didn't have the flu. Beth, I'm ashamed to admit this, but I want you to know the truth."

Beth put her hand over his on the table. "It's okay. Whatever it is, you can tell me."

"Chaz and his dad took a new client and his son out for happy hour that night. They asked me to go with them. The son is taking over his dad's business, and Chaz's dad thought it would be good to have us there to talk through some newer, more innovative strategies than they'd been using. The son is one of those arrogant types who thinks he knows everything. Anyway, he had too much to drink. He was getting loud, harassing the server, that kind of thing."

"Ah. Like the jerk at the brewery."

"Exactly like that." Andre shook his head, as if trying to forget the incident. "I said I needed to leave because I had plans with you. We were walking to our cars, and the guy started taunting me, calling me henpecked... and worse names I won't repeat. I told him to back off, that he'd had too much to drink and was out of line. I tried to keep my cool because we wanted their business."

"I think I can guess what happened next. I remember, when I saw you a few days later, your lip was swollen."

"Yes. The guy took a swing at me, and I hit him back. I shouldn't have done it, I know. But when drunks act like that, it brings back my dad's rants."

Her eyes showed sympathy for Andre's past experiences. "I can understand that. But you're right, you can't go getting into fights with every drunk idiot you encounter."

"I know, I know. But the thing I felt worst about was that I missed your class, that I broke my word to you."

He looked so sad, Beth's heart broke.

"I told Chaz and the old man that I didn't want to be mixed up in any more sticky situations. They've been very good to me, but I wasn't going to do just anything that came along anymore." He pulled her close. "I told them I have a girl who makes me want to be a better man."

Beth sighed and took in everything Andre had told her. "I'm glad you told me. It helps me understand you so much better."

Andre gazed out the window without speaking for a long moment.

"What are you thinking?" she asked.

"I'm just remembering what you said upstairs about Danny. That you thought he was 'the one.'" His look was sincere when his eyes met hers. "I hope you've met another guy who could be 'the one.'"

Chapter Twenty-Nine

"We swear, Beth, we had *no* idea about any of this. We are just as stunned as you." Bruce Collins held his wife's shaking hand.

Josh sat nearby, silently taking it all in. Beth had relayed the story to them in parts, ending with Reilly. She managed to remain tempered, her hysteria and tears seemingly depleted, at least for the time being.

A week had passed since the revelation about Reilly. Beth had given herself a serious pep talk before making the hour-long trip north to see her in-laws. She'd talked to herself the entire way through the mountain roads flanked by tree branches bowing slightly under the weight of ice. They appeared glassy and fragile, like they were barely holding on. Beth knew that feeling. Her emotions ran the gamut—anger at Danny for his infidelity, confusion about the source of the money, naivety that she'd not suspected anything, and heartache for Reilly.

Mostly, she'd thought about Reilly. She was an eight-year-old girl, blameless for the sins of her parents. Beth tried to imagine her. She fell asleep at night conjuring up images of her. *Does she have Danny's unruly hair? His deep-blue eyes? His mercurial personality?* Beth wondered if Danny had ever met her. She couldn't fathom him knowing about his daughter and not wanting to be present in her life. Reilly had been born shortly after Danny and Beth's wedding. Toni said he'd only recently learned about her. *But how recently?*

Those were questions for Madison Fisher.

Now, in the elder Collinses' living room, Louise pulled a tissue from the sleeve of her cardigan and blew her nose. Beth could tell her failing health made the news harder to bear. She looked even older than she had when Beth arrived. Danny's death was enough of a burden to live with. These revelations threatened to burst the dam.

"Beth, have you given any thought to what you will do next? I'm sure you're reeling from all of this." Bruce's eyes were kind, so much like Danny's—the Danny they'd all thought they knew.

"I've thought of little else. I'm planning to go to New York and pay Madison a visit. Reilly's birth certificate has an address for her, but I looked her up, and she lives at a different New York address now."

"Oh my, that will certainly be unpleasant." Louise shook her head.

Beth paused before continuing. "Danny is gone. He took his sins with him, but Reilly is here. I want to meet her. I hope Madison will let me. If she does, would you like to meet her too?"

Bruce and Louise nodded in unison, and Louise answered, "She's our granddaughter. We want to be part of her life." She looked sympathetically at Beth. "Of course, we always thought you and Danny would make us grandparents." She let out a ragged breath as tears sprang to her eyes.

"I know. I did too. But Reilly is here, and none of this mess is her fault. She's an innocent child. And she has grandparents and an uncle she deserves to know about."

Bruce's expression was strained, deep lines prominent around his blue eyes. "Beth, you're her family too. If my son had lived—and I'm struggling not to speak ill of him at the moment, despite my anger and disappointment in him—you would have been part of Reilly's life when he eventually came clean." He rose and drew Beth into a hug. "She will be lucky if her mother allows you to be in her life."

"Thank you, Bruce, but let's not get ahead of ourselves. I'm not sure Madison will welcome me with open arms."

"She may not, but Louise, Josh, and I are the child's blood relatives. Surely, she'll let us see her."

"I hope so."

"We'll take her to court if we have to, but hopefully, it won't come to that. This is all so shocking."

"It is," Beth agreed. "And I have so many unanswered questions—not just about Reilly and Madison but about Danny's clandestine money activities. I still have some digging to do."

Josh loudly cleared his throat as Beth stood to leave. "Beth, I'll walk you out."

She said a teary goodbye to Danny's parents, promised to keep them in the loop, and walked with Josh to the front door.

He shuffled his feet and dug his hands deep into his pockets. "Listen, there's a coffee shop about a mile from here on Worthingham Ave. Do you know it?"

His face was so pale that Beth feared her brother-in-law might faint. "Yes, I know it."

"Can you meet me there? Give me a few minutes to make sure Mom and Dad are okay. Especially Mom." He looked back at his parents, who were huddled on the sofa, murmuring quietly.

"Okay. Yes. I'll see you there soon."

Beth drove to the coffee shop and waited in the parking lot for Josh. He'd looked strange when he asked her to meet him. She told herself it was just the shock of the revelations about Danny. He probably wanted to speak candidly to her away from his parents so as not to upset them more. They all had a lot to process.

She cut the engine and pulled her coat tightly around her. She'd gone through the five stages of grief after Danny's death—denial, anger, bargaining, depression, and acceptance. Though she hadn't necessarily experienced them linearly, and she'd felt stuck in some for longer periods than others, she'd finally arrived at acceptance. Beth wasn't sure that would be the case after being gobsmacked with all she'd learned about her husband recently. This was much less natural than death—even an untimely one.

Josh's Jeep pulled into the parking lot next to her, and they went inside and ordered coffee. When the server left, Josh drummed his fingers on the table. Beth waited for him to speak, confused by his nervous demeanor. He seemed reluctant to look her in the eye.

Suddenly, her eyes flew open wide. "Oh my God." Beth drew in a sharp breath. "You knew."

Josh groaned and massaged his forehead. "No. Well, yes, I knew some of what was going on, but I didn't know about Reilly. I swear, Beth, I'm just as shocked as you are about her."

The server returned with their coffee, but Beth didn't touch hers. She felt as if she might be sick. "Okay. Start talking."

Chapter Thirty

"It's weird, you know, how random life is. We're just trillions of cells, bouncing around every day, trying to get it right. But we're really at the mercy of the universe." Josh exhaled loudly and leaned in close to Beth, keeping his voice low. "If I hadn't been doing a favor for an old friend of mine, I might never have known a thing about any of this."

Josh was a residential real estate agent. Living about thirty miles north of Beth and Danny's house—about halfway between them and his parents—his usual territory was north of Stradmore. He began by telling Beth how he'd coincidentally seen Danny coming out of a Bank of Greater Pennsylvania branch in a town neither of them typically had reason to visit.

"That's the bank affiliated with the LLC."

"Right. I was in that area one day, about two years ago, give or take. My friend's sister was going through a divorce, and he asked me to meet with her about listing her house for sale. As you know, that bank is a few towns over from where you and Danny lived and even farther from where I live and normally do business. Anyway, I had just met with Sophie—my friend's sister—and was driving home. I was at a red light at an intersection near the bank. I spotted a car in the parking lot that looked like Danny's but dismissed it as ridiculous since it was so far from his office. That is, until I saw Danny leaving the bank, head down, hands stuffed in his coat pockets. I drove into the lot and pulled into the spot next to him. When he reached his car and saw me, the color drained from his face. I rolled down the window and was all casual, like, 'Hey, dude, fancy meeting you here! What's going on?' Danny's eyes darted around the parking lot. He was clearly shaken up that I'd seen him."

"Did he explain what he was doing?"

"Not at first. He made up a story about working on a case with complicated banking issues."

"You didn't believe him?"

Josh shook his head. "No. I know my brother. He was nervous, stumbling over his words. Not himself at all. I could tell he was making it up as he went along."

"Did you call him out on it?"

"Not on the spot. Danny said he was in a hurry, needed to get back to the office, yada yada. He said we'd catch up later, and he took off."

"You just let him go?"

"Yes. But I couldn't get it out of my mind... how he looked... his haunted expression. I called him the next day and asked him to grab a beer after work."

"And he agreed to meet you?"

"It took some convincing. I told him I could come by the house if that was easier. He nixed that idea immediately. That's when I knew he was hiding something." Josh studied his hands before locking eyes with Beth. "From you."

The server approached to refill their coffees but retreated when she saw the barely touched mugs.

"We met the next day at a little dive bar on the edge of town. Honestly, I wasn't even sure he'd show up. When he did, he looked more stressed than I'd ever seen him. He took off his coat, and I noticed he'd lost some weight. His eyes were rimmed with dark circles. When he sat down, his leg bounced up and down so rapidly, I joked he would spill our beers. He was in no mood for kidding around, though."

Beth nodded, gazing distractedly past her brother-in-law and out the window. "I remember that period when Danny was losing weight. He also wasn't sleeping well. I heard him pacing the halls in the middle of the night. When I questioned him, he said he had a complicated case and the client was being difficult. I had no reason to doubt him."

"Of course you didn't. We all know how seriously Danny took his work."

"But that wasn't it, was it?"

"No." Josh picked up his mug but put it down again without drinking. He toyed with packets of sweeteners in a ceramic bowl between them. "Beth, I won't lie. This will be tough to hear. I hoped Danny would fix his mess and you'd never have to know about it. When he died, I kept my mouth shut, hoping it had died with him."

"Tougher to hear than learning Danny had fathered a child with another woman?" Beth's soft voice and slumped shoulders exhibited the weight of it all.

"Maybe. I don't know. It's all tough to swallow."

"Continue."

Josh sagged, elbows spread, hands resting one on top of the other on the table. "Danny said he was in trouble financially. He needed money. Lots of it and fast."

Beth knit her eyebrows in confusion. "Financial trouble? We were very comfortable. We didn't have money troubles."

"He said *he* had financial problems. Not the two of you. No matter how many times I asked, he wouldn't tell me the nature of the money issues, but I pressed him hard on what he was doing at the Bank of Greater Pennsylvania branch." He sighed heavily. "Beth, to get the money he needed, he was stealing from his clients."

Beth reeled back as though struck in the stomach. "No. I don't believe that!"

"I know, I know. I didn't either, but he finally told me exactly what he was doing." Josh rubbed his eyes with the heels of his palms. "He stole from his clients' estates. He came up with the idea because he had a few cases where the beneficiaries were, as he called them, 'bratty pains in the ass.' You know the type—spoiled rich kids who just want a big fat check. They don't want to do any of the work beneficiaries typically have to do to settle an estate. They're happy to give the lawyer handling the estate carte blanche because all they care about is the bottom line—how much money they're getting.

"It started with a situation where one of the assets of the deceased was a house that the kids wanted to sell, of course, to collect the money."

Beth's unblinking eyes remained fixed on him, so he forged on.

"The house was in disrepair, and Danny told the heirs that extensive work needed to be done to get the house on the market. By the way, he'd often call me when he wasn't sure which repairs were necessary to sell a house and which ones buyers would likely be okay handling, so I knew these estate cases were sometimes convoluted. Anyway, Danny told this family the house needed a new roof and updates to the kitchen and baths. Then there would be the added cost of things like trash removal after those projects were completed. But they couldn't be bothered. They told Danny to handle everything and take the funds from the estate to pay for the repairs."

"So, okay, these surviving kids are brats. Where does the LLC come in?"

"Think about it. Danny needs money. The family members can't be bothered with the necessary work, so they give Danny free rein to manage the costs associated with settling the estate."

Beth nodded slowly as clarity descended on her. "Danny forms an LLC to bill the estate for the cost of the work."

"Bingo. Then it goes something like this: He hires a roofer. Let's say, for argument's sake, that the new roof costs fifteen thousand dollars. Danny inflates the cost and bills the estate twenty-five thousand dollars. The LLC keeps the difference, and neither the beneficiaries nor the roofer is the wiser. The roofer gets paid, and the spoiled kids won't bother to check if the amount is correct. They believe Danny. It's not like they're going to call the roofer to verify the invoice. The estate holds plenty of money. Twenty-five grand is peanuts."

"So, the roofer gets their fifteen thousand, and Danny keeps the rest in his LLC." Beth held her head in her hands. "Then he wires money from the LLC to Reilly's trust to pay Madison for her care."

"Apparently. I didn't know about that. He wouldn't tell me what he needed the money for, only that he needed a lot of it."

"What did you say when he told you? Did you yell at him about how effed up it is? Did you tell him to stop?" Beth's voice grew shrill as the questions tumbled out of her like a waterfall.

"God, yes! I couldn't believe what I was hearing. *My* brother, the stand-up guy who helps people with their legal issues, big or small, whether they can pay or not. I met with him several times to plead with him to stop. I was like, 'Dude! Do you hear yourself? You have to stop this. This is nuts!' But he had this wild look in his eyes. He said he *had* to do it... that he had no other way to get the amount of dough he needed. I begged him to tell me what he needed it for, but he said it was better that I didn't know." Josh paused to get his breath. "I even threatened to tell you about it."

Beth drew in a sharp breath. "How did he react to that?"

"How do you think? He lost his shit. Started screaming at me and saying he'd never speak to me again. He said he was doing everything he could to protect you from his problems. He even threatened to disappear if I told you. I wasn't sure what he meant by that, but it scared me. I didn't know if 'disappear' meant 'run away' or... worse." He brushed a tear from the corner of his eye. "Beth, he was so desperate. I kept quiet so Danny would know he had someone to talk to. I didn't want to alienate him and drive him further underground."

"I understand, Josh. I just wish he had trusted me enough to tell me the truth."

"Beth, Danny worshipped you. He wanted to be the guy you thought he was."

"Not someone who would steal money from his clients. Jesus."

"Yep. And he apparently did it several times. He chose estates like that one, where he considered the beneficiaries greedy or lazy and didn't care about anything but collecting a lot of money from dear old Mom and Dad."

"Well, as awful as they sound, it's still their money. It doesn't excuse what Danny did."

"Oh, I agree one hundred percent. He also pulled the same stunt a few times when the beneficiaries lived far away. Danny convinced them it would be easier for him to take care of things like repairs and landscaping so the family members wouldn't have to incur the cost of traveling to hire contractors and oversee the work. They were grateful to Danny for taking care of those things in their time of grief." Josh looked disgusted.

"God Almighty, I can't believe Danny would do something like that. It's like we're talking about someone else. It's like a movie."

"I know. I think he was so desperate, he told himself the bratty rich kids wouldn't miss the money he stole. He figured they'd still get a windfall when the assets were distributed, even after Danny skimmed his share. The ones that really bothered him were the ones who gave him free rein because they lived far away, not because they were selfish. They trusted him. That ate away at him."

"It should have! All of it should have eaten away at him, bratty beneficiaries be damned!" Beth slammed her fists on the table, sending cold coffee sloshing out of their full cups.

"Yep. Only, I swear, Beth. I had no idea the funds in this LLC were being transferred to a woman who'd had Danny's child. I did not know about Reilly. He wouldn't tell me why he needed the money so badly. I figured it was gambling debt or something like that." Josh looked up at the ceiling. "Come to think of it, a few of the estate cases were ones he did for his buddy's firm in New York. I bet that's how he met Madison Fisher."

"Madison's occupation is listed as a paralegal on Reilly's birth certificate." Beth considered everything she'd just heard. "I wonder why Danny needed *so much* money. The withdrawals from the trust every month were pretty hefty. More than I would think typical child support would be."

"That's a question for Madison. And I wouldn't hold my breath that she'll brew some tea and want to have a friendly chat with you."

A long moment passed in which neither Beth nor Josh spoke. Beth felt crushed under the weight of all that she'd learned about Danny. It was like one of those soap operas starring a decent, up-standing guy, and one day, his evil identical twin blows into town and turns everything on its head.

Finally, Josh cleared his throat. "Beth, I'm sorry I didn't tell you. Believe me, I wrestled with it daily when Danny was alive. When he died, I hoped it would disappear without you ever having to know about it. At first, I worried that if it was gambling debt, or worse yet, something to do with drugs, the people he owed money to would come after you. But time passed, and nothing came of it, so I decided to let sleeping dogs lie. I didn't want that to be your lasting memory of my brother."

"I can't fault you, Josh. You did what you thought was best." *Just like I did all those years ago.*

"I had no idea you were chasing down mysteries about Danny's secretive financial activities. If I had, I would have at least supplied you with this piece of the puzzle. I hate that you've been tackling it alone."

"Well, now that you mention it, Molly knows, and... well..." Beth's cheeks turned pink above a shy smile.

"What? Wait, seriously? You've started seeing someone?"

"I have. Recently. He's very nice. I think you'd like him. I mean—" Beth was flustered, but Josh came to her rescue.

"Stop! No need to sell me. I think it's great, Beth." He took her hand across the table. "Listen, it's been over a year. The Danny shit show notwithstanding, you are a great girl and deserve to be happy. I'd love to meet him sometime."

Beth's phone dinged. Pulling it from her purse, she saw a text from Andre. "Speak of the devil."

Andre: *How's it going? Still with D's parents?*

Beth: *No. Coffee with Josh. Heading home soon.*

Andre: *All good?*

It was all Beth could do not to burst into maniacal laughter at Andre's question.

Beth: *Went well with Bruce and Louise. Details later. See you tonight?*

Andre: *Absol-tively! I mean, posil-utely!*

Beth smiled at Andre's easy humor. She and Josh stood and hugged. He started to let go but then pulled her in for a second embrace.

"Go home and decompress. Be good to yourself. Give yourself time to process. This has been a lot."

"You're telling me. It feels so strange to be so angry at a dead man, a man I loved, a man I thought I knew! A man who has a child I knew nothing about."

"I know. He's my brother, but it's like I never knew him." Josh held her by the shoulders. "Please, keep in touch. Don't be a stranger."

A strangled laugh escaped her. "I'm not going anywhere. Through all of this, I feel like a new Beth is emerging. And I think you'll like her."

Chapter Thirty-One

Beth was grateful for the time alone during her drive home. The day had left a tightening in her chest, deep pulsing knots in her shoulders, a stifling grip on her heart, but with each passing mile, she felt oxygen return to her lungs and found it easier to breathe.

Snippets of previous conversations crept into her thoughts as she navigated the winding roads. Amelia's words—from Dr. Roth's office—took on an especially new meaning. "My parents thought my grandfather had quite a bit more money than he apparently did… They figured my grandmother could afford to live out her days comfortably with no money worries… Anyway, my grandmother lives with my parents now." Beth's cheeks burned with shame at Amelia's last remarks. "They thought the world of your husband. He helped them through a rough time." At the time, Beth had been buoyed that, despite Danny's secrets, he'd shown them kindness and compassion. Now she choked back a sob, thinking that he might have stolen from Amelia's family. *How many others were there?*

As she pulled into her driveway, the last of the January sun descended behind the mountains. After texting Andre to let him know she was home, Beth called her parents and asked them to come over the next day after the café closed. She wasn't looking forward to that conversation, but she knew she couldn't put it off.

She changed into yoga pants and a sweatshirt and went downstairs to open a bottle of cabernet. "Ugh," she groaned at realizing she had no wine in the house. The bell rang, and she yanked the front door open to see Andre, wine bottles and bags of takeout containers in hand.

"You are a sight for sore eyes."

"Awesome! That's just what a guy wants to hear from his beautiful girlfriend!"

"I was talking to the wine." Beth winked as Andre pulled her close. "But I'm happy to see you too."

Andre spread the food on the counter. "I figured you haven't eaten all day. I wasn't sure what you were in the mood for, so I got a little bit of everything. And the way I grilled the staff at each place about gluten, you'd have thought I was the DA grilling them on the witness stand. Not a speck of gluten anywhere near these eats."

Smiling, Beth opened a bottle of red and studied the man she had fallen for. In light of everything, she was comforted by the fact that he was there to go through it with her. Even months after she'd accepted Danny's death, Beth couldn't fathom getting involved with another man. She had been filled with dread that she was doomed, that it would happen again—she would learn to love again, then he would be cruelly taken from her. Instead, she had Andre, as sturdy as a rock, whistling cheerfully as he brought plates and silverware to the table. *Surely,* she thought, *most men would leave skid marks speeding away from a circus like my life.* Not Andre. With every newly uncovered transgression, he was by her side, assuring her he was all in. And now, over carefully selected gluten-free calamari, she would tell him that her "damn near perfect" husband had been stealing money from his clients to secretly support his child. No one wished for a boring life, but lately, boring sounded pretty good to Beth.

As they ate, she recounted what Josh had told her. Andre listened intently, eyes wide, nodding, shaking his head at times, rubbing Beth's arm but saying little. When she finished, she pushed her plate away and gulped her wine.

"Had enough yet?"

She shook her head and held out her glass, which Andre hastily refilled.

He exhaled audibly and took Beth's hand in his. "Wow. I can't imagine what you're feeling. I'm sure it's hard to put into words."

"It's just so hard to conflate this man with the Danny I knew. He wasn't perfect, but my God, stealing money from clients, hiding that he has a child… not to mention that he obviously cheated on me. I can't stop wondering if it was a one-night stand or if Danny and Madison had a relationship. Maybe he even loved her."

She traced the rim of her wineglass with her index finger, lost in melancholy that Danny might have loved another woman while Beth walked down the aisle into his waiting arms, while they promised in front of their families and friends to love and cherish each other forever. "It's frustrating that I can't confront him, you know? I can't yell at him. I can't tell him how much he's hurt me. I can't throw things or pound my fists on the wall to show him how angry I am. I loved him, damn it!" Then her expression softened into something resembling empathy. "I also can't help him. I can't give him a chance to express what he has to say for himself. I go back and forth between wishing he were here so I could listen and support him and wishing he were here so I could bash him over the head. The noise in my brain is deafening."

"Everything you're feeling is perfectly natural and understandable. It'll take time. I'd venture that some parts of this saga will sting for a long time, maybe permanently. And you'll accept other parts of it. But I have faith that you will move past it and be happy again. I intend to help see to that." Andre stood and pulled Beth to her feet.

"Wait," she whispered, imploring him with her eyes. "You're not leaving, are you?"

He took her face in his hands and kissed her tenderly. "I hope not."

"I want you to stay."

"Should I put the leftovers—"

"Leave them." Taking his hand, she led him upstairs.

The air was electric between them, and they started fast, hungry. But wanting to savor every touch, every kiss, they pulled back. They undressed each other slowly, each gently exploring the other's body. His hands curved around the back of her head, lightly gripping her hair. She moaned and leaned into him. Beth lost herself in Andre's kisses, so satisfying and yet leaving her wanting more. Clinging to each other, she caressing the sinewy muscles on his back, he gently grazing her throat with his lips, they moved to the bed.

That night, Beth didn't fall asleep alone on top of the comforter.

She awoke hours later, his body wrapped around hers, the memory of their lovemaking filling the space in her mind that had been overflowing with Danny's wrongful deeds. The room had grown chilly, and she pulled Andre's discarded shirt, a blue-and-white button-down, from the floor and slipped into it. His musky, masculine scent clung to it, and she drew the collar up to her nose, breathing him in. He opened one eye, and Beth could tell by his lazy smile that he approved of this most intimate gesture between lovers. She laid her forehead on his chest. He kissed the top of her head, wrapped his arms around her, and they didn't stir until late morning.

Chapter Thirty-Two

The chaotic sounds of Fresh Start were music to Beth's ears. It allowed her to escape her own noisy head, where random TV stations played at the same time, each showing a different movie—not in a harmonious way but battling it out for Beth's attention with earsplitting volume and flashing pictures. She thought about the way streaming services boasted a list of Suggested for You shows based on previous choices. The cacophonous list in her aching head screamed, *Secret Love Child*, *How to Steal from Your Clients*, and *What Your Wife Doesn't Know*. She wanted desperately to pull the plug on all of it.

The show she didn't mind watching repeatedly in her head was her blissful night with Andre. She hadn't wanted it to end. Waking up in his arms that morning, she wanted to stay barricaded there with him forever, under the blanket, away from her chaotic life. When they reluctantly dragged themselves out of bed, she'd showered and washed her hair, but his scent lingered on her even now.

"Hey, girl!" Red, tray of glazed cinnamon buns in hand, greeted Beth as she came in through the kitchen. "Just in time to sample one of these beauties."

She was glad to be back with her café family. "I'll take you up on that. I smelled them from the parking lot." Beth dropped her bag and coat in her office and fired up her computer before going out to greet the rest of the staff.

"You okay?" Lucy's squinted eyes showed her concern. "You've been an absentee boss lately—not that we're complaining. How 'bout it, Frank?" She winked at her coworker.

"Oh, yeah." Frank laughed while mixing up a huge bowl of pasta salad. "We have all kinds of wild parties when you're not here. I'm surprised the neighbors haven't called the cops."

The cops. Given everything I've learned, I'm a little surprised I haven't had a visit from them myself. "Yes, I'm good. I know I've been a missing person these last few weeks, popping my head in like some kind of nosy neighbor instead of the owner. I had some personal stuff to take care of. But it'll all get sorted. Thanks for holding down the fort." She poured a mug of coffee and briskly rubbed her hands together. "So, catch me up. What have I missed? I've tried to respond to all your texts and emails, but I'm sure we have things to discuss."

Lucy pulled a large glass dish of baked French toast from the oven. "Same old, same old around here. Business is good. Everything has been smooth. Oh, but I do want to talk to you about next month's cooking class. It's a class for kids, so I thought it would be fun to do breakfast foods. Like this." She tilted the French toast dish so Beth could get a better look.

"Mmm, great idea. I think kids will have fun with that. Let's nail down a date today and start advertising on social media and our website. Gemma can make some signs to display here."

They continued discussing café matters until it was time to open. The morning was busy, a steady stream of regulars and newcomers enjoying breakfast, chatting easily with both staff and other customers. Beth was swiping a credit card for a takeout order when a family of four she'd never seen before entered and sat at a table near the bay windows.

The family included a mother, father, and two children, a boy and a girl. They looked like any other family who might happen into Fresh Start on any given day. Gemma greeted them, placed menus on the table, and asked if they would like something to drink while they looked over it. After they ordered coffee for the adults and orange juice for the children, they perused the menu, throwing out suggestions on what to order.

Beth found herself moving closer to them. The father said something to the boy, who Beth guessed was about five years old, and tousled his son's hair as they debated between scrambled eggs and pancakes. The mother studied the Specials board as she sipped the coffee Gemma delivered and noted that the baked French toast sounded good. She pulled off her scarf and stuffed it in her coat sleeve.

Nothing about them seemed remarkable. But Beth couldn't take her eyes off the girl. Her long blond hair was twisted into a French braid that trailed down her slender back. Hazel eyes sparkled and lit up her face as she spotted something on the board that appealed to her. She closed the menu, and Beth could see chipped polish, bright pink, on her short nails. On the back of her chair hung a small purse from which the girl extracted a book of riddles. The rest of the family offered guesses as the girl read to them from the tattered pages.

"I go all around the world but never leave the corner. What am I?"

The boy shrugged, and her parents said, "I give up."

The girl beamed. "A postage stamp!"

They all chuckled.

"Good one!" the father said.

The girl looked to be about eight years old. The same age as Reilly.

Danny's daughter.

Beth studied the girl. *Is this what Reilly is like? Does she test her mother with riddles? Does Madison polish her nails? Does Reilly have friends, sleepovers with sleeping bags, and favorite well-worn stuffed animals? What kind of clothes does she wear? Is her hair long, worn in a braid or a ponytail, or short, framing a delicate face that might resemble her father's?*

Zoe had just turned seven, and Sydney was six years old. Beth wanted them all to meet. She hoped they could be friends. Though Reilly was a bit older, Beth knew she could count on her nieces to welcome her.

Gazing at this family, this girl, Beth was overcome with the desire to meet Reilly.

She said a silent prayer that Madison would let her.

That evening, the air outside Beth's kitchen window was bitter and still, too quiet, like the world was bracing for something. Just like Beth. Her family was due to arrive any minute. The weight of the news she was about to deliver settled on her like the frost on her windowpanes—heavy, quiet, inevitable.

Beth pulled a tray of barbecued chicken thighs from the oven. Her hands shook slightly, an outward sign of her stress about the evening ahead.

"What can I do to help?" Andre asked.

"Could you set the table? They should be here soon." She cut open a thigh and shoved the tray back into the oven. "Not quite done." Next, she stirred au gratin potatoes bubbling in a casserole dish. "So, I've been workshopping my spiel. How does this sound? 'Mom, Dad, Danny has a secret love child, and he was stealing money from his clients to support her. Would anyone like another biscuit?'" She pinched the bridge of her nose.

Andre played along. "Hmm. Not bad, but maybe offer the biscuits first. It will be harder to shriek with a mouthful of carbs."

"Good point. And I should wait until everyone has had at least one glass of wine."

Andre nodded as he placed silverware next to the plates. "Maybe we should mix up a pitcher of something stronger."

"I'm second-guessing my decision to ask Hannah and Nic not to bring the kids. If I ever needed Ethan and Henry to fling cherry tomatoes at each other during dinner, it's tonight." Beth lifted the back of her hand to her forehead and leaned against the counter.

"I'll gladly take one for the team, but who should I target?" Andre teased, easing her tension. "Seriously, Beth, it will be all right. You'll see. From what I've observed so far, your family sticks together and can handle anything."

"Yeah, I guess you're right. But it'll be brutal to hear. I'm afraid they'll feel like Danny died all over again—or more likely that the Danny they knew never even existed."

Andre pursed his lips.

"What?" Beth asked.

"Nothing."

"No, you look like you want to say something. What is it?" Beth dried her hands on a dish towel and threw it onto the counter.

Andre looked into Beth's eyes. "It's just... I don't know. Part of me wants to feel sympathy for Danny—"

"*Sympathy?*" Beth asked incredulously.

"Yes. To steal from his clients? He must have felt cornered, like the walls were closing in." His look turned sad. "I've felt that way at times too. And Lord knows, it made me do some things I regret."

"Yes, but—"

"Let me finish. I *want* to feel sorry for Danny, but I can't. He had a great life, and he had you, a wonderful girl, but it wasn't enough for him. He should have woken up every day, thanking the universe for his good fortune. But instead, he was unfaithful to you, and he committed crimes against his clients. He kept Reilly from her family. When I think about all of that, he doesn't deserve sympathy."

Beth slumped onto a counter stool.

"I'm sorry, Beth. I shouldn't bad-mouth Danny. You have enough to deal with."

She embraced him, tears in her eyes. "It's okay. It's not like you're saying anything that isn't true."

They continued working together in the kitchen until Beth's parents and sisters arrived, desserts in tow. After greetings and hugs, Andre gave Beth a confidence-boosting look, and she led everyone into the family room, where a tray of wineglasses sat on the coffee table.

"Dinner isn't quite ready. Let's have a glass of wine in here. I need to talk to you about something."

Andre disappeared momentarily to the kitchen and returned with a bottle of red and a bottle of white.

As he poured, Hannah teased, "This better be good. Syd was furious that she couldn't come. She finally said, and I quote, 'Fine. A grown-up dinner sounds stupid and boring anyway.'"

Richard whistled. "She's going to give you a run for your money when she's a teenager."

Laura sipped her wine and joked, "It's called karma. So, Beth, what is it you need to tell us? Is everything all right at Fresh Start?"

Her mother looked so worried, Beth almost lost her nerve.

"Yes, everything there is fine. Great, actually." She inhaled deeply, and Andre squeezed her shoulder. "I need to tell you some things I've found out about Danny."

She had everyone's rapt attention as the air seemed to leave the room. As Beth stoically told her family the whole saga, the only other sound in the room was an occasional gasp.

She was exhausted by the time she got to the news about Reilly. The family's reactions were varied and colorful. Laura covered her mouth in shock as Richard put a steadying arm around her.

Nicole managed, "But... but... how...? Oh my God," and Hannah succinctly offered, "Holy shit!"

"Yep," Beth agreed. "That about sums it up."

After they absorbed the initial blow, Beth stood. "I'm going to get dinner on the table. Take a few minutes to chew on all of that, and I'll see you in the dining room."

Andre followed close behind. "I'll help you."

Alone in the kitchen, Beth leaned against his chest and cried softly. "That was harder than I thought it would be."

"You did great, hon. It's out there now. It's a lot to take in, but do you feel better for telling them?"

"Yes, I hate hurting them, but it was good to get it off my chest. The secrecy was killing me. You know, I've been thinking about something. I shared the years-long secret about my abortion with you—God, that's the first time I've said it out loud in years. And now all this stuff with Danny. It's the secrecy that ruins us, not the deeds. Just getting it all out there feels like a weight has lifted... like healing is possible. It's taught me to move forward, no more secrets. They don't do anyone any good."

Andre held her a moment longer but said nothing.

She wiped her face with the back of her hand before passing him the salad bowl and biscuits. "Anyway, I hope everyone still has an appetite."

As expected, Beth's parents and sisters had a myriad of questions and comments over dinner. By the time she served coffee and dessert, the conversation had mellowed.

Hannah finally asked the question on everyone's mind. "What will you do now, Beth?"

Beth sighed and pushed her pie plate away from her. "I'm going to New York. I need to talk to Madison. Since the one person I really want to talk to isn't here, she's the only one who can give me answers."

"And Bruce and Louise claim they knew nothing about any of this?" Laura had barely touched her dessert.

"That's right, and I believe them. If you had seen how shocked they were, you'd believe them too."

"Are you going to call Madison before you go? You know, to warn her. Or are you planning to just show up?" Nicole walked around the table, refilling coffee cups.

"I tried to find her phone number, but the only one for a Madison Fisher in that area has been disconnected. I did find her address, and I think it actually may be better if I just show up. Hit her with the element of surprise. Lord knows I've gotten my share of surprises these last few weeks." She began clearing the table. "Now it's her turn."

Moving into the kitchen, the family insisted that Beth sit down while they cleaned up.

"Beth, do you think Madison will let you see Reilly?" Richard looked around at the rest of his family. "I think I speak for everyone when I say we'd all like to meet her. She's a child and blameless in all of this." Amid enthusiastic nods, he continued. "I know we don't have any legal right to see her, but Danny was her father, and you're Danny's widow. Will that count for anything?"

"Yeah, you'd think Madison would be happy to have more people in Reilly's circle who care about her, right?" Hannah asked. "Maybe she'll be reasonable."

"I hope so." Beth closed her eyes and tried to picture Danny's daughter for the thousandth time. "But I really have no idea what to expect."

Chapter Thirty-Three

"You ready for this?"

"As ready as I can be." Beth placed her phone—open to a navigation app with Madison Fisher's address as their destination—in the holder where Andre could see it. A month had passed since the bombshell revelations about Danny, and she knew it was time to confront the mother of his child. "Thanks for driving. I'm so distracted, I shouldn't be behind the wheel."

"I had no intention of letting you do this by yourself or letting you drive." Andre gave Beth's thigh a gentle squeeze and backed out of her driveway. As he headed toward Route 95 North, he asked, "Have you decided how you want to approach Madison? We've tossed around different scenarios, but you weren't sure of the best way to handle it then."

Beth sighed and laid her head back on the seat. "I'm still conflicted. My gut says staying calm will make for a more productive conversation, but I'm not going to lie, that won't be easy. The thought that Danny cheated on me with her is enough to make me fly into a rage." She pensively gazed out the window. "But then I remember that it was Danny who broke my trust, not Madison. She owed me nothing. Who knows? If it was a one-night stand or a fling, she may not have even known he was engaged."

"True, I hadn't thought of that, but she obviously found out at some point that you and Danny got married. It sure seems like she was extorting money from him."

Beth snorted sarcastically. "You mean because of the inordinate amount he was paying her?"

"Yes. Didn't you say her withdrawals were somewhere around four thousand dollars a month? That's some serious money."

"Mm-hmm. But they didn't start out that high. Initially, they were around two thousand, but they had increased to four by the last payment."

"Exactly. That's what gives me the feeling she was putting the squeeze on him. You know, an ante-up-or-I'll-tell-your-wife kind of thing." Andre hit the brakes intermittently as traffic on I-95 picked up.

"And maybe that pressure made Danny so desperate that he started stealing from his clients. To keep her quiet."

"Could be."

"But I have to prepare myself for the possibility that Danny and Madison were in a relationship. That would be even harder for me to accept." She turned in her seat to face Andre. "But if that was the case, she wouldn't be shaking him down for more money, right?"

Andre stroked his chin. "I agree with that logic. If they *were* involved, it's unlikely she would do that—assuming that's what she was doing."

Beth blew out an exasperated breath. "I just don't understand why he wouldn't come to me. I mean, I know it wouldn't have been easy. It would have been excruciating, especially if they did love each other. But something tells me they weren't in a relationship. Everything I've learned points to Madison extorting money from him in exchange for her silence. I can't imagine another reason Danny would resort to such appalling behavior."

"It's hard to say, babe." Andre lightly stroked her arm. "Desperation does strange things to people."

After a brief stop along I-78, Andre and Beth continued on to New York and Madison Fisher's address in a suburb of Nassau County. A quiet area in the town of Hempstead, it had a friendly vibe with its many restaurants, shops, and parks. Beth found herself comforted that Reilly lived in such a neighborhood. Driving past a small park, she wondered if Reilly walked the paved paths with her mom or played on the swings with her friends, laughing as they challenged each other to see who could soar the highest.

Or if she'd ever played in the park with Danny.

Every street sign brought her closer, every turn a step she couldn't undo. It was true that Beth had tried to rehearse what she might say to Madison, but with the woman just moments away, all the words she'd imagined felt wrong—too harsh, too careful, too big, too small. She didn't know how the conversation would start. She only knew it had to—and that once it did, there would be no taking it back.

They drove until they found the house they were looking for, a small two-story brick stand-alone with dark-green shutters and an enclosed front porch. Pulling up to the curb in front of the house, Andre turned off the car and took Beth's hand. She made no move to get out, and he didn't rush her.

Her heart pounded, and she struggled to control her breathing. After a long moment, she spoke. "Okay, let's go. Not knowing is worse than anything Madison could tell me."

Frozen flower beds in front of the house showed signs of once-thriving plants, but neglect was evident in patches of unpulled dead weeds surrounding overgrown bushes. On the porch, a child's purple bike lay on its side, streamers hanging limply from dirty handlebars. Next to the front door, one of the three house numbers was gone like a missing tooth, only a discolored shadow of the number visible next to the others. Beth shot Andre a look under raised eyebrows.

Neither said anything as Beth rang the doorbell. No sounds were perceptible inside, and Beth wondered if the bell was working.

She knocked loudly, but still, no one answered. "Let's try the back of the house. I'm not leaving until I talk to her."

They followed a stone path that led around the side of the house to the backyard. On a small patio outside sliding doors, faded outdoor furniture sat uncovered, exposed to the winter elements. Beth climbed two paint-peeled wooden steps and knocked loudly on the sliding doors. The blinds were closed, so it was impossible to see anything inside.

Again, no one answered, and Beth turned to Andre. "Now what? We've come all this way."

"Maybe she's at work." He consulted his iWatch. "Let's go to one of the coffee shops we passed in town and come back later."

"Hello?"

Behind them, in the yard, a female voice startled them, and Beth's hand flew to her chest as she and Andre took in a woman who looked to be in her late fifties. She wore jeans and an oversized sweatshirt that billowed like a sail in the winter wind. Her dark hair just brushed her shoulders, and she held it back with her hand as it blew around her angular face.

Thin brows knotted as she gazed curiously at the two strangers banging on the window. "Can I help you?"

Beth stammered, "I'm... That is, we're... um... We're looking for Madison Fisher. Is this her house?"

"Who are you?" The woman hugged her middle against the cold temperature.

Every muscle in Beth's body was coiled just a bit too tightly, and the thought of fleeing flashed through her mind. But she had come this far. She wasn't about to turn back. "I believe my husband—late husband—knew Madison."

"Knew Madison how?"

Beth looked her directly in the eye. "He was Reilly's father."

The woman's shoulders sagged. "I'm Patricia Whitmore. I live next door."

"So you know Madison well?"

"I *knew* her well." Patricia's expression softened, and her eyes filled with mist. "Maddie passed away a short time ago."

Andre grabbed Beth's elbow as she lost her footing on the steps. They both gaped open-mouthed at her, and Patricia motioned toward her house.

"You better come next door with me."

The house was homey and neatly kept, the kitchen bright and cheery with pale-yellow scallop-edged curtains framing windows above spotless countertops.

"I don't really know much about Madison," Beth confessed, seated next to Andre at Patricia's kitchen table.

"It's a sad, sad story all around." Patricia poured steaming coffee into three mugs and placed a plate of chocolate chip cookies on the table. She lowered herself into a chair next to Beth and folded her hands in front of her. "She was a good person. She loved Reilly. The child was almost four years old when they moved here. I knew Maddie was a single mom, but I didn't pry. She seemed to manage okay.

"Maddie mostly kept to herself. At first, we were friendly but not necessarily friends. I grow tomatoes and peppers in my garden, and I'd take some over to her. She'd make vegetable soup and bring some to me—that kind of thing.

"She enrolled Reilly in a local preschool after they moved in, and I'd see other kids come over for playdates on Fridays, when Maddie only worked half a day. Sometimes, the other moms would stay. They'd sit on the patio while the kids played in the yard. It seemed like a happy enough existence, even if"—she glanced sheepishly at Beth—"there wasn't a father in the picture. Eventually, we became better friends. Her mother died several years ago, and Maddie never met her own father. She was an only child, so I guess you could say I was kind of a mother figure to her—and a grandmother figure to Reilly."

"It sounds like they were lucky to have you," Beth said sincerely. Though she found it hard to believe under the circumstances, she felt something akin to sympathy for Madison—a fatherless woman raising a fatherless child.

"Maddie was a paralegal at a law firm in town, and she had a young woman—Brandy—pick Reilly up from school and babysit until Maddie got home. I was her backup babysitter if Brandy was sick or couldn't make it for some reason."

Beth and Andre exchanged a look when Patricia mentioned Maddie's employment.

Patricia smiled as though recalling fond memories. "I loved watching Reilly. My own two kids are grown and out on their own. I keep waiting for one of them to make me a grandmother, but so far, they haven't. My husband died a few years ago. Reilly livened things up around here. She breathed life into this empty house, so polite and curious and smart. She loves to do puzzles and play brainteaser games."

Like Danny.

"Then Reilly started school full-time and got involved in all kinds of extracurricular activities. She took dance class and played soccer. Those things cost money. And understandably, she wanted the latest fashions and sneakers and book bags like the girls at school. Maddie was finding it harder to afford everything. She started working longer hours to earn more money, but that took her away from Reilly and her activities, which she didn't like."

Patricia refilled their mugs. Beth curled both hands around hers and imagined what it must have been like for Maddie to struggle on her own to raise the child she had with Danny.

"One Saturday, I kept Reilly while Maddie worked all day on a big case for her boss. She looked so exhausted when she came to pick up Reilly." Patricia gazed out the kitchen window at the bare trees in her backyard, their branches pointing every which way like bony fingers. "I probably overstepped, but I couldn't help it. I asked her, 'Honey, you can tell me to mind my own business, but doesn't Reilly's father help you financially? Doesn't he pay child support?' I'll never forget the sadness in her eyes when she said, 'Reilly's father doesn't know about her.'"

"How long ago was that?" Beth studied Patricia intently.

Patricia looked at the ceiling as if doing the math in her head. "Let's see, I'd guess it was about two and a half years ago."

Beth nodded, the timeline making sense with everything she knew so far.

Patricia continued. "I told her to file for child support. She needed the money. I could see how raising Reilly on her own wore on her. But Maddie waved off the idea, told me I wouldn't understand... I didn't press the issue." She sighed heavily. "But then, something changed. Shortly after that conversation, Maddie seemed different."

"Different how?"

"It's difficult to describe. She became sullen and more, I don't know, closed off? She'd pick up Reilly when I babysat and rush out the door instead of sticking around for a few minutes like usual. Often, she was on her phone when she arrived, and she seemed irritated. She'd cut the calls short when I was within earshot, but sometimes, she looked like she'd been crying."

She was probably talking to Danny, Beth thought.

Patricia pursed her lips. "On one particular day, Maddie had been on the phone when she arrived. After ending the call, she snapped angrily at Reilly to get a move on and gather her things to go home. She even cursed at her. She'd never behaved that way before. I mean, I know parents lose their patience with their kids—I did more times than I can count—but it seemed like her frustration had some-thing to do with the call. It upset Reilly. I shooed her into the kitchen for a brownie and milk and told Maddie to have a seat in the living room so she could cool off. I asked her what was going on, though I wasn't sure she would tell me.

"She started crying. She said she'd taken my advice and con-tacted Reilly's father. Apparently"—Patricia shook her head and ex-haled loudly—"Maddie and Reilly's father had slept together one time when he was in town working on a case. They'd been working late and had stopped at a bar for a drink afterward. One drink turned into two then three... They ended up at Maddie's apartment—she lived in the city at that time—and, well, nine months later, Reilly was born."

Beth hadn't realized she'd been gripping the table's edge. As the blood drained from her face, she said softly, "So it's true. Danny didn't know about Reilly until about a year before he died."

"Yes. After Maddie told him, it seemed like all hell broke loose. I don't know all the details, but Maddie was furious with him. Appar-ently, she had aggressively pursued him after their one night togeth-er, but he said it was a terrible mistake made by two people who'd had too much to drink. He said it could never happen again. He ei-ther pleaded with her to leave him alone or didn't take her calls. She wanted to see him, but he refused. Then Maddie found out she was pregnant."

Beth spoke quietly, her voice laced with sadness. "Based on Reil-ly's birthdate, Danny was engaged to me at the time of his one-night stand with Maddie."

Andre rubbed her back.

Patricia nodded, looking like she was putting together missing puzzle pieces in her mind. "I guess Maddie had her reasons for not telling your husband about Reilly for so many years. Maybe she was angry that Danny didn't want a relationship with her. I don't know.

But when she did come clean, Danny insisted on a paternity test. When the test proved Danny was Reilly's father, she went after him for child support."

Andre chimed in. "We don't think Maddie filed through regular child support channels. Danny was paying Maddie through a trust account. Beth just discovered that."

"Huh. Is that so? That might explain..." Patricia's voice trailed off.

"Explain what?" Beth pleaded. "Please, Patricia. I'm trying desperately to piece together exactly what happened. Danny's gone. Maddie's gone. You're the only person who can fill in the gaps."

Patricia stood and offered more coffee, which both Andre and Beth declined. "Well, at first—after Maddie told Danny—like I said, she was broody and sullen. But after some time went by, she seemed to bounce back. She was more relaxed, more like her old self. She went back to working regular hours and didn't seem as stressed about money."

"That must have been when Danny started paying her," Beth mused.

"I guess so. But then Maddie started *really* spending money. On things that surprised me. Almost like money was no object." Patricia tilted her head and squinted as though unraveling a mystery. "It was like she went from struggling one day to having more money than she knew what to do with the next. She not only spent money on Reilly, but she also bought herself a new wardrobe, jewelry, whatever she wanted."

Beth and Andre exchanged a knowing look. Beth pictured the printouts that showed the hefty deposits from Danny into the trust account.

Beth's eyes pleaded with Patricia. "Do you know if Danny ever met Reilly?"

"I don't know. Not to my knowledge. But Maddie made a few comments to me when I mentioned that things seemed to have picked up for her financially. Things like 'Well, Reilly's dad can keep his cushy life, but he's going to make damn sure Reilly and I have one too.' I flat-out asked her if Reilly's father wanted to meet her."

"And?"

Patricia looked embarrassed for Maddie. "She said something like 'He says he wants to meet his daughter, but *I* hold the cards. I'll make him jump through hoops a while longer. Then I'll decide.' As I said, Maddie changed dramatically."

Beth reared back in her chair. "That's terrible! You know what she was doing, right? She was extorting money from Danny and using Reilly as a pawn. That doesn't sound like Maddie had her daughter's best interests at heart."

"I know it sounds bad, and it is if that's what she was doing. Please believe me. Maddie tried to be a good mother, and for the most part, she was. I think when she told Danny about Reilly, she thought he'd come running. She didn't expect that he'd be happily married, though I can't imagine why. She had to know he had a life. But when he didn't ride in on a white horse to give her the happily ever after she wanted, things took a sharp downward turn."

"How do you mean?"

Patricia gathered the empty mugs and untouched cookies and carried them to the sink. Gazing out the window, she could see directly into Madison's backyard. Her expression turned wistful, and she spoke without turning around. "It pains me to think about it. I can't help feeling that if I had done more, Maddie would still be alive."

Chapter Thirty-Four

Beth and Andre gave Patricia a moment to compose herself. Her face showed the strain of a person who wished she'd done things differently. Beth knew that feeling well.

"What happened with Maddie?" Beth asked gently.

Patricia's eyes were awash in grief, and creases lined her face. "As I said, Maddie started spending indiscriminately. But it was more than that. She went out more at night. She'd stay out late and ask if Reilly could spend the night here. I was fine with that; I was even glad that she was doing things with friends. She was a young woman. She deserved to have a life. But something seemed off."

"What do you mean?"

"At first, she seemed happy when she dropped off Reilly before going out. She took more interest in her appearance—new clothes, wearing makeup, fixing her hair. But then that changed. She'd stay out very late. Sometimes, I'd see her coming home in the morning when I was already up making coffee. She stopped caring about how she looked. She also started going out during the week instead of just weekends. A few times, I spent the night at her house so I could get Reilly off to school." Patricia shook her head, a move that caused a tear to drop from her lashes. "On one of those mornings, Reilly went into her mother's bedroom to say goodbye before school. Maddie was so out of it, Reilly couldn't rouse her. It scared Reilly. It scared her a lot. I decided I couldn't keep my mouth shut any longer. After Reilly got on the bus, I went back into Maddie's house. I shook her until she woke up. I'll never forget how she looked. She was a complete mess. Mascara smeared all over her face, hair matted and tangled. Sleeping in her clothes from the night before. I laid into her. I told her how upset Reilly had been. I told her she'd been behaving irresponsibly and demanded to know what was going on."

"So, you think she was drunk and passed out?"

Patricia pinched the bridge of her nose. "That was her story, but she wasn't being entirely truthful. You know, hindsight is twenty-twenty. But sometimes, we only see what we want to see."

Beth nodded. *Don't I know it.* "So it wasn't just drinking."

"No. And I should have known. I should have pressed harder. She'd been losing weight, sleeping more, missing work. Until then, I'd never known her to miss work. Her moods were erratic. That day—the day Reilly couldn't wake her—I should have told her I knew she was using drugs. It had been going on for a few months, but I buried my head in the sand and told myself Maddie was just living her life, staying out late, having fun with friends. I guess I thought if I didn't hassle her, she'd get it out of her system." She choked back tears. "I should have been more forceful, insisted she get help. I should have offered to help her with Reilly while she got clean."

"Patricia, I can see how tortured you are by this, but you know you can't force someone to get help. They have to want to do it."

"I know. I know all of that. But if I had confronted her, kept after her, supported her, maybe..."

"What happened, Patricia? Did Madison overdose?"

"You see it every day on the news. But it wasn't an overdose that killed her." Dropping her head into her hands, she released a guttural sob. "She'd been partying at someone's house. Reilly spent the night at my house, and Maddie never came home, never called. I was furious. I decided when she finally came home, I would confront her and tell her if she didn't get help, I would call Child Protective Services."

Beth's eyes widened in shock.

"Yep. I was livid. As the hours passed, I worked myself into a lather. I was so angry with her. I couldn't wait for her to get home so I could lay into her."

Her voice lowered to barely more than a whisper. "But she didn't come home. Instead, I got a call from a police officer. They went through her phone and contacted me because my number was one she frequently called and texted. Maddie had been partying with a bunch of people at someone's apartment in the city. They took some pills."

Her tears flowed freely now, and Beth's heart broke.

"Apparently, Maddie had bought pills that looked like legitimate opioids but had fentanyl pressed into them. One of the other people there called an ambulance when they couldn't wake her. She was already gone at that point. The officer came here to talk to me. He explained that dealers mix fentanyl with other drugs because they can sell them cheaper. The dose Maddie took was lethal and killed her almost instantly. Of course, he didn't know all of this for sure until they investigated the incident, but that's what they learned later—after they tested the other pills.

"A young woman, a mother, gone—just like that. Such a senseless tragedy. I couldn't have been more devastated if she were my own daughter." Patricia blew her nose and swiped her hand under her eyes. "And there's Reilly."

"Oh my God." Beth placed a sympathetic hand on Patricia's arm. "Both Reilly's parents are gone. I... I don't even know what to say. I came here to ask Maddie if she would be willing to let us—Danny's family and mine—see Reilly." She gave Andre an anguished look. "When did Maddie die?"

Patricia gulped and shuddered as she regained control. "About a month ago."

Beth mustered every bit of compassion she possessed. "Patricia, where is Reilly?"

Without answering, Patricia stood and left the room as Beth and Andre exchanged puzzled looks.

She returned and placed a card on the table in front of Beth. "Reilly is in foster care. This is the name of her caseworker."

Beth picked up the card and studied it.

"I've petitioned the court for guardianship, at least temporarily. Reilly knows me and is comfortable here. The caseworker—Susan Blackburn—is helping me. She's trying to find relatives, but so far, she's come up empty. She's looking for Reilly's father. I only knew his first name. I didn't know he died. If Maddie knew, she didn't tell me."

Andre had been listening intently. "I wonder if Danny's death pushed Maddie over the edge."

"What do you mean?" Beth cocked her head, her eyes squinting inquisitively.

"Well, I'm just trying to piece things together. Let's say Maddie contacts Danny, tells him about Reilly, and hopes they can have a future together. He tells her he's happily married and that's not going to happen. Maddie is distraught, but she gets Danny to start paying her. He wants to meet Reilly, but Maddie figures she's in control and can shake him down for more and more money. Think about it. She's having a grand old time pulling the puppet strings, making Danny dance. She starts spending money on herself, goes out partying more... you know—if Danny doesn't want to be with her, at least she's going to make sure he pays up." Andre leaned forward and placed both elbows on the table, his expression sad. "Then... one day, she learns Danny died. Patricia, you say Maddie was a good person at heart, and I believe you. Maybe when she learned about Danny's death, she was overcome with guilt about extorting Danny, using Reilly as a pawn. Maybe that's when her behavior became more erratic, even risky. She started hanging out with a bad crowd, and... well, we know the rest."

Patricia looked down at her hands folded in her lap. "I suppose that makes sense. Not knowing all the facts is torture. I wanted to go through her phone, but the police still have it. I think they were trying to figure out who sold Maddie the pills, but it's almost impossible. These dealers are good. They use burner phones. They contact people through social media and can create and delete accounts at will. They're despicable. I also wanted to get inside her house to search for any clues left behind, but I'm not allowed to go in because I'm not a relative. Maddie did not have a will—at least not one anyone can find. There's a name for that, but I can't remember what it is."

"Intestate," Beth said. "That's the word used when a person dies without a legal will. I'm not sure how it works in New York, but in Pennsylvania, if a person dies without a will, the state's intestate laws determine how their assets are distributed to their heirs."

"Right. That's it. Susan said that since Reilly is a minor, the state of New York will step in. They'll sell the house and determine any other assets, then hold it in a fund for her. It all sounds very complicated to me."

"Yes, it sounds messy. And much more so without a will." Beth paused and put her hand over Patricia's on the table. "Patricia, Maddie was an only child, and her parents are deceased—at least her mother is, and she never met her father—but Danny does have relatives. They're also Reilly's relatives." Beth saw Patricia's worried expression and rushed to continue. "No, no, I agree, Reilly knows you and would be comfortable here. That seems like the best arrangement, at least until a permanent solution can be reached. I hope the court agrees."

Patricia's face relaxed again. "I can't bear to think of that poor girl in foster care. In the meantime, while we wait to hear about that, Susan helped me file a petition for visitation. She said the court will often grant visitation for a close friend who is not a family member if it's in the child's best interests and if there's an existing relationship with the child.

"I hope to hear something any day now. I spoke to Reilly before she left with Susan. That poor child. Her eyes were sunken as though she were a ghost. She was so distraught about Maddie. She asked why she couldn't stay with me. I thought my heart would shatter on the spot. I told her I would do everything I could to make that happen." She shook her head, eyes closed. "Her entire world has been upended. She lost her mother, and now, she's with strangers. Don't get me wrong—Susan is great, and she's trying her best to have Reilly stay with me, but the system is flawed, and things move slowly."

Beth placed her elbows on the table and pressed her fingers into her temples. Making circular motions with her fingertips, she agonized about what to do next. Though she'd only met her today, Beth knew in her heart that Patricia loved Reilly and her motives were pure. Beth had come hoping to meet the woman Danny had had a child with and to convince her to let Beth and her family into Reilly's life. In a few short hours, another layer of sadness and shock had been added to the story.

Beth felt a wave of heaviness, exhaustion. She longed for the weightlessness she experienced when swimming underwater, hair splayed out behind her, arms gliding in front of her, moving together in sync. She ached to clear her head of things like stealing money, LLCs, trust accounts, secret daughters, fentanyl deaths, and court petitions.

"Patricia, if it's okay with you, I'd like to reach out to Susan Blackburn. Reilly *does* have family—her father's family—and the court needs to know that."

Patricia held her breath.

"But having said that, you're clearly an important part of Reilly's life. In fact, it sounds like you're the most stable person in her life. I agree with you that the best place for Reilly—at least for the time being—is with you, and as I said, I hope the court sees that." Beth's eyes implored her. "But if the court grants you guardianship, would you be willing to let us see Reilly?"

Patricia was silent for a long moment before she nodded, subtly at first. "Yes. I'd agree to that." Beth exhaled, and Patricia added, "But only if she wants to."

Chapter Thirty-Five

The next six weeks were nothing short of a whirlwind. After leaving Patricia's, Beth relayed the sad story of Reily's mother to both her family and Danny's. Everyone agreed it was more important than ever to try bringing Reilly into the fold.

In her quiet moments, Beth fought to separate her anger and disappointment toward Danny from potentially forming a relationship with his daughter. After all, she was only human. Thoughts of the man she'd married now felt like the ghost of Danny past. Every fond memory was tainted by a portrait of an adulterer, liar, and thief. Falling asleep at night, she reminisced about their marriage and wondered which portions were real and which were part of Danny's secret life. Some nights, it drove her practically to madness, and Andre wrapped her in his arms when she couldn't stop tossing and turning.

But maybe Reilly would be a salve, a bright spot in her parents' tragic story. Beth kept reminding herself that Reilly was a little girl, blameless of her parents' sins. A little girl whose entire life had recently and suddenly been torn apart. The adults in her life owed it to Reilly to behave as grown-ups and put her interests first.

"I'm so nervous, I can hardly sit still." Louise wrung her hands and leaned against her husband in the back seat of Beth's car.

"I'm sure you are, but Patricia is very nice and easy to talk to. I'm certain it will go fine. And I'm confident that when she meets you, she'll want Reilly to meet you too." Beth turned and offered an encouraging smile.

Andre nodded from the driver's seat.

Bruce added, "It's certainly been a few months of change, hasn't it? Processing everything we've learned about Danny has been difficult, to put it lightly. I wake up every morning thinking I must have had a bad dream." He reached forward and gave Andre a friendly slap on the shoulder. "Andre, I'm so glad Beth met you, and we're very happy we're getting to know you. Beth will always be family to us. We'll get through this together."

"Thanks, Bruce. I feel the same way."

After Beth and Andre's initial meeting with Patricia, Beth had decided it was time for Danny's parents to meet Andre. They'd been spending more and more time together, and it was clear that Andre wasn't going anywhere.

That gathering had gone smoothly, Beth's family joining them at her house for pizza. Danny's parents had confessed they were more nervous about facing Richard and Laura than meeting Andre, given the recent bombshells about their son. Beth's parents had assured them that they held no ill will toward them, but Richard couldn't help adding that he wished he could give Danny a piece of his mind. His parents hadn't argued and had admitted they shared that sentiment. Josh and Andre had hit it off instantly, discovering they had many of the same interests. The two families struggled to come to terms with the fact that a young man they all loved had not been who they'd thought he was. Despite that, it hadn't taken long for Andre's casual, easygoing manner to set the tone, and everyone had managed to relax and enjoy themselves.

Beth and Patricia had been in constant contact since they met. To everyone's delight, the court granted Patricia visitation rights, and she'd seen Reilly twice a week since the decision. Patricia reported that Reilly seemed to be okay, but a palpable gloominess clouded the girl's previously happy demeanor, especially when she spoke of Maddie.

Then, just yesterday came even better news—the successful hearing on Patricia's emergency petition for guardianship. The court approved temporary guardianship, taking tearful, heartfelt testimony from Patricia, who was represented by a lawyer in the firm that had employed Maddie. Though the order was temporary, Patricia was hopeful she would be awarded permanent custody of Reilly at a hearing set for that summer. As was typical, the court ordered an investigation from a social services agency and mental health professionals, who would visit Patricia and file reports with their recommendations. The judge would also conduct a confidential interview with Reilly. Patricia—as well as Beth—hoped that after the court considered the evidence, it would determine it was in Reilly's best interests to award Patricia custody.

The fly in the ointment for Patricia was that Reilly did, in fact, have biological relatives, which made it harder for Patricia to make a case to have permanent custody. Patricia and Beth spoke about this at length, though, and both agreed that Patricia was the right choice. Though Bruce and Louise were blood relatives, they'd never met Reilly. Louise's failing health made Patricia's case even stronger. She was the only one—at least for the time being—who had a relationship with Reilly.

As Beth and Patricia had decided, Beth, Andre, Bruce, and Louise were traveling to New York for Danny's parents to meet Patricia. The hope was that after getting to know them, Patricia would agree to let them meet Reilly. Bruce and Louise had a legal right to have contact with her, but they were reasonable people and understood that dragging Patricia and Reilly through court hearings would not be in Reilly's best interests.

It was an unseasonably warm March day as the foursome drove north to Hempstead. A chill still clung to the morning air, but the sun peeking through the tree branches promised that spring was near, and the forecast predicted afternoon temperatures in the mid-sixties. As they neared Patricia's neighborhood, Beth reflected on everything that had happened over the last several months. It was staggering to think that it had all begun when she'd referred Frank to the water restoration company Beth and Danny had hired. She shook her head and groaned. *Alice in Wonderland* had nothing on her. When Beth had begun her trip down the rabbit hole, she couldn't have imagined ending up here.

Andre parked in front of Patricia's house. He and Beth glanced briefly at Madison's house and were silent for a moment. Andre took Beth's hand, and she nodded and opened the car door.

She turned to Bruce and Louise. "This is it. Nice little neighborhood, right?"

"Yes," Louise agreed. "When I think of New York, the city always comes to mind. I forget there are quaint suburbs here just like everywhere else."

Bruce took his wife's arm and led her up a path next to flower beds, where thawing soil gave way to the hint of spring perennials coming back to life.

Not for the first time, Beth marveled at how life went on, no matter how chaotic a person's circumstances. The sun rose and set. Rain and snow fell. Seasons came and went. Here were Patricia's phlox, their rich-pink blooms just beginning to emerge as ground cover, oblivious to all that had occurred in these two houses since last spring.

As they rang Patricia's doorbell, Beth gestured toward Maddie's house and told her in-laws, "That's where Maddie and Reilly lived."

Bruce and Louise took in the house where their granddaughter had grown up, unknown to any of her family. Louise's eyes misted.

"Louise," Beth said. "Patricia told me that Maddie was a good mother before she spiraled downward. Reilly was happy and well taken care of."

"That does bring me some comfort. This is all so overwhelming."

The door opened, and Patricia, dressed in black jeans and a light-blue cable-knit sweater, offered a warm smile.

Beth hugged her. "Patricia, this is Bruce and Louise Collins. Reilly's grandparents."

"Who's ready for more coffee?" Patricia made the rounds and topped off everyone's mugs.

The group had been chatting amiably for the past hour and a half. Patricia had told Bruce and Louise all about Reilly—her speed on the soccer field, her perfectly timed moves in dance class, her love of old game shows on television. Bruce and Louise listened attentively as Patricia described their granddaughter's activities. Beth watched as they pictured Reilly running down the field with her hair streaming behind her, engaging in typical activities for an eight-year-old. They told Patricia about themselves, that they lived a pretty quiet life in retirement. They traveled, though not as much as they used to. Louise admitted that her health had slowed them down a bit.

Beth, Bruce, and Louise also told her about Danny, at least the Danny they knew.

"He was incredibly curious and very bright, even as a little boy. He couldn't let anything rest. His favorite word was 'why,' and he questioned everything he was told. Honestly," Louise recalled, "I always thought he'd go into science. We were surprised when he chose law."

Beth added, "And he was a hard worker, extremely focused and serious. But when he shut down his computer, he left the work behind and was the easygoing jokester in the room, the guy everyone wanted to hang out with. At least"—Beth's voice cracked, and sadness crept into her eyes—"he was that way for years. Until the year or so before he died."

"You know, Reilly has that same quality. She's serious about her schoolwork but the life of the party when she's with her friends."

Louise clasped her hands in front of her. "Patricia, do you have any photos of Reilly?"

Patricia stood and opened the glass doors of built-in shelves that lined one wall of her living room. She took out a photo box and placed it on the coffee table. Everyone held their breath as Patricia sifted through its contents. Andre put a comforting arm around Beth's shoulders. Finally, Patricia selected a few photos and laid them in front of her anticipatory guests.

At the sight of the first photo, Beth drew in a sharp breath, and Louise's hands flew to her chest.

"Oh!" Louise gasped. "It's like I'm looking at my son's photo! Bruce, look at this."

Even if Danny hadn't requested a paternity test, there would be no mistaking that Reilly was his daughter. Her dark, shiny hair was pulled back into a sleek ponytail, which brought out the deep blue in eyes identical to her father's. She struck a comical stage pose in a jazzy dance costume with wide sleeves. In the next photo, her hair was down, and just above her left eyebrow, a small cowlick caused her hair to flop over her eye. Beth envisioned Danny pushing back his hair, floppy in exactly the same way—as though he'd styled it like that. In the photo, Reilly was with a young blond woman, and they were laughing at something outside the picture's frame. Beth picked it up and studied it.

"Yes," Patricia said softly. "That's Maddie. Before, well, you know..."

Louise patted Patricia's arm, and Beth and Andre sighed in unison. They looked through a few more photos, Patricia reminiscing and adding context. Afterward, no one spoke for a few minutes, each lost in their own thoughts and memories.

Andre finally broke the silence. "This coffee cake is delicious, Patricia." He took the last bite and wiped his mouth with a napkin.

"Thank you, and, Beth, I'm so sorry. I didn't know you have celiac disease and can't eat anything with gluten. I'll know for next time."

"No worries, Patricia. How could you have known?"

"Well, I'd like to learn more about it. Reilly enjoys baking. She and I can experiment with gluten-free recipes. Or"—she exhaled and smiled broadly—"maybe the three of us can whip up something when you visit next time."

"Are you saying what I think you're saying?" Beth's eyes widened as she grasped Louise's hand.

"Yes." Patricia's face relaxed in a peaceful expression Beth hadn't seen since they met. "I think it would be great for you to meet Reilly." The group let out a collective yelp, and Patricia added, "I'll talk to her first and explain who you are. I'll need to go slowly. Lord knows that girl has been through enough. But I really think she will warm up to the idea of meeting you. Right now, she feels so lost and untethered. Maybe knowing she has some family will give her something to connect to."

Louise embraced her. "Oh, Patricia, we can't thank you enough. Learning everything we have about our Daniel—well, it's been a nightmare, to say the least. Reilly is the bright spot in the whole sordid mess."

"Wait until you get to know her. She really is wonderful. I just met all of you, but I can tell you have nothing but good intentions where Reilly is concerned."

Not wanting to overstay their welcome, the four of them stood to leave.

Patricia retrieved jackets and purses and showed them out. "I'll be in touch."

Chapter Thirty-Six

There are some things one can't prepare for, some situations for which there is no point of reference, no one to advise or give pointers from experience. When traveling to a new destination, there would always be someone who'd been there to ask about the restaurants and amenities. When buying a new car, it was easy to ask others who'd had the same car about the gas mileage. Even something risky like skydiving had a pool of people who could describe the rush of soaring through the air while praying the chute would open.

But whose advice can a woman seek when meeting her dead husband's eight-year-old secret love child for the first time? Beth would be hard-pressed to find someone who could recount that experience for her. There were no websites or Facebook groups to consult, no my-dead-husband-had-a-secret-child-with-an-extortionist blogs. That was what Beth thought as she and Andre headed north to make the familiar trip to Patricia's, where Reilly now lived.

The court's decision to give Patricia temporary custody had restored some normalcy to Reilly's life with a woman she knew and loved. And they'd cleared the first hurdle—Reilly was open to meeting her father's family.

When Patricia had called with that news, Beth had gripped her cell phone so tightly that she'd had red indentations on her hand when the call ended. Patricia had recounted her conversation with Reilly to Beth, and it had moved Beth to tears. Beth's pulse raced as Patricia told her how she'd gently explained to Reilly that she had family on her father's side who would like to meet her. Her little face was serious as Patricia described Reilly's grandparents, Beth, and Andre. She also mentioned that Reilly's father had a brother, so she also had an uncle. Not surprisingly, Reilly had multiple questions about Beth. Patricia lovingly and painstakingly told her that her father had passed away recently, but he was married to a very nice lady who would love to meet Reilly. The girl's eyes opened wide when Patricia told her that Beth's sisters also had children, some close to Reilly's age. Though Reilly didn't say it, Patricia interpreted her wide-eyed look to mean she was pleased at the idea that she might belong to an actual family.

She reported that the girl took in the information slowly, like painting a picture of something never seen before and, therefore, only imaginable. Reilly went to her room and lay on her bed, staring at the ceiling, contemplative but not upset. Patricia feared that after thinking about it, Reilly would get cold feet and refuse to have anything to do with Beth or Danny's family. Instead, as she cooked pasta and meatballs—Reilly's favorite meal—the girl emerged from her room, sat down at the kitchen table, and peppered Patricia with a string of questions typical for an eight-year-old girl in her rare situation.

As they ate, Patricia told Reilly all about her visits with Beth, Andre, Bruce, and Louise. She colorfully described their pleasant personalities and laidback demeanors and promised Reilly that she would be present if Reilly decided she would like to meet any or all of them. Reilly asked Patricia why none of these family members had reached out before, and Patricia took both the girl's hands in hers and assured her that they only recently found out about Reilly, and when they did, they contacted Patricia immediately.

By the time Reilly cleaned her plate and drained her milk glass, she told Patricia that they should invite them to the house for dinner. Patricia said Reilly could take time to think about it, but the girl's deep-blue eyes lit up, and she smiled wider than Patricia had seen in months.

Before they ended the call, Patricia told Beth with a laugh that Reilly had already started planning the menu, and she anticipated scouring several grocery stores to find everything Reilly had in mind. "I cut her off when she proposed we have ice cream sundaes *before* dinner," Patricia joked. "But you can't blame her for trying! Seriously, Beth, Reilly is so excited to meet all of you. I have a really good feeling about this. It's been such a tough time for her, and this is the first thing I've seen her hopeful about in ages."

After much back and forth, Patricia had suggested Beth and Andre come alone for the first meeting, and if that went well—which she had every reason to believe it would—they would invite the others.

Beth had labored over whether to bring Reilly a gift. She'd asked Patricia for suggestions, but Patricia had assured her it wasn't necessary. Beth didn't want to seem like she was trying to buy the girl's affection, but she thought a small gesture might be nice. She'd remembered Patricia mentioning that Reilly liked puzzles and brainteasers and that she had a sweet tooth—*what eight-year-old didn't?*—and had put together a small gift bag of puzzle books and candies.

Now, she clutched the bag to her stomach, nervously pulling on the curly ribbon tying the handles together. "Maybe I shouldn't have brought this. Maybe she won't like the candy I chose. I should have included some colored pencils or markers for the puzzles. How will she do the puzzles without markers? I'm such an idiot!"

Andre glanced at her and smiled slyly. "Yep, you're right. This whole thing is going to go south because you didn't bring markers. We should probably just turn around and go home."

Her cheeks blazed red, and she shook her head as if to dislodge her absurd ideas. "Okay, maybe I'm overthinking. But I'm so nervous."

"Of course you are. Who wouldn't be? This is huge."

"I just want it to go well. I want... I want her to like me so I can get to know her. She's Danny's daughter. Never mind all the terrible things he did—she's a little girl who deserves a happy, stable life."

Andre turned onto Patricia's street. "Beth, Reilly is going to like you for the same reason everyone likes you—you're a good person. You're real and kind and easy to be around. Reilly will see that, and I'm willing to bet you two will hit it off instantly. Kids have great instincts."

"Even though I didn't bring markers?" Beth winked at him before opening her car door.

"Even with that monumental blunder."

Andre rang the doorbell when Beth's shaking fingers prevented her from doing so. As they waited, she felt perspiration building near her hairline.

Grabbing Beth's trembling hand, Andre assured her, "It'll be fine."

Patricia pulled open the door and drew them both in for a bear hug. Over Patricia's shoulder, Beth took in a young girl seated on the stairs, peering through the posts. She wore khaki joggers and a long-sleeved navy T-shirt with sparkly hearts on the front. Beneath dark hair swept up in a high ponytail, deep-set blue eyes searched her guests' faces. Beth drew in a sharp breath at Reilly's serious and careful countenance, so much like her father's in new situations.

The magnitude of the moment overtook Beth. Her heart went out to the vulnerable child, Danny's child. Eight years old was such a delicate age, all sharp eyes and soft edges. The girl's leg bounced as she fidgeted, and she seemed not to know what to do with her hands.

Neither spoke at first. Beth felt the air between them stretch thin, as though one wrong word might tear it open. Patricia nodded, and Beth approached Reilly slowly, as if she were a squirrel who might flee at any sudden movement.

"You must be Reilly. I'm Beth, and this is my friend Andre. We've been looking forward to meeting you." She smiled, warm and genuine.

Reilly stood. "Hi."

"Why don't we all sit down?" Patricia led the way to the living room. "Who'd like coffee? Reilly and I baked three kinds of cookies that I know she can't wait to show off."

They took their seats, Reilly eyeing the bag Beth still clutched.

"Oh, this is for you, Reilly. I just wanted to... I wasn't sure if you liked..." Beth stammered.

Reilly thanked Beth and accepted the bag. "Miss Patty, is it okay if I open it?"

"Of course."

Beth held her breath, hoping the small token would break the ice.

"Twix is my favorite! And look at this puzzle book with animal trivia questions. I'm going to beat you at that game, Miss Patty!"

Patricia laughed. "I have no doubt about that."

"Do you like animals, Reilly?" Andre asked.

"Yes, especially mammals. Did you know there are over five thousand species of mammals in the world?"

Beth and Andre shook their heads, and Beth answered, "I did not know that. I'll have to study before I play that game with you."

Reilly beamed, looking pleased with herself for teaching adults something new.

Patricia retreated to the kitchen to get the coffee, and Andre followed her. "Right behind you, Miss Patty," he quipped.

She playfully swatted his arm. "As a little girl, Reilly had trouble with 'Miss Patricia,' so we came up with an easier version."

When Beth and Reilly were alone, the conversation lagged for a moment before Beth finally spoke again. "Reilly, I'm so happy that you agreed to meet us. You've been through a lot lately. I want you to know that there is no pressure for you to do anything you don't want to do."

Reilly sat on her hands, her feet swinging back and forth beneath her, and she studied the floor. "Did you know my mom?"

Beth spoke softly. "No. I never met her. I'm so sorry about what happened to her, Reilly."

Patricia had told Beth that she and Susan Blackburn thought it best not to divulge Maddie's drug use and the cause of her death to Reilly until she was a bit older. Her mother's death was enough for her to handle.

"I can't imagine how hard it is to lose your mom at such a young age."

Reilly's large eyes searched Beth's face, and her serious look returned. "Miss Patty said you knew my dad. She said he was in a car accident and died."

"Yes, that's right. It happened about two years ago."

"Were you in the car too?"

"Yes, I broke my arm and had some other bumps and bruises, but otherwise, I was okay." *Except I lost your unborn brother or sister.*

"And you were married to my dad?" The words landed with a strange weight—on one hand, simple and true, and on another, too complicated to label.

"Yes."

Reilly nodded, appearing to take that in. "I used to ask my mom about my dad. Why he didn't live with us or come to see me."

The way she said it struck Beth. Not dramatic or looking for pity. Just a quiet, terrible statement spoken by someone too young to carry such a heavy burden.

"Reilly, I'm sure this is all a lot for you to understand." Beth let out a breath. "Honestly, it's a lot for grown-ups like me to understand."

Reilly smiled at that.

"But one thing I can tell you for sure: Your dad didn't know about you until very shortly before he died. If he had, he would have been part of your life. He would have been very proud to be your dad."

"Mom didn't really talk about him. Why didn't she want him to know about me?"

Beth's heart caught, not because of who Reilly was but because of who she wasn't. She wasn't guilty—of anything. She was a blameless child standing in the middle of a truth she hadn't asked for. "I can't answer that. I'm sure she had her reasons. I wish they were both here so we could ask them all these questions." Beth moved closer to Reilly. "I won't pretend to know everything your parents were thinking or why they did the things they did. I just know that I hope you and I can get to know each other and be friends. If you want, you can also meet not just your dad's family but mine too. My sisters have kids who would love to meet you."

Reilly studied Beth as if contemplating everything she'd said. Then a shy smile took shape on her small face. "Is Andy your boyfriend?"

Beth returned her grin. "It's Andre, yes. And I think you'll like him." She lowered her voice conspiratorially. "And I know you'll kick his butt at that trivia game!"

Patricia and Andre returned with coffee and a platter of cookies.

"What's so funny?" Andre asked.

"Oh, nothing." Beth winked at Reilly, who was still giggling as she passed out plates.

"Beth, Miss Patty and I used a special flour in these cookies so you can eat them. What's it called again?"

"Gluten-free flour."

"Right. We have chocolate chip, peanut butter, and vanilla sugar cookies." She pointed at each type. "Which one would you like to try?"

"Well, why choose? I think I'll try all three!"

Reilly beamed as she offered the platter to Beth and Andre. They chatted as they nibbled on the cookies, Andre confessing he liked the chocolate chips best and helping himself to a few more.

"Chocolate chips are my favorite vegetable!"

Beth shook her head and said she couldn't decide—she loved all three. After a few minutes, Reilly asked Beth if she would like to see her bedroom.

Beth enthusiastically followed her up the stairs. She had no idea what to expect when Reilly swung open the door, but it only took a few seconds to see that Patricia had gone to great lengths to give the child a space where she would feel comfortable.

A twin bed stood under a window adorned with rainbow curtain panels tied back with pink tasseled rope. A pale-pink comforter with purple stars complemented the walls, painted the same shade as the stars. Several colorful pillows on the bed made Beth wonder how there was room for Reilly in it, but then she recalled Syd's and Zoe's beds, which were laden with pillows, dolls, and stuffed animals. In one corner hung what could only be described as a hammock, which was filled with stuffed animals of every kind. Above the bed, a neon wall sign spelled out "Reilly." Along one wall, a shelf with books stood about as tall as the little girl. But the thing that caught and held Beth's eye was a string of lights with photos clipped to it that stretched from the ceiling to the far wall.

Reilly took Beth's hand and led her inside.

"Wow, Reilly, what a great room! Did you and Miss Patty pick out all these decorations?"

"Well, some of it is from my room next door." She shuffled her feet and stared at the floor. "But then when I came to Miss Patty's, we added some more stuff. Isn't the neon sign cool? We got it on Amazon!"

Beth chuckled. "Good old Amazon. If you can't find it there, it can't be found." She moved to the photos on the string of lights. Several photos were of Reilly with her mother, who Beth recognized from photos Patricia had shown them on an earlier visit.

Reilly pointed to them individually. "That's me and my mom at my soccer game. And that one is at my school bake sale. This one is when we went to the beach in New Jersey. It's a different state. Have you ever heard of New Jersey?"

Beth laughed, thoroughly enjoying such a sincere conversation with this enchanting child. "As a matter of fact, I have, and I really like the beaches in South Jersey. I love going to the boardwalk."

Reilly's eyes lit up. "Me too! We got orange and vanilla soft ice cream there and French fries in a huge bucket!"

"Yes, not good for the waistline but loads of fun, that's for sure. If you like it that much, maybe we could all take a day trip there together sometime."

Reilly nodded vigorously as they examined more photos.

She sat on the bed and was quiet for a minute. Then she looked up with beseeching eyes. "Do you have any pictures of my dad?"

Beth reached into her pocket for her phone. Her heart breaking, she took a seat next to Reilly. "Yes, I do." She scrolled through her photo library, surprised at how few pictures she'd taken since the accident. "Here we go. This is your dad and me on a trip we took a few years ago. And here we are taking a goofy selfie at brunch. This one is your dad struggling with Christmas lights on our front porch. He wasn't too happy that I snapped that one."

Beth studied Reilly for her reaction.

The girl held the phone close to her face as she examined the images. Finally, she asked, "I look like him, don't I?"

"Yes, Reilly, you do. Not only do you have the same hair and eye color, but the shape of your face is just like his. What's really uncanny is how some of your facial expressions are a mirror image of his."

"What does 'uncanny' mean?"

"Good question! Let's see, it means that it's fascinating that you and he have the same facial expressions, though you never met."

Reilly opened her mouth to respond, but Patricia's voice from downstairs interrupted her.

"Reilly, don't hold poor Beth hostage up there!"

"Coming!" Reilly answered, her face turning red. "Sorry, Beth."

"Don't be sorry at all. If I visit again, maybe you can show me some of your book collection. I love reading, and I'd really like to see what kind of books you're interested in."

Back downstairs, Patricia and Andre had cleared the dishes and mugs and packaged some of the remaining cookies for Beth and Andre to take home.

"I'll hide the chocolate chips when she's not looking," Andre told Reilly with a wink.

Reilly bounced up and down. "Beth, Miss Patty said you have your very own restaurant. Do you think I could go there sometime?"

Beth was powerless to stop the mist forming in her eyes as Andre grabbed her hand and squeezed it. "I would love that, Reilly. You and Patricia are welcome to visit anytime."

"Well, we should be going." Andre leaned forward, hands on his thighs.

"Yes, Patricia, thank you so much for having us. And, Reilly, it was so great to meet you."

"Wait!" Reilly ran upstairs amid confused shrugs from the adults. She returned in a minute with a kid's instant polaroid camera. "Miss Patty, take a picture of me and Beth and Andre. I want to hang it in my room."

As Patricia squinted through the viewfinder, Beth and Andre stood with Reilly between them, and whether Beth's or Reilly's grin was wider was entirely too close to call.

Chapter Thirty-Seven

"A daughter? Your deceased husband has an eight-year-old daughter." Lucy gaped at her.

Frank and the others were silent as Beth opened their monthly meeting by telling the staff about Reilly. Fresh Start was set to open in thirty minutes, but everyone was glued to their seats.

"Yep. How's that for an agenda item? And I bet you thought the most interesting thing to come out of this meeting would be the new spring menu."

"You're not kidding," Frank finally said. "I was going to ask if you thought it would be too wild to throw some bean sprouts into the spring stir fry. This news beats the pants off that."

Red and the rest of the staff found their voices.

"Jesus, Beth. We knew you were chasing down a mystery these last few months, but I never dreamed it would be something like this. How are you doing? Are you okay?"

"How did you find out?"

"And you've met her?"

"Her mother died too?"

Beth put up her hands, palms facing out. "Whoa, whoa. One at a time!" She filled in some of the gaps, leaving out that Danny had been stealing from his clients. Though she'd had no part in it, that portion of Danny's past still caused her deep hurt and shame. She and Andre had had countless conversations about it, Beth wondering if she could somehow make restitution to the families he'd cheated.

Andre's opinion was that it would be almost impossible to figure out who he'd stolen from and how much money he'd taken.

"Aaaaand, there's more. Reilly and Patricia will be coming here soon to visit the café. I hope to see Reilly regularly and for her to get to know my family and Danny's. She's had a devastating few months. Patricia is wonderful, but I want Reilly to know she has other people in her life—if she wants us in it, that is."

Lucy stood and shrugged into the chef's jacket that she wore for protection from splashing when cooking soups and chilis. "Lord, Beth, you should write a book."

"Right? I've thought about it."

She gave Beth a quick hug. "Well, you can count on us. Bring Reilly around. We'll show her the glamour of running an eating establishment."

The others murmured their agreement and went about readying the café to open.

Beth watched them with admiration. She'd had months to process everything bit by bit. It wasn't lost on her how it all sounded when relayed all at once. The stuff of soap operas. *No one can say things are dull around here.*

Though it was not yet warm outside, it wasn't brutal anymore. The wind still carried a chill, but it no longer cut. Spring approached the way healing sometimes did—gradually, imperceptibly. The day had arrived for Patricia and Reilly to visit Fresh Start for the first time. Beth found herself clinging to the signs of spring's arrival, signs of cautious hope that even after long periods of darkness, something bright might dawn.

Allie wiped down the tables for the third time. She checked the temperature in the display case and straightened the containers.

Then she put on a clean apron as she glanced nervously out the window.

Beth chuckled. "Allie, she's a little girl, not the health inspector."

Allie briskly rubbed her hands together. "I know. I don't know why I feel so nervous. I guess it's because, well, Reilly is kind of your daughter."

Beth's hands flew to the sides of her head. "Well, damn, Allie, now *I'm* nervous!"

"Oh God, I'm sorry!" She fanned her face briskly with her hand. "It's just, I've been thinking about something since you told us about Reilly a few weeks ago. I never mentioned this, but my mother died when I was very young. My dad remarried a really nice woman. Mom and Dad had both grown up as only children, but Andrea—that's my stepmom—is from a big family."

Beth listened raptly.

"Anyway, Andrea's family accepted my brother and me into the fold immediately. They became our family, and it's been a godsend. I guess I'm just thinking it could be the same for Reilly."

Beth gently touched her arm. "Thank you for sharing that, Allie. I hope that's exactly how Reilly will feel. I'm not trying to replace anyone or fix what's broken. I just hope to build something from all that was left behind."

Truth be told, Beth's eyes had been opened since finding out about Danny's sordid past and Reilly. Before, she'd seen only what she'd wanted to see when it came to Danny. In her mind, he had been her path to fulfillment, and that was all she'd focused on. She'd always taken a supporting role in life, waiting for a leading man to take the stage and deliver happiness at her feet. Reilly had changed her perspective. That little girl had been through unimaginable tragedy. Her entire life had been turned upside down. And there she was, pulling herself up by her bootstraps and forging ahead. If Reilly could move forward and carve out some joy for herself, then Beth could too. Maybe it was time to start going after happiness herself. And maybe there was more than one path.

Just then, a noise at the door caught their attention. Patricia entered first, followed closely by Reilly, who beamed as if she were going backstage to meet Taylor Swift.

"Hey there, come on in!" Beth made a sweeping gesture with her palm up. "This is it. Welcome to Fresh Start!" She hugged them both and ushered them inside.

Patricia and Beth had set up the visit the week before, Patricia reporting that Reilly asked at least three times a day when they could see the café. They'd decided that Patricia would bring Reilly to Fresh Start for lunch then they would go to Beth's to meet other family later.

Reilly, clad in jeans, an oversized long-sleeved striped top, and Crocs, looked around and exclaimed, "This is so cool, Beth! You own this whole place?"

Beth and Allie laughed.

"Yep, I do. I guess it is pretty cool." She took Reilly's hand and smiled at Patricia. "Until the wrong food order is delivered or the refrigeration goes on the fritz. Come on, I'll show you around. This is Allie, one of our servers."

"Hey, Reilly, nice to meet you!"

Beth continued the tour and introductions, the staff greeting the pair enthusiastically. When she entered the large, bustling kitchen, Reilly appeared as fascinated as if she had been flown through space to a different planet.

As they settled at a table for lunch, Reilly asked, "Is Andre coming?"

Lucy chortled and said under her breath, "Even the kid knows he's a keeper."

Beth rolled her eyes at the chef. "No, he's working, but he'll be at the house later."

Chatting as they ate, Beth told them about some of the attractions in the area that Reilly might be interested in on a future visit.

Noticing several bracelets woven from colorful string on Reilly's wrists, Beth commented, "Your bracelets are pretty, Reilly. Did you make them?"

Reilly shifted in her seat, touching the bracelets individually. "I made some of them. Some of them my friends made. We trade them." She touched one made from rainbow string, and sadness clouded her eyes. "My mom made this one. I made one just like it for her. She never took it off."

Beth was horrified that she had brought up a painful memory for Reilly and silently implored Patricia for help, but the older woman nodded gently, as if telling her it was okay.

Beth gently touched Reilly's arm before continuing. "That's really nice, Reilly. It must have been very special to her because you made it. It's wonderful that you have something she made that you can wear always."

The blue moment seemed to pass. "I have a box with hundreds of strings in all kinds of colors. I'll show it to you next time you come to my house."

"That would be great."

Promising to stay out of the way, Reilly asked if she could go back into the kitchen and watch the staff. Frank loved an audience and gave Reilly a front-row seat to what he called "watching the magic happen."

After Reilly left the table, Beth hit her forehead with the heel of her hand.

Patricia rescued her. "Beth, it's fine, really. This kind of thing happens a lot. And it's different every time. Sometimes, she talks happily about Maddie, and other times, she cries. Some days, she's quiet and sullen. Other days, you wouldn't even know anything had happened.

It's a process." She offered a bittersweet smile. "You've visited her a few times now. Have you noticed that she seems to be doing better?"

Beth sighed. "Yes. You're right. I just feel guilty when I inadvertently bring up something that makes her sad."

Beth and Patricia had had several Zoom meetings with Susan Blackburn in the last few months. The caseworker visited Reilly frequently at Patricia's and was pleased that the girl seemed to be coping as well as possible. Though she was quieter than before, she continued to do well in school and get together with her friends. She was comfortable at Patricia's and enthusiastic about seeing Beth and her family. Susan also told Patricia and Beth that Reilly talked openly to her about Maddie. She explained that children experience many feelings, thoughts, and behaviors after the sudden death of a parent. Susan had further stressed the importance of helping Reilly understand that it was okay to grieve in different ways at different times and to reassure her that, over time, she would start to feel less sad.

"This is uncharted territory for me," Beth lamented.

"You and me both, Beth. You and me both."

"What should I call them?" Reilly took a break from arranging grapes, cheese, and crackers on a tray. She was on her knees on a stool at the island in Beth's kitchen, leaning her chin on her hand.

"Hmm, that's a good question. What would you like to call them? I think they'd be fine with whatever you're comfortable with." Beth had discussed the issue with both Patricia and Susan, and all had agreed it should be up to Reilly how she addressed her newfound relatives. "Also, nice job with that tray. How's it going over there, Andre?"

Andre stuck toothpicks into sliders to keep them from toppling over. "All good. A perfect job for my skill level," he joked.

Reilly grabbed a few toothpicks and jumped in to help. Then she wrinkled her nose. "I would feel kind of weird calling my dad's parents Grandma and Grandpa since I never met them, even though they are my grandparents."

Beth laughed. "I'll tell you something funny. My nieces and nephews don't call my mom Grandma."

"Why not?"

"She thinks it makes her sound old. And honestly, I kind of agree. She doesn't look like a typical grandmother. They call her LaLa. It's a play on her name, which is Laura."

"That's funny! Does Louise look like a grandma?"

Beth leaned in conspiratorially as the doorbell rang. "She does, but I'll deny saying that if anyone asks."

Reilly giggled and swung her legs down off the stool as Beth gave her a quick hug.

"Seriously, Reilly, don't worry about what to call them. They're all just happy to meet you. And wait until you see how fast this peace and quiet disappears!"

"She's not kidding, Reilly," Andre agreed. "When they're all together, it's slightly less chaotic than a circus."

Proving Beth and Andre correct, they spilled in the door like they always did—noisily and disorderly, everyone talking at one time.

"Ethan, get back here and take off your shoes!"

"Syd, move your backpack out of the way so no one trips over it. Oh crap, I left the whipped cream in the car! Eric, will you go get it?"

"This package was on your front porch, Beth. You should bring your deliveries in right away. Someone could steal them."

Beth stifled a laugh and gave Reilly a what-did-I-tell-you look as the wide-eyed girl took in the lot of them all at once. Keeping her arm around Reilly's shoulder, Beth shooed them into the family room.

There was no guide for this kind of moment, no script or correct words. Just hope that something could grow here, where so much had been lost. Beth noticed Louise's hands trembling and Bruce's look of wonder, and her heart ached for these grandparents meeting their granddaughter eight years too late.

Finally, the adults quieted the kids, and all the attention shifted to Reilly. When Beth introduced her, amid her nieces and nephews clamoring around their new cousin, a lone tear rolled down Louise's cheek as her eyes fixed on her son's daughter.

Chapter Thirty-Eight

As spring brought warmer temperatures and longer days, Beth and Reilly continued their visits. When Beth went to New York, they walked to the park near Patricia's and to Reilly's favorite pancake house.

"They're good but not as good as yours," Reilly assured Beth with a mischievous grin.

In Pennsylvania, Beth took Reilly to the weekend open market in the square, where they sipped fruit smoothies and admired local artisans' wares. Often, they wandered along walking paths, Beth letting Reilly take the lead when talking about Maddie and Danny. She was heartened—and more than a bit awestruck—by Reilly's maturity and resilience.

Reilly's school was closed for spring break in April, the same week as Beth's nieces and nephews, and Beth asked if she would like to spend a few days at her house. She started to sell the idea to Reilly during a FaceTime call, but the girl let out an elated whoop before she even mentioned the egg hunt in the park or the baking class at Fresh Start.

Patricia laughed as she picked up the phone Reilly had tossed onto the sofa. "Given the fact that she's already packing, I'd say that's a yes. I knew when you floated the idea by me that she'd be thrilled. Thanks, Beth."

"Don't thank me. I'm happy to have her. The other kids will be thrilled. And I'm sure you could use a break. I know you love Reilly, but what you've taken on is no easy task."

"Well, now that you mention it, it will give me a chance to do some shopping for baby items..."

"Baby items," Beth repeated. "Wait, what? Oh! Your daughter? You mentioned a while back that she and her husband were going to start trying."

"Yes, she's pregnant! Due around Thanksgiving." Patricia's entire face lit up when she spoke of her future grandchild.

"Oh, Patricia, I'm so happy for all of you."

"Thanks, I knew you would be. But back to the spring break visit, based on the frenetic sounds coming from upstairs, Reilly is packing for a month rather than a few days. I better get up there and get things under control."

Beth laughed. "Sounds good. We'll firm up the details later."

That evening, Beth, Andre, and Reilly walked around the square, trying to decide what to have for dinner.

"Burgers?" Andre posited. "A place at the end of the block has bottomless fries. Just sayin'."

"Pizza!" Reilly held Beth's hand, swinging their arms as they strolled.

"Pizza sounds good to me," Beth agreed. "And, Andre, the pizza places have fries too."

"As always, you're a master of diplomatic relations, babe."

Reilly scrunched her face. "What does that mean?"

"It means I just convinced Andre he got his way, but we're getting pizza!" Beth gave Andre a satisfied grin. "Let's cross here. The best pizza place is a few blocks over."

Several minutes later, seated at a window booth, Reilly's expression turned to worry. "Oh, Beth, I forgot! You can't eat pizza because of gluten."

Beth ruffled her hair, touched by the girl's concern. "That's true—sometimes. But this place has an excellent cauliflower crust, so I'm good to go."

Reilly studied the menu with interest, Beth helping her with unfamiliar words. "I've never heard of cauliflower crust, but I want to try it."

"Count me in," Andre added.

"Okay, they're smaller than regular pizzas, so how about we get two? And yes, Andre, we'll get fries." Beth gave him a playful look. "What toppings do you want?"

After they ordered and the server delivered their drinks, Reilly played with her straw and stared out the window.

"Reilly?" Beth asked. "Is everything okay?"

"Yes. I was just thinking..." Her voice trailed off.

Beth shot Andre a worried look as she put her arm around the girl. "What is it? You can tell us anything."

Reilly turned to Beth, her dark eyes wide. "I think I might have met my dad once."

Beth felt the air leave the room. "You did? Do you remember when?"

"One time, my mom and me went to a pizza place kinda like this. She said we were meeting her friend there. When you showed me pictures of him on your phone, I couldn't tell. But then I saw more pictures at your house. I think he was the friend who met us for pizza. I'm pretty sure." She rolled and unrolled her napkin.

Beth was momentarily paralyzed, so Andre jumped in. "How do you feel about that, Reilly? Are you glad you got to meet him?"

"Yeah, he was nice. He asked me about school and soccer. But he told some stupid jokes." Reilly smiled, as if warmed by the memory. "I think that's the only time I saw him. I asked my mom once if we would see him again, but she seemed really sad and didn't answer me. I never asked her again after that."

As they had more and more recently, Beth's thoughts of Danny turned angry that he and Maddie had created such a mess of their lives and caused this poor girl so much pain. She found her voice. "Reilly, I don't know why your parents did the things they did, but I know this. When your dad found out about you, I believe with my whole heart that he wanted to meet you and be part of your life. Maybe they were working toward that."

Reilly was quiet, as though considering that. "Sometimes, in bed at night, I ask my mom questions out loud. It sounds kinda dumb, but Susan said it might help, even if she can't answer me."

Beth gave Reilly another squeeze as the server arrived with their food. "I don't think it sounds dumb at all. I'll tell you a secret. Sometimes, I do that with your dad too."

And I'm trying to get in the right frame of mind to read that letter.

Beth sat on the edge of the tub that night as Reilly brushed her teeth before bed. They were talking about the upcoming cooking class at Fresh Start.

Reilly spit out a glob of toothpaste and swished water around her mouth. "You should do a pizza-making class. That would be fun. We could use gluten-free crusts like the ones we had tonight and let people choose which toppings they want to put on them."

"It would be fun, wouldn't it? Frank and I have talked about it many times because we'd like to put pizza on the menu. The problem is we have no pizza ovens at the café."

"Why can't you make pizza in the ovens you have? You have a lot of them."

"Well, those ovens don't get hot enough to make pizza. The best temperature for baking pizza is like seven hundred degrees."

"Whoa, that's really hot! One time it was ninety-nine degrees outside, and Miss Patty said she could fry an egg on the sidewalk. She didn't try it, though."

Beth laughed. "I can hear her saying that." She tapped her chin with her index finger. "You know what, though? I just got a catalog of all kinds of new restaurant equipment. I saw this thing called a pizza steel in there."

"A pizza *steal*? You mean you *steal* the pizza?" Reilly's eyes grew to saucers.

"No, nutty bird, *steel* as in a type of metal." Beth chuckled, playfully hitting Reilly on the arm with the hand towel. "It's a steel baking sheet that gets hot enough to make pizza."

"Like a cookie sheet?"

"Yes, but cookie sheets are much lighter than the steel ones. They get the oven temperature up to between six and seven hundred degrees. I'll look into getting some."

"Can I please be there when you do the pizza-baking class? Pleeeease! It will be so fun."

"Of course you can! It was your idea. We may need to name a pizza after you."

They made their way to the guest room where Reilly slept.

"Hmm, what toppings would be on The Reilly?"

Reilly pulled down the comforter and climbed in bed. "I think pepperoni, cheese, marshmallows, and M&Ms."

"Gross! I don't think we'll sell too many of those." She kissed Reilly on the cheek. "Sleep tight. Big day tomorrow—cupcake-baking class and you get to decorate your cupcakes for Easter."

"Yesssssss! Me, Sydney, and Zoe are going to make bunny faces on ours. Henry said he just wants to eat the icing."

"Good night, Reilly," Beth said, heartened by the relationship forming between Reilly and her cousins. Before she turned off the light and closed the door, she took in the beige walls, navy-blue comforter, and overstuffed armchair in the room, and another idea took shape in her mind.

Chapter Thirty-Nine

"Up here!" Beth called from the guest room when she heard Andre come in the front door. She was almost finished applying painter's tape around the trim and doorframe. Hearing him bound up the stairs, she smiled to herself. *He's like a big kid.*

He dropped the bags he'd been carrying and pulled her in for a kiss. Taking in the taped trim, six-foot ladder, and drop cloths, he whistled. "Wow, you didn't waste any time, did you?"

"Nope. Why wait? School will be out in a few weeks, and I want the room finished before Reilly's next visit." A strand of hair escaped her ponytail, and she blew it out of her face.

After Reilly had fallen asleep the night they'd talked about the pizza-making class, Beth had gone downstairs and excitedly told Andre about her idea. Andre, supportive to the end, had said he thought it was great and that he was sure Reilly would be thrilled.

They always had a blast when Reilly visited, but a few days here and there went by too quickly. Truthfully, Beth hated that Reilly lived out of her carry-on bag when she was at Beth's and stayed in a bland room that embodied none of Reilly's colorful personality. When they went to Hannah's or Nicole's houses, Reilly wandered through the kids' bedrooms, touching their dolls and stuffed animals, running her fingers along the books' bindings on the shelves, and examining the knickknacks on the dressers. Beth had purchased a few items for the guest room at her house, but she worried Reilly still felt like a visitor. The room was comfortable enough, but it wasn't decorated to the liking of an eight-year-old girl.

It didn't sit well with Beth. Reilly was Danny's daughter. *Doesn't she deserve a room of her own at his house?* Danny might have failed Reilly by keeping her a secret, but Beth was determined to make her feel like part of the family—because she was.

Beth—always careful not to go around Patricia—called her friend to discuss her idea. She asked if Reilly could spend half the summer in Pennsylvania with her. Of course, Patricia was welcome to visit as often as she liked. Beth also thought Reilly might like to go to Avalon, New Jersey, for vacation with the whole Peterson crew in July.

Patricia was moved by Beth's desire to welcome Reilly into her home and her family. "I really think Reilly will love the idea, Beth."

"Patricia, I hope you know I'd never try to impose on your time with her. She thinks you hung the moon. No one could ever mean to her what you do."

She could hear Patricia choking up at her words. "Of course I don't think that. And truthfully, hanging out with all of you has to be more fun than spending all her time with an old lady like me."

"Old? Be real! You run circles around all of us."

Patricia laughed. "I don't know about that, but the reality is, it's not a contest. I believe the more people children have in their lives who love them, the better. My relationship with Reilly is wonderful, but you and Andre and your family have given her something I can't—a big family. In the span of half a year, despite losing Maddie, she's gained not only you but grandparents, aunts, uncles, and cousins. It's been so good for her. Especially after everything she's been through."

"I think we're all pretty lucky. Honestly, when I found out what Danny had been up to before he died, *and* that he'd been unfaithful, *and* that he had a child, I thought I'd never get past my anger. But as much disappointment and sadness as Danny caused me, Reilly has given me that much joy. You know something, Patricia? I used to think the only way I'd ever be happy was if Danny and I had a house with a white picket fence, two point five children in matching outfits, and a piping-hot dinner on the table every Sunday. But Reilly's opened my eyes. She's made me get over myself and see things in other ways. I view the world entirely differently these days."

"Beth, you're going to make me cry. But listen, I love your idea. Go ahead and tell Reilly about it, and we'll figure out the dates and details later."

Beth had been so excited, it was all she could do not to race upstairs and wake Reilly that night to tell her.

"Awesome! And I'm going to fix up the guest room here and make it Reilly's own. I'll have her pick out paint colors, curtains, bedding, and—"

"Slow down there! Don't give her too much free rein. She might break the bank!" Patricia couldn't keep the glee out of her voice. "And, Beth, I'm on my way to bed now, but I want to talk to you about something another time. An idea of my own I'd like to run past you."

"You got it, Patricia. Thanks."

That had been a few weeks earlier, and now Beth and Andre were preparing the room to paint. Reilly, who was over the moon both about spending part of her summer at Beth's and decorating her room, had picked out a matching tie-dye comforter and curtains. Beth had chosen one of the colors in the bedding, a soft blue, to paint the walls. A large shell-shaped beanbag chair would replace the armchair, and a white dresser, vanity, and nightstand would take the place of the nondescript maple furniture. Beth planned to take Reilly on a shopping trip for wall decorations and incidentals to complete the room and make it her own.

She poked through the bags Andre brought with him. "Great, you got paint trays, rollers, brushes... I think we're set. Do you mind opening that can of paint and stirring it while I finish taping? This part is time-consuming!"

"You got it, boss." Andre grabbed the paint can opener and popped off the lid. "Great color. You finally narrowed it down."

Beth laughed. "Yeah, nothing like choosing a paint color to educate you on how many shades of blue there are! This one will look good with the bedding and window treatments."

"Window treatments. Uh-huh. Another phrase you've taught me. I thought they were called curtains. I'm such a commoner." Andre gave her an impish grin.

"Well, I've never seen a commoner dressed like you paint a room. You better change your clothes and shoes unless you want them coated with—what's this paint color?—oh, yeah, cornflower."

"See? I would just call it—"

"I know, commoner. You'd call it blue." She grabbed some loose pieces of tape and stuck them on his shirt as she embraced him.

"Ooh, if I get to make out with the foreman, this will be the best job I've ever had." He brushed a strand of hair from her face and kissed her. Taking a step closer to her, he bumped into the paint can, sending a puddle splashing onto the drop cloth.

"Ugh! Go change your clothes."

Turning around, he stepped directly in the puddle of paint. "Uh-oh."

"You're worse than the eight-year-old!" Beth teased as he continued toward the door. "Stop! Take off your shoes. You'll track paint everywhere."

She shook her head as he stepped out of his shoes. "Maybe you'll start a trend. You know, like Christian Louboutins, except the shoe bottoms will be cornflower blue."

"That could catch on," he called from her bedroom. He returned wearing a T-shirt and shorts.

"Much better. Give me your shoes. I'll take them down to the laundry room and clean the bottoms with detergent and warm water before the paint dries."

When she returned, she cast a satisfied look around her. "The room is all prepped. We have the rest of the day to paint." They decided Beth would take the tedious job of painting around the windows, trim, and door, and Andre would roll the walls.

Beth disappeared into the bedroom to change while Andre resumed stirring the paint.

"I'll be there in a minute," she called. "In the meantime, my laptop is just outside the door. I have a YouTube video queued up with tips on painless painting. It's like 'Painting for Dummies.' Would you open it?"

"Sounds perfect for me. I bet the first tip is, don't step in the paint!" Andre whistled as he tackled his task.

Beth returned as Andre clicked on several open tabs on the toolbar. "You've got a lot of pages open. Do you want me to close some of them?"

"No, let them go. I'll do it later. It's a bad habit of mine. I also don't shut down or restart my computer as often as I should."

Andre clutched his chest. "I'm crushed. You have bad habits? I thought you were perfect. Next, you're going to tell me you bite string cheese instead of peeling it."

"Is that a deal breaker?"

"I could try to live with it, but it won't be easy."

They worked methodically for a few hours and finished the first coat. Just before the sun set, Beth stood back and admired the job. "Looks good, don't you think?"

Andre groaned and massaged his lower back. "Yes, but let's quit for today and have dinner. This is taxing on the old bod."

She dabbed at his nose with her brush, leaving a small smudge. "Okay, Grandpa. Can you walk to the shower, or do you need a wheelchair?"

"I think I can walk—if you join me." He grabbed her hand and led her from the room.

"You warm up the water, and I'll be right there." She picked up her laptop as she left the room and began closing some of the open tabs. As she x-ed out of various pages, one—a photo—caught her eye. Something about it gave her pause, but she couldn't put her finger on why. She stared at the image until Andre's voice jolted her from her reverie.

"Come on. I'm lonely in here!"

Shedding her clothes as she headed for the bathroom, she forgot all about the image on her computer screen.

Chapter Forty

Summer was just around the corner. Trees were thick with leaves, deep green and rustling with every breeze. Beth opened the windows as she put the finishing touches on the walls in Reilly's room. She could hear sprinklers ticking and smell burgers grilling. It all made her think of second chances, how growth could happen with light, warmth, and time.

Beth and Patricia had decided Reilly would spend the first few and last few weeks at Patricia's and the middle weeks with Beth. Reilly was overjoyed about joining Beth's family in Avalon, and Patricia had accepted their invitation to spend a day at the beach with them as well.

On a visit to Beth's in May, Reilly and Beth shopped for finishing touches for Reilly's bedroom. Beth would never forget the wonder on the girl's face when she saw the room's transformation after it was painted and had new furniture, bedding, and window treatments.

"Wow! It's so cool!" she'd exclaimed as she opened dresser drawers and hopped onto the bed, wrapping herself in the tie-dye comforter. "You did all this for me?"

Beth's voice cracked when she answered. "Yes, Reilly. I want you to know you have another home here."

Beth surprised herself sometimes. So much of the anger she'd felt toward Danny had melted away the more she spent time with Reilly. She still occasionally cried for the man she thought he'd been and the father he'd never gotten the chance to be. The emotion that astonished her most was her gradual acceptance of the dichotomy between the man she'd married and the one who'd lied, stolen, and cheated. Even with everything that had come to light, she believed deep down that Danny was not entirely bad. True—he'd done awful things. But Beth felt in her heart that he'd felt cornered, like a wild animal, and had reacted in kind. *Had he lived, would he have come clean?* He would have had to. He couldn't hide Reilly forever.

Reilly would arrive in Stradmore in a week, and Beth and her family could hardly wait. As she pulled into the parking lot at Fresh Start, she marveled at the irony of ironies: Beth, not Danny, had the opportunity to be a parent to Reilly.

The kitchen was bustling with preparations for the upcoming day.

"Good morning, everyone," Beth greeted the staff as she headed straight for the coffee pot. "Gemma called in sick this morning, so yours truly will be serving with Allie."

"Not surprised. That girl looked like something the cat dragged in yesterday." Lucy shook her head. "Did you reach out to Nicole to see if she's available?"

"Nah, I'll do it. It's been a while, but hopefully, it's like riding a bike." Beth studied the Specials board.

Red laughed. "True that. Except during the lunch rush, the wheels fall off the bike and it runs off the road and bursts into flames."

"I'll be fine. Busy is good."

The morning went by smoothly, and the staff was preparing for lunch when Officer Kingston came through the door.

"Hi, Offi—uh, Adam. How are you?"

"I'm good, Beth. Look at you. They put you to work!"

"Yes, Gemma's sick, so you know—desperate times call for desperate measures."

"I guess you could say—wait for it—one of your servers is down!"

"Ah! Clever. What can I get you to drink?"

"I'll have a seltzer, please."

"Okay, I'll get that while you decide on lunch."

As Adam ate, Beth recalled he had sent her some emails she'd never responded to. Most were meant to be updates on the accident investigation that didn't seem to include any updates. She'd long since given up hope that the police could identify the driver or the man who'd robbed Danny and her. It seemed to Beth that the investigation had come to an end, albeit an unsatisfying one. "Adam, I'm sorry I didn't respond to your emails, but it's looking more and more like we won't get answers to our questions."

Adam swiped at his mouth with a napkin as his face reddened. "It's okay. Mostly, I was keeping you in the loop, not expecting a response. Some of them included photos from the scene. After I sent them, I wanted to kick myself. The last thing you need to see is photos that remind you of that awful night."

"Don't feel bad. I know you and the department did your best." Beth sat down next to him and cleared her throat. "Listen, Adam, over the course of the last year, I've found out some things I didn't know about Danny."

"What kinds of things?"

Beth sighed at the magnitude of the officer's question. She looked around, making sure no one was within earshot. "Some of them are personal, but I also discovered that he defrauded some of his clients. Estate clients."

"You mean he stole from them?"

Beth's cheeks blazed in anger and shame. "Yes. I don't have much specific information. I learned about it through some financial discrepancies I found."

Adam leaned back in his chair and studied Beth through narrowed eyes. "Wow. Okay. Well, my initial thought is that lawyer should be arrested, but in this case..."

"I know. A little late for that."

"Yeah. That's out of my wheelhouse. I can put you in touch with an agency that handles things like that—most times, the FTC is a resource for reporting frauds and scams. This is an odd case, though. Usually, it's the people who've been defrauded who report the activity."

"Okay. Thank you, Adam. Send me that information, and I'll go from there. I need to get to work. Looks like the lunch rush is upon us."

As Beth walked away, the officer called out, "Beth? You don't think there's any connection to, you know, everything that happened, do you?"

Beth turned and shrugged. "There's no evidence of any connection. As you've said, the accident appears to have been totally random." An image flashed in her mind of one of the photos from the accident scene but quickly vanished when the lunch crowd began pouring in.

The steady stream of customers finally slowed down ninety minutes later. A few people straggled in for the next hour until closing time. Beth and Allie wiped all the tables and counters and filled the condiment containers. Then Allie swept the floor while Beth retreated to the kitchen to help pack away food and load the dishwasher.

When Lucy and Frank tossed their aprons in the linens bin and said their goodbyes, Beth locked the back door and sank into her office chair. Then she dug into the café's clerical work, but an unshaped, unsettled feeling wouldn't leave her alone. As she worked on payroll, her thoughts drifted to the task she'd begun at home that morning before Gemma called in. Beth had set her mind to figuring out who the clients were that Danny had stolen from to pay Maddie. She couldn't stop thinking about them, not that she had any idea what she would do if she identified any of them. She figured the best place to start would be surfing around his laptop, but she had one major problem—she didn't know his password.

After Danny died, the firm he'd previously worked for had stepped in and reassigned his cases. Beth had been grateful and allowed them to use an IT specialist to access his active files. Though the firm had been successful in referring Danny's clients to other attorneys, she wanted to dig around and see if she could find anything—emails, documents, or some correspondence—that might help her identify any of his victims, but she didn't want to get an IT person involved.

She'd stored passwords for accounts they'd shared in a secure file, but she'd never known the password to Danny's laptop. There had never been any reason to. Until now.

The shower felt heavenly after the busy day at Fresh Start. Beth stood on sore feet under the stream of warm water and racked her brain about Danny's password. Their shared passwords were ones typically considered obvious and widely unrecommended—birthdays, anniversaries, and the like. They'd tacked on a few numbers and special symbols, but she had to admit that a determined person could probably figure them out. As she rinsed shampoo from her hair, she tried to get inside Danny's head during the last year of his life. She could only imagine his desperate state of mind.

Think, think...

She turned off the water and grabbed her towel. Rubbing the steamy mirror in a circular motion, she watched her face slowly appear. *That's it!*

After hurriedly wrapping her hair in the towel and throwing on her robe, she trotted to her bed, where she'd left Danny's laptop that morning. She sat cross-legged and flung open the computer to the login page. Sending up a silent prayer, Beth typed in "Reilly" but received an invalid-password message. Next, she typed in the name in all lowercase letters. Same result. Not wanting to get locked out altogether, she sat back and thought hard before continuing. The Forgot Password button taunted her. She'd clicked on it earlier but could not get the password sent to any email except Danny's—and Beth couldn't log in to that either.

"Oh!" Beth jumped up and ran down the stairs. She flicked through a stack of materials on Danny's desk until she found the envelopes from the safe-deposit box. Finding the date she was looking for—Reilly's birthday—she returned to the laptop in the bedroom. She felt her heart pounding in her ears as she typed, "Reilly128."

Nothing.

"Ugh." Noticing the time, she gave up. Andre was due to pick her up soon for dinner. She turned her attention to dressing and doing her hair, but she was still distracted when he arrived, right on time.

He planted a kiss on her mouth. "Hey, gorgeous. Give me a minute to change my shirt, and we'll get going." Andre had gradually brought some clothes and personal items to Beth's, and lately, they'd begun talking about moving in together.

In the car, Andre studied Beth's serious face. "What's going on in that overworked brain of yours?"

Beth sighed. "I can't stop thinking about the people Danny stole from. They probably worked their whole lives to accumulate money for retirement and to leave to their heirs. I just can't stomach the idea that he took that from them."

Andre quickly responded. "So, what do you plan to do? I can see the wheels turning."

"I don't really know. I'm starting by trying to get into Danny's computer."

"How will that help you find the names of his victims? Didn't his old firm take his files and reassign his cases?"

"Yes, but his personal computer is still at the house."

"Do you think he corresponded with them through his personal email?"

"Who knows? I don't even know what I'm looking for. It's not like I think I'll find emails that say, 'Hey, asshole, I know you stole our money and I want it back.' My guess is that the victims don't even know they were defrauded. I just want to poke around for any clues."

Andre cocked his head and nodded slowly as he pulled into the parking lot at the restaurant. "Hmm. Have you found anything yet?"

"Hardly. I can't even figure out his password." She turned toward him, practically knocking over the Yeti in his cupholder. She caught it before it fell and sighed deeply. "Lately, I've been beating myself up for not having *any* clue what Danny was doing. Some of the signs are so obvious now. How could I have missed every single one?"

Andre took Beth's hands in his. "Here's a little story I heard a long time ago. I think it will help you understand." He cleared his throat. "A man rides up to the Mexican border on his bicycle. He has a bag of sand on the back of his bike. The guard at the checkpoint, certain the man is smuggling something, insists on searching through the bag. He finds nothing but sand and lets him cross. The next week, the same thing happens. Again, the guard rips open the bag but finds only sand and allows the man across the border on his bicycle. This goes on every week for a year. Every week, the guard is certain the man is smuggling something in the bag, but he never finds anything but sand. Eventually, the man on the bicycle stops showing up."

Beth's forehead creased in puzzlement. "I don't get it. So the man wasn't smuggling anything?"

Andre looked immensely satisfied. "One day, the guard meets up with the man at a cantina in Mexico. He gives him a friendly slap on the back and says, 'Hey, buddy! I know you were smuggling something. It's all I think about. It's driving me crazy. Just between you and me, what was it?'

"The man sips his beer and answers, 'I was smuggling bicycles.'"

Chapter Forty-One

The only sound in the house was the hum of the air conditioner as the late-July day succumbed to night. Beth switched on a lamp and settled on the sofa with Danny's computer on her lap. She checked on Reilly, who'd been packing for days for the upcoming family trip to Avalon, and was relieved to find her asleep. The girl was so keyed up that Beth worried she would be up all night.

Andre stirred next to Beth as she woke the computer screen.

"I must have dozed off. You and Reilly were up there a long time. She's really jazzed about the beach trip, huh?"

Beth laughed and shook her head. "She sure is. She's packed enough for a month." She rubbed his leg. "How about you? Are you packed? We leave in less than a week."

"Me? Oh, yeah. All I need is my Speedo and a toothbrush, right?" he quipped.

"Oh, thanks for that visual. I won't be able to unsee it!"

He stretched and winked at her. "What are you working on so intently?"

"Still trying to figure out the password to Danny's personal email."

Andre sat up straight and rubbed his face with both hands. "I can't figure out Danny's endgame."

Beth looked up and tilted her head. "What do you mean?"

"Well, did he intend to keep stealing from his clients to support Reilly till she was eighteen? Did he plan to invest some of their money and replace it before anyone was the wiser? And what about Reilly? Did he plan to keep her from you forever?"

"Now you sound like me. Trying to sort it all out is enough to give you a migraine. If Danny had survived, I think something would have eventually given way. I'd love to believe he was planning to replace the money he took, but we'll never know."

Andre seemed to consider that. "I guess a lot of people have *some* secrets they keep from the ones they love to protect them. And I bet most of them think they can clean up their messes before anyone gets hurt." He stood and kissed the top of Beth's head. "I'm going to hit the bathroom, then I'll pour us a glass of wine."

Andre left the room, and Beth stared at the screen in front of her. She touched the keys lightly, willing a light bulb to go on in her head. *The password has to have something to do with Reilly.*

After a few more misses, Beth typed in "RCF128." The infuriating but now-familiar Invalid Password message flashed at her. Ready to give up for the night, on a whim, she typed, "RCF128$."

Bingo. Danny's home screen materialized.

"Yes!" Beth practically jumped off the sofa.

"What's going on?" Andre set Beth's wineglass on the coffee table and sank down next to her.

"I got it! Danny's password. I finally figured it out!" She frowned. "Now I just have to hope he used the same password for his email."

"Way to go, but I was hoping your enthusiastic 'Yes!' was your answer to the question I telepathically sent you." He removed the laptop from her legs and kissed her neck.

She wrapped her arms around him and lay back on the sofa. "Yes. Definitely yes."

Later, Beth propped herself up in bed and opened Danny's laptop again. Beside her, Andre's rhythmic breathing signaled a deep sleep. She kept the lights off so as not to disturb him. She needed to be up early to get to Fresh Start, so she vowed to spend no more than one hour browsing through Danny's email. Luck had finally smiled on her—the email password was the same as his login.

The first several messages yielded nothing of interest. The ones that weren't junk were ordinary correspondence of both a personal and professional nature. She was just about to give up when one message caught her eye. The name rang a bell, but Beth couldn't immediately place it. *Evan Montgomery. Where have I heard that name?*

The subject line read: *Question About Dad's Estate.* She sat up straighter and opened the message.

Dear Mr. Collins,

I'm going through the file you sent with Dad's financial information. Thank you for putting together such a comprehensive profile. I must say, though, that I'm surprised at the amount of funds in his investment portfolio. I was under the impression that the number was much higher and that my mother would be better off financially. At any rate, thank you for your attention to detail in handling Dad's estate. I've mailed a check to cover your fee.

Sincerely,

Evan Montgomery

Montgomery. Montgomery. It finally came to Beth. Montgomery was Amelia's last name, the nurse at Dr. Roth's office. Beth groaned softly as she thought of the unsuspecting family Danny had taken advantage of. She read through additional messages, but none questioned the amount of money in their family member's estate.

Just before Beth logged out, the sender name on an email grabbed her attention. *Barto. That sounds familiar.* Fatigue won out, and Beth, unable to give the name any context, closed the laptop and slid under the covers next to Andre. But she fell asleep with the name Barto on her mind.

To Reilly's delight, the day had finally arrived. The morning temperature pushed eighty degrees, though it was barely eight a.m. Andre had loaded beach chairs, sheets, towels, and nonperishable foods in the car the day before, and now, he and Beth packed the rest of their bags and food for the ninety-minute drive to Avalon.

"Okay, I think that's everything. And I do mean *everything*. I had no idea a week at the beach required this much stash." Andre slammed the hatch and bumped it with his hip for good measure.

"I know, right? It looks like we're moving out." Beth emerged from the house with coffee and called over her shoulder. "Come on, Reilly! We're all set."

Reilly bounded out the front door with a bag of snacks and activities for the ride. After locking up the house, they piled into the car and settled in for the drive.

Beth gripped her travel mug and placed Andre's in the cupholder. "Reilly, did you remember your water bottle?"

When Reilly confirmed she had, Andre backed out of the driveway.

"Avalon, here we come!"

Light traffic made the drive uneventful, and they arrived at the beach rental under two hours later. Beth relished the salty, breezy scent that greeted her as soon as they crossed the bridge leading to the South Jersey beach towns. Before going into the house, Beth led Andre and Reilly down a winding dune path to the beach and beamed as they took in Avalon's charm. The whole town was bathed in golden morning light, and the soft breeze carried the faint sound of seagulls and the rhythmic crash of waves onto the sand. The familiarity of it gave her comfort, and she was doubly heartened to share it with Andre and Reilly.

Richard and Laura had left earlier than everyone else and had already gotten the keys from the real estate office. Hannah, Eric, Nicole, and the rest of the kids rolled up shortly after Beth and Andre. The house was impressive—six bedrooms, four full bathrooms, a modern kitchen, large living area, and a game room with a pool table, a ping pong table, and a dartboard. The best part, according to the adults—who had to transport chairs, umbrellas, and coolers in search of the perfect spot each day—was the fact that it was merely half a block from the beach.

After several trips from the cars to the house, everyone agreed they should refrigerate the perishable food, deposit bags in the assigned bedrooms, and get the kids—who were bursting with excitement—ready for the beach. They could make up the beds and unpack clothes later.

The girls wasted no time changing into bathing suits and were slathering sunscreen all over themselves when Hannah put up her hand.

"Hold up, girls! You're not going anywhere without us." She shooed Ethan and Henry into their bedroom and helped them into their swim trunks.

Richard and Laura offered to go to the grocery store, and Beth joked that they were smart to steal an hour of peace and quiet. Outside, Eric and Andre staged everything going to the beach.

After she changed into her bathing suit and cover-up, Beth carried her toiletries into their designated bathroom. Needing to brush her teeth after drinking coffee the whole way there, she dug through her bag for toothpaste. "Damn, I must have forgotten to pack it." She sent Laura a text asking her to pick up an extra tube and went in search of Andre's toiletry bag. She finally found it, a bright-red nylon bag with a company logo.

"Beth, come *on*!" Reilly and Zoe yelled. "We want to go to the beach!"

"Jeez, I'm coming!" She quickly brushed her teeth and headed outside to join the others. During the short walk to the beach, Beth enjoyed the kids' excited chatter, but she was distracted by something she couldn't name, something that tugged at the corners of her mind but scurried away before she could make sense of it.

She positioned her chair close to Andre's on the beach and took his hand. "I'm so glad you're here."

He kissed her hand. "Not nearly as glad as I am."

She watched Reilly happily shrieking as she jumped waves with Richard and Sydney. "I think Reilly has had a great few weeks. It's going to be so hard to send her back to New York next month."

"I know. It's amazing how she's already so much a part of your family. And think about the craziness of it all—you and Danny wanted a family. He had a child he kept secret. His financial antics led you to Reilly, and it's *you*, not Danny, who gets to be part of her life. It's nuts when you really think about it."

"Yeah, definitely not a typical situation, by any means."

"And, Beth, your instincts were spot-on. After everything she's been through, you arrived in Reilly's life and rescued her from a world of sadness and loss."

Beth listened to Reilly's laughter over the crashing waves. Her voice was barely audible when she responded, "I'm not sure who saved whom."

As usual, the week-long family vacation flew by. Long days on the beach, early-morning fishing, excursions into town and to the nearby Ocean City boardwalk, game nights, and multiple trips to ice cream shops later, the crew was relaxed, sun-kissed, and blissfully exhausted, the kind of tiredness that signaled a great time.

Packing to return home was never as enjoyable as packing before a trip. Beth and her sisters tackled the refrigerator and the "keep" versus "throw out" dilemma. Then she headed upstairs to help Reilly pack her clothes.

The girl was uncharacteristically quiet, prompting Beth to ask, "Is everything okay?"

Reilly picked at the henna tattoo she'd gotten in Ocean City. Her sad eyes met Beth's. "The vacation went so fast. And soon, I'll have to go back to New York. I'm... going to miss you and Andre and my cousins."

Beth's breath caught in her throat. *My cousins.* It was true. Reilly had a bona fide family now. Beth was so consumed with how much she would miss Reilly, she hadn't considered that the child might feel the same way.

"I mean, I love Miss Patty, and I can't wait to see my friends, it's just..." Her voice trailed off as a large tear balanced on top of an eyelash.

Beth put her arms around her. "I know what you mean. I'll tell you what. Why don't I talk to Miss Patty and see if we can work out more time in Pennsylvania for you? Your school has lots of breaks and long weekends. I'm sure we can figure something out. How does that sound?"

Reilly wiped her face with the sleeve of her hoodie and nodded vigorously. They folded Reilly's clean clothes and placed them in her suitcase and threw her dirty ones in the laundry bag.

"Okay, you're in good shape here. I'll go see if Andre's all packed."

Up in the bathroom, Beth thought about Reilly as she packed her makeup, hair products, and toiletries. She wondered if it was harder or easier for the girl to live next door to the house she'd shared with her mother. *Does it cause her pain or provide a sense of comfort and familiarity?* Reilly never talked about that, and Beth wasn't sure it was appropriate to ask. She made a mental note to ask Susan her thoughts about it.

She finished packing her own things and decided to help Andre since he was outside hosing off beach chairs. As she gathered the last of his toiletries, the nagging thought she hadn't been able to shake crept into her mind again. She rubbed her temples, willing it to become clear.

Just then, Andre appeared at the doorway. "We're ready to load the rest of our stuff into the cars. Why does it always seem like you go home with so much more than you bring to a vacation?"

Beth tossed a giant stuffed gorilla he'd won on the boardwalk at him and smirked. "I have no idea."

Chapter Forty-Two

"Avalon called. It wants its sand back. I'm pretty sure I brought half the beach home in my beach bag." Beth stood in her backyard, shaking it out for at least the tenth time.

Andre banged his shoes against the side of the deck. "And the other half is in my shoes. I didn't even wear these to the beach. How do they have so much sand in them?"

"It's one of life's great mysteries. I even found sand in my purse."

The vacation behind them, Beth and Andre transitioned to working and following a schedule again. Fresh Start had been closed for the week, and Beth had arranged to meet the staff there to prepare the café to reopen the following day.

She transferred a load of beach towels from the washer to the dryer and called upstairs to Reilly, "We're leaving in five minutes, Reilly!" Then she turned to Andre. "How late will you be working today? Do you want to meet back here for dinner? I'm thinking something light since I ate my weight in French fries and ice cream last week."

He pulled her close to him. "It looks great on you. Yes, I'll be back in time for dinner. I'm meeting with the boss to go over my new accounts." He kissed her and grabbed his keys as Reilly bounded down the steps. "Bye, Reilly. See you later."

At Fresh Start, everyone talked about their time off as they prepared food for the upcoming week. Frank had enjoyed a staycation with his wife. Lucy described a fabulous time with friends at an all-inclusive in the Caribbean, and Red had accompanied her daughter and family to Gloucester, Massachusetts. Her favorite part had been whale watching, but she joked that her daughter was always so worried about her kids falling into the water or otherwise hurting themselves that it took some of the enjoyment out of it.

"Don't get me wrong," she assured them. "I'm all about making sure the children are safe, but my daughter is overprotective to a fault. If she could, I think she'd Bubble Wrap them."

Frank yelled from the walk-in, "It's good to let them get a few bumps and bruises, right? Toughens 'em up!"

"You know it," Lucy added, a mischievous twinkle in her eye. "When I was a kid, there were only two ways to depart this life—natural causes and talking back to your parents."

Reilly told the staff all about their week in Avalon and said it was the best trip she'd ever been on. She showed off her henna tattoo, which was fading a little every day.

"What was your favorite part of the trip?" Frank asked.

"Burying Ethan and Henry in the sand!"

"Well, I hope you unburied them and didn't leave them there." Frank winked at her as he breaded chicken cutlets.

Reilly howled as she followed him around the kitchen.

When all were satisfied that the café was ready to open the following morning, they locked up and headed home. Reilly gazed out the window as Beth drove.

Notably quieter than she had been with the Fresh Start staff, she sighed before asking, "How many more days do I have with you before Miss Patty comes for me?"

"Five. She's coming this weekend. We'll have a cookout with the whole family before you leave."

"Will I miss the movie night and sleepover at LaLa and Pop's?"

Beth's heart broke. All four grandparents—Louise, Bruce, Laura, and Richard—loved that Reilly used their grandparent monikers.

"No, you'll be here for that. They specifically planned it for before you leave."

Later, at dinner, Andre talked about his work and how glad he was that they had no travel plans in the near future. His boss had assigned him two new accounts, businesses whose profits had declined considerably over the last twelve months. He was anxious to roll up his sleeves and get to work figuring out how his firm could help.

"I love seeing you so excited about that, Andre. You don't usually talk much about your work."

"Well, Mr. B.—that's what I call the boss—has been scaling back and delegating more and more work to the younger guys like Chaz and me. He's always been a bit of a workaholic." He chuckled, shaking his head. "Chaz jokes that his dad's idea of scaling back will be working eighty hours a week instead of ninety."

Reilly pushed away from the table. "Beth, I'm finished. Can we play Uno tonight?"

Beth didn't answer. She was lost in thought about—*what?* She couldn't pinpoint it.

"Beth?"

"Huh? Oh. Yes, let's load the dishwasher, then we'll play."

"You okay?" Andre studied Beth's creased forehead.

"Yes. I'm fine," she answered, but she didn't convince either of them.

All week, Beth tried to steal some time to resume surfing Danny's computer, but the busy days got away from her. She had an almost morbid fascination with his email, like he was speaking from the grave. An odd feeling told her that the messages would help her get inside his head and offer some insight into his frame of mind. The Danny who'd lied, cheated, and stolen was not the man she knew. *Or was he?*

She had to admit there had been signs—the sullen, sour moods after traveling to New York, the hushed phone calls he took in private, his erratic attitude toward money, spending indiscriminately one day and inexplicably tightening the reins the next.

Lots of signs. *Had I ignored them? Had I been so desperate for a family that I disregarded obvious signs to make our marriage seem perfect?*

His emails were the only actual words she had left of him. Except that letter. She'd lost count of how many times she'd gripped the envelope, wanting to tear it open but not ready to read what Danny had written. *Would it be an explanation? A plea for forgiveness?* She wasn't ready, not yet.

Beth turned her attention to the pasta salad she was making for the cookout. The occasion was bittersweet. On the surface, the sunbathed day would be filled with laughter, food, and games, but underneath it all was the sorrow around Reilly's upcoming departure back to New York to get ready for the school year. Beth had taken Reilly school shopping, and though she'd chosen several tops, jeans, and sneakers she loved, the girl's mood had been melancholy.

Beth poured the gluten-free pasta into a strainer and checked her watch. Patricia would arrive soon, earlier than the others, because she had something she wanted to discuss with Beth. Shaking the excess water off the pasta, she dumped it into a bowl to refrigerate just as the doorbell rang.

"Patricia, come in! So good to see you."

They embraced warmly, and Patricia handed Beth a blueberry cobbler.

"I've been baking with the gluten-free flour you suggested, and I love it. And get this. My neighbor across the street was just diagnosed with celiac disease, so I've been helping her out with recipes. It's amazing how I never knew a single person who has it, but since meeting you, I feel like every week, I hear of someone else."

"I'm not surprised. Celiac awareness is improving all the time. And look at you, helping the cause." Beth led her to the back porch and offered her a cold drink.

Patricia looked around. "Where's Reilly?"

"She went with my dad and the girls to grab a few last-minute things from the grocery store for my mom."

"That's nice of him."

"Yes, well, I think Mom does it partially to get him out of her hair." Beth laughed. "Sit down and let's talk. We have some time before everyone else gets here. Is everything okay? You sounded serious on the phone."

Patricia sat up straight and took a deep breath. Placing her palms on her thighs, she began, "You know my hearing for permanent custody of Reilly is coming up next month. I've been thinking about something all summer. I even spoke to Susan about it. Reilly loves me. I know that. And I couldn't love her more if she were my own granddaughter. I want to be part of her life always. And truthfully, Beth, I loved Maddie too. I know she and your husband made terrible mistakes, and of course, I'm disappointed in her about that, but at her core, she was a good person. I don't expect you to feel any sympathy toward her. But I feel like I owe it to Maddie to do what's best for Reilly."

Beth blinked hard. "What are you saying?"

"I've been doing research and, as I said, talking to Susan. She's a wonderful resource and a wealth of knowledge about these things."

"What things?"

Patricia took Beth's hand. "As you know, in New York, the law allows a nonfamily member to petition for legal guardianship of a minor child. That's what I'm doing."

"Yes."

"But that person—in this case, me—can recommend that another qualified person, one who has an established relationship with the child, be awarded guardianship."

Beth could barely breathe. "You mean..."

"Yes. Beth, I don't know how we got here, but here we are. Reilly is the biological daughter of your late husband, who had a fling with my next-door neighbor. All of that sounds like a fictional miniseries, but the outcome is real. Reilly is real. Maddie and Danny are gone, but you and I are here. You rescued Reilly from a life of sadness and loss, a life with no real family."

"*You* did that, Patricia."

"Truthfully, we both did. I love that kid. You know I do. And I want to be in her life forever, but..." Her voice cracked as her eyes filled with tears. "You've given Reilly a family. I'm most angry at Maddie and Danny for depriving her of that from the start, but *you* gave that to her. She loves being with you and Andre and your family."

Beth was crying openly now.

"Would you consider petitioning for legal guardianship of Reilly? I'd write a formal recommendation, and Susan will help with all the red tape. Of course, we would both sit down with Reilly and talk about what she wants. Susan and the judge will do that too. It wouldn't happen overnight. It would be a process, one that everyone is comfortable with." She paused and swiped her hand under her damp eyes. "It's a lot to think about. You don't have to answer right now. Take your time."

Beth grabbed Patricia and pulled her into a bear hug. "Oh, Patricia, I don't need time to think about it. It's all I've thought about over the last few months. I love Reilly as much as if I'd given birth to her, and she's part of our family whether she lives with you in New York or here with me. My answer is yes, yes, *yes*!"

Patricia's hands flew to her chest. "I was so hoping you'd say that! Let's talk to Reilly before we leave for New York." She stood, exhaling loudly.

They both turned at the sound of Richard arriving with the girls.

"Beth, I know you've been through hell. But think about it. You saved that child."

Beth shook her head vigorously. "Andre said the same thing. But I think Reilly and I saved each other."

Chapter Forty-Three

It was a beautiful day for a cookout. Blessedly, the typical August humidity gave way to blue skies and drier, cooler air. Beth and Patricia were bursting with their secret about Reilly's guardianship but promised each other they would keep it to themselves until after the cookout.

Andre wasn't fooled. "What's up with you two?" he asked as he flipped burgers on the grill. "You look like the cat that ate the canary."

Beth kissed his cheek as she placed hot dogs in a row next to the burgers. "I have no idea what you're talking about."

"If you say so, but that twinkle in your eye says otherwise."

There was enough food for an army—burgers, dogs, an array of side salads, and desserts. After everyone was sufficiently stuffed, those who could still move played beanbag toss and bocce ball. At nightfall, Andre made s'mores, and Richard lit sparklers for the kids, who chased each other around the yard, squealing in delight. When the family left with promises of coming back to see Reilly off the following morning, Beth shooed Reilly upstairs to take a bath.

"I'm too tired," the girl complained.

"Just a quick one, and then Miss Patty and I will meet you in your room."

While Reilly bathed, the women shared their plan with Andre.

"Oh my God, that's amazing. Beth, I'm so happy for you—for us! Patricia, this is so generous of you, so selfless."

"Patricia is a big part of Reilly's life. If Reilly agrees to try our idea, we'll work out frequent visits." Beth squeezed Patricia's shoulder. "And of course, if Reilly does come here to live but then decides she'd rather live with you—as difficult as that would be for us—she can go back to New York. We all want Reilly to be happy."

"I'm done!" Reilly called from upstairs.

"Did you hang up your towel and brush your teeth?" Beth called back, rising from her spot on the sofa.

"Yep!"

Beth chuckled as she climbed the stairs with Patricia. She could hear Reilly running back to the bathroom, most likely to retrieve her wet towel from the floor. "Come on up with us, Andre. You'll be an important part of this if Reilly is on board. You're part of the package."

Andre trotted to the stairs. "Nowhere else I'd rather be."

Beth sprayed conditioner on Reilly's wet hair and helped her brush out the tangles. "So, Reilly, we have something we want to talk to you about."

Reilly turned to face Beth. "Okay."

"Miss Patty and I—and Andre—have been talking about an idea we had. We want you to know that whatever you think of the idea is fine. You don't have to do anything you don't want to do." She paused, and Patricia nodded. "We were thinking that you might like to live here in Pennsylvania with Andre and me. You'd go to school and play soccer here and continue taking dance or join other activities if you want. You could visit your friends and Miss Patty in New York anytime, and she would come here often to see you." Beth paused to let the girl absorb her words.

Reilly looked from Beth to Patricia to Andre. "You mean, I'd live here with you, like, all the time?"

Beth nodded.

"And I'd get to see Zoe and Sydney and everyone whenever I want?"

"That's right. You and the girls would go to the same elementary school. And Zoe went to soccer camp this summer, so Aunt Nicole can help with details about you joining the team."

Reilly's face grew serious as she moved next to Patricia. She folded her hands in her lap. "Miss Patty, will you be okay all alone if I stay here?"

Patricia didn't speak at first, as if she didn't trust her voice. "Yes, Reilly, I will miss you, but we'll see each other often. And remember, my daughter is having a baby soon, so I'll help take care of her. You can come visit me anytime you want, and I'll come here to see you. I love you. I'll always be a part of your life."

Reilly looked around. "So, this would be my room? My house?"

"Yes."

No one spoke for a long moment until Beth asked, "Do you have anything you want to say, Reilly? You don't have to answer right now. You can take your time."

"That's right," Patricia added. "In fact, you're so tired. Why don't you let the idea sink in, and we'll talk again in the morning?"

Reilly climbed into bed. All three adults gave her a good-night kiss and left the room. As Beth turned off the light, she wasn't sure, but she thought she saw a smile spreading across Reilly's face.

Beth, Andre, and Patricia all agreed that the discussion with Reilly had gone well but that the girl needed time to consider the magnitude of what they were suggesting. They talked through some of the details that would be first on the list to take care of if Reilly decided to live with Beth—especially registering her at the local elementary school and finding a pediatrician—then turned in for the night.

Beth and Andre held hands in bed and spoke quietly about Reilly. She rolled onto her side to face him. "You know, Andre, if Reilly decides she'd like to live here, what would you think about moving in here permanently as well? We've broached the subject many times but haven't discussed it seriously."

"I was just thinking about that. I think we haven't decided formally because I spend so much time here that it doesn't really matter what my official address is."

"I know. I feel like we live together already. I love that about us. Sure, you run home to get your mail and other items you haven't brought here yet, but that's about it."

"But to your point, I agree that if Reilly moves in, it might be better if we all live together."

"Yes, I think the stability would be good for her."

"Plus," he teased, kissing her forehead, "you can't bear the thought of being away from me for longer than an hour."

"Yes, that, too, you nut." She yawned loudly and snuggled closer to him. Before she closed her eyes, Beth caught a glimpse of Danny's laptop on a chair near the bed. As she drifted off to sleep, she vowed to resume surfing his email as soon as possible.

Beth was in the kitchen the following morning, pouring a cup of coffee, when Reilly appeared at the doorway.

"Good morning!"

Reilly rubbed the sleep from her eyes and padded to the table. "Do you have to go to the café today?"

"Yes, but I'm going in a little later. I wanted to be here when everyone comes over to see you before you leave." She offered Reilly a warm smile. "How do you feel this morning? Do you want to talk?"

Reilly sat up rod straight in her seat. "Beth, I really want to live here with you and Andre and the rest of the family. I thought about it until I fell asleep last night, and I want to do it."

Beth grabbed her and hugged her so tight that Reilly laughed and said, "Ow! You're squishing me."

"I'm sorry, I'm just so happy!" Beth's eyes misted over.

"Are you sure Miss Patty won't be mad?"

"Reilly, listen, no one will be mad no matter what you decide. We all love you and want you to be happy. You've had a very difficult year, and we want to do whatever is best for you. That means doing what makes you happy. Wherever you live, we're all here for you. That won't change."

Reilly's face brightened. "When can we tell Miss Patty?"

"Tell me what?" Patricia glided into the kitchen, ruffled Reilly's hair, and grabbed a coffee mug.

Beth and Reilly relayed Reilly's decision to Patricia, and the older woman tenderly embraced Reilly.

"I think you're going to love it here. I'm so glad you will be surrounded by family who loves you. And don't forget, you've still got an old gal in New York who loves you too."

"You mean the old gal who walks three miles every morning?" Beth teased. "I should act so old."

Jumping from one foot to the other, Reilly clapped her hands. "So, does that mean you'll go back to New York today without me?"

Both women laughed.

"Slow down, Reills." Beth wrinkled her nose. "Patricia, how should we proceed? I mean, I know there is the process of petitioning the court and having hearings, but school starts here in a few weeks."

"Maybe the best course is for me to take Reilly back to New York to pack up more of her things. That will give you a bit of time to make some calls and settle the issue of registering Reilly for school. Then I could bring her back, or you can come pick her up."

"Sounds like a solid plan to me."

A commotion at the patio door grabbed their attention. Hannah held a bouquet of balloons, and Laura carried a tray of pastries. Nicole followed with a large gift bag. The kids excitedly pushed past them and made a beeline for Reilly.

Sydney cried, "We're going to miss you, Reilly! When are you coming back?"

Reilly's grin stretched across her entire face as she hugged her cousins. "Guess what? I'm not going to live in New York. I'm staying here!"

"What's going on?" Laura set the tray on the counter.

"We have news!" Beth directed everyone to the deck.

Andre, showered and dressed for work, joined the fray. "I didn't know we were having a party this morning."

Beth grinned from ear to ear, and he seemed to get her meaning.

He hugged her before scooping up Ethan and following the others out the door. "I call a chocolate doughnut!"

When the two women were alone in the kitchen, Patricia touched Beth's arm. "Are you sure you know what you're getting yourself into?"

Beth's expression was calm. "Yes. One hundred percent. I've always dreamed of being a parent." She shook her head, chuckling. "Naturally, I thought I'd be starting at the rattle stage, not friendship bracelets, but I'm ready. I love Reilly. We all do. Having said that, I know parenting is difficult and there will be challenges. But I can handle that." She gazed out the sliding door at Reilly and the rest of the family. "I've evolved so much over the last year. I know now not to ignore something just because I don't want to face it. I painted over the cracks when it came to Danny and my marriage instead of seeing the deeper issues. I wanted a family so desperately that I pretended things were perfect. I pretended *Danny* was perfect. People are human. They make mistakes. Good people do bad things. It doesn't mean they're inherently bad. I only saw things in black-and-white, no gray areas." She pulled herself up to her full height. "But that Beth doesn't live here anymore. My eyes are open wide. I don't need perfect. I just need honest and real."

Andre slid open the door and stuck his head inside. "Help a guy out, will you? You can't expect me to play hide-and-seek without even a cup of coffee. I'm not firing on all cylinders yet!"

Beth grabbed the coffee pot. "Honest and real," she repeated.

Chapter Forty-Four

The end of summer brought with it a feeling that routine and structure were about to replace easy, carefree days. Parents fell into organization mode while kids pushed back, clinging to every last drop of summer freedom.

Beth crossed another item off her list. She entered Reilly's pediatrician appointment into the calendar on her phone. Then, pen between her teeth, she punched in the number to the school district administration building. After gathering the information necessary to get Reilly ready to start school, she turned to her laptop to access the website Nicole had given her for the local soccer program.

Opening her computer, she silently chastised herself again for leaving so many tabs open. She clicked on them one by one to close them. The photo Officer Kingston had sent her of the robber's footprints at the accident site appeared on the screen. As she closed the tab, something struck a chord with her, but she didn't know why. Her phone rang, startling her. Patricia's number lit up the screen.

"Hi, Patricia! How are you?"

"Good. Just checking in to see how getting Reilly ready to start the school year is going."

The women talked for a few minutes, comparing notes on what still needed to be done. Beth also told Patricia she planned to take Reilly to see Bruce and Louise in September because Louise wasn't feeling well enough to travel.

"I'm so relieved they're on board with you petitioning to be Reilly's guardian."

"Oh yes, they're thrilled that Danny's daughter is coming to live with me, especially after I promised to visit them with Reilly as often as possible."

Satisfied that everything was on schedule, they agreed that Beth and Andre would pick up Reilly the next week and ended the call.

Beth returned to her laptop and surfed the soccer webpage for the name and contact information of the program coordinator. Then she closed out of the site and grabbed her purse and keys to head to Fresh Start.

On the drive, she chatted with Molly, who was as excited as everyone else that Reilly would be moving in with Beth.

Molly was already planning a girls' day out, complete with lunch and manicures. "Seriously, Beth, I'm so happy things have fallen into place for you. My God, when you think about the last year and a half..."

Beth promised they would get together as soon as Reilly arrived in Pennsylvania then hung up, but the footprint photo niggled at the back of her mind. *I should delete that thing. It hasn't amounted to anything.* But it was still in her thoughts as she entered the café.

Business was booming. Families were out in full force, school shopping. Beth moved around the dining area, delivering orders, clearing tables, and chatting with customers. When the crowd thinned, she worked on the schedule and menus for upcoming cooking classes, uplifted that Reilly would be there to participate in them.

That night, alone in her house, she curled her legs under her on the sofa. Andre had to work later than usual and planned to pick up takeout on his way home. Cradling a glass of wine, Beth opened Danny's laptop and logged in. She scrolled through message after message, finding nothing incriminating. Many of them were junk or run-of-the-mill correspondence. She combed through them nonetheless, looking for additional messages referencing family members' estates, but came up empty.

Weary of the fruitless task, she was about to log out when, on a whim, she went back and read the message from Amelia's father. Sorrowfully, she recalled Josh's explanation of how Danny had duped unsuspecting families, either brazenly stealing from so-called "brattier" heirs who wouldn't bother to check invoices or inflating prices of repairs then funneling money to his LLC. Those families had trusted Danny with their delicate information when they were at their most vulnerable, and he'd betrayed them. It made Beth sick to her stomach. Though Beth didn't know Amelia's siblings, Amelia didn't strike her as a spoiled brat, so she guessed Danny had pulled the latter stunt on them. She sat back and exhaled loudly.

Then another thought struck her. Danny had been damn lucky he hadn't messed with the wrong people, the kind of people who would come looking for revenge if they found out what he had done. The kind of people who might harm him. *God, am I watching too much TV?*

Something hovered outside the periphery of her mind, unclear but definitely there. *What is it? What am I missing?* She scrolled back to the few messages expressing surprise at the amount in their family members' estates. They were all pleasant enough on the surface but conveyed a sad undertone. She didn't recognize any of the names.

Chapman. Dessendo. Ross. Adelson. Barto.

Barto. She stared into her glass, a thought taking shape. *Barto.* The walls began closing in. Her hands trembled, causing wine to slosh up and down the sides of the glass. She set it down and rose from the sofa on shaky legs. As she climbed the stairs, her heartbeat thumped in her ears. Making her way to the bathroom, Beth was eerily reminded of the day she opened the safe-deposit box at the bank. As on that fateful day, she feared she stood on the precipice of something from which there would be no going back. Something she couldn't unsee. Couldn't unknow.

Gripping the counter with one hand to steady herself, she slowly pulled open the drawer where Andre kept his toiletries. Moving aside various items, she located what she was looking for—his red toiletry bag, the one with the company logo.

Barto Consultants & Advisers.

Chapter Forty-Five

Beth was in the basement when she heard Andre's footsteps approaching from above. Her heart pounded in her ears. She looked upward, listening to him make his way to the kitchen to drop the takeout food on the counter, food she had no prayer of swallowing, given the boulder-sized lump in her throat. The footsteps upstairs ceased, and Beth wondered if Andre could sense something was amiss. She wondered if her distress was palpable.

Andre's steps overhead resumed, heading toward the living room, and Beth imagined him looking for her in the stillness of the house. Typically, she would call out to him, "Up here!" or "In the laundry room, be right out!" but tonight, Andre was met by silence. She remembered she'd left the laptop open in the living room, pictured him frozen in place at the sight of the email from Anthony Barto, frantically trying to piece together what Beth knew. The item she'd been holding slipped from her fingers and hit the cement floor with a clatter. Andre had to have heard the noise in the otherwise-dead-silent house. Suddenly feeling creepily calm, she waited for him to descend the stairs.

He approached the basement door, which stood ajar. A single bulb above the steps illuminated him as he descended slowly. "Beth?"

She didn't answer. She wanted him to come closer, needed his face entirely visible to her. At the bottom of the steps, he came into view. The light was dim in the dank basement, and Andre's shadow made him look distorted, as though she both literally and figuratively saw him in a different light.

"Beth? What are you—"

He gasped, and Beth followed his gaze as he took in the item she'd dropped at her feet—her old cell phone. The one taken from the accident scene.

Andre opened his mouth to speak but closed it again. He blinked, once, twice, then sat heavily on the bottom step, as though gravity had doubled. His head sank into his hands, and a strangled sob escaped his throat.

She laughed softly, a sharp, bitter sound. "I couldn't get that image out of my mind. It drove me crazy, the way that photo from Officer Kingston nagged me. But I couldn't figure out why." Beth thumped her forehead with the heel of her hand.

Andre stared at her, and she was almost amused at the terrified look on his face.

"Remember how cute I thought it was when you stepped in the blue paint you spilled? How I scolded you to stay on the drop cloth and not track paint onto the carpet?"

"Beth, God, I'm so sorry. Please, let me—"

But she continued, her eyes so vacant it appeared as though she'd forgotten he was there. "Then, tonight, it hit me. When I saw the name *Barto* in Danny's email then on your toiletry bag." She yanked a large piece of wrinkled fabric off the floor behind her. "It finally hit me. I'd seen those footprints before. The first time was the night we first kissed. I watched you walk to your car. It was snowing, and your steps made perfect footprints. Of course, those footprints disappeared." She shook out the drop cloth she'd gathered from the floor. "But these didn't."

Andre finally stood and gaped at the image of his footprints on the drop cloth that Beth held in front of her like a piece of prized artwork.

"I spread this out next to the photo from the police. The footprints are a perfect match." Beth wobbled on her feet. Her legs felt hollow. She let the cloth fall next to her. Remembering the phone, she kicked it. It spun in circles on the floor and ended up at Andre's feet. Her eyes bored holes straight through him. "Jesus Christ, Andre. Start talking."

Chapter Forty-Six

His hands shook as he wiped the tears that soaked his face and shirt front. He asked softly, "Can we go upstairs?"

Beth, awash with exhaustion, managed, "I don't think I can make it up the steps right now." She felt as if the ground had been ripped out from beneath her. Again. Her mind struggled under the weight of it all. *How is this happening again? Is anyone who I thought they were?* The conflicting desire to both run as far from him as possible and stay to demand answers gripped her. Her thoughts swirled wildly in her head like a storm.

She wanted to throttle Andre for keeping secrets from her. He knew what discovering Danny's had done to her, how his betrayals had upended her life. And yet, she wanted to hear what he had to say. God help her, she loved him. She desperately wanted to believe he would have an explanation, something to make it all make sense.

He approached her as one might a frightened puppy, as though she might flee. Folding chairs lined the basement wall like spectators at a macabre show. Andre grabbed two and hastily set them up facing each other. He motioned to Beth. "Sit. Please. I can't begin to tell you how sorry—"

"No. Stop with the apologies. Start explaining." Wearily, she let him lead her to a chair and sank into it.

Andre rubbed his face with both hands and loudly cleared his throat. "Right. Okay. My boss's family is one that Danny stole from."

Beth couldn't speak. Her nod was almost imperceptible. Andre reached gently for her hand, but she pulled it away, and a tear slipped down Andre's cheek.

"Beth, no one was supposed to die. You have to believe me. I would *never* get mixed up in anything like that. Neither would the Bartos. They have their faults, but they would never try to kill anyone. We were just supposed to scare him. Mr. B. asked that guy to do it."

"Who was he? Did you know him?"

"No, no." Andre vehemently shook his head. "All I know is he went by the name Bear. Maybe a nickname or a play on his real name. I don't know. I didn't want to know. He was just some dude, you know the type, always 'between jobs.' He did odd jobs for the Bartos—mowing, handyman projects—stuff like that. Mr. B. asked me to ride along with him to run Danny off the road and shake him up a little. You know, scare him into repaying the money. He thought Bear was a wild card and wanted someone with him to keep things under control.

"I don't even know why I agreed, Beth. I guess I figured I owed it to them. They've been good to me. They are the reason I could get my mom her own place where she'd be safe, away from my dad." His eyes pleaded with her. "I'm not condoning it, just explaining.

"Anyway, I warned that idiot he was driving too fast in the pouring rain, but he brushed me off, like he was on some sort of big-time vigilante mission. He wouldn't listen, just kept driving recklessly. His idiocy got him killed too."

Andre dropped his head in shame. "When we crashed into your car, I was screaming at him, but my screams got lost in the pounding rain. It happened so fast. The impact, the shattering glass."

Beth squeezed her eyes shut at the memory.

"Sorry, Beth. I hate to make you relive it."

"Keep going. Tell me everything."

"When our car came to a stop, I was banged up and, honestly, shocked to be alive. I knew Bear was dead. He was bleeding profusely from his head, and I didn't feel a pulse. After that, it was a blur. I was disoriented but full of adrenaline and somehow pried myself out of the car. There was this awful hissing noise. All I could think about was getting to your car to see if you two were alive."

Beth practically whispered. "You knew I was in the car?"

Andre's face crumpled. "Yes. Mr. B. knew you two were at that party. Someone he knows was also going and told him that you and Danny would be there. He found your address. That's how he knew the route you'd take to get home."

"So this Barto guy didn't care if he got *me* killed?" Beth's face twisted in horror.

"No, no, Beth, I swear. *No one* was supposed to get killed. He was so pissed off that Danny had stolen from his family—it was his uncle's estate—that he wanted to make a statement, let Danny know they were on to him, and scare him into paying back the money. That's all."

"I don't understand. If Barto and his family knew Danny stole from his uncle's estate, why didn't they go to the police?"

Andre closed his eyes and sighed. "They couldn't. Let's just say I get the feeling Mr. B.'s uncle was no choir boy. I don't imagine they'd want the authorities looking into how he made all his money."

Beth nodded as realization dawned on her. She stared at the drop cloth as though it were a snake that might strike her. "So you came over to our car. The unidentified footprints at the scene are yours." It was a statement, not a question.

"Yes. I was frantic. Your car was all dripping fluids and groaning metal. You were moving, but Danny wasn't. It all happened in seconds. I grabbed my phone to call for help, even though I knew it would implicate me. I just wanted to get help. But just then, a car pulled over, and I heard a woman screaming into the darkness, asking if anyone was alive, saying she was calling an ambulance. I panicked, Beth. I took your wallets and phones to make it look like a robbery because I knew my footprints would be at the scene. I swear, I *was* going to call an ambulance, but that couple arrived and called instead. So I got the hell out of there."

Beth rubbed her forehead. She struggled for thoughts coherent enough to form questions. When she spoke again through trembling lips, her voice cracked. "So, you just *left*?"

"Not at first. I stumbled a block or two away and waited behind a building to make sure an ambulance came. It did, within a few minutes. Then I walked—I don't even remember how long—before getting an Uber to a hotel and collapsing into bed. Later, I had Chaz pick me up. He took me back to New York, and I went to the ER to get my cuts and scrapes cleaned up."

"Didn't the ER staff ask how you got your injuries?"

"I'm sure they did. I was so out of it. I was so racked with guilt, I didn't care much what happened to me." Andre shook his head at the memory. "Anyway, Chaz's family knows everyone. I saw him talking privately to one of the staff. They stitched me up without asking questions."

Beth had listened intently, but now she sat back and exhaled forcefully. "I need some water."

Andre ran upstairs and was back in under a minute.

"So, how is it that you turned up at Fresh Start?"

"Jesus, Beth, the guilt was killing me. I was obsessed with knowing what had happened to you and Danny. Then I read that you were the only survivor of the crash. I felt absolutely awful. I couldn't live with myself. I had to know that you were okay. I just wanted to check on you. I even sent a card to your house. I didn't sign it. It was a stupid, impulsive thing to do, but I wasn't thinking straight."

She looked up at the ceiling, recalling opening it. "I remember that card. I was baffled by it but still too numb and grief-stricken to care much who'd sent it. So, then you came to my café? What, were you stalking me?"

"No, no, nothing like that. I just really wanted to meet you. I wanted to look you in the eye and see if you were okay."

"Okay? *Okay?* My whole *life* was torn apart!" She shrieked, grasping both sides of her head.

"I know. And, God, I know how lame it sounds. But I couldn't stop myself. Like I said, I was obsessed. I wanted to know the girl behind all that pain. It sounds crazy, but in a weird way, I wanted to help you. Then I met you, and something happened to me. I couldn't get you out of my mind. I wanted to know more about you. We hit it off immediately. You remember that, right? Then we spent time together and got to know each other. And, Beth, I didn't mean to fall in love with you. But I did."

He took her hands in his, and this time, she let him.

She replayed every moment they spent together, his kindness, his sense of humor, the way he held her when she cried over revelations about Danny.

Beth was quiet for several moments. "That accident brought us together," she said, more to herself than to Andre.

"Yes. And it was an accident, Beth. A tragic one, but an accident just the same. I'm sorrier than I can say. There's not a minute of the day when I don't hate myself for all the pain it's caused you. I don't want to lose you. I love you. More than I ever thought I could love someone." He searched her face desperately for any clue as to what she was thinking. "Can you ever...? Do you think you can find it in your heart to forgive me?"

Chapter Forty-Seven

Beth loved this time of year. Neighborhood kids trotted to the bus stop, laughing and chattering, the new school year in full swing. Warm sunlight still bathed the daylight hours, but mornings and evenings were crisp and cool. That morning, walking Reilly to the bus stop, she'd clutched her cardigan in front of her with one hand and grasped her coffee mug with the other.

She smiled, thinking about how excited Reilly was to go to school today. In the world of an eight-year-old, it didn't get much better. It was her new friend Josie's birthday, and she was treating the class to cupcakes. The teacher would be reading a book to the class, one of Reilly's all-time favorites, and soccer practice began after school today. Reilly had practically floated onto the bus.

The transition with Reilly had gone smoothly, even with the un-nerving events of the last few weeks. Reilly loved school and was making friends. She and Beth were settling in together, forming routines, a new kind of belonging crafted from shared sorrow and hope for brighter days ahead.

Things with Andre hadn't gone quite as easily, but still...

It was stunning, really. The whole thing could have blown sky-high. *Should have* blown sky-high. For the second time in under two years, Beth grieved—not just for Danny and the man she'd learned he wasn't but for the honest and real relationship she'd thought she'd built with Andre. The one that felt like healing from the first, like hope that she could find happiness after Danny died.

Danny. She shook her head at the thought of his letter—tucked away in her nightstand drawer—which she'd finally read. It didn't say anything she didn't already know. She'd read it so many times, she had it memorized:

My Dear Beth,

The only way you're reading this is if I'm not here to explain myself. Tomorrow is not guaranteed, so I'm leaving this letter in the event I never get to tell you everything. By now, you know about Reilly. I swear, Beth, it was one drunken night that meant nothing. It's the worst regret of my life, one that I thought I could put behind me and never have to hurt you by telling you about. But then there was Reilly.

I found out about her when she was six years old. Her mother kept it from me. I met her only once, and she's amazing. My punishment is that I betrayed you, and that betrayal resulted in a child whom I do not know. I'm not trying to paint myself as a victim. I deserve all the pain I've created, but you and Reilly don't.

As despicable as being unfaithful to you is, it's nothing compared to the depths I sank to after learning about Reilly. I've entered a world that a decent person like you can't even imagine. If something happens to me as a result, I have no one to blame but myself. I put myself in danger.

Beth, if I'm gone before I can beg your forgiveness, please reach out to Reilly's mother. The best thing for Reilly would be to have you in her life. And maybe the best thing for both of you is to be rid of me.

Love,

Danny

She'd read it the morning after the confrontation with Andre in the basement.

Andre. It made her head spin. He was in the car that had killed Danny and her unborn baby. That night, finding her cell phone and wallet buried in a box of Andre's belongings in her basement had knocked the air from her lungs. At first, she'd replayed his confession in her head on a continuous loop. *But, no, he didn't really confess, did he? I figured it out.* That felt like the greater betrayal, but underneath it all was an important truth. Danny was responsible for the events that had caused the accident. He had been unfaithful to Beth, impregnated another woman, and stolen from his clients to support his secret child.

As unbelievable as the situation was, the least complicated part for Beth was that she still loved Andre. It was still there, clashing with the shock that he had been at the accident.

Her new grief was more complex than her sorrow over losing Danny and discovering her old life wasn't what she'd thought. This grief was tangled with questions about what it meant to love someone new when that love was woven into the worst day of her life.

Her initial emotion was anger. She could have turned Andre in to the police. *But to what end?* Every dreadful thing that had happened had been set in motion by Danny, not Andre. He'd stolen from the Bartos, and they'd wanted their money back. Danny did that. Actions had consequences. She'd thought he was nearly perfect, incapable of such heinous acts. She'd ignored signs, painted over the cracks. *Danny* stole from the Bartos, and *Bear* caused the accident. *Who would be served if Andre were the only one to pay?*

After everything, she kept coming back to Andre. Beneath the pain and shock was one persistent truth. She still loved him. She knew what it felt like to lose someone in one shocking instant, and she didn't want to lose someone she loved a second time, not if there was a way forward.

She didn't fool herself into thinking it would be easy. She didn't forgive him, not completely, not yet. But she was willing to make space for a future with him. Because if she'd learned anything, it was that love wasn't black-and-white. She could love her late husband despite his secrets, lies, and crimes. She could love the child he had as a result of an affair. She could love a man who was peripherally involved in the whole sordid mess.

Beth didn't get to rewrite the beginning, but she could damn well decide what came next. What was done was done, and it might never make sense. No one would come down from a high mountain and make all the hurt disappear.

The pain of the past, no matter how unfair or who was to blame, was *hers* to carry. Or to put down.

And that in itself felt something like freedom.

Acknowledgments

Though writing a novel seems like a solitary endeavor, it takes many eyes, hands, and hearts to turn dreams into published books, and I'm grateful for everyone who accompanied me on this journey. My heartfelt thanks to:

Lynn McNamee, owner of Red Adept Publishing, for having faith in my story and me. Thank you for your tireless work to get our stories out into the world. Special thanks to Red Adept's wonderful editors, staff, and mentors.

Diane Byington, my talented content editor, for helping me turn "old Beth" into "new Beth."

Amanda Kruse, my outstanding eagle-eyed line editor, with whom no unnecessary adverb is safe!

Barbara Conrey and Sarahlynn Bruck, the best critique partners an author could ask for. Your expertise, time, and support mean the world to me.

My beta readers, especially Barbara Conrey, Renee Anderson, and Amy Obritz, for your thoughtful feedback.

Victoria Beltzner, paralegal extraordinaire, for your invaluable help with the parts of my book involving legal issues. You're one smart cookie.

Fellow RAP authors for their warm welcome and support. I'm so happy to be part of this team.

Special thanks to the admin and members of Bookish Road Trip Facebook group. BRT is hands-down the best forum to engage with readers, authors, and travelers. If you haven't done so, check it out.

My family—a circus of the very best kind. I love you all.

My mom—there's no one quite like you. No matter what you are going through, you're always there to support us.

Barbara Conrey—I know I mentioned you above, but you deserve double billing. Thank you for your friendship, generosity, and honest guidance. You're the best.

A Letter From Lee

Dear Reader,

My heartfelt thanks for choosing to read *Painting Over Cracks*. If you enjoyed it, I'd be so grateful if you would take a moment to leave a review on your favorite social platform. Reviews are a vital part of a book's journey. They not only help authors reach new readers—they also help readers discover books that resonate with them.

A few words about celiac disease. Like my protagonist, I live with this autoimmune condition that affects many aspects of daily life, far beyond simply avoiding gluten. For millions of people like me, it's not a trend or a choice but a serious illness that is difficult to navigate. If you'd like to learn more or find support, please visit the Celiac Disease Foundation at celiac.org.

Thanks again for making space in your heart for my characters and their story. You can learn more about me and my work at www.leebukowski.com or connect with me on social media. I always love hearing from readers.

All the best,

Lee

About the Author

Lee Bukowski writes stories about complicated relationships of every kind. The messier, the better. Faced with navigating difficult situations, her characters grab the reader and take them along for the ride. Her goal is to lead both her characters and readers to personal growth and self-discovery.

After she'd raised her two daughters and taught seventh-grade English for sixteen years, the writing bug bit her. In 2017, she obtained an MFA in English and Creative Writing.

Lee lives near her large family in Reading, PA, and is admittedly useless until she's had two cups of morning coffee. She loves reading, traveling, and trying cocktails with creative names. Lee is a *Seinfeld* aficionada and a Billy Joel superfan with a live-concert count of fifty shows. Rumors of stalking charges are greatly exaggerated.

Read more at https://www.leebukowski.com/.

About the Publisher

Dear Reader,

We hope you enjoyed this book. Please consider leaving a review on your favorite book site.

Visit our site to find more quality books!

Read more at https://RedAdeptPublishing.com.

www.ingramcontent.com/pod-product-compliance
Lightning Source LLC
Chambersburg PA
CBHW020912060726
47591CB00004B/1199